Ao Haru Ride

The scent of air after rain...
In the light around us, I felt your heartbeat.

8

IO SAKISAKA

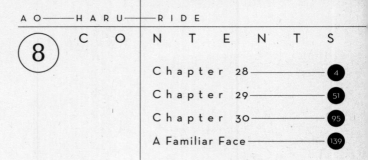

C O N T E N T S

S T O R Y T H U S F A R

Futaba Yoshioka was quiet and awkward around boys in junior high, but she's taken on a tomboy persona in high school. It's there that she once again meets her first love, Tanaka (now Kou Mabuchi), and falls for him again.

Kou becomes closer to his classmates, but the friendlier, happier Kou doesn't remain for long. His personality quickly changes once Yui, his old classmate from Kyushu, shows up.

Futaba realizes that Kou is spending time with Yui out of empathy. Futaba confronts her and asks her to let Kou go. But why would Yui let go of the guy she likes?

Futaba decides to tell Kou her feelings to get closure for herself.

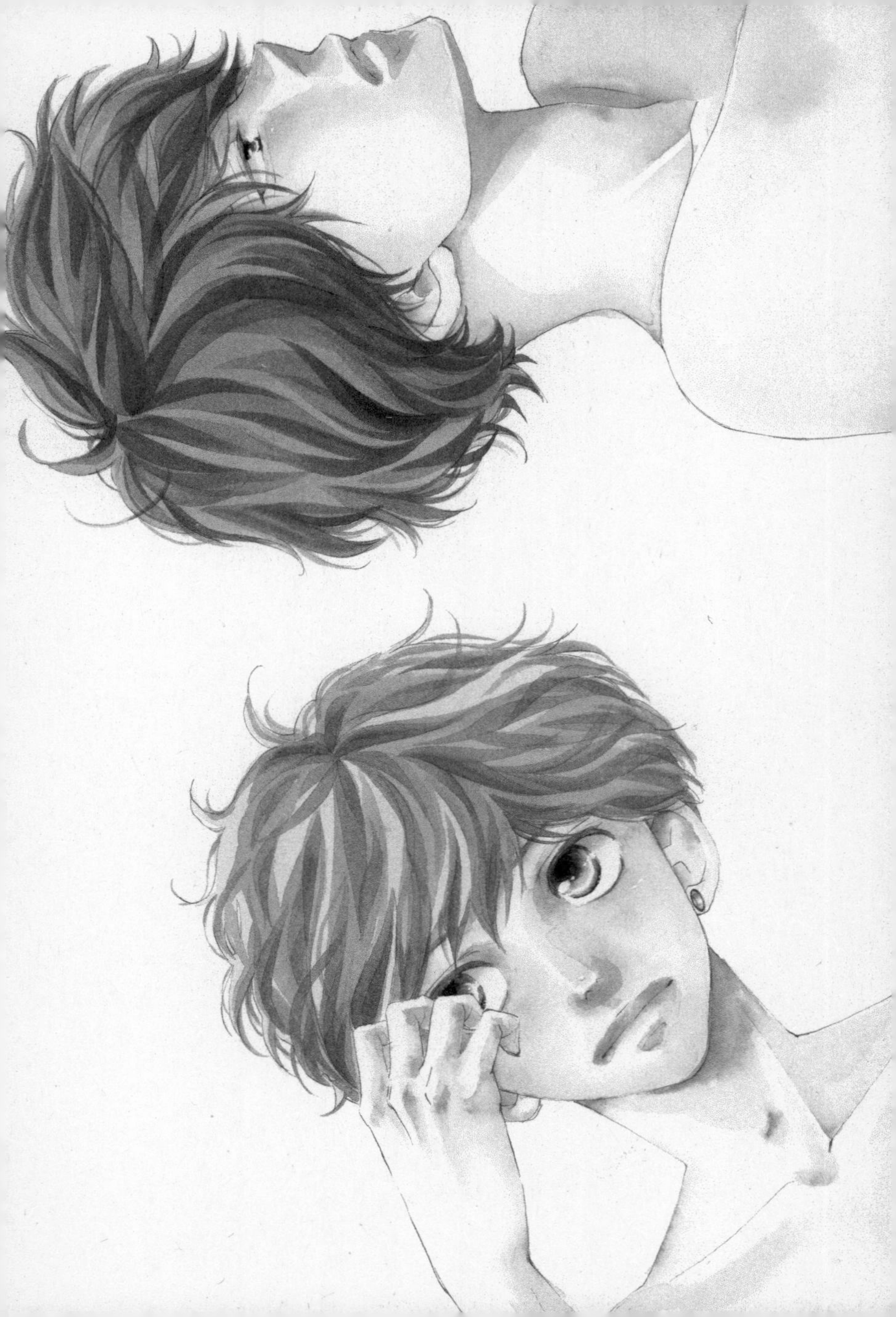

Ao Haru Ride

The scent of air after rain...
In the light around us, I felt your heartbeat.

CHAPTER 28

IO SAKISAKA

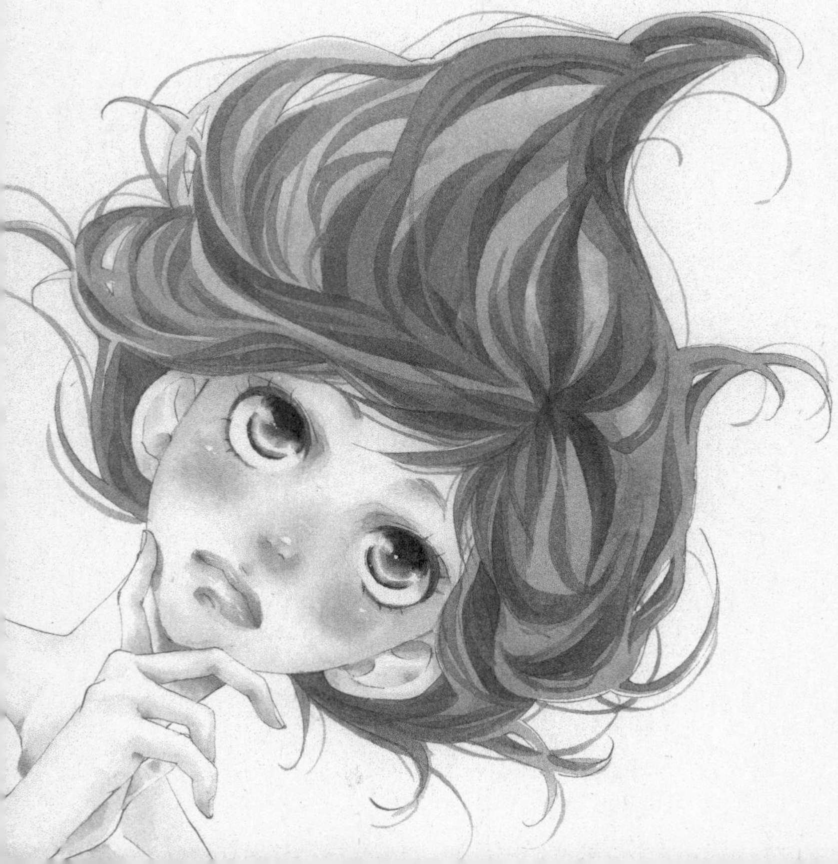

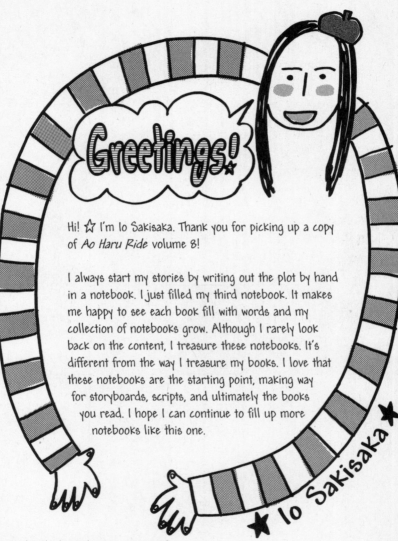

Greetings!

Hi! ☆ I'm Io Sakisaka. Thank you for picking up a copy of *Ao Haru Ride* volume 8!

I always start my stories by writing out the plot by hand in a notebook. I just filled my third notebook. It makes me happy to see each book fill with words and my collection of notebooks grow. Although I rarely look back on the content, I treasure these notebooks. It's different from the way I treasure my books. I love that these notebooks are the starting point, making way for storyboards, scripts, and ultimately the books you read. I hope I can continue to fill up more notebooks like this one.

★ Io Sakisaka ★

And with that, I hope you enjoy this volume and read through to the end!

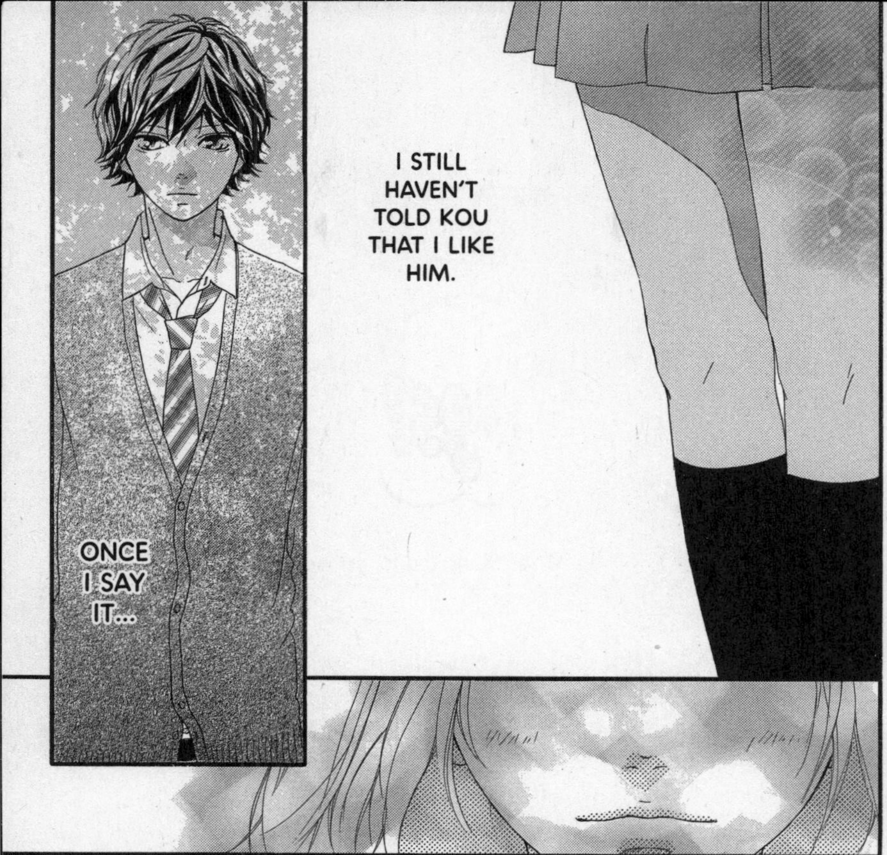
I STILL HAVEN'T TOLD KOU THAT I LIKE HIM.
ONCE I SAY IT...

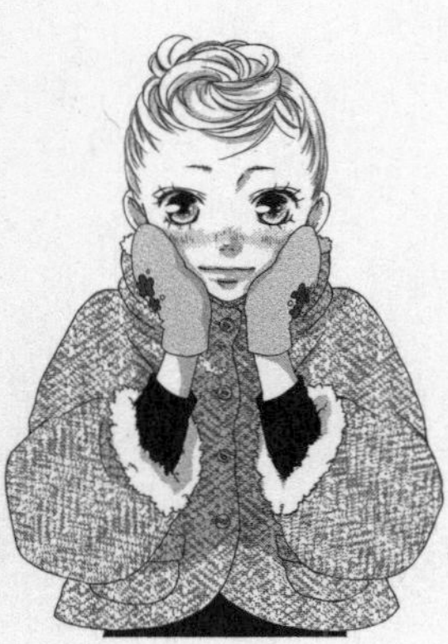

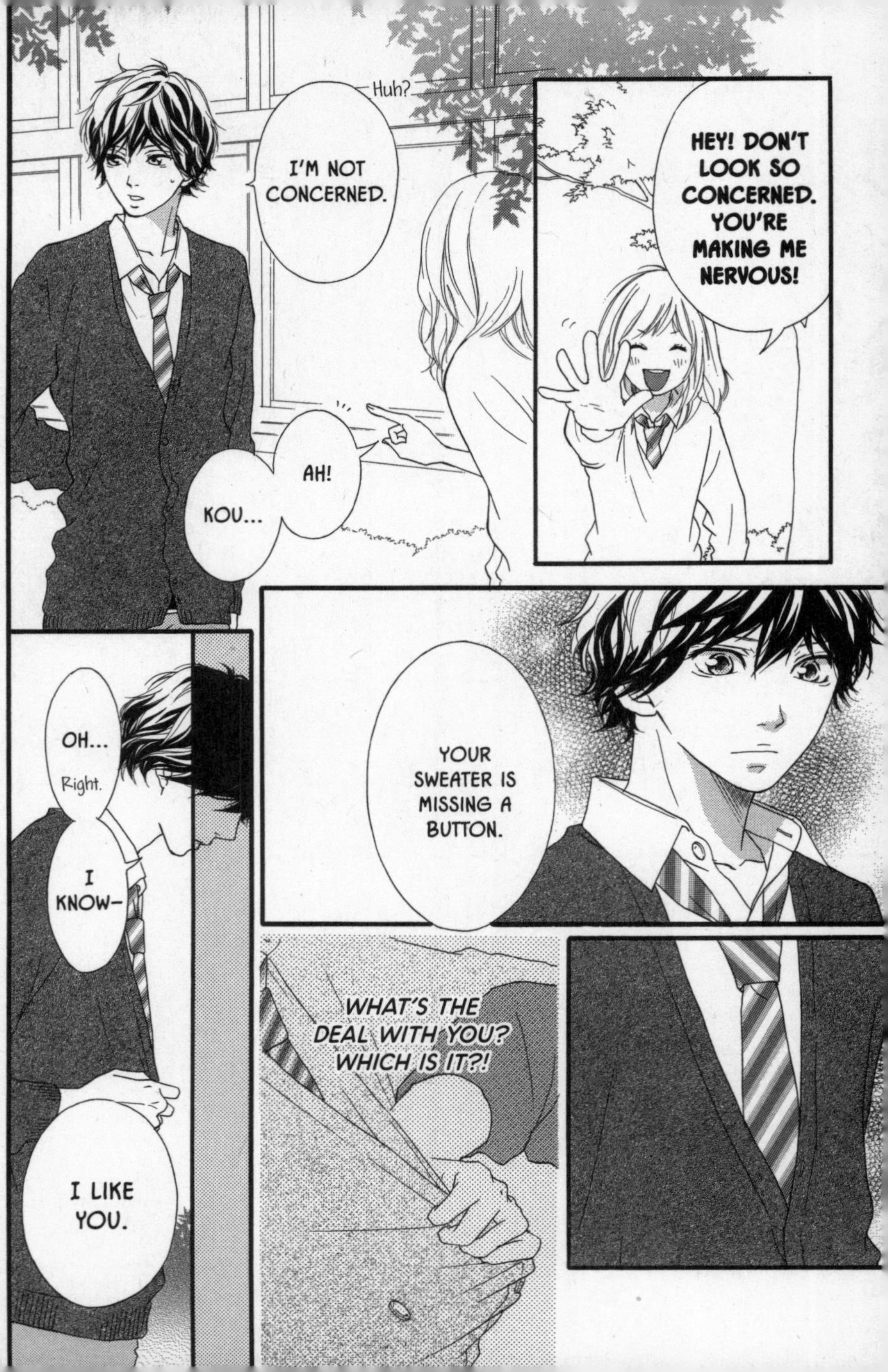
HEY! DON'T LOOK SO CONCERNED. YOU'RE MAKING ME NERVOUS!
Huh?
I'M NOT CONCERNED.
AH!
KOU...
YOUR SWEATER IS MISSING A BUTTON.
WHAT'S THE DEAL WITH YOU? WHICH IS IT?!
OH...
Right.
I KNOW—
I LIKE YOU.

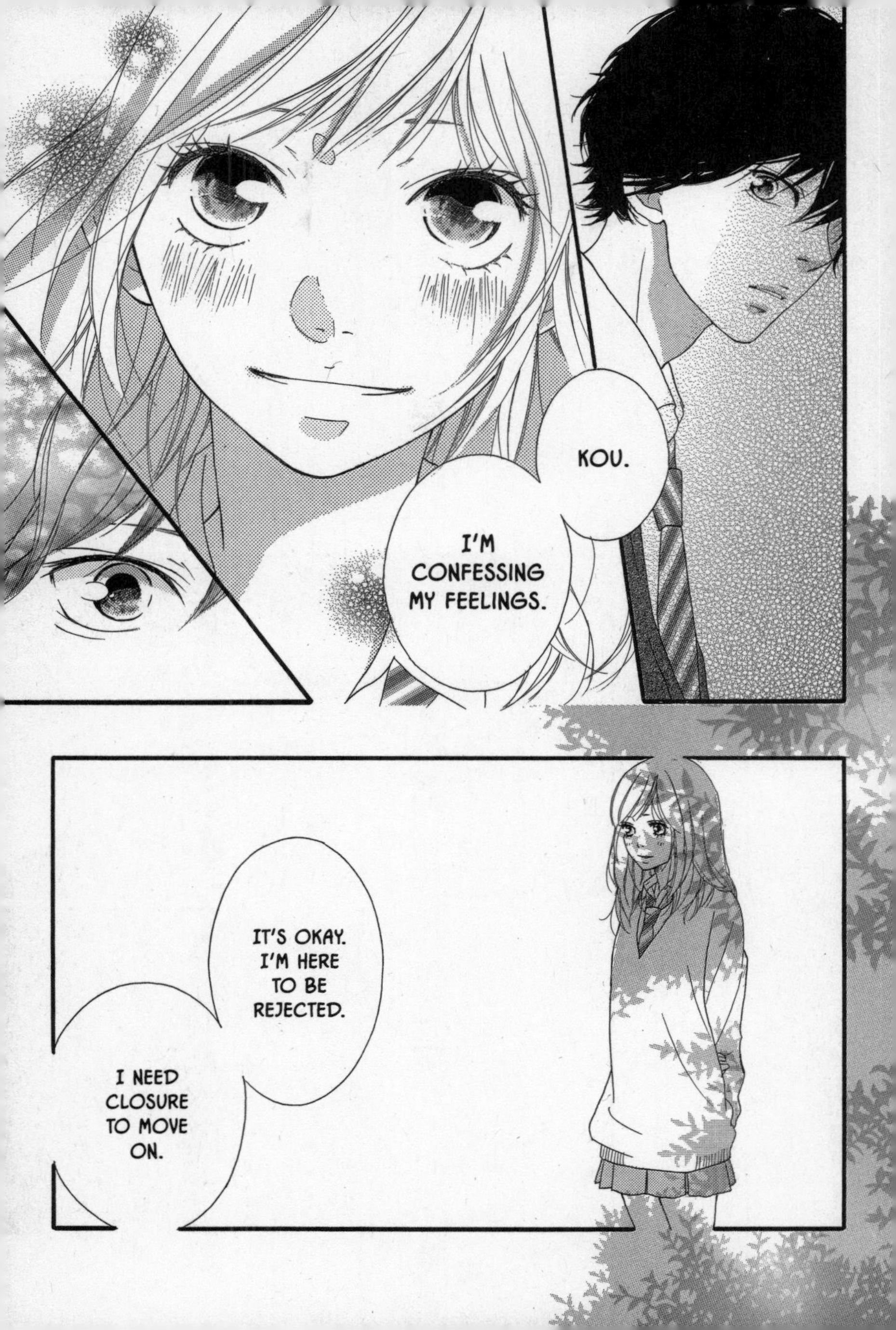
KOU.
I'M CONFESSING MY FEELINGS.
IT'S OKAY. I'M HERE TO BE REJECTED.
I NEED CLOSURE TO MOVE ON.

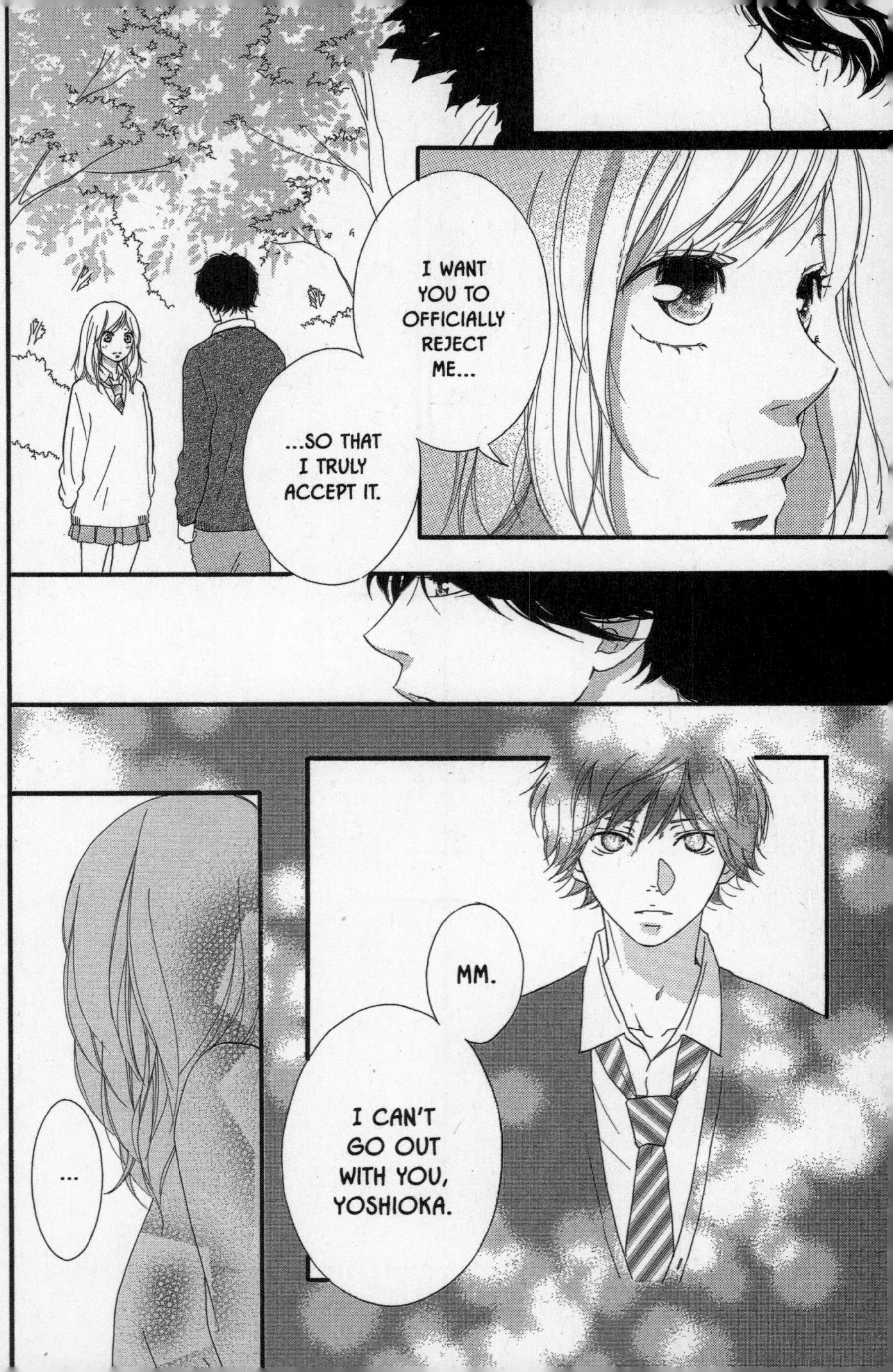
I WANT YOU TO OFFICIALLY REJECT ME...
...SO THAT I TRULY ACCEPT IT.
MM.
I CAN'T GO OUT WITH YOU, YOSHIOKA.
...

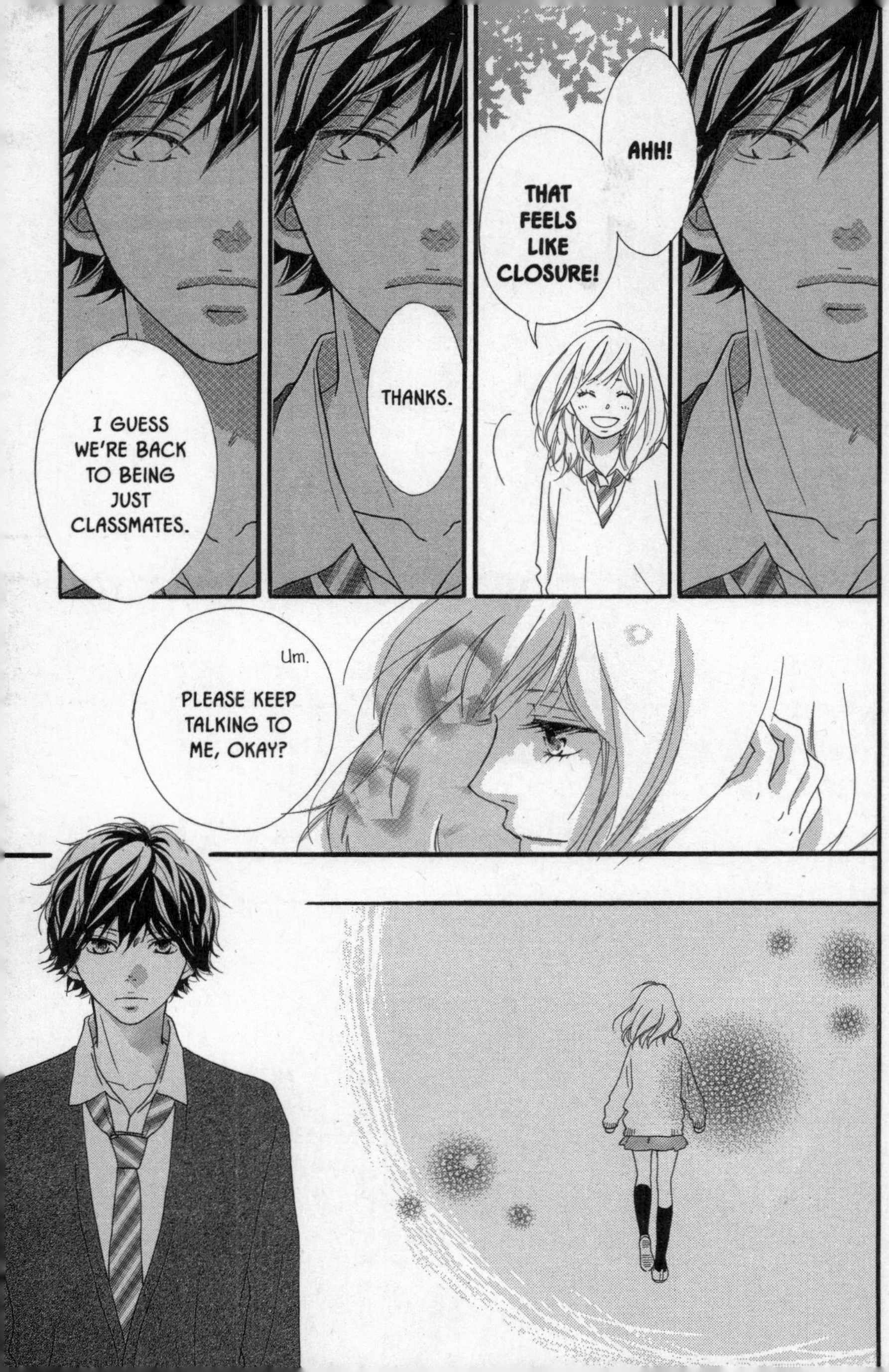
AHH!
THAT FEELS LIKE CLOSURE!
THANKS.
I GUESS WE'RE BACK TO BEING JUST CLASSMATES.
Um.
PLEASE KEEP TALKING TO ME, OKAY?

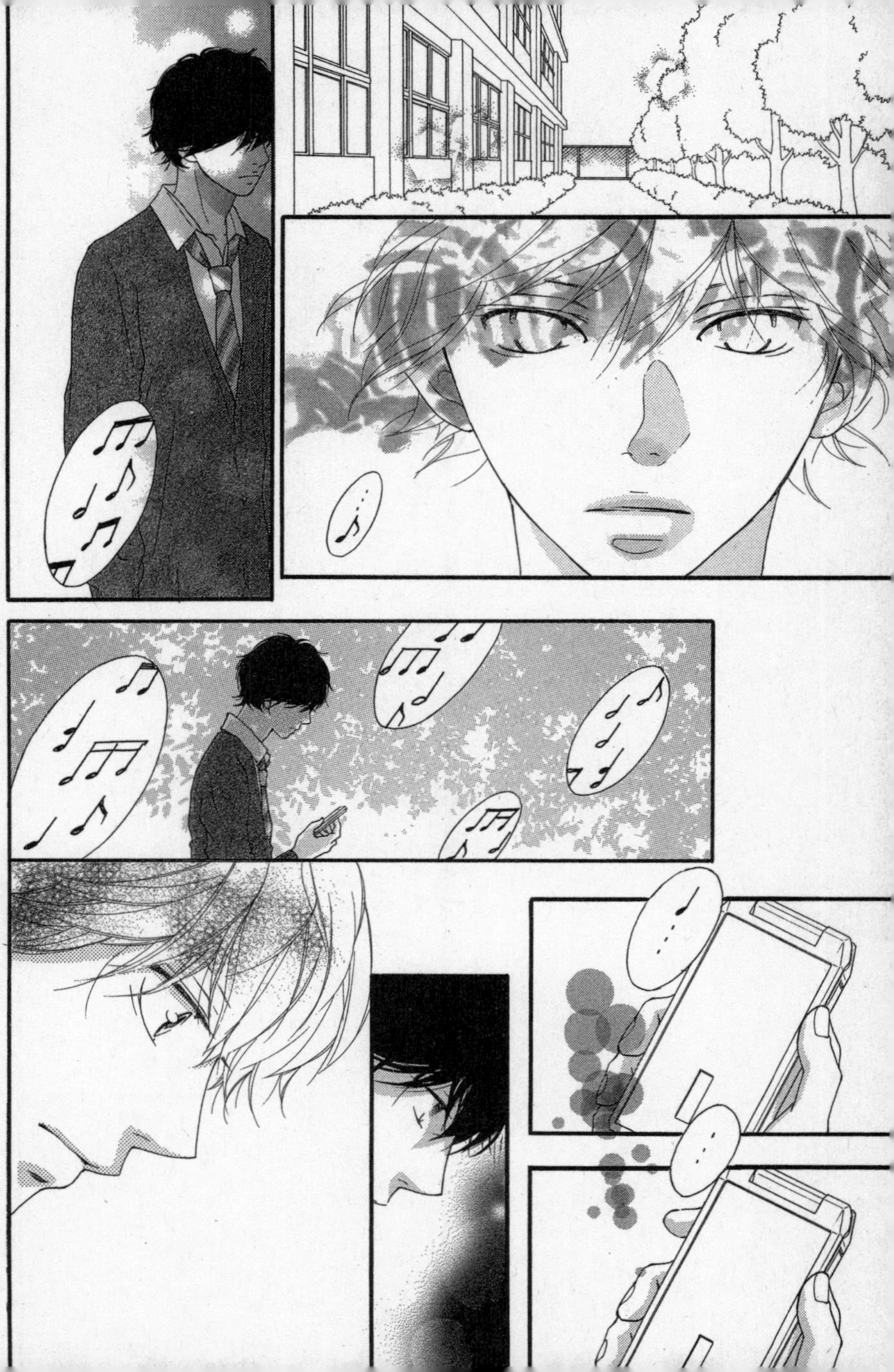
…♪
…
…

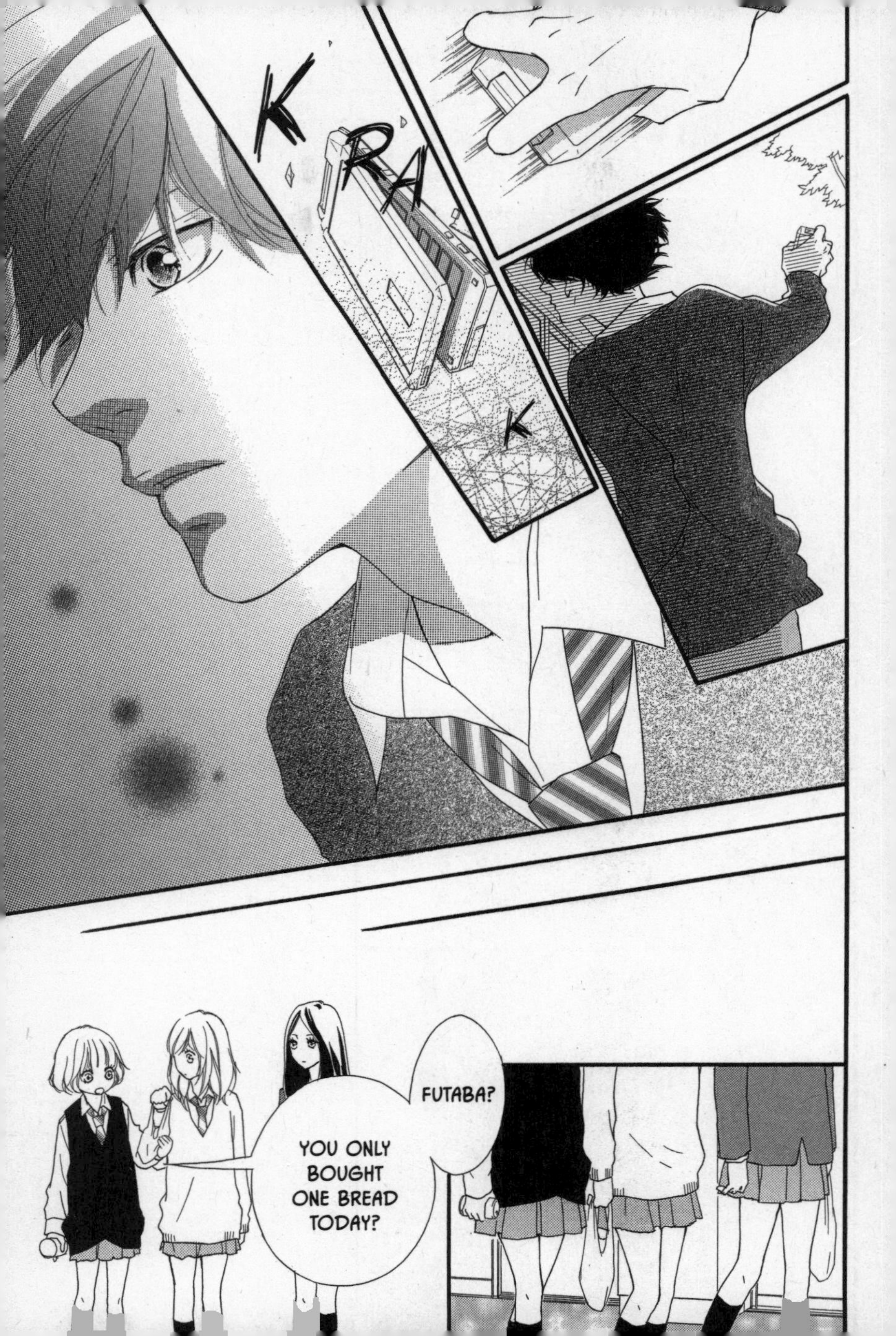
KRAK
FUTABA?
YOU ONLY BOUGHT ONE BREAD TODAY?

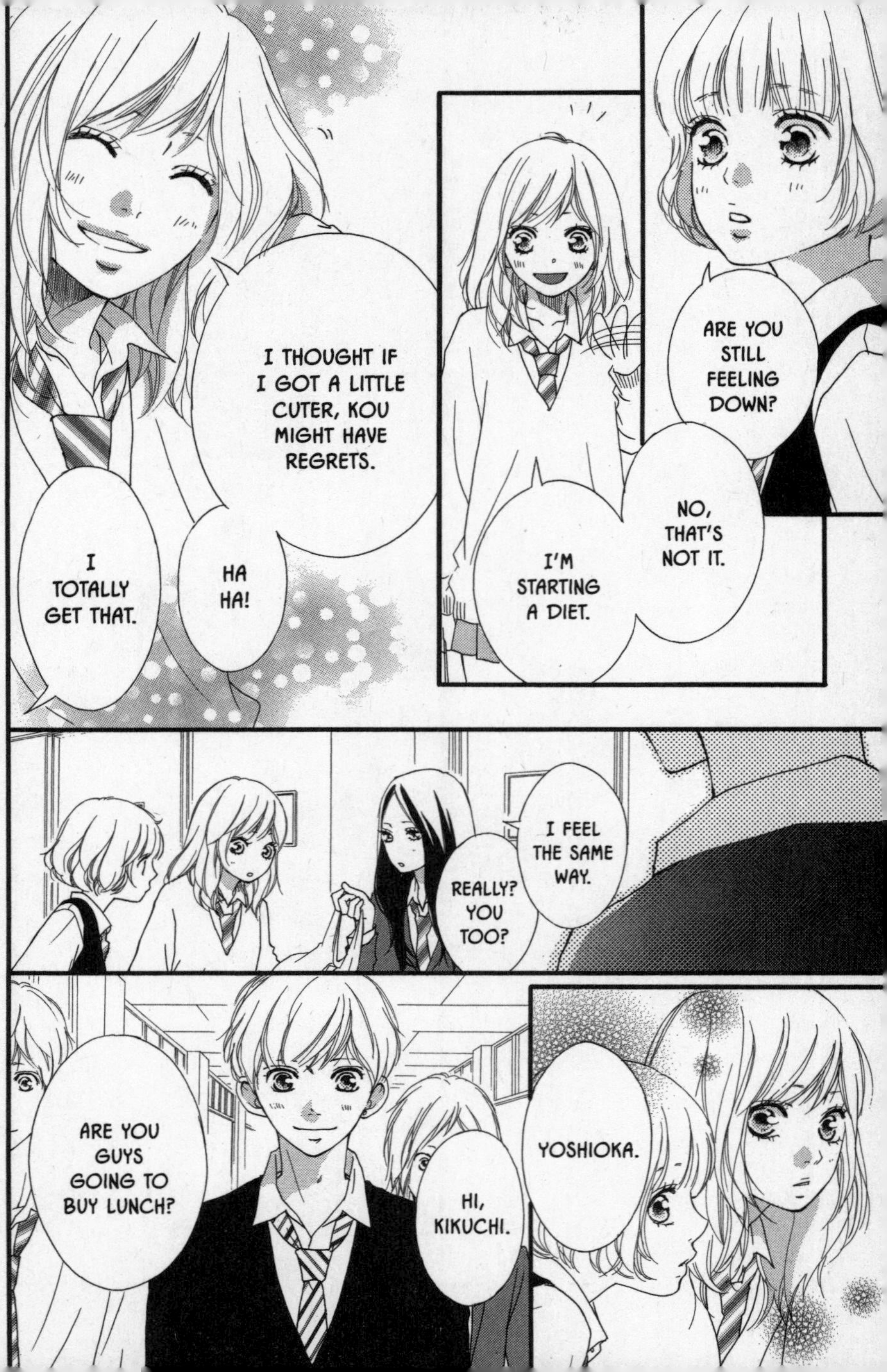
ARE YOU STILL FEELING DOWN?
NO, THAT'S NOT IT.
I'M STARTING A DIET.
I THOUGHT IF I GOT A LITTLE CUTER, KOU MIGHT HAVE REGRETS.
HA HA!
I TOTALLY GET THAT.
I FEEL THE SAME WAY.
REALLY? YOU TOO?
YOSHIOKA.
HI, KIKUCHI.
ARE YOU GUYS GOING TO BUY LUNCH?

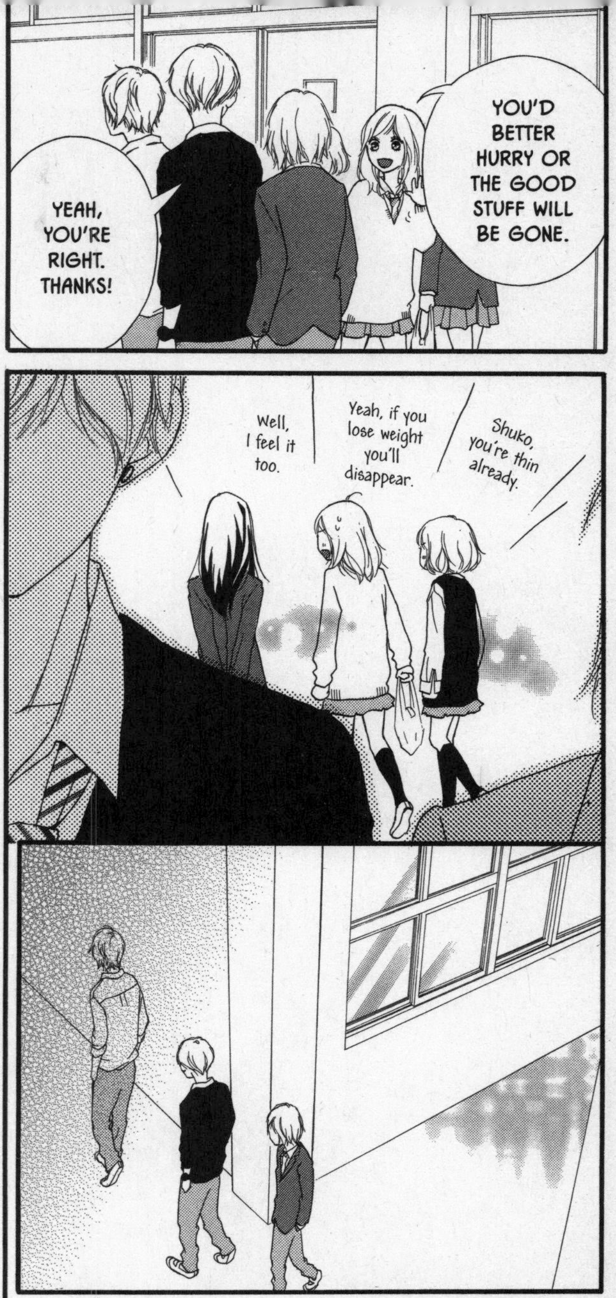
YOU'D BETTER HURRY OR THE GOOD STUFF WILL BE GONE.
YEAH, YOU'RE RIGHT. THANKS!
Shuko, you're thin already.
Yeah, if you lose weight you'll disappear.
Well, I feel it too.

Lately I've been getting so many unsolicited text messages that I've been turning off my phone. I turn it back on once per day, and when I do I get a barrage of stupid texts that I then have to delete. I'm worried I may mistakenly delete important messages in this process, but I am not willing to make the effort to change my settings to block incoming messages. Why is that? It must be my personality. Meanwhile, the flip phone (that I forced myself to use for longer than necessary for some reason) has started to break, so I think it's time for an upgrade. When I do, I think I will change my phone's text address. The new phone I want is sold by a different carrier, so I'll need to change it anyway. I think it's a good thing. But, while I write this, I can also see myself continuing to use my fat old flip phone for a while longer.

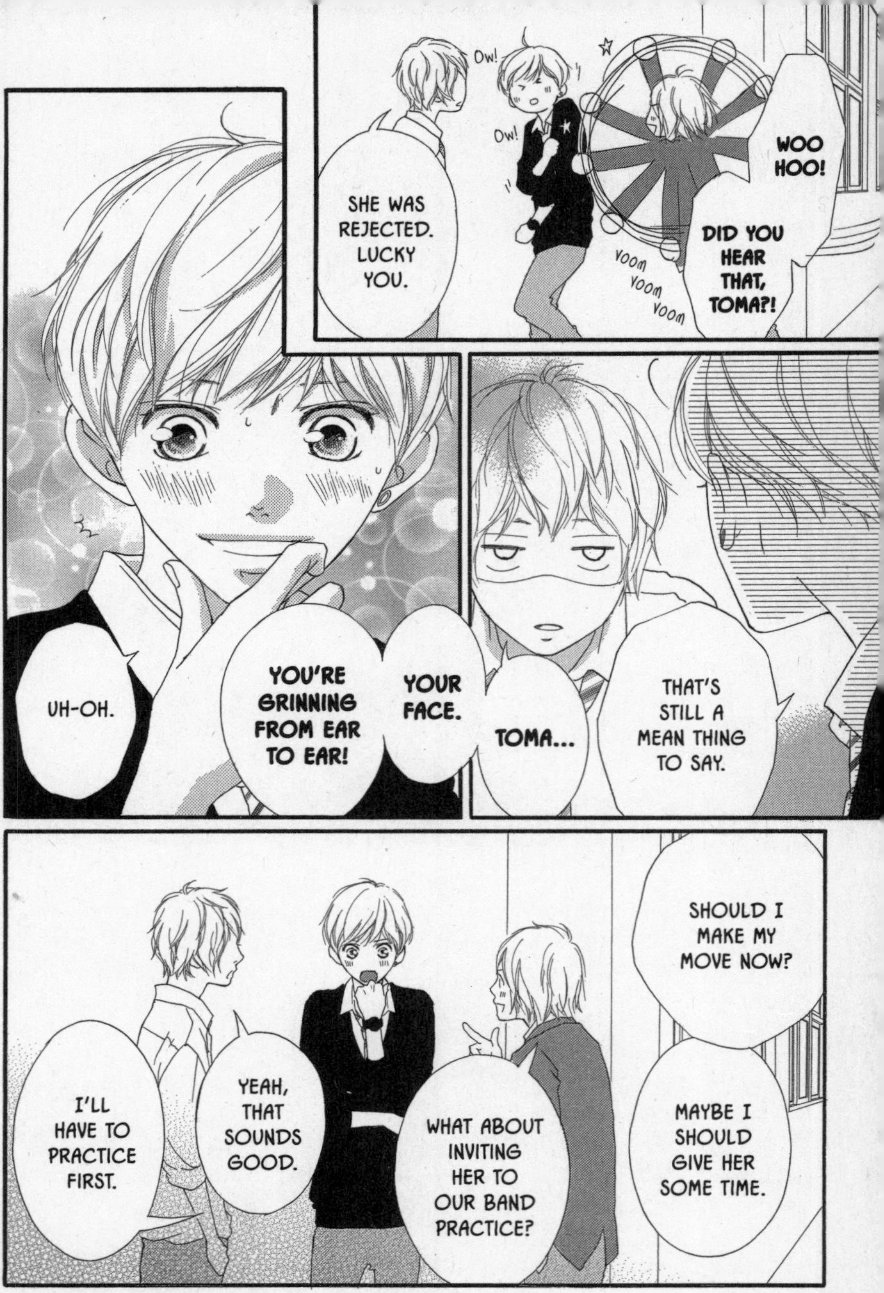
WOO HOO!
DID YOU HEAR THAT, TOMA?!
VOOM VOOM VOOM
OW!
OW!
SHE WAS REJECTED. LUCKY YOU.
THAT'S STILL A MEAN THING TO SAY.
TOMA...
YOUR FACE.
YOU'RE GRINNING FROM EAR TO EAR!
UH-OH.
SHOULD I MAKE MY MOVE NOW?
MAYBE I SHOULD GIVE HER SOME TIME.
WHAT ABOUT INVITING HER TO OUR BAND PRACTICE?
YEAH, THAT SOUNDS GOOD.
I'LL HAVE TO PRACTICE FIRST.

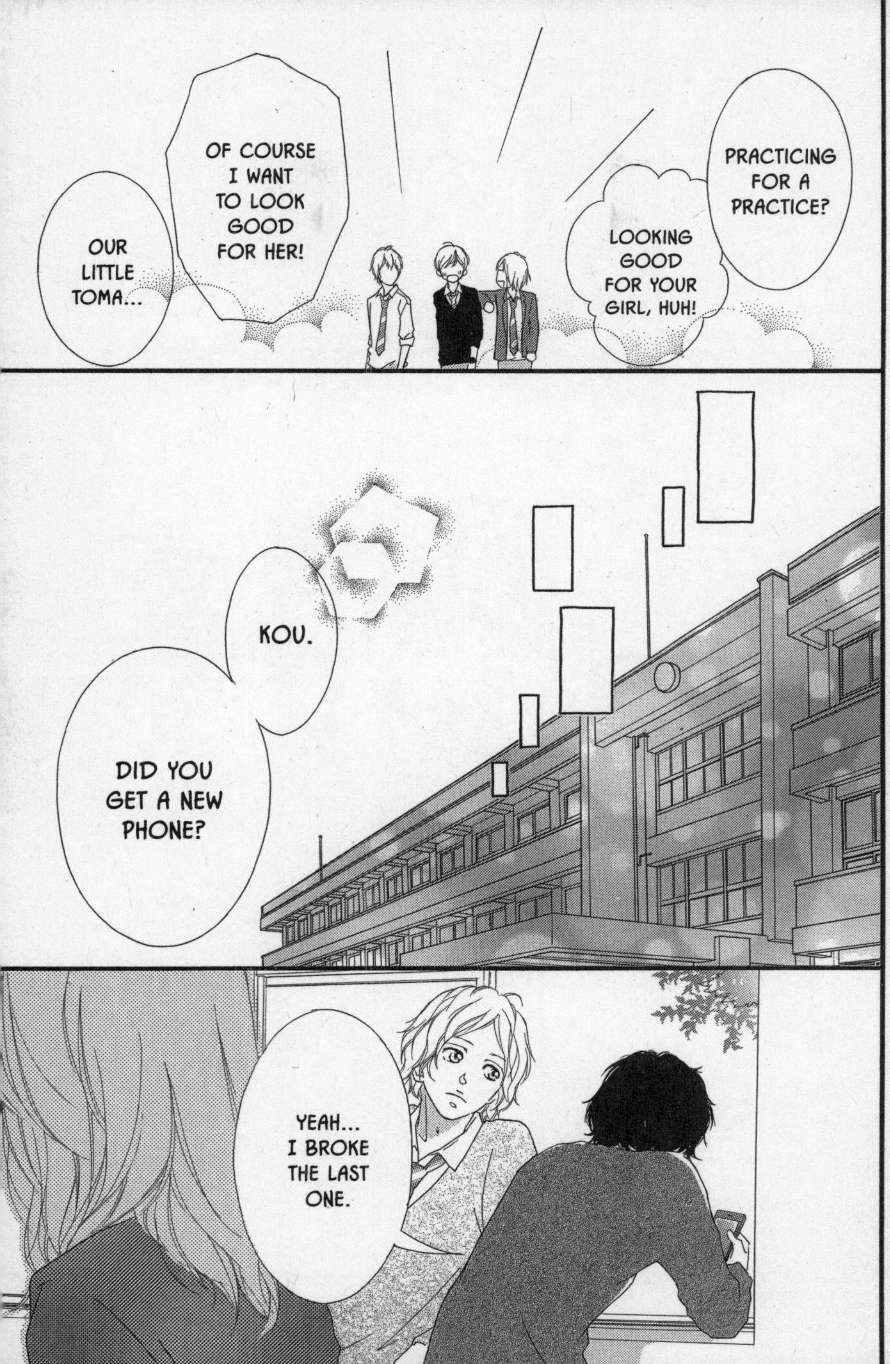
PRACTICING FOR A PRACTICE?
LOOKING GOOD FOR YOUR GIRL, HUH!
OF COURSE I WANT TO LOOK GOOD FOR HER!
OUR LITTLE TOMA...
KOU.
DID YOU GET A NEW PHONE?
YEAH... I BROKE THE LAST ONE.

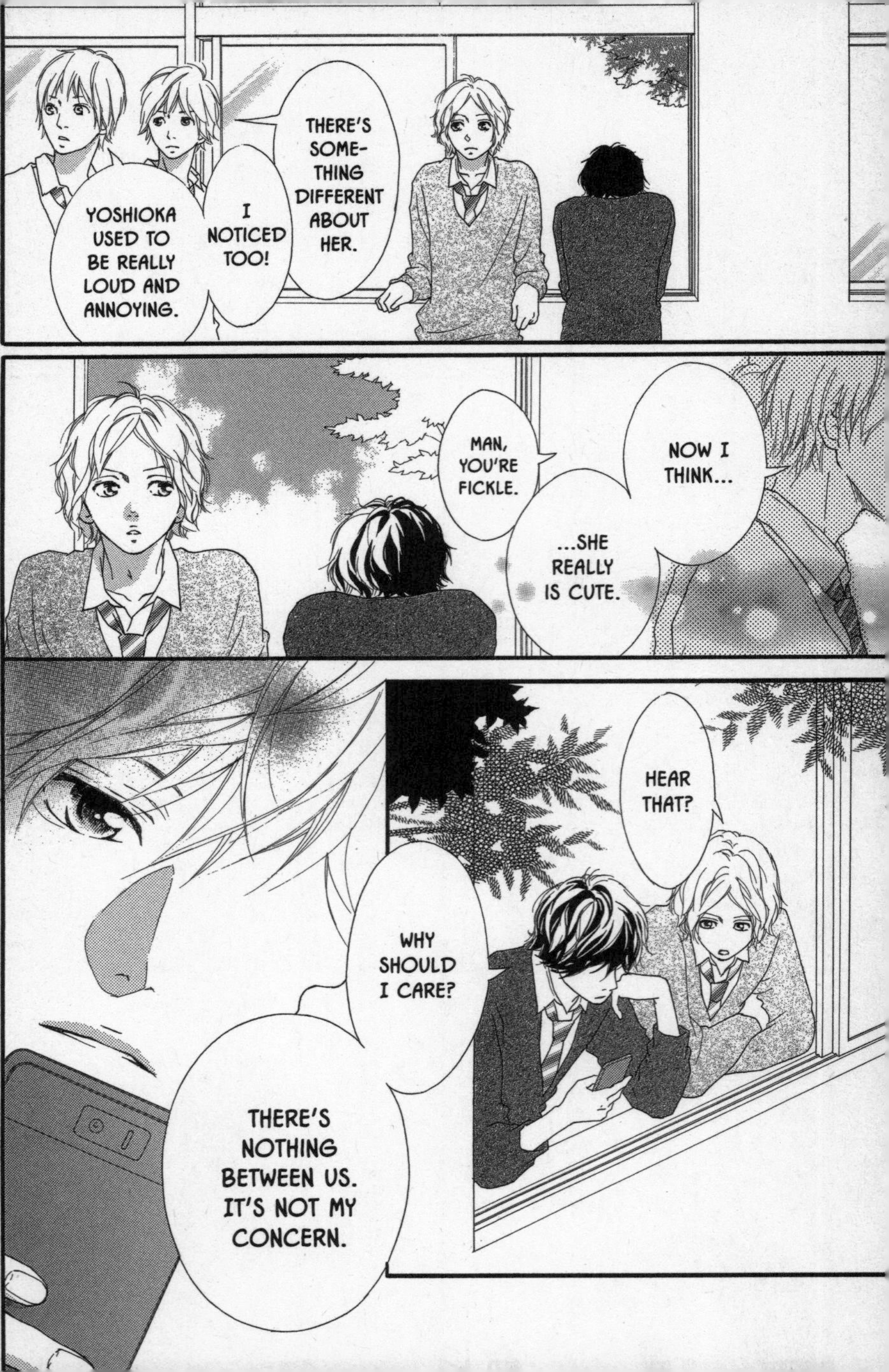
THERE'S SOME-THING DIFFERENT ABOUT HER.
I NOTICED TOO!
YOSHIOKA USED TO BE REALLY LOUD AND ANNOYING.
NOW I THINK...
...SHE REALLY IS CUTE.
MAN, YOU'RE FICKLE.
HEAR THAT?
WHY SHOULD I CARE?
THERE'S NOTHING BETWEEN US. IT'S NOT MY CONCERN.

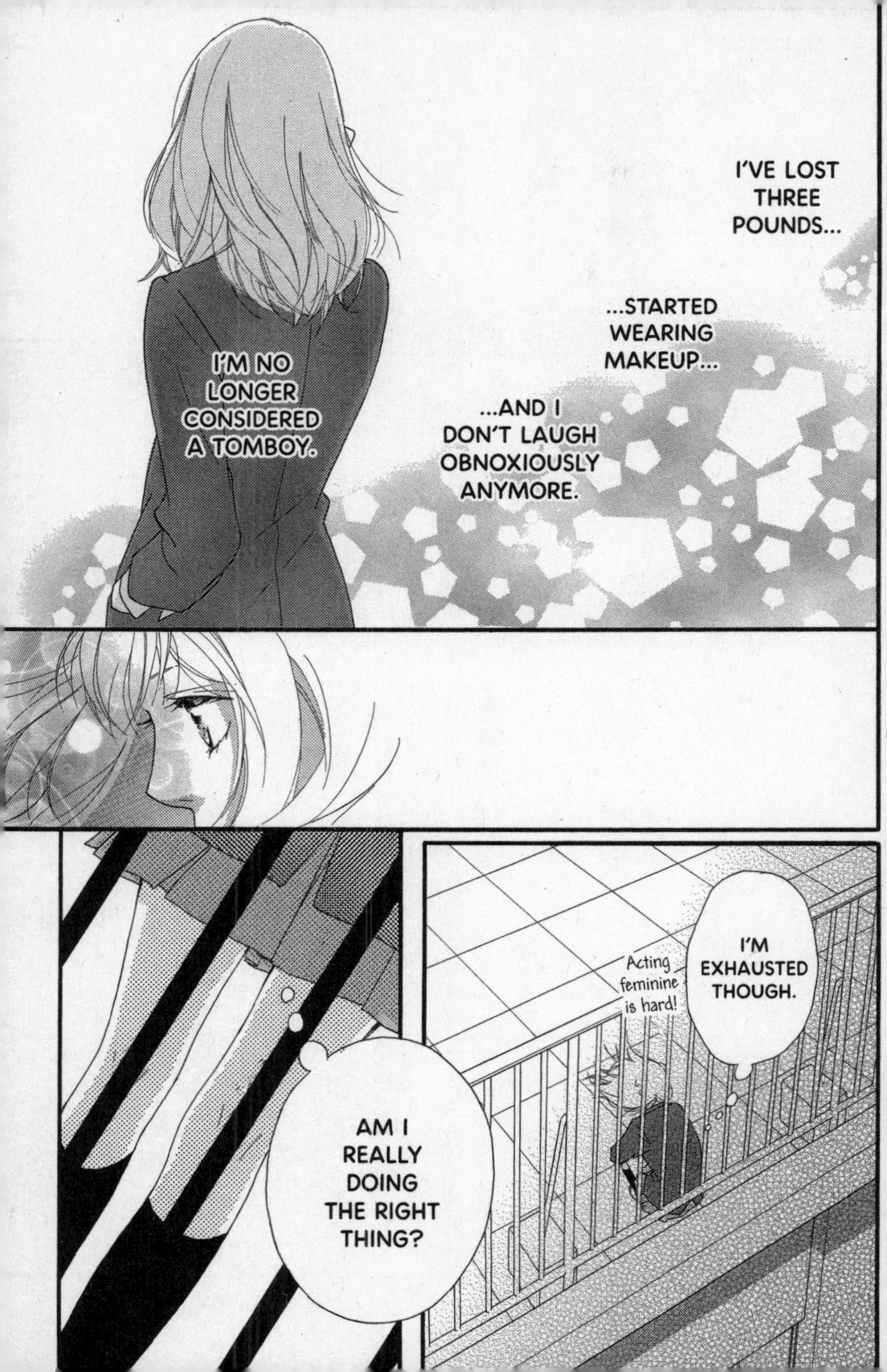
I'VE LOST THREE POUNDS...
...STARTED WEARING MAKEUP...
...AND I DON'T LAUGH OBNOXIOUSLY ANYMORE.
I'M NO LONGER CONSIDERED A TOMBOY.
I'M EXHAUSTED THOUGH.
Acting feminine is hard!
AM I REALLY DOING THE RIGHT THING?

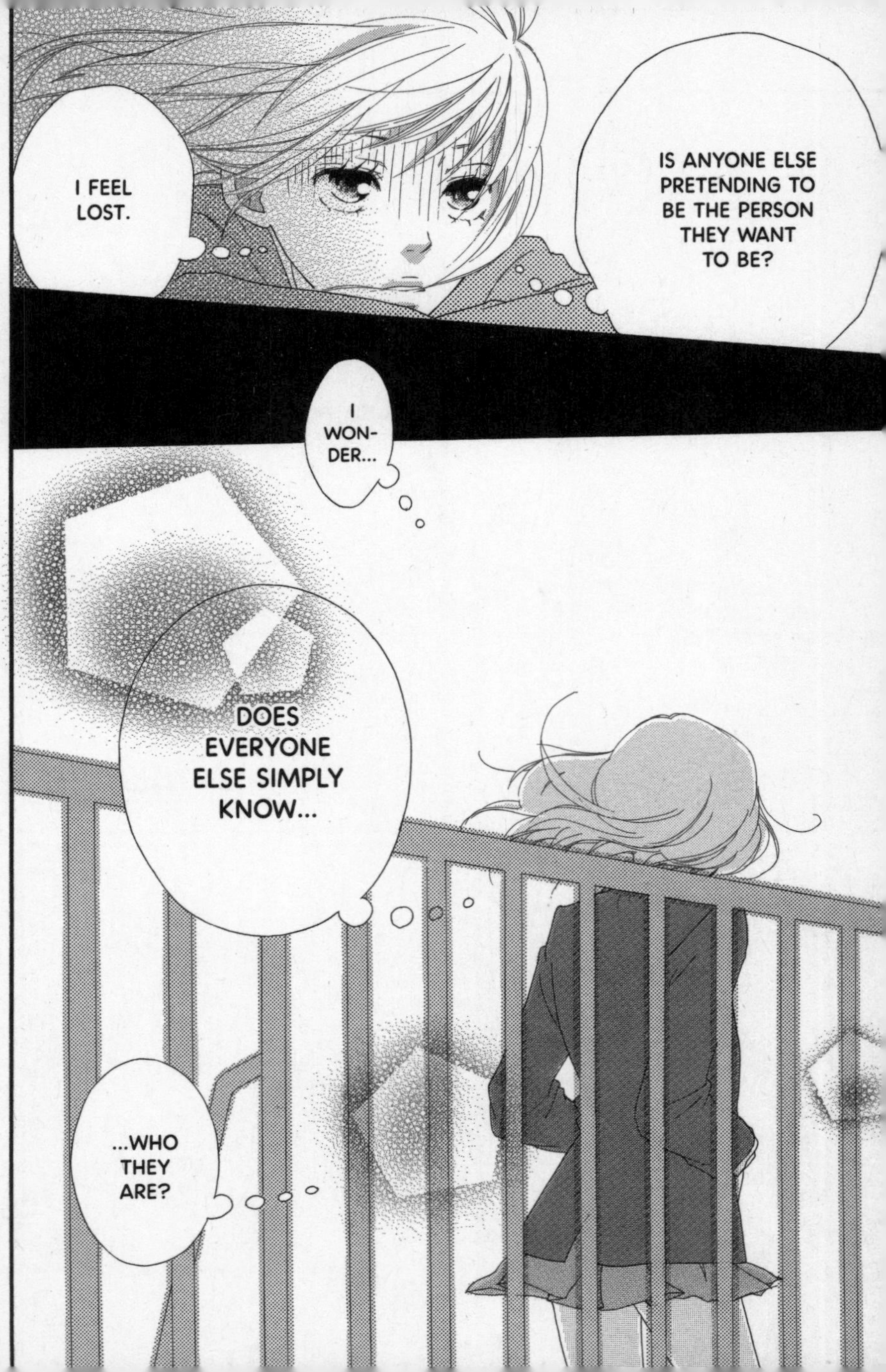
IS ANYONE ELSE PRETENDING TO BE THE PERSON THEY WANT TO BE?
I FEEL LOST.
I WONDER...
DOES EVERYONE ELSE SIMPLY KNOW...
...WHO THEY ARE?

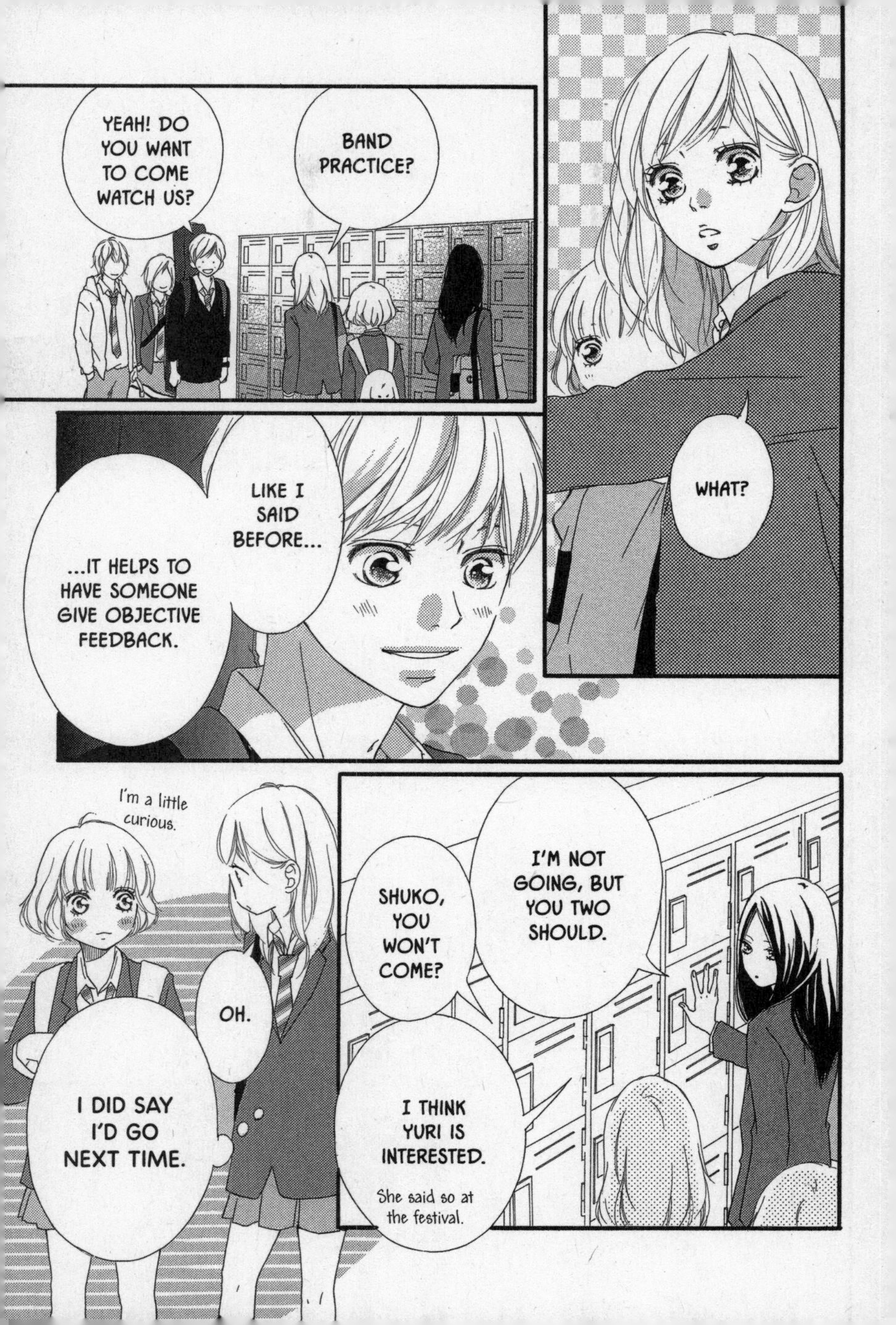
WHAT?
BAND PRACTICE?
YEAH! DO YOU WANT TO COME WATCH US?
LIKE I SAID BEFORE...
...IT HELPS TO HAVE SOMEONE GIVE OBJECTIVE FEEDBACK.
I'M NOT GOING, BUT YOU TWO SHOULD.
SHUKO, YOU WON'T COME?
I THINK YURI IS INTERESTED.
She said so at the festival.
I'm a little curious.
OH.
I DID SAY I'D GO NEXT TIME.

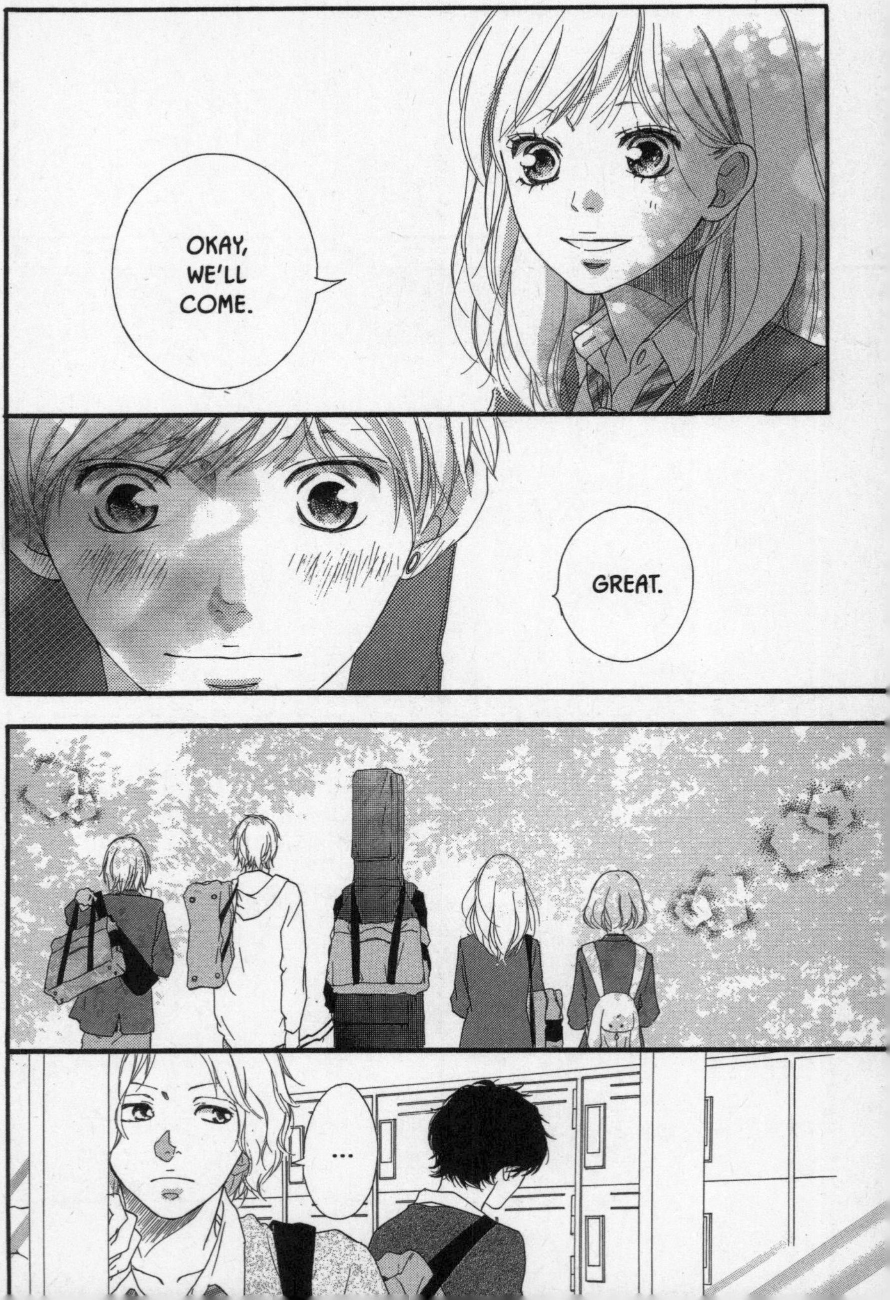
OKAY, WE'LL COME.
GREAT.
...

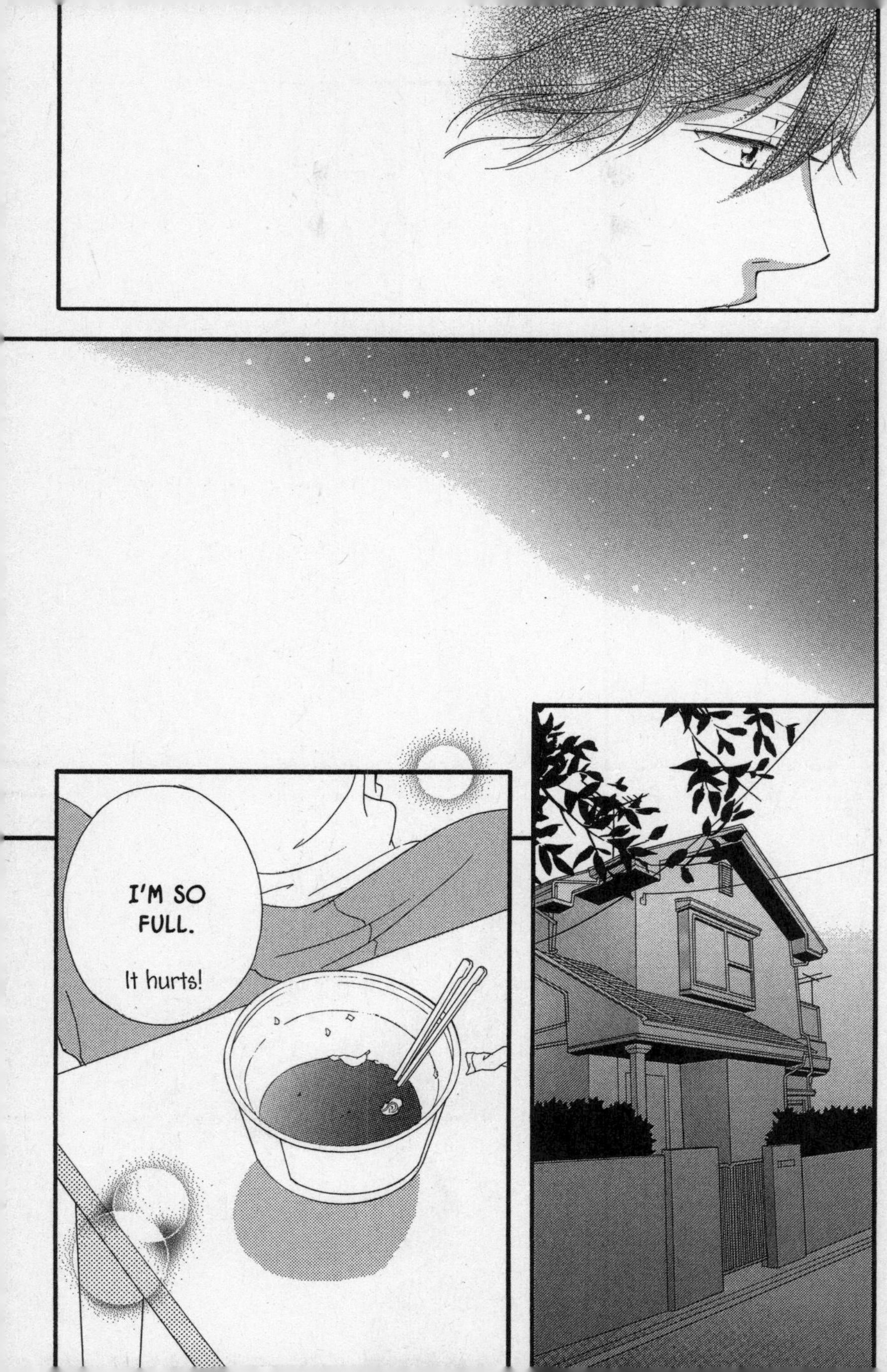
I'M SO FULL.
It hurts!

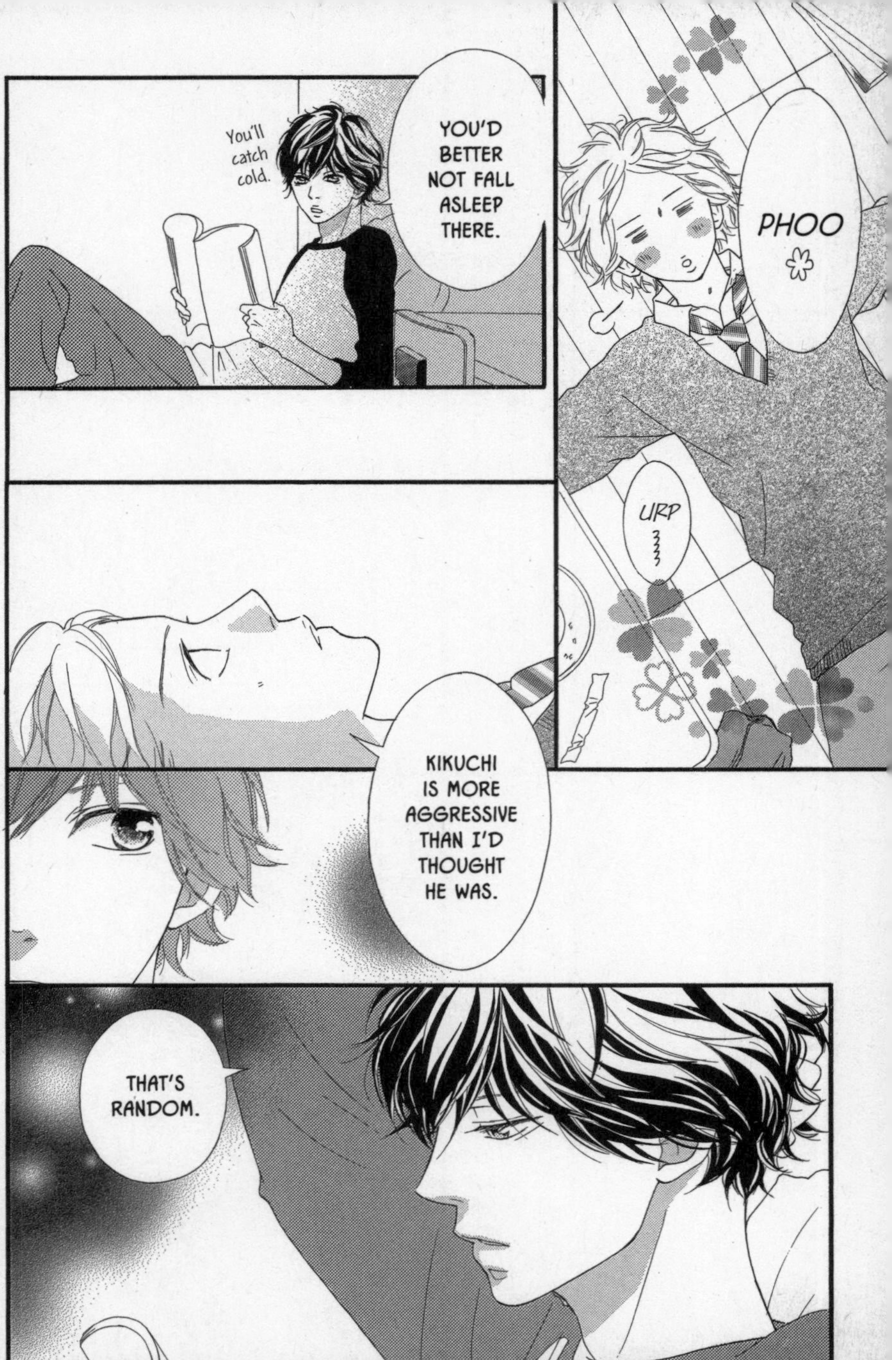
PHOO
URP
YOU'D BETTER NOT FALL ASLEEP THERE.
You'll catch cold.
KIKUCHI IS MORE AGGRESSIVE THAN I'D THOUGHT HE WAS.
THAT'S RANDOM.

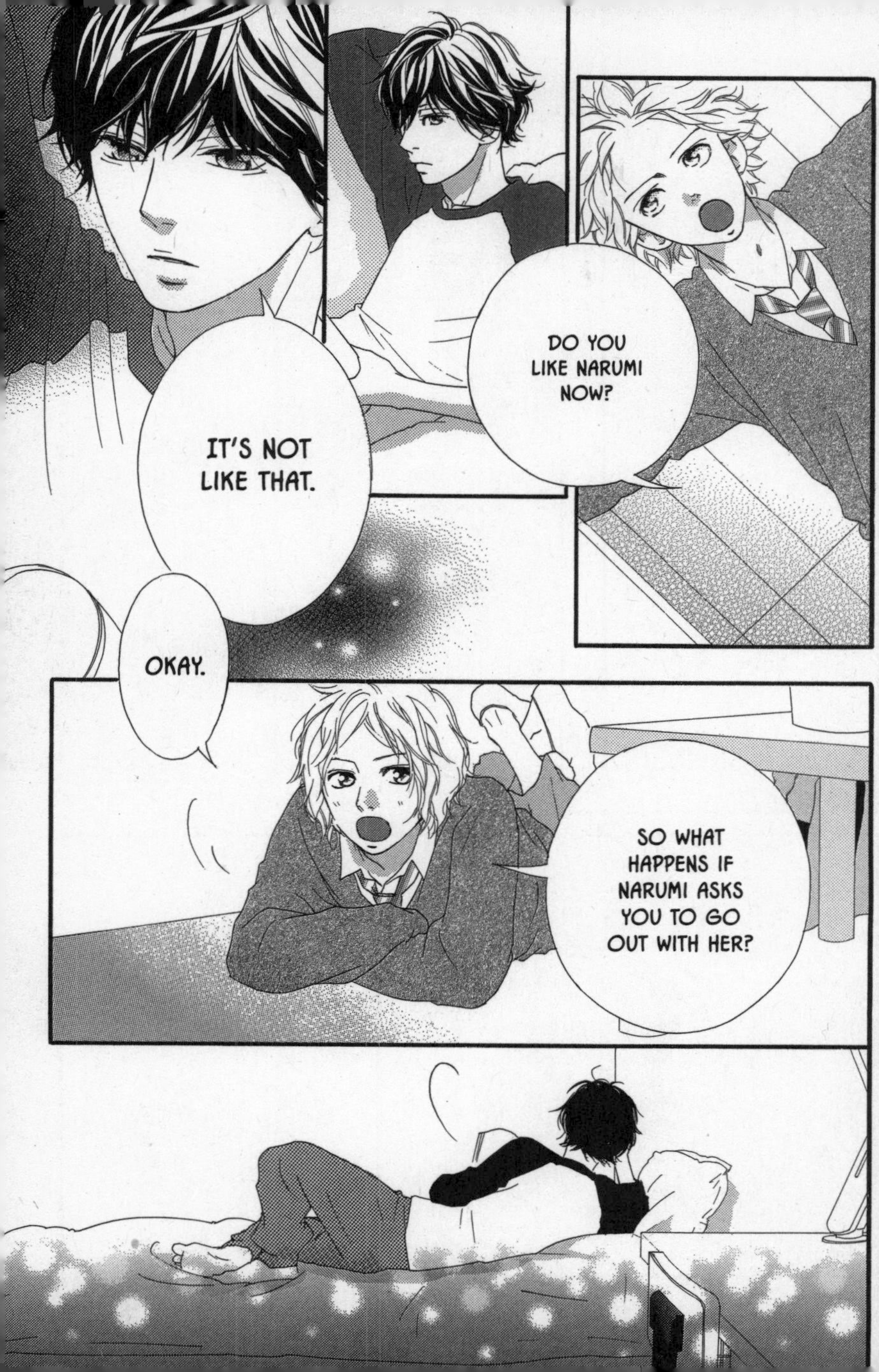
DO YOU LIKE NARUMI NOW?
IT'S NOT LIKE THAT.
OKAY.
SO WHAT HAPPENS IF NARUMI ASKS YOU TO GO OUT WITH HER?

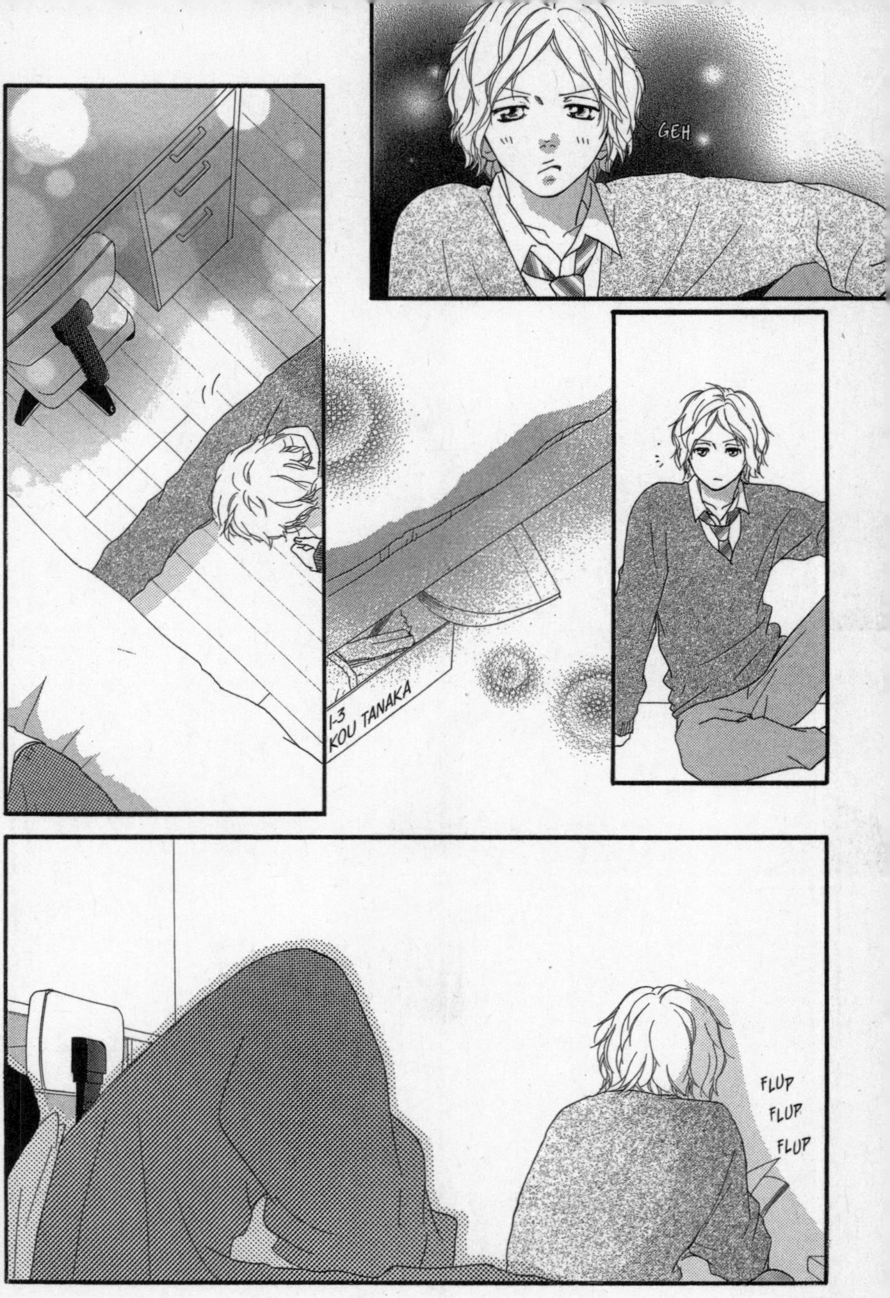
GEH
1-3
KOU TANAKA
FLUP
FLUP
FLUP

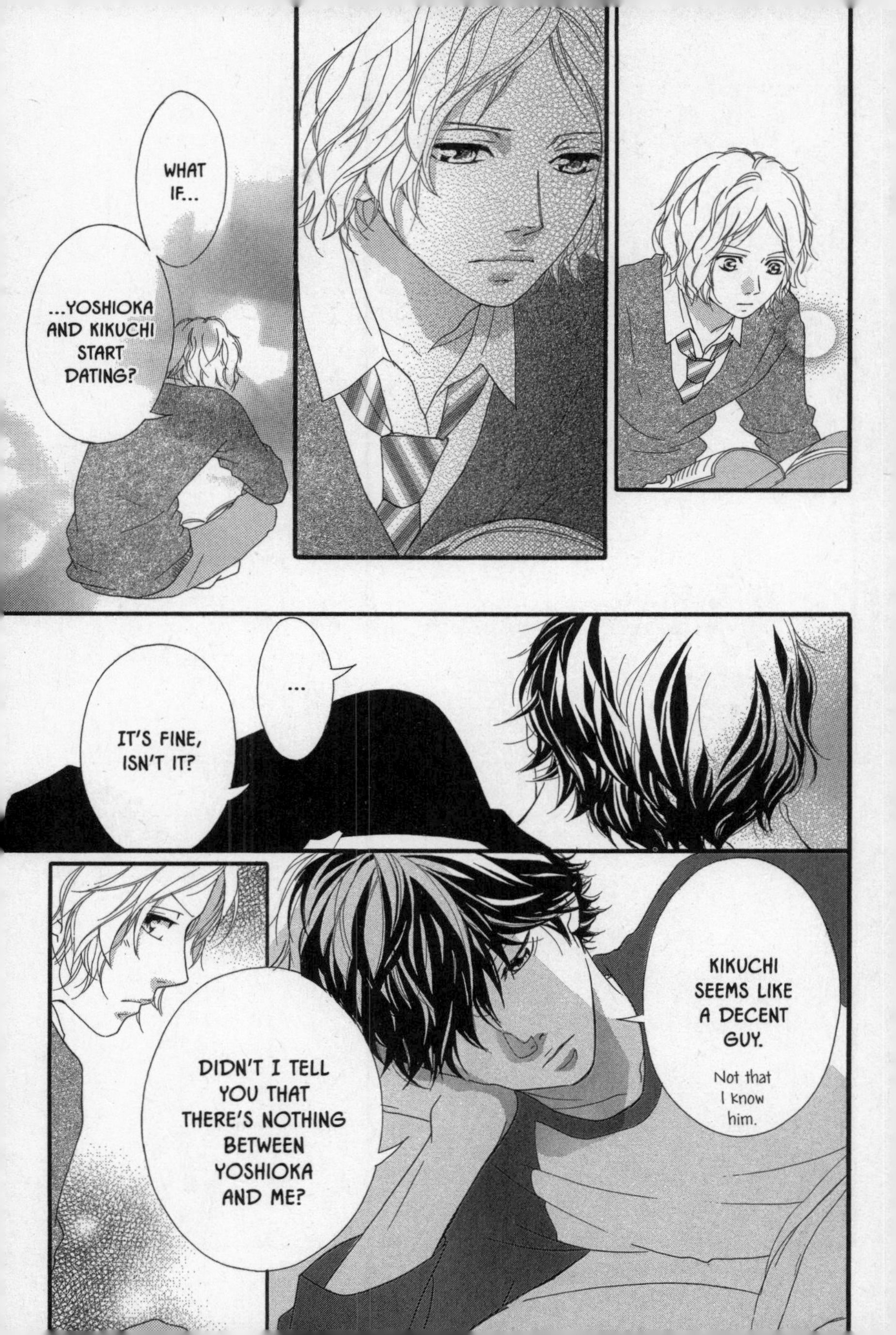
WHAT IF...
...YOSHIOKA AND KIKUCHI START DATING?
...
IT'S FINE, ISN'T IT?
KIKUCHI SEEMS LIKE A DECENT GUY.
Not that I know him.
DIDN'T I TELL YOU THAT THERE'S NOTHING BETWEEN YOSHIOKA AND ME?

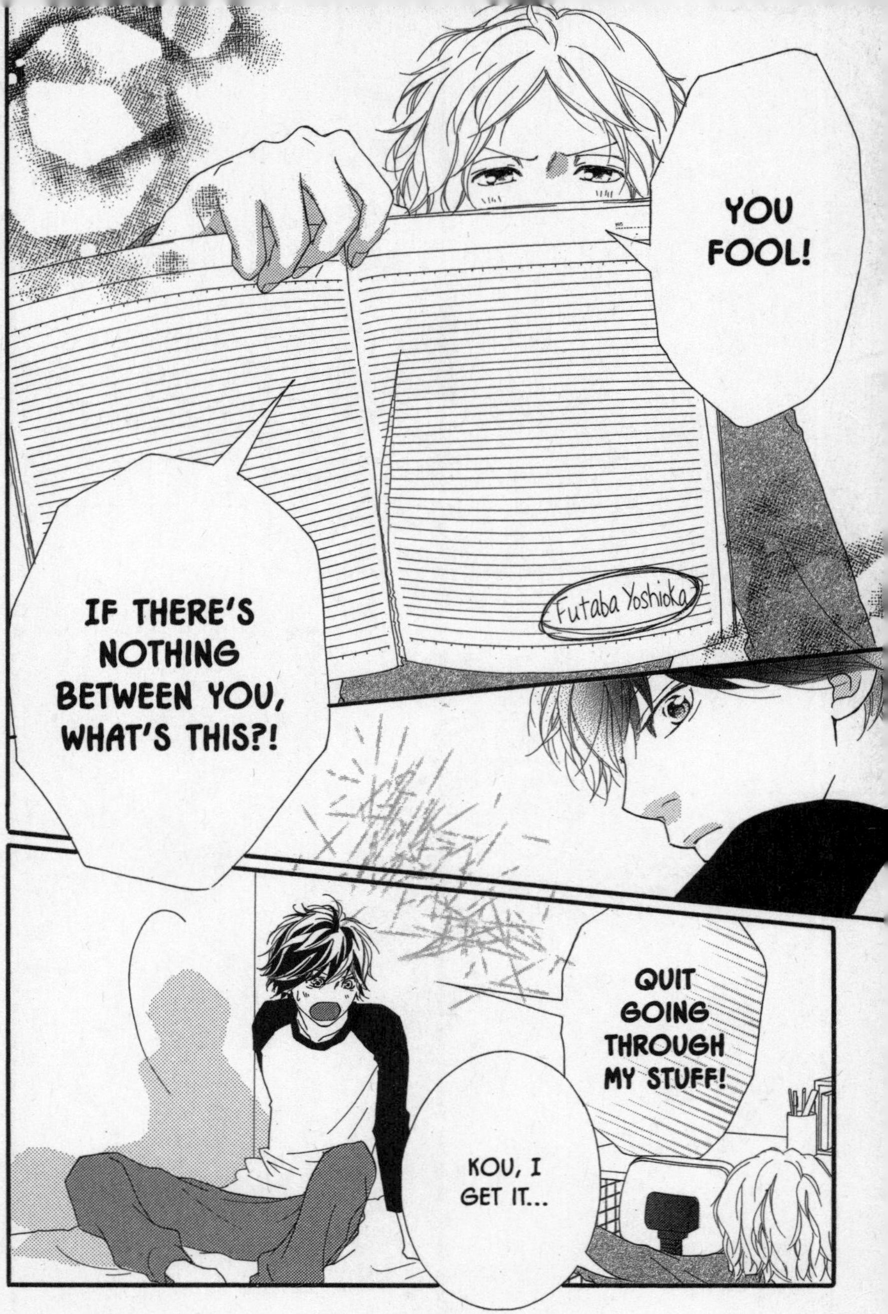
YOU FOOL!
Futaba Yoshioka
IF THERE'S NOTHING BETWEEN YOU, WHAT'S THIS?!
QUIT GOING THROUGH MY STUFF!
KOU, I GET IT...

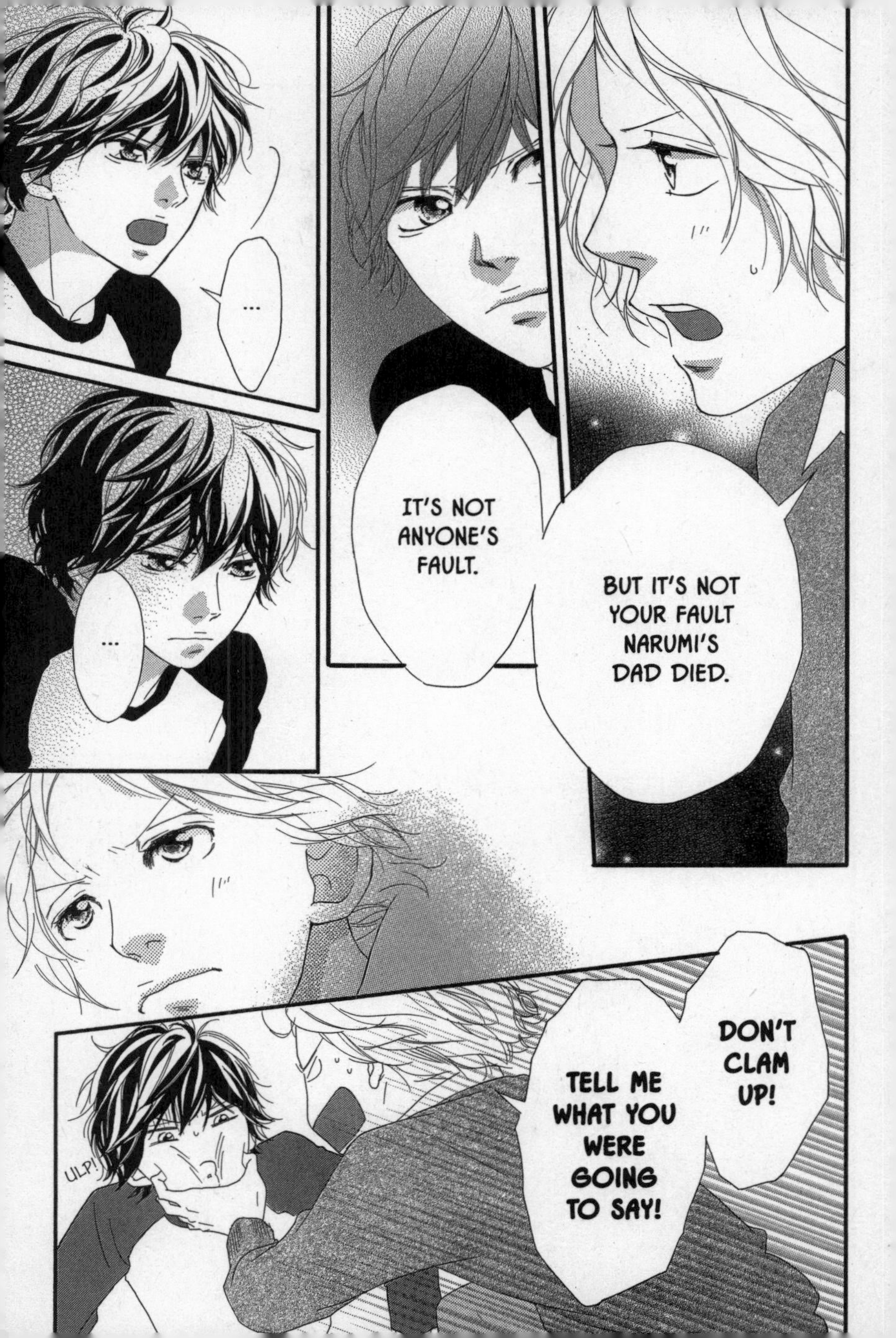
BUT IT'S NOT YOUR FAULT NARUMI'S DAD DIED.
IT'S NOT ANYONE'S FAULT.
...
...
DON'T CLAM UP!
TELL ME WHAT YOU WERE GOING TO SAY!
ULP!

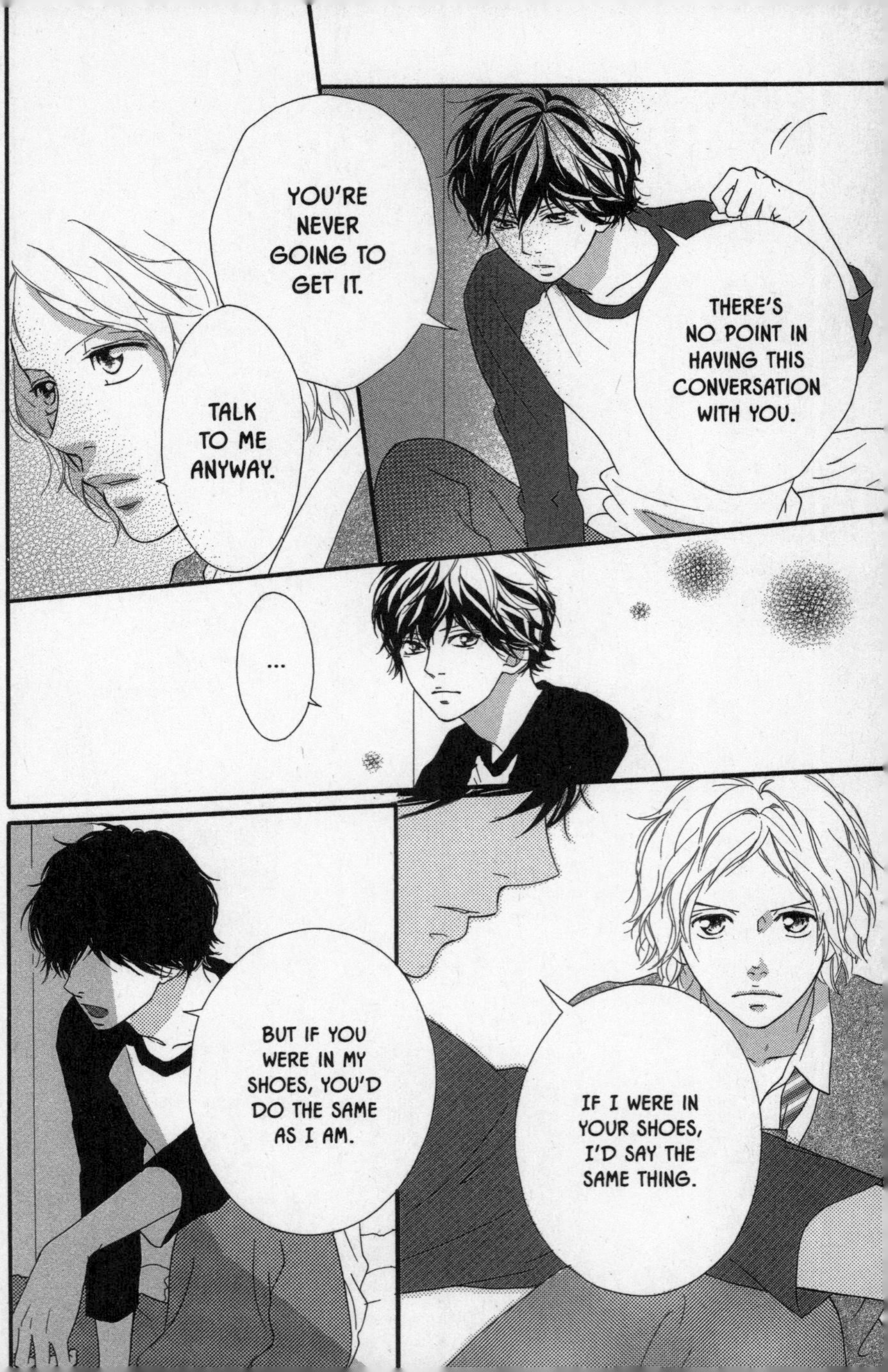
THERE'S NO POINT IN HAVING THIS CONVERSATION WITH YOU.
YOU'RE NEVER GOING TO GET IT.
TALK TO ME ANYWAY.
...
IF I WERE IN YOUR SHOES, I'D SAY THE SAME THING.
BUT IF YOU WERE IN MY SHOES, YOU'D DO THE SAME AS I AM.

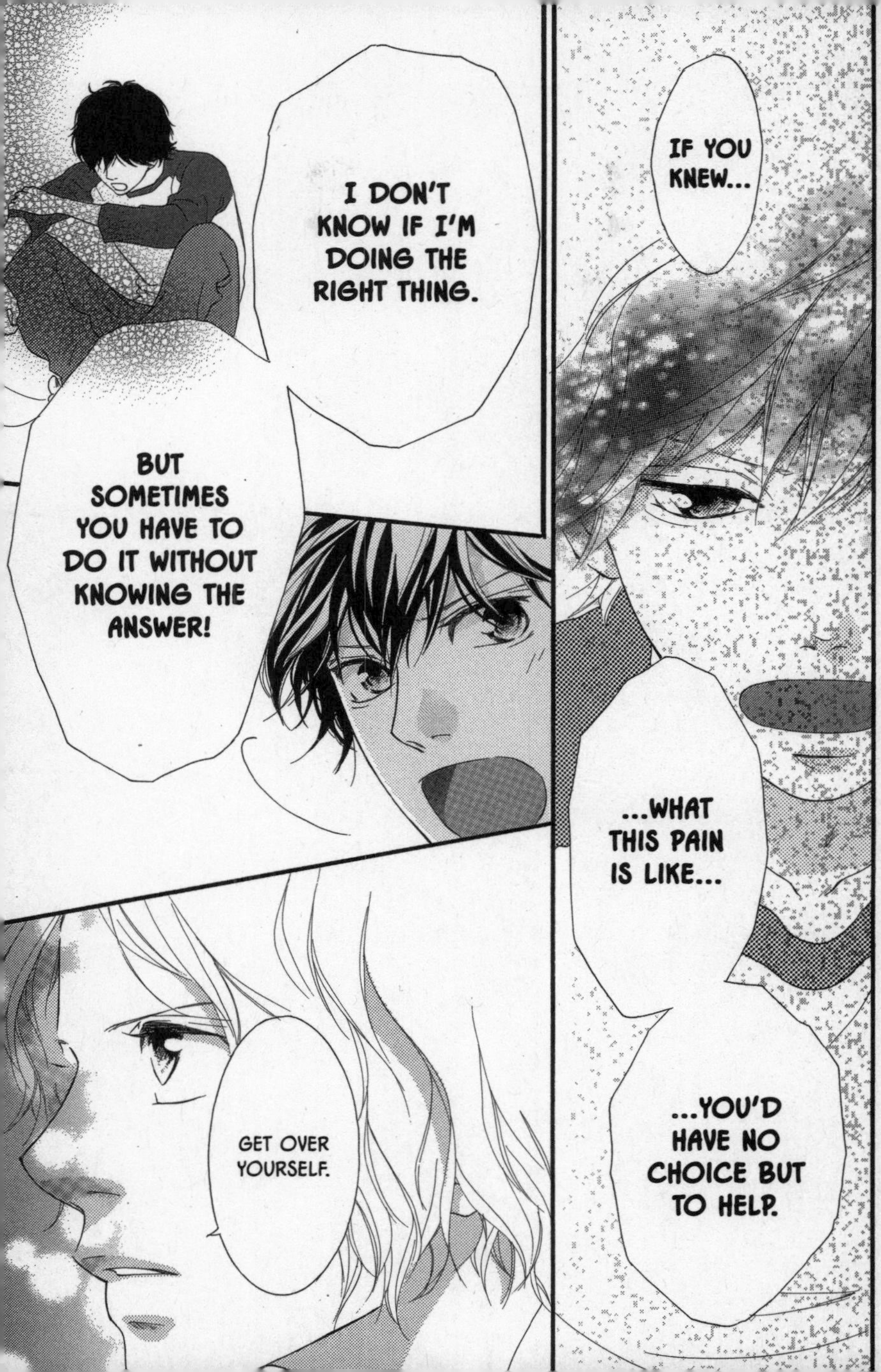
IF YOU KNEW...
...WHAT THIS PAIN IS LIKE...
...YOU'D HAVE NO CHOICE BUT TO HELP.
I DON'T KNOW IF I'M DOING THE RIGHT THING.
BUT SOMETIMES YOU HAVE TO DO IT WITHOUT KNOWING THE ANSWER!
GET OVER YOURSELF.

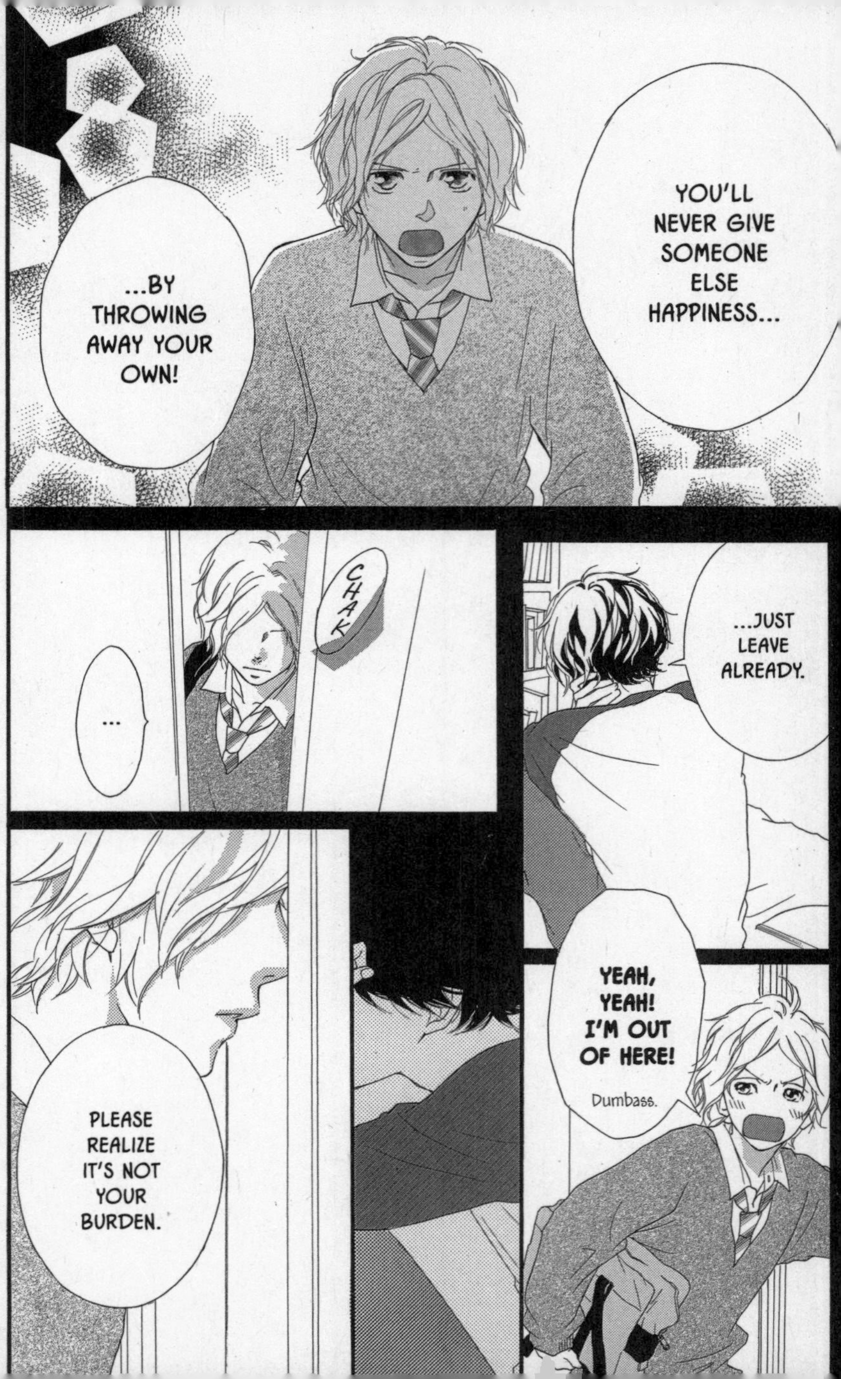
YOU'LL NEVER GIVE SOMEONE ELSE HAPPINESS...
...BY THROWING AWAY YOUR OWN!
...JUST LEAVE ALREADY.
CHAK
...
YEAH, YEAH! I'M OUT OF HERE!
Dumbass.
PLEASE REALIZE IT'S NOT YOUR BURDEN.

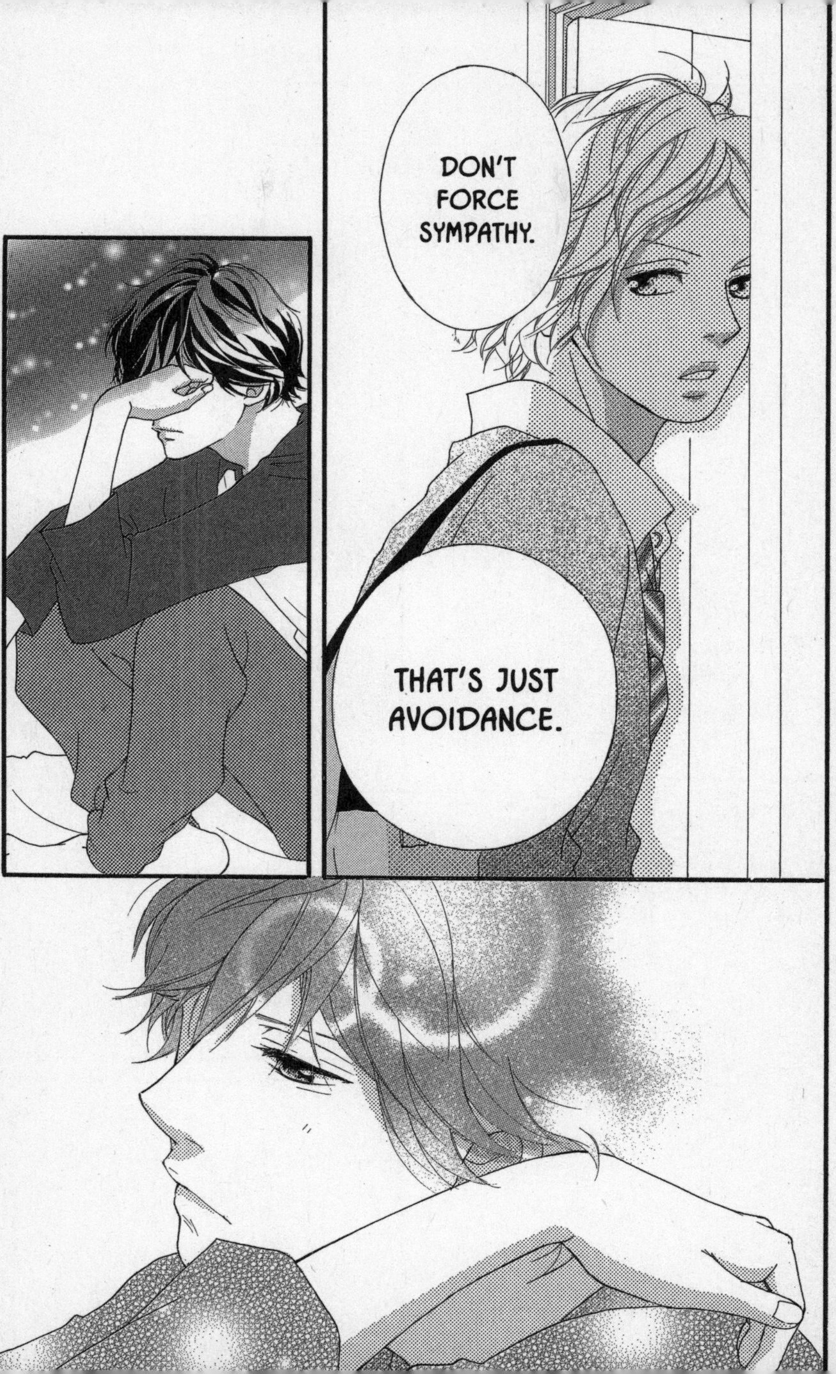
DON'T FORCE SYMPATHY.
THAT'S JUST AVOIDANCE.

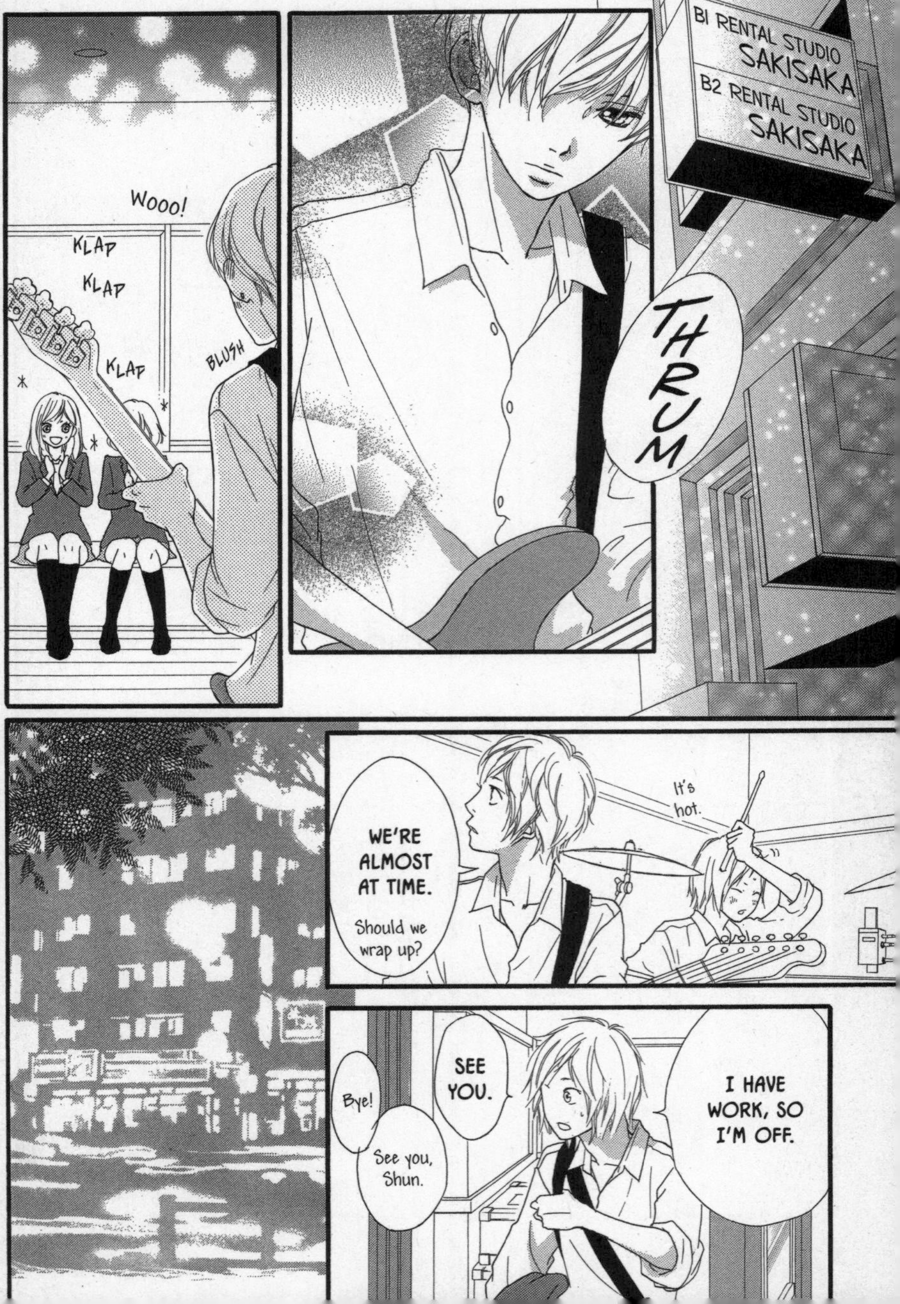
B1 RENTAL STUDIO SAKISAKA
B2 RENTAL STUDIO SAKISAKA
THRUM
WOOO!
KLAP
KLAP
KLAP
BLUSH
It's hot.
WE'RE ALMOST AT TIME.
Should we wrap up?
I HAVE WORK, SO I'M OFF.
SEE YOU.
Bye!
See you, Shun.

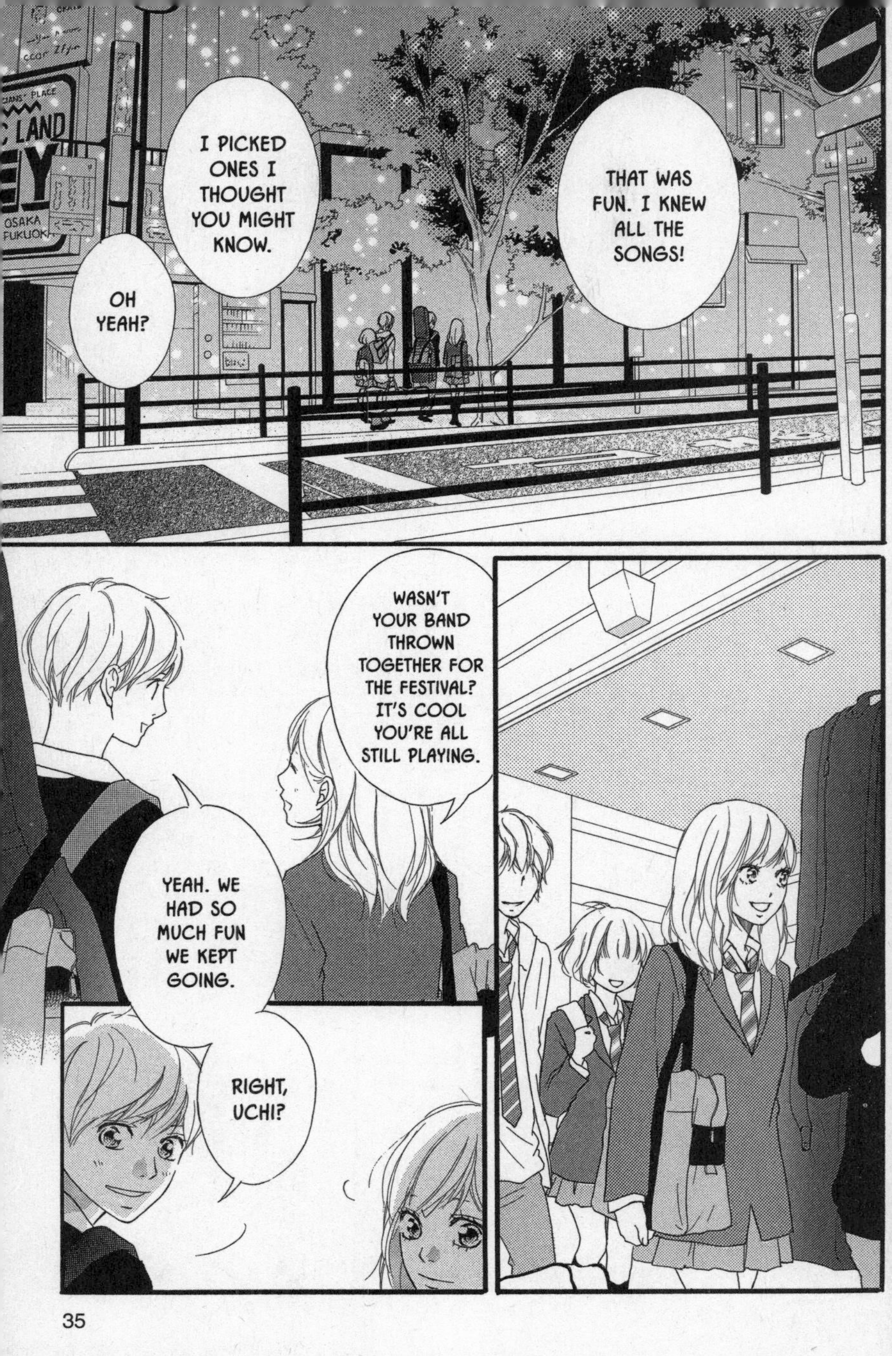
THAT WAS FUN. I KNEW ALL THE SONGS!
I PICKED ONES I THOUGHT YOU MIGHT KNOW.
OH YEAH?
WASN'T YOUR BAND THROWN TOGETHER FOR THE FESTIVAL? IT'S COOL YOU'RE ALL STILL PLAYING.
YEAH. WE HAD SO MUCH FUN WE KEPT GOING.
RIGHT, UCHI?

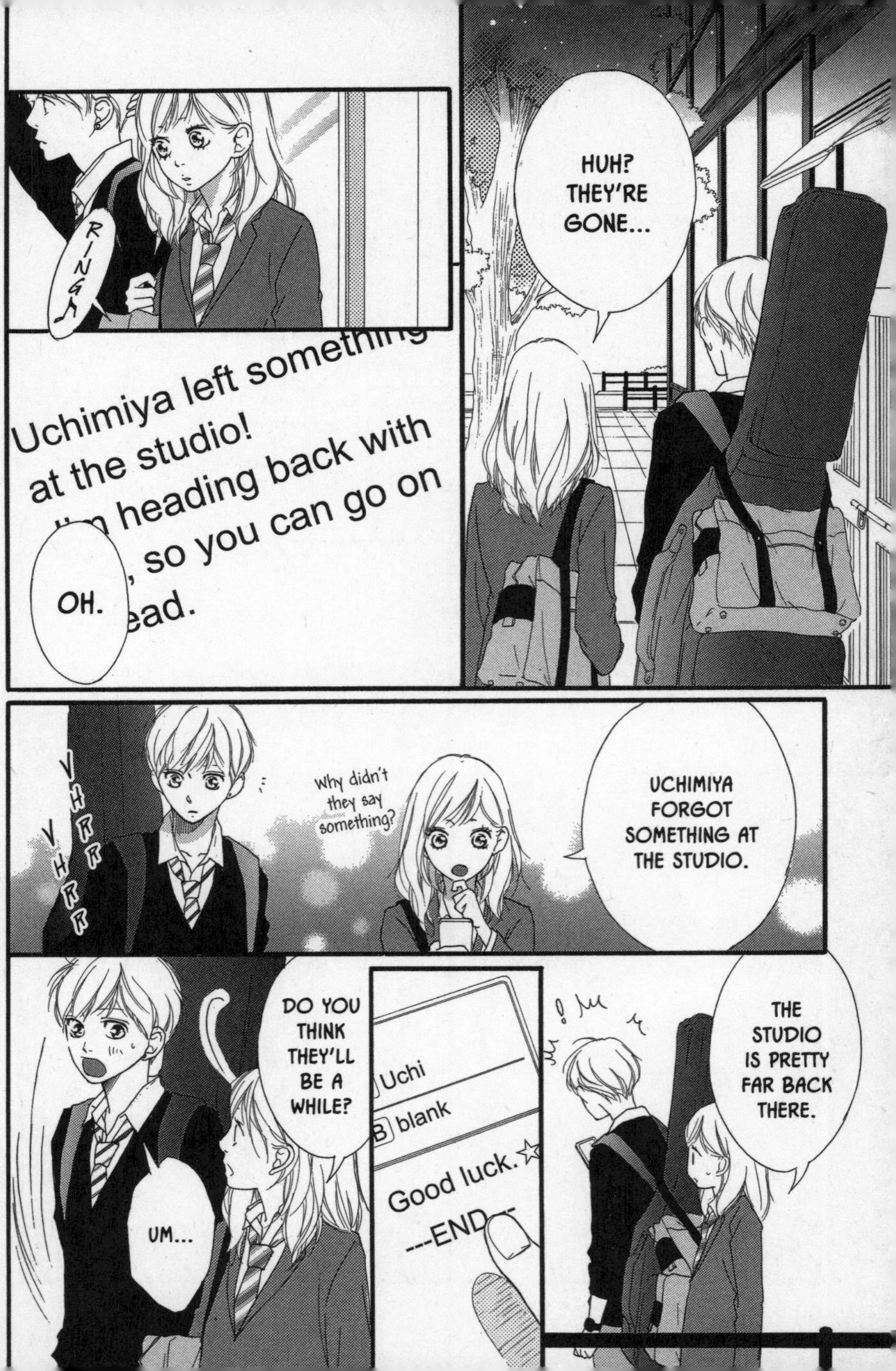
HUH? THEY'RE GONE...
RING♪
Uchimiya left somethin
at the studio!
heading back with
, so you can go on
ead.
OH.
UCHIMIYA FORGOT SOMETHING AT THE STUDIO.
Why didn't they say something?
VHRR VHRR
THE STUDIO IS PRETTY FAR BACK THERE.
Uchi
blank
Good luck.☆
---END---
DO YOU THINK THEY'LL BE A WHILE?
UM...

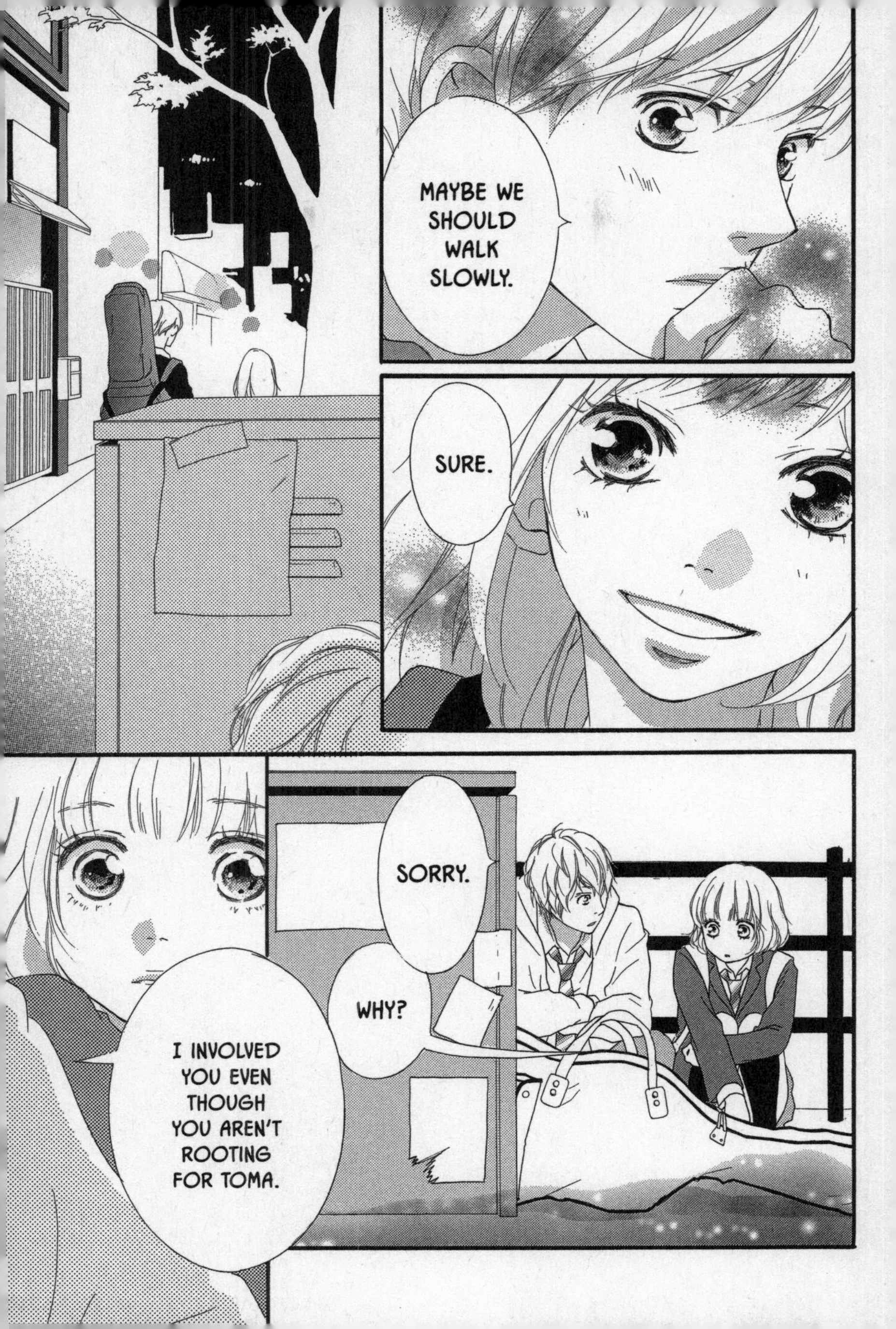
MAYBE WE SHOULD WALK SLOWLY.
SURE.
SORRY.
WHY?
I INVOLVED YOU EVEN THOUGH YOU AREN'T ROOTING FOR TOMA.

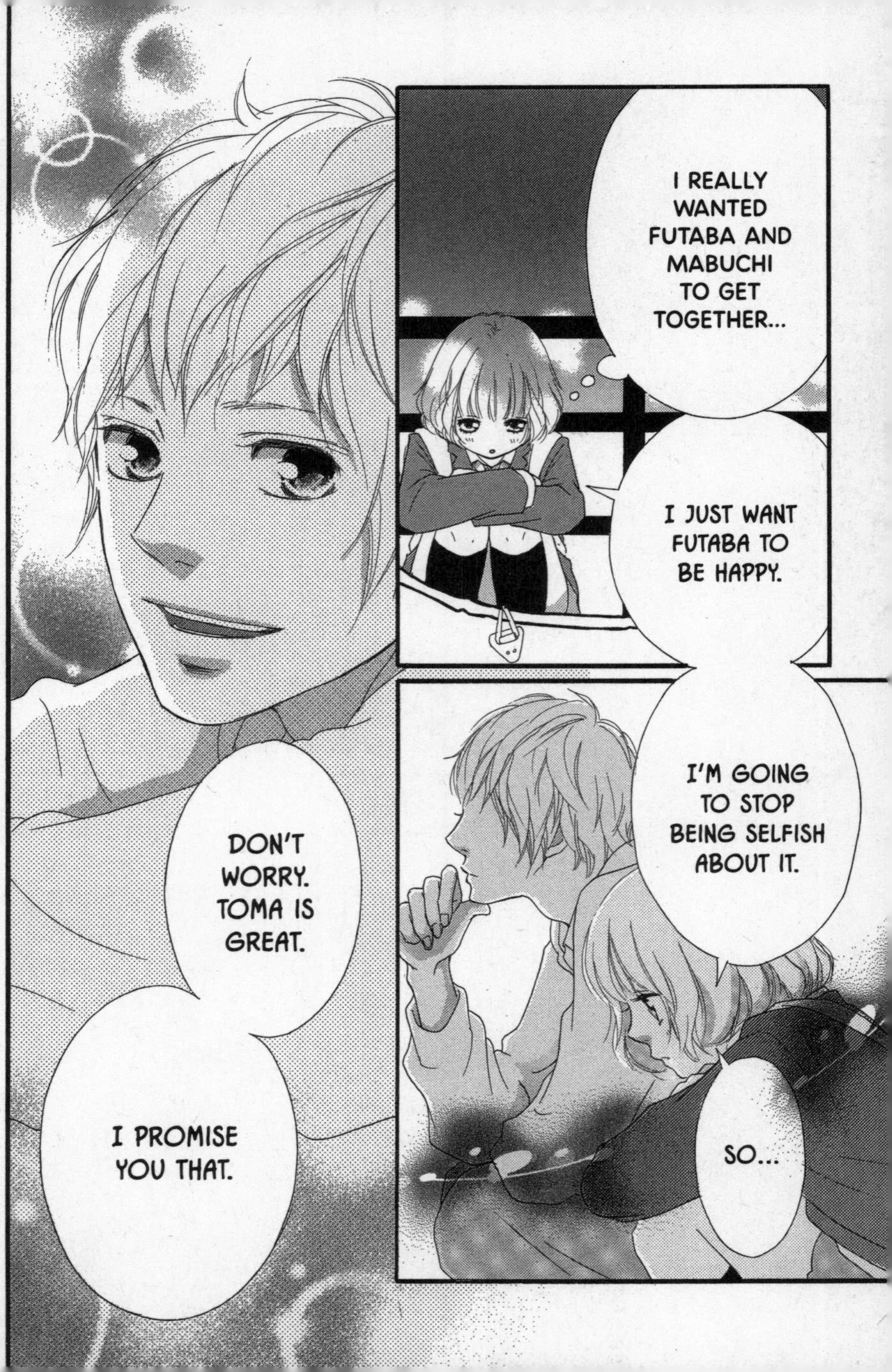
I REALLY WANTED FUTABA AND MABUCHI TO GET TOGETHER...
I JUST WANT FUTABA TO BE HAPPY.
I'M GOING TO STOP BEING SELFISH ABOUT IT.
SO...
DON'T WORRY. TOMA IS GREAT.
I PROMISE YOU THAT.

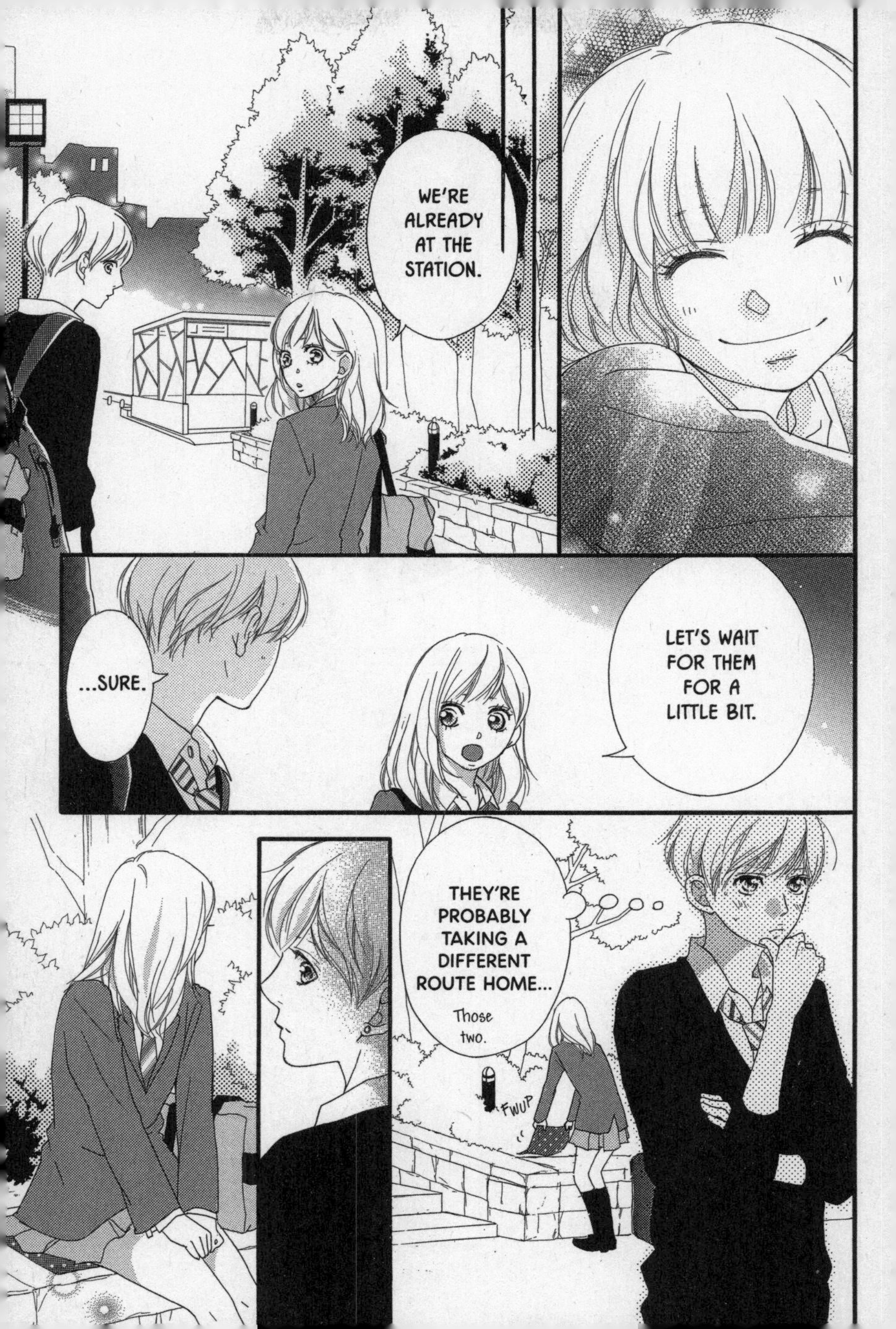
WE'RE ALREADY AT THE STATION.
LET'S WAIT FOR THEM FOR A LITTLE BIT.
...SURE.
THEY'RE PROBABLY TAKING A DIFFERENT ROUTE HOME...
Those two.
FWUP

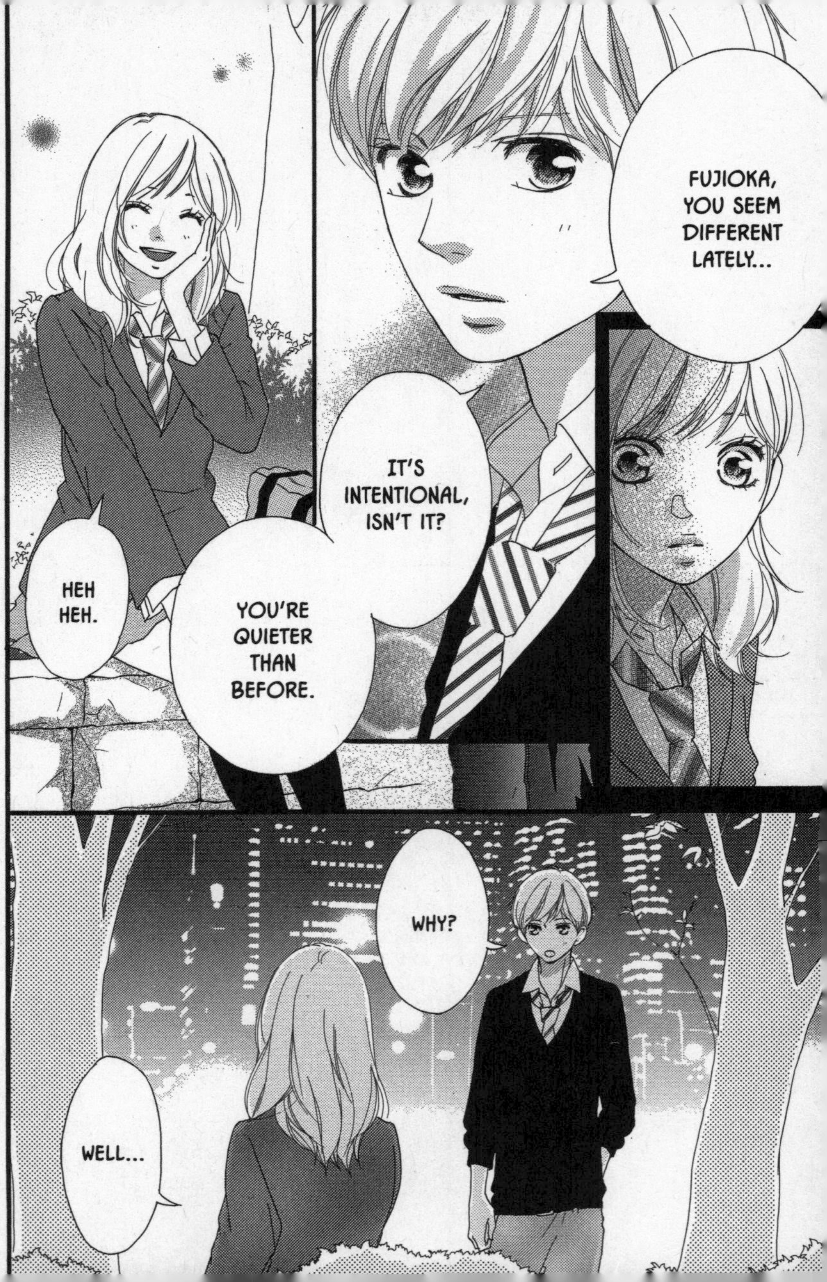
FUJIOKA, YOU SEEM DIFFERENT LATELY...
IT'S INTENTIONAL, ISN'T IT?
YOU'RE QUIETER THAN BEFORE.
HEH HEH.
WHY?
WELL...

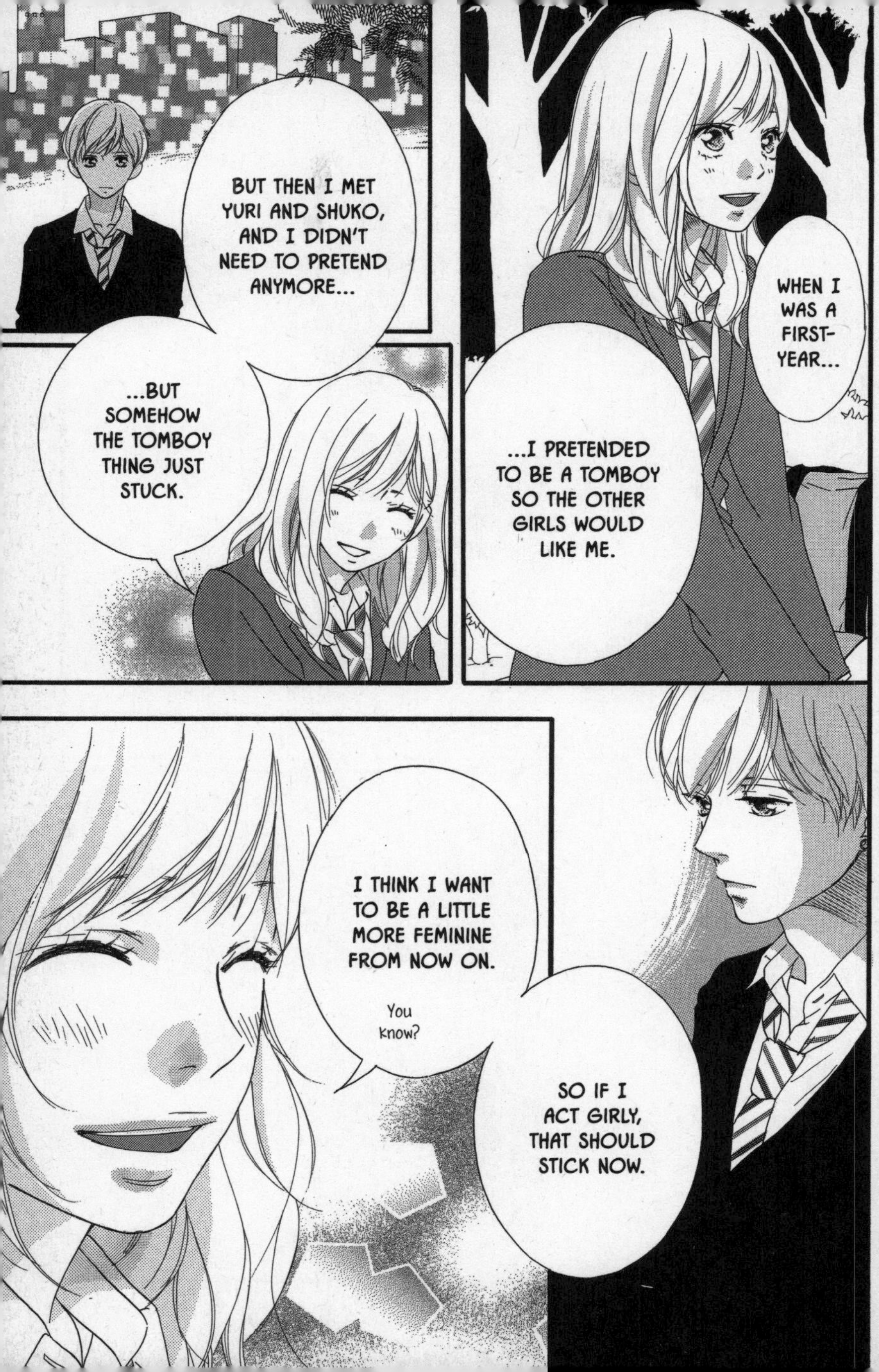
WHEN I WAS A FIRST-YEAR...
...I PRETENDED TO BE A TOMBOY SO THE OTHER GIRLS WOULD LIKE ME.
BUT THEN I MET YURI AND SHUKO, AND I DIDN'T NEED TO PRETEND ANYMORE...
...BUT SOMEHOW THE TOMBOY THING JUST STUCK.
I THINK I WANT TO BE A LITTLE MORE FEMININE FROM NOW ON.
You know?
SO IF I ACT GIRLY, THAT SHOULD STICK NOW.

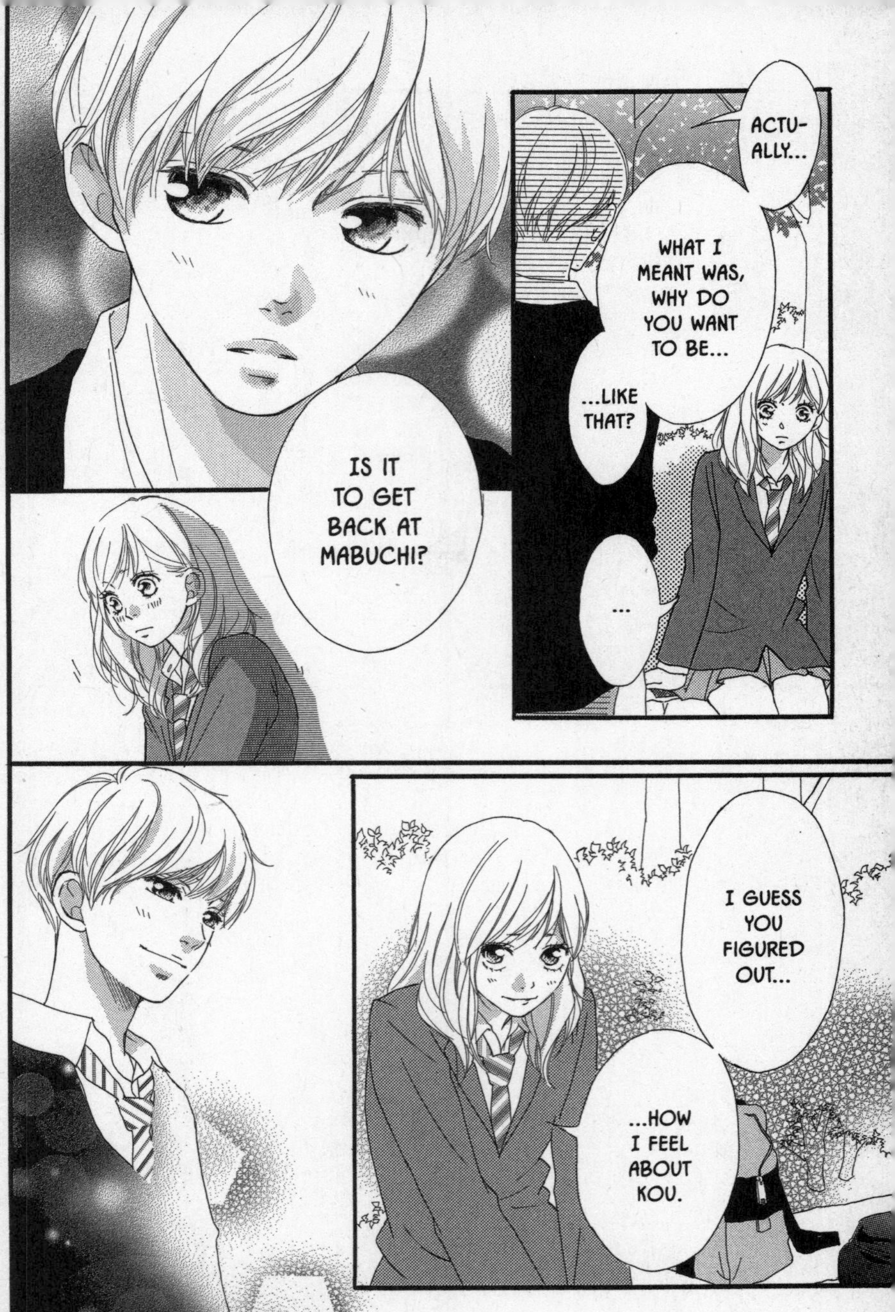
ACTU-ALLY...
WHAT I MEANT WAS, WHY DO YOU WANT TO BE...
...LIKE THAT?
...
IS IT TO GET BACK AT MABUCHI?
I GUESS YOU FIGURED OUT...
...HOW I FEEL ABOUT KOU.

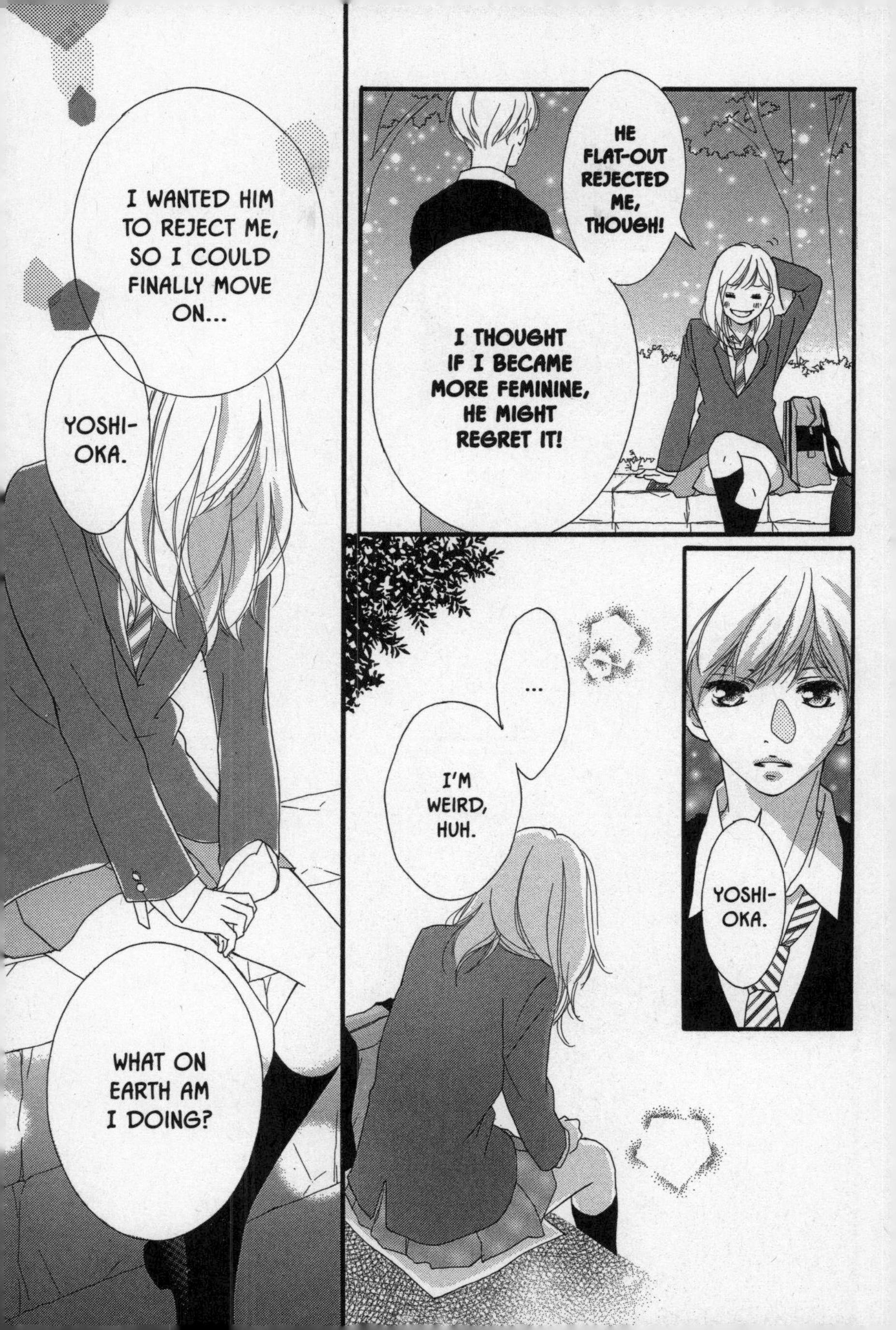
HE FLAT-OUT REJECTED ME, THOUGH!
I THOUGHT IF I BECAME MORE FEMININE, HE MIGHT REGRET IT!
YOSHI-OKA.
...
I'M WEIRD, HUH.
I WANTED HIM TO REJECT ME, SO I COULD FINALLY MOVE ON...
YOSHI-OKA.
WHAT ON EARTH AM I DOING?

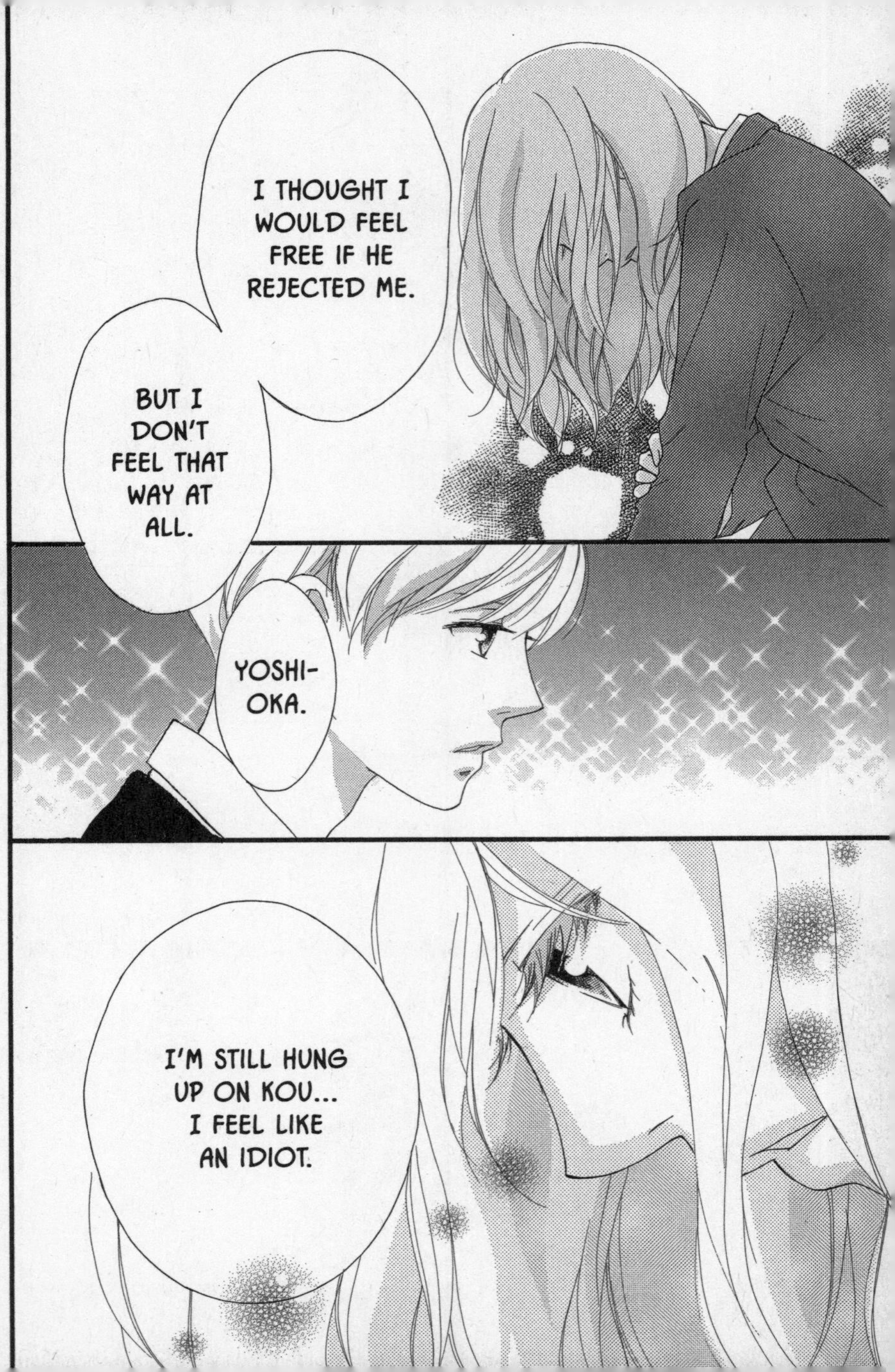
I THOUGHT I WOULD FEEL FREE IF HE REJECTED ME.
BUT I DON'T FEEL THAT WAY AT ALL.
YOSHI-OKA.
I'M STILL HUNG UP ON KOU... I FEEL LIKE AN IDIOT.

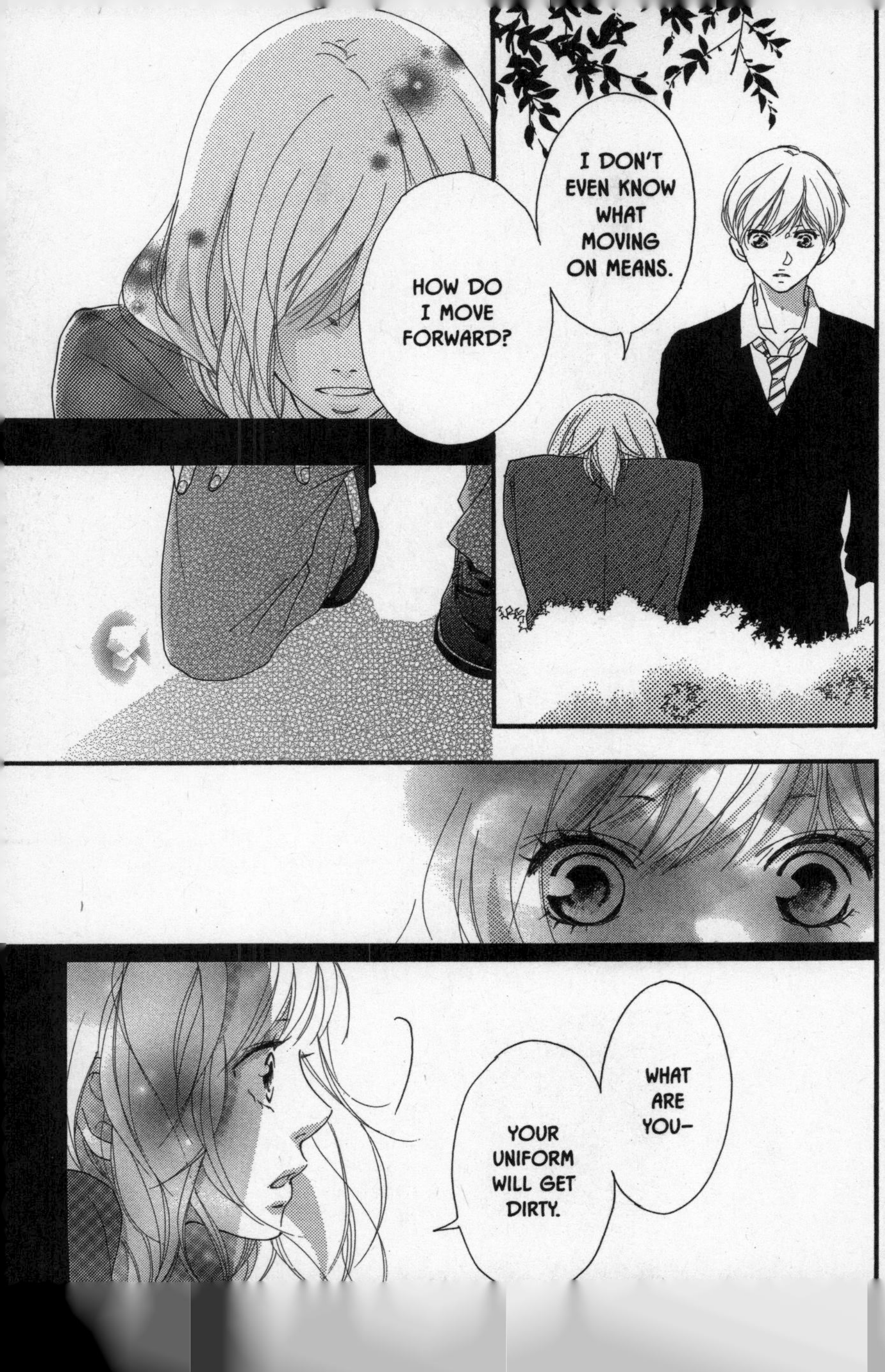
I DON'T EVEN KNOW WHAT MOVING ON MEANS.
HOW DO I MOVE FORWARD?
WHAT ARE YOU–
YOUR UNIFORM WILL GET DIRTY.

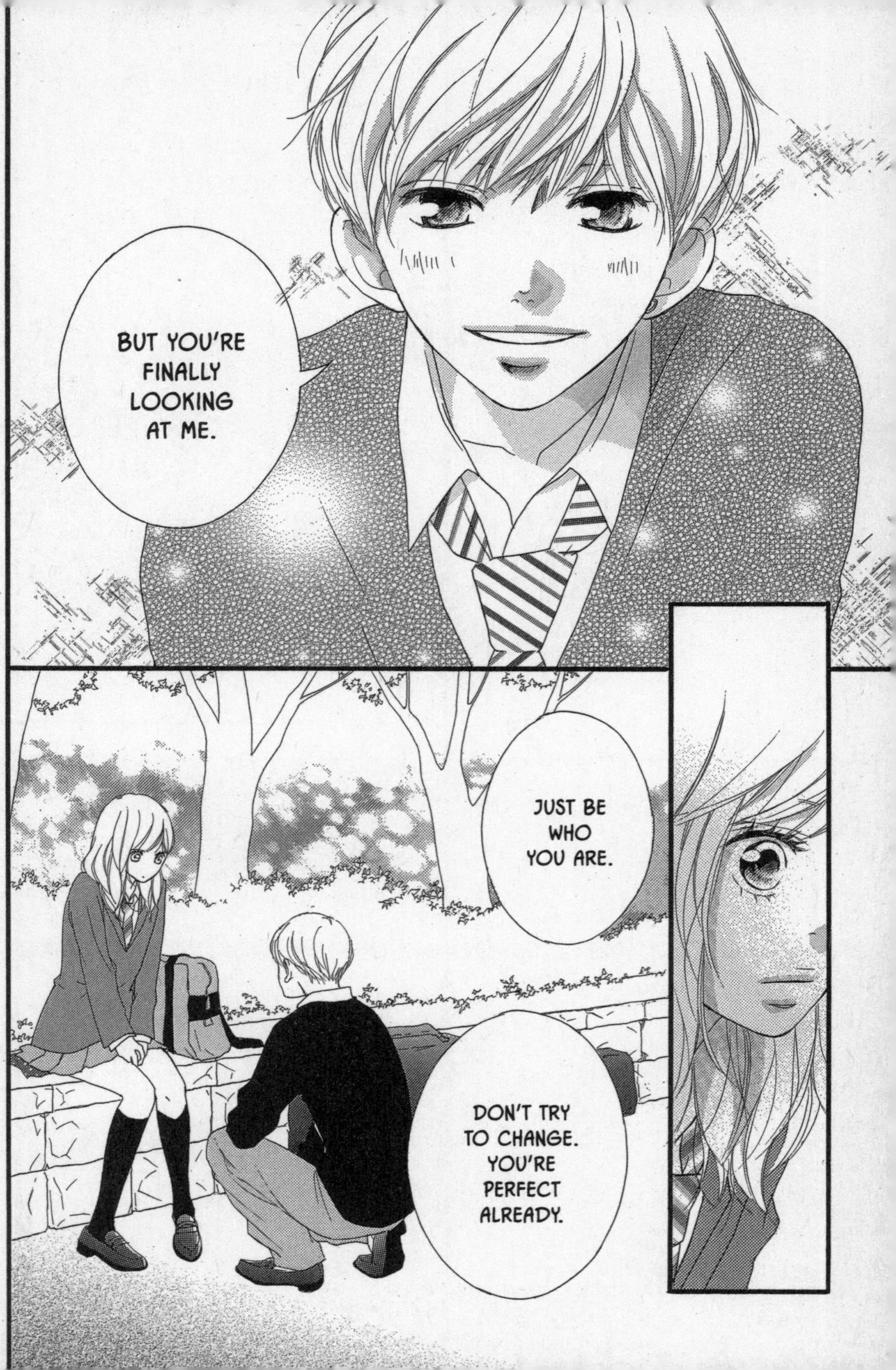
BUT YOU'RE FINALLY LOOKING AT ME.
JUST BE WHO YOU ARE.
DON'T TRY TO CHANGE. YOU'RE PERFECT ALREADY.

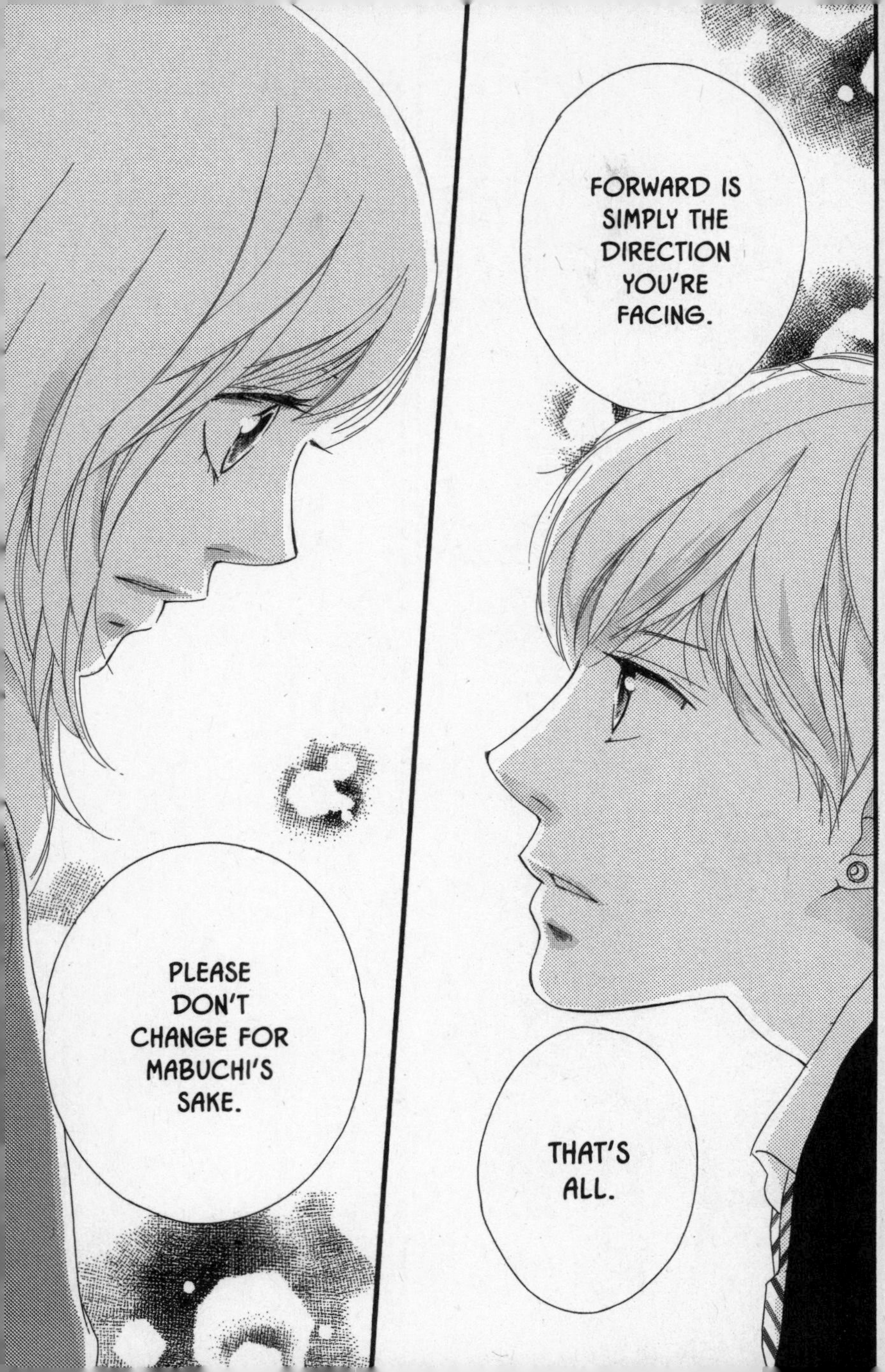
FORWARD IS SIMPLY THE DIRECTION YOU'RE FACING.
THAT'S ALL.
PLEASE DON'T CHANGE FOR MABUCHI'S SAKE.

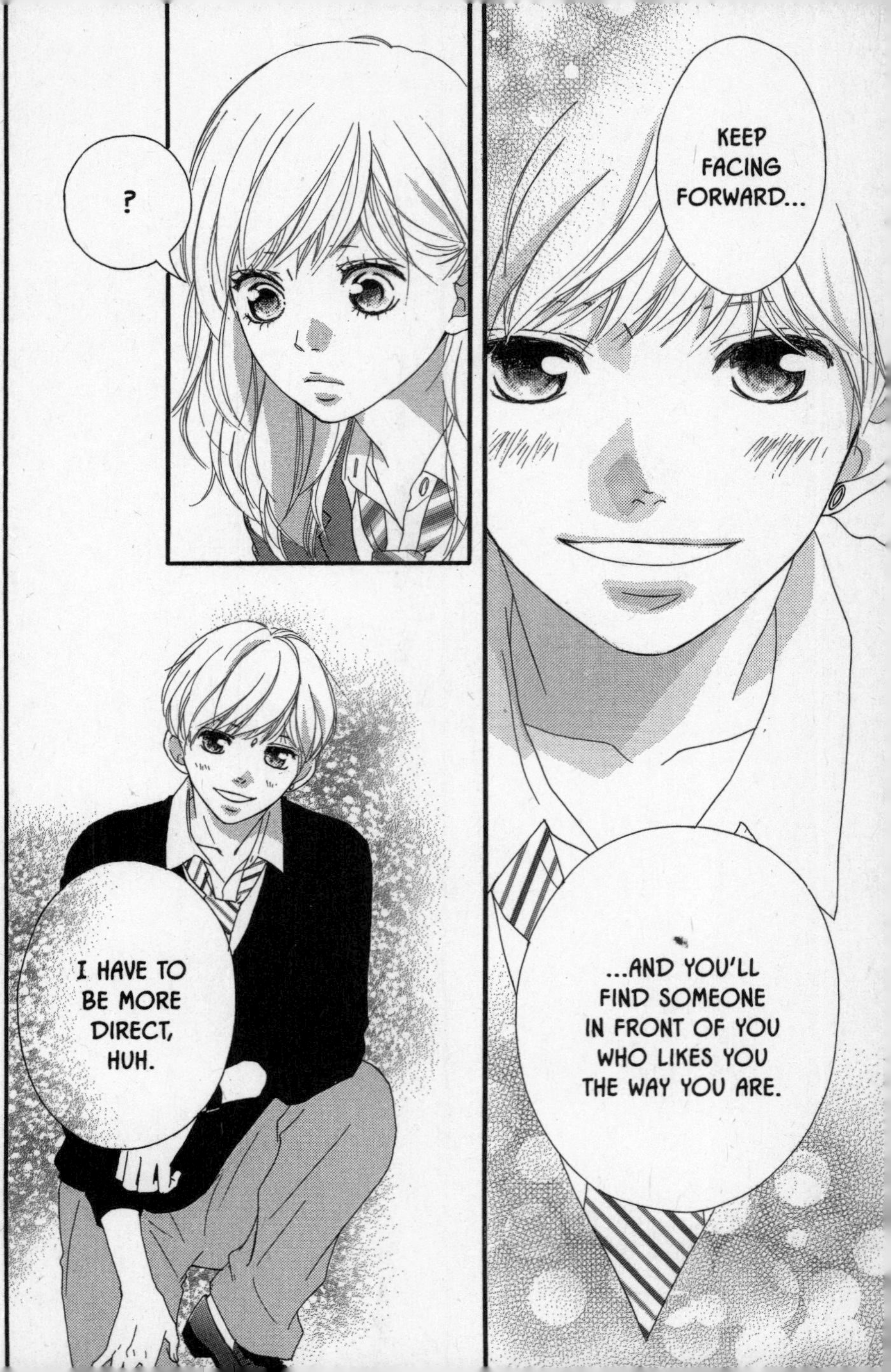
KEEP FACING FORWARD...
...AND YOU'LL FIND SOMEONE IN FRONT OF YOU WHO LIKES YOU THE WAY YOU ARE.
?
I HAVE TO BE MORE DIRECT, HUH.

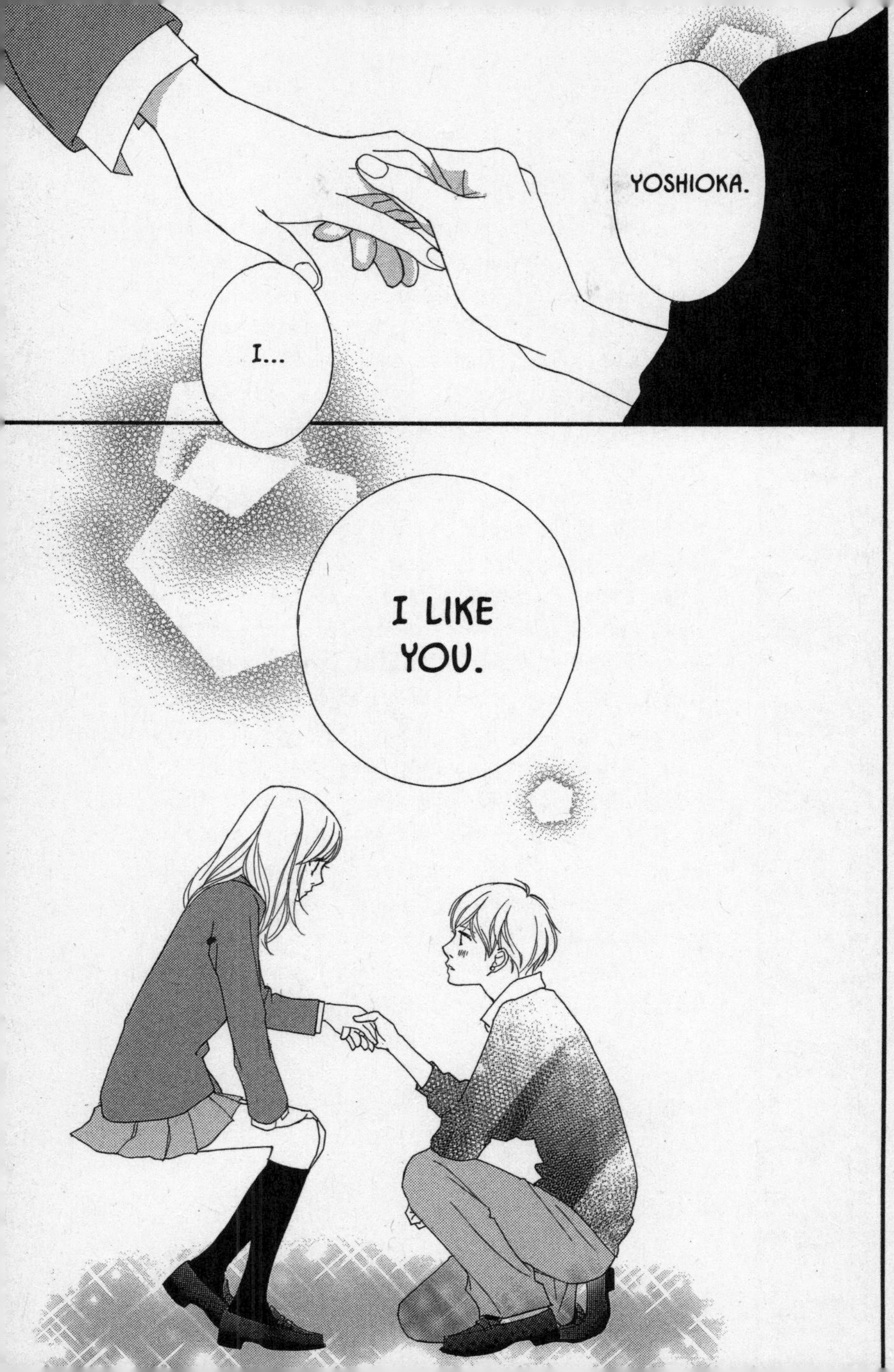
YOSHIOKA.
I...
I LIKE YOU.

When I was a student, I watched all the movies that were aired on TV. Even as an adult when I had less work than I do now, I loved renting a ton of movies at once and spending the whole day watching them. What's sad is that I can't remember what happened in most of them. Basically I would remember if they were really good or if I loved them, which didn't do much in terms of recommending those titles to others.

There was one black-and-white movie—I can't remember when I saw it (back in junior high?)—that was shown on TV in the middle of the night. Although I don't really like black-and-white movies, I watched it, and when it ended I was overcome with this mysterious feeling that I absolutely had to watch it again! I wrote down the TV station and the name of the movie (it was my first time writing down the name of a movie for this purpose), and as expected, I completely forgot what the movie was about. I do remember I thought it was great(!), and I have a lasting image of the swing that appeared in the movie. Although I misplaced the note almost immediately after writing it, I think I must've really wanted to watch the movie again. I somehow miraculously remembered the title recently and thought to look it up online to see if it had come out on DVD, even though it was old. Well, I found out that it's so famous it's even on Blu-ray now. Whoa! I ordered it, and I'm just waiting for it to arrive. The movie is called *To Kill a Mockingbird*, and I'm pretty proud of myself for remembering the title. Right now I'm super keen to finally watch it again and to find out if I experience the same feelings I did before. I'm really excited!

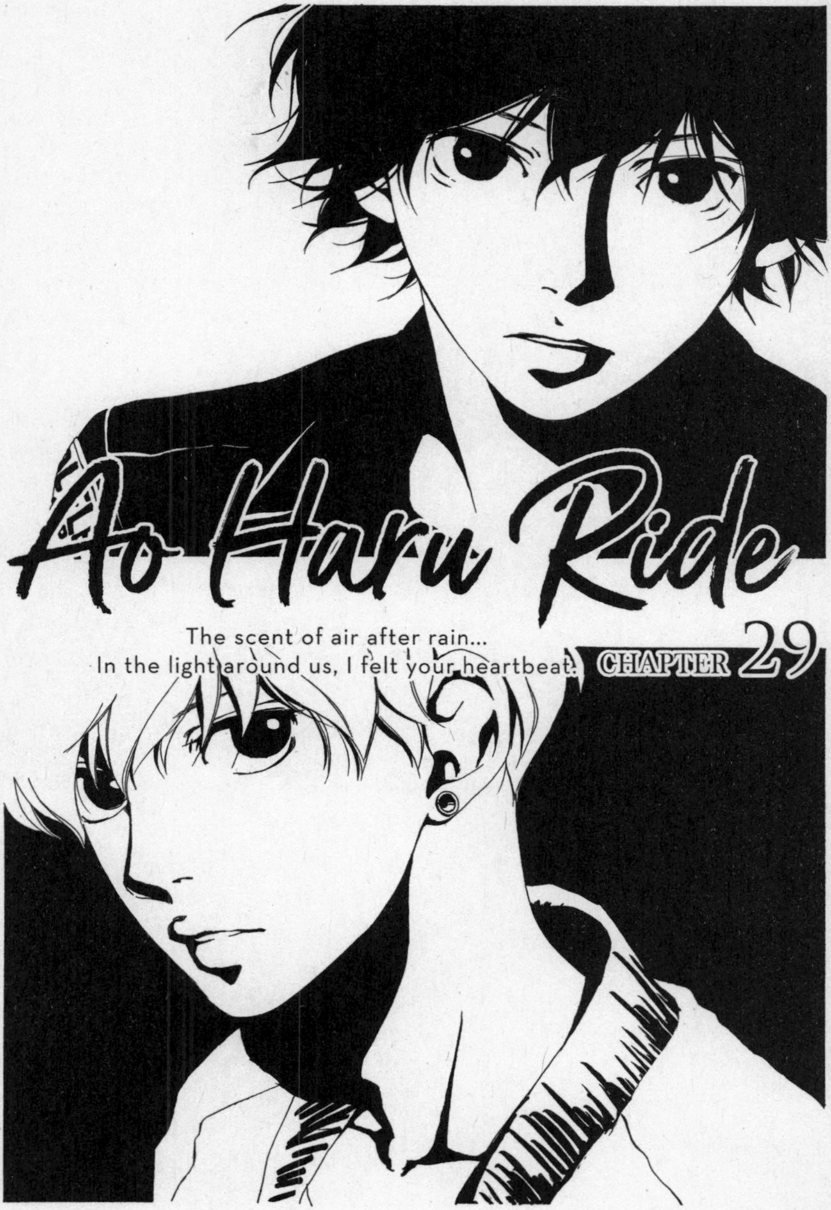
Ao Haru Ride
The scent of air after rain...
In the light around us, I felt your heartbeat.
CHAPTER 29

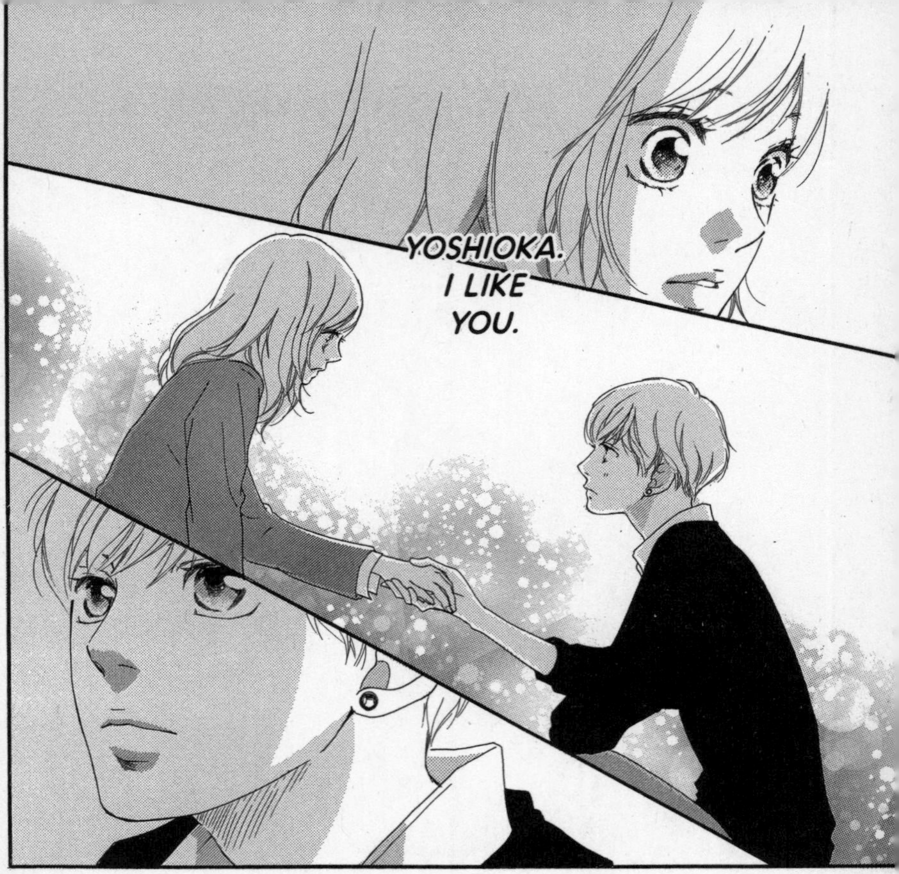
YOSHIOKA. I LIKE YOU.

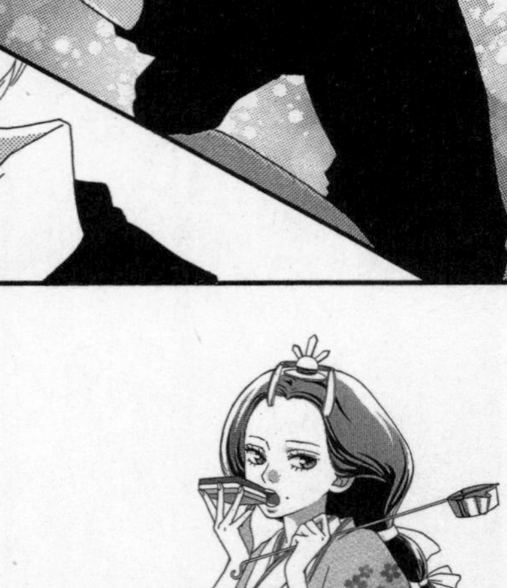

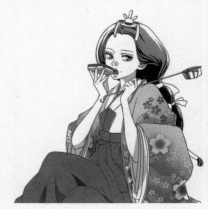

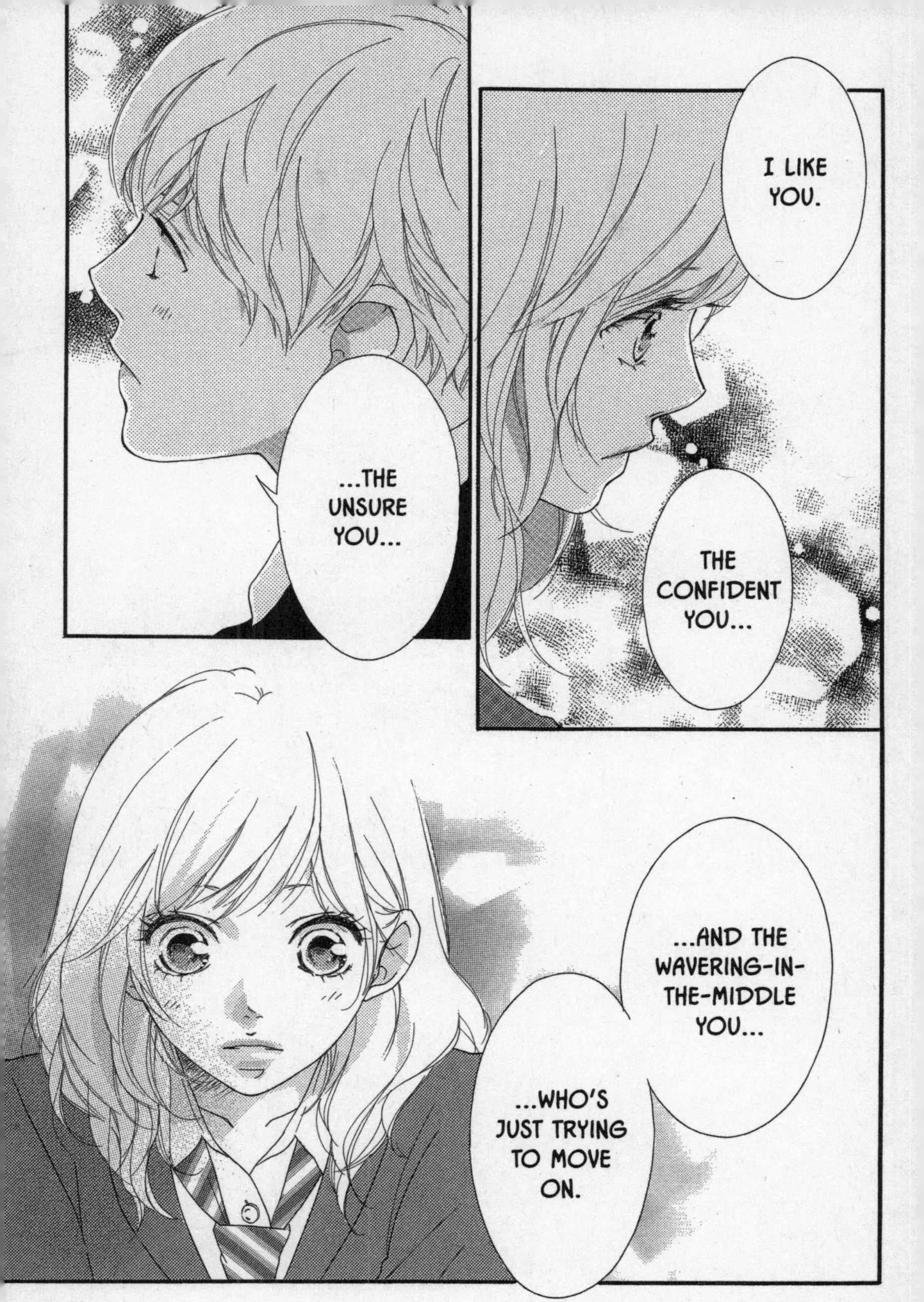
I LIKE YOU.
THE CONFIDENT YOU...
...THE UNSURE YOU...
...AND THE WAVERING-IN-THE-MIDDLE YOU...
...WHO'S JUST TRYING TO MOVE ON.

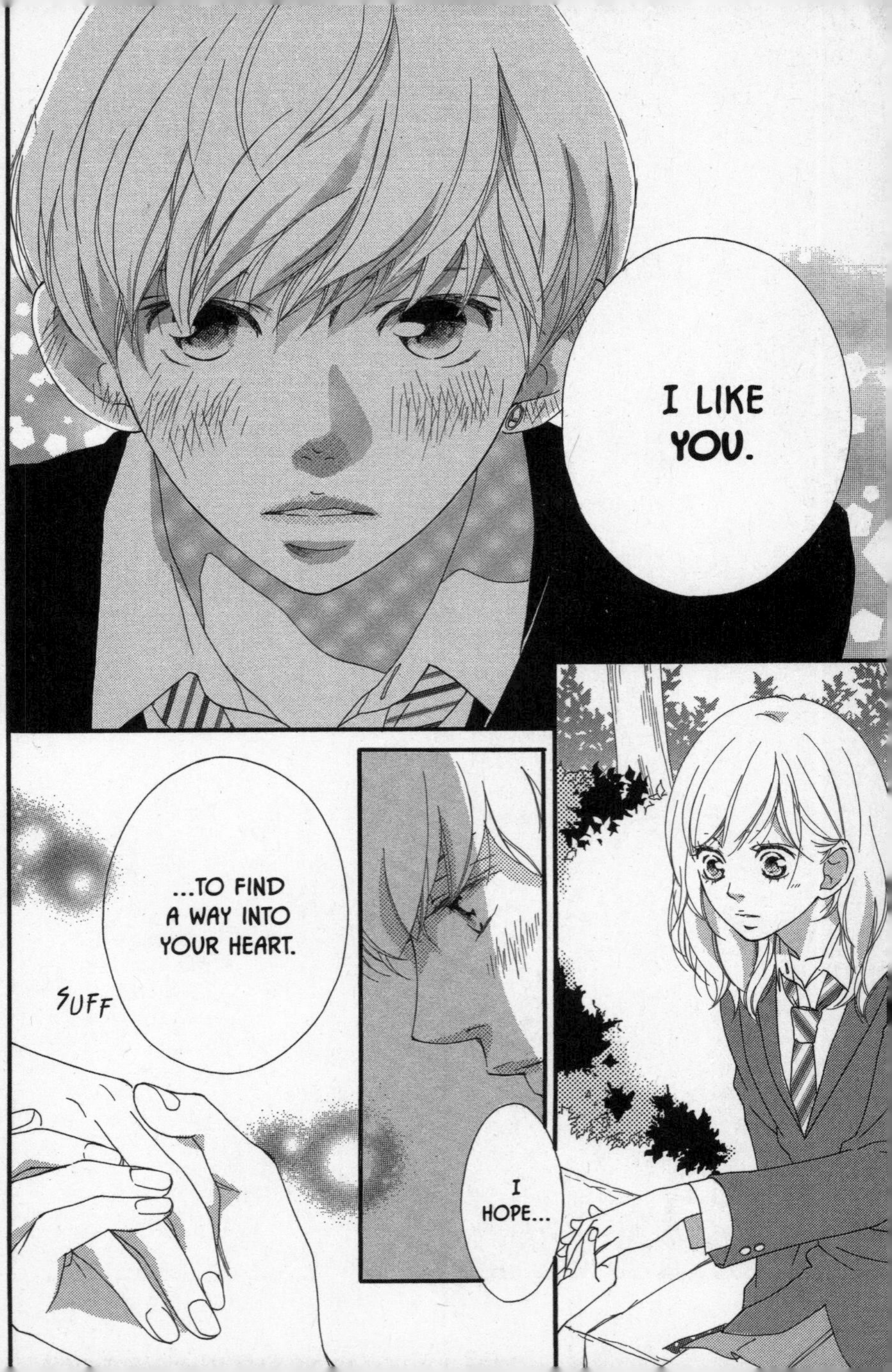
I LIKE YOU.
I HOPE...
...TO FIND A WAY INTO YOUR HEART.
SUFF

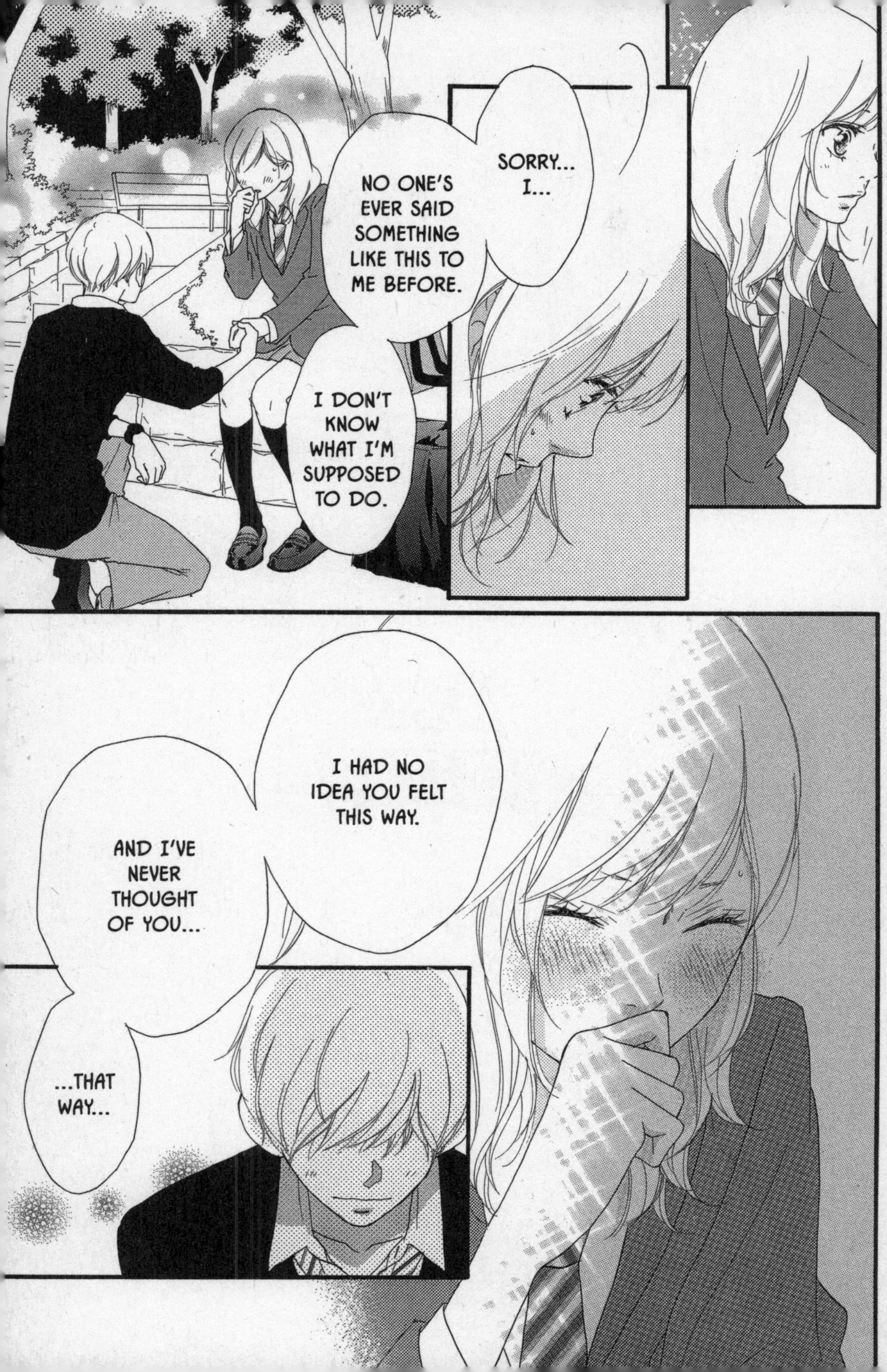
SORRY... I...
NO ONE'S EVER SAID SOMETHING LIKE THIS TO ME BEFORE.
I DON'T KNOW WHAT I'M SUPPOSED TO DO.
I HAD NO IDEA YOU FELT THIS WAY.
AND I'VE NEVER THOUGHT OF YOU...
...THAT WAY...

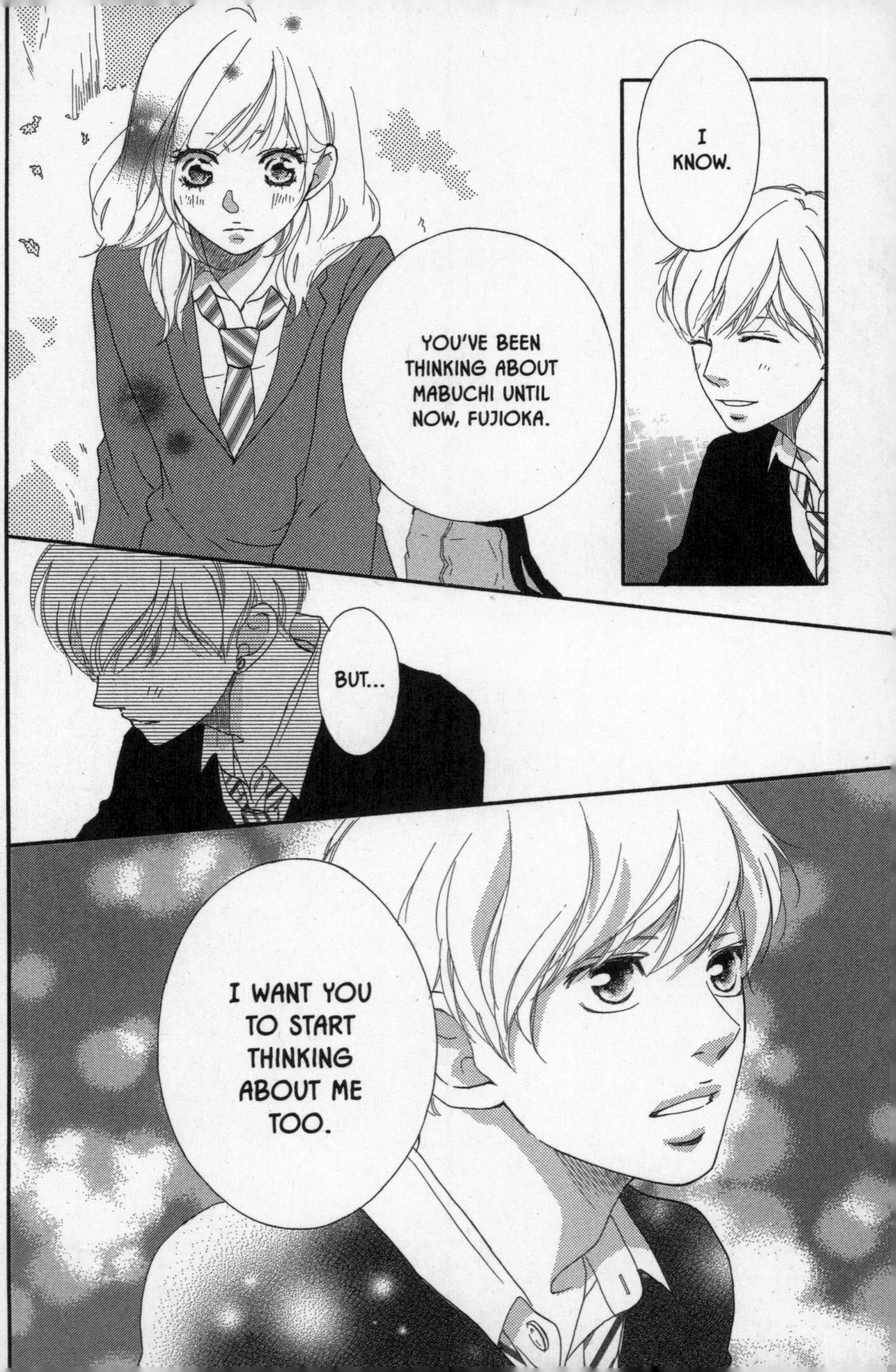
I KNOW.
YOU'VE BEEN THINKING ABOUT MABUCHI UNTIL NOW, FUJIOKA.
BUT...
I WANT YOU TO START THINKING ABOUT ME TOO.

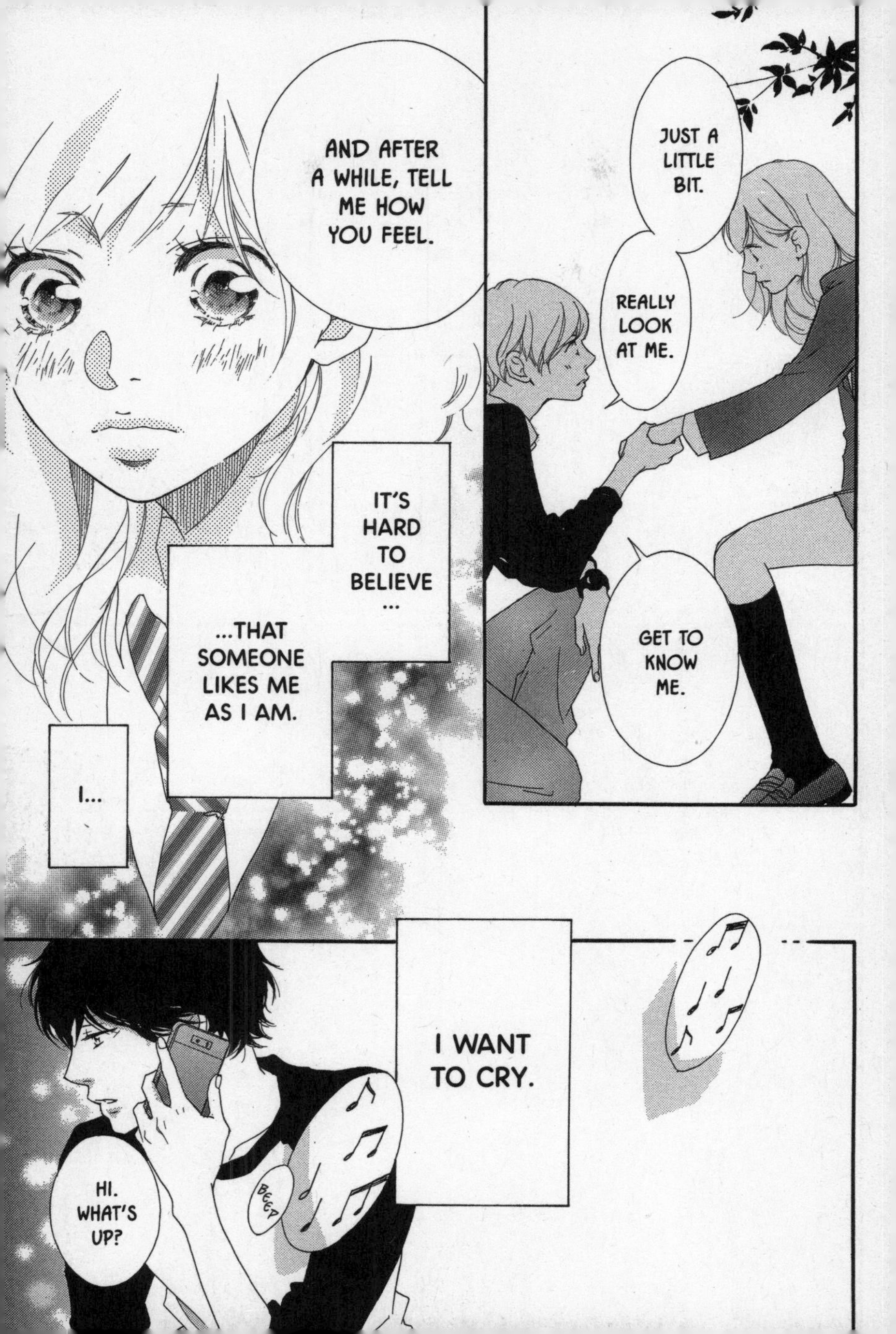
JUST A LITTLE BIT.
REALLY LOOK AT ME.
GET TO KNOW ME.
AND AFTER A WHILE, TELL ME HOW YOU FEEL.
IT'S HARD TO BELIEVE...
...THAT SOMEONE LIKES ME AS I AM.
I...
I WANT TO CRY.
BEEP
HI. WHAT'S UP?

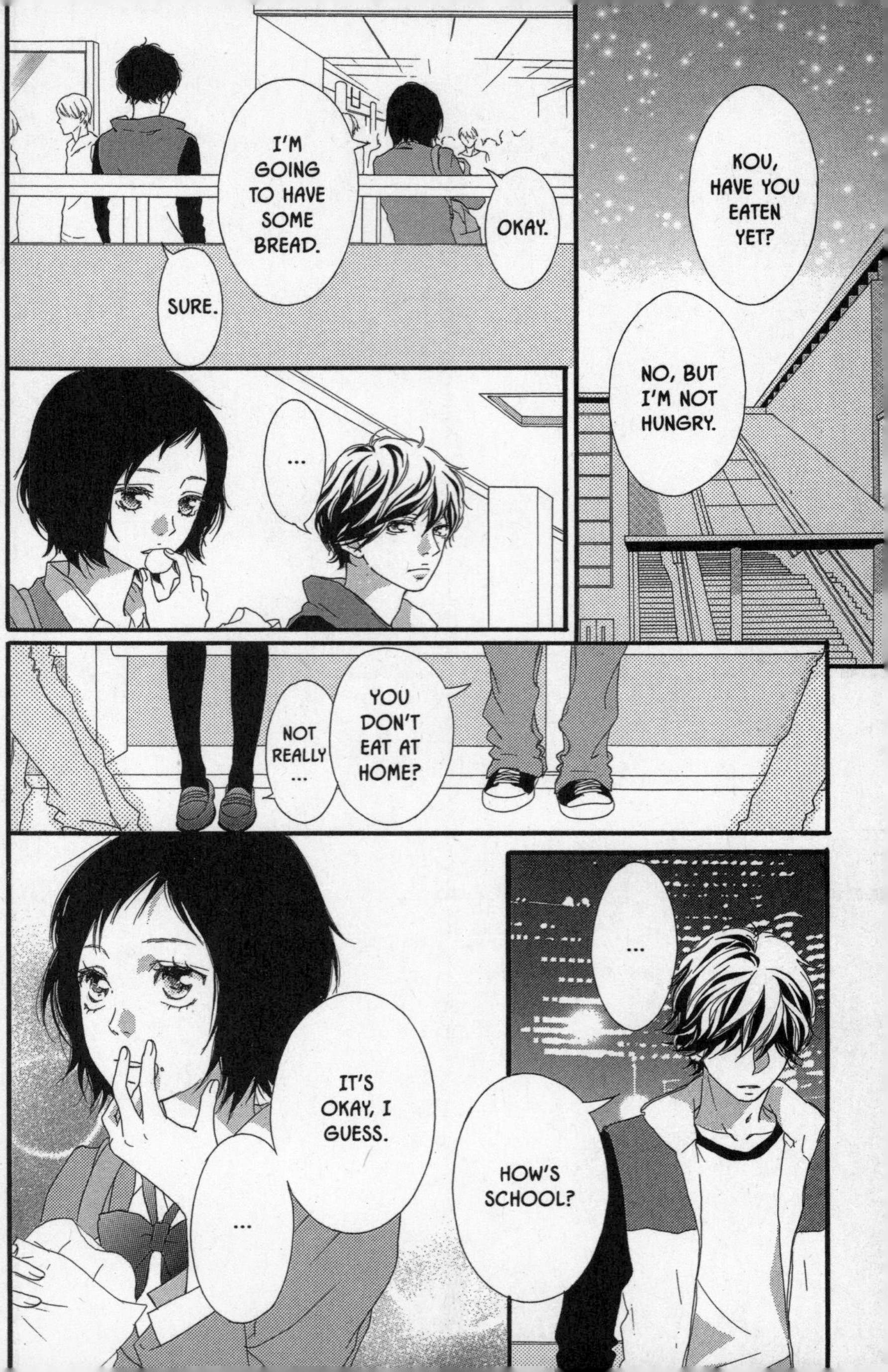
KOU, HAVE YOU EATEN YET?
NO, BUT I'M NOT HUNGRY.
I'M GOING TO HAVE SOME BREAD.
OKAY.
SURE.
...
YOU DON'T EAT AT HOME?
NOT REALLY ...
...
HOW'S SCHOOL?
IT'S OKAY, I GUESS.
...

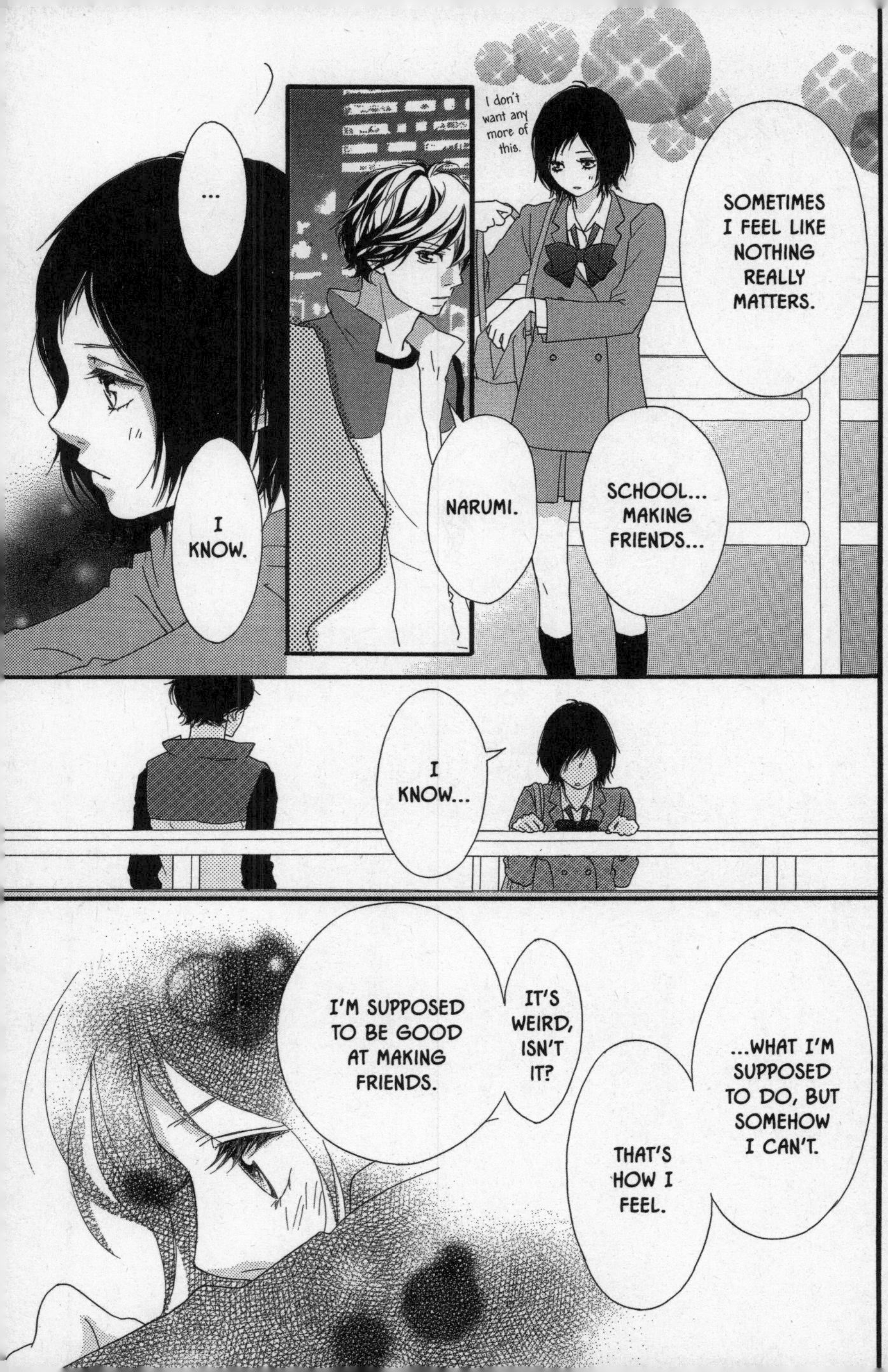
SOMETIMES I FEEL LIKE NOTHING REALLY MATTERS.
I don't want any more of this.
SCHOOL... MAKING FRIENDS...
NARUMI.
...
I KNOW.
I KNOW...
...WHAT I'M SUPPOSED TO DO, BUT SOMEHOW I CAN'T.
THAT'S HOW I FEEL.
IT'S WEIRD, ISN'T IT?
I'M SUPPOSED TO BE GOOD AT MAKING FRIENDS.

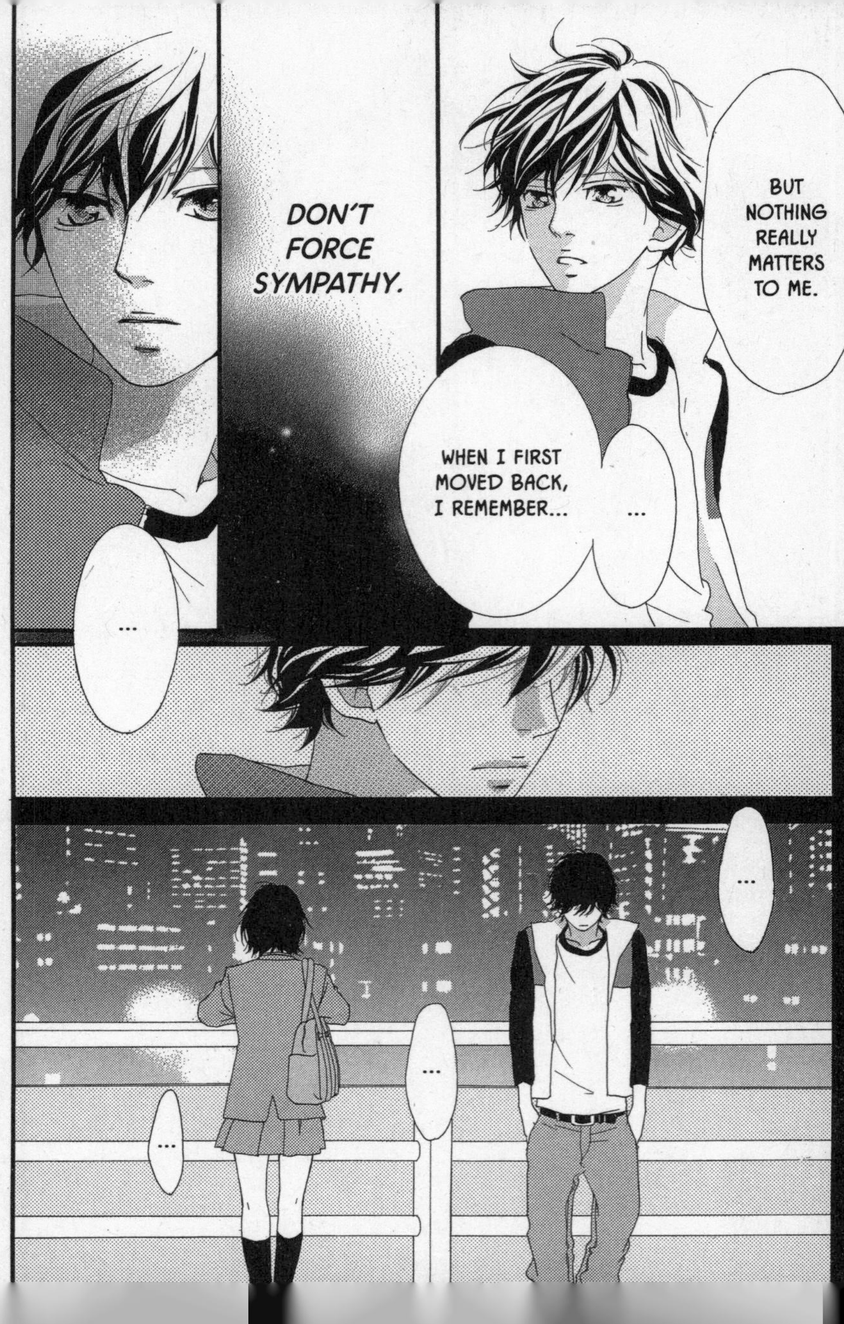
BUT NOTHING REALLY MATTERS TO ME.
...
WHEN I FIRST MOVED BACK, I REMEMBER...
DON'T FORCE SYMPATHY.
...
...
...
...

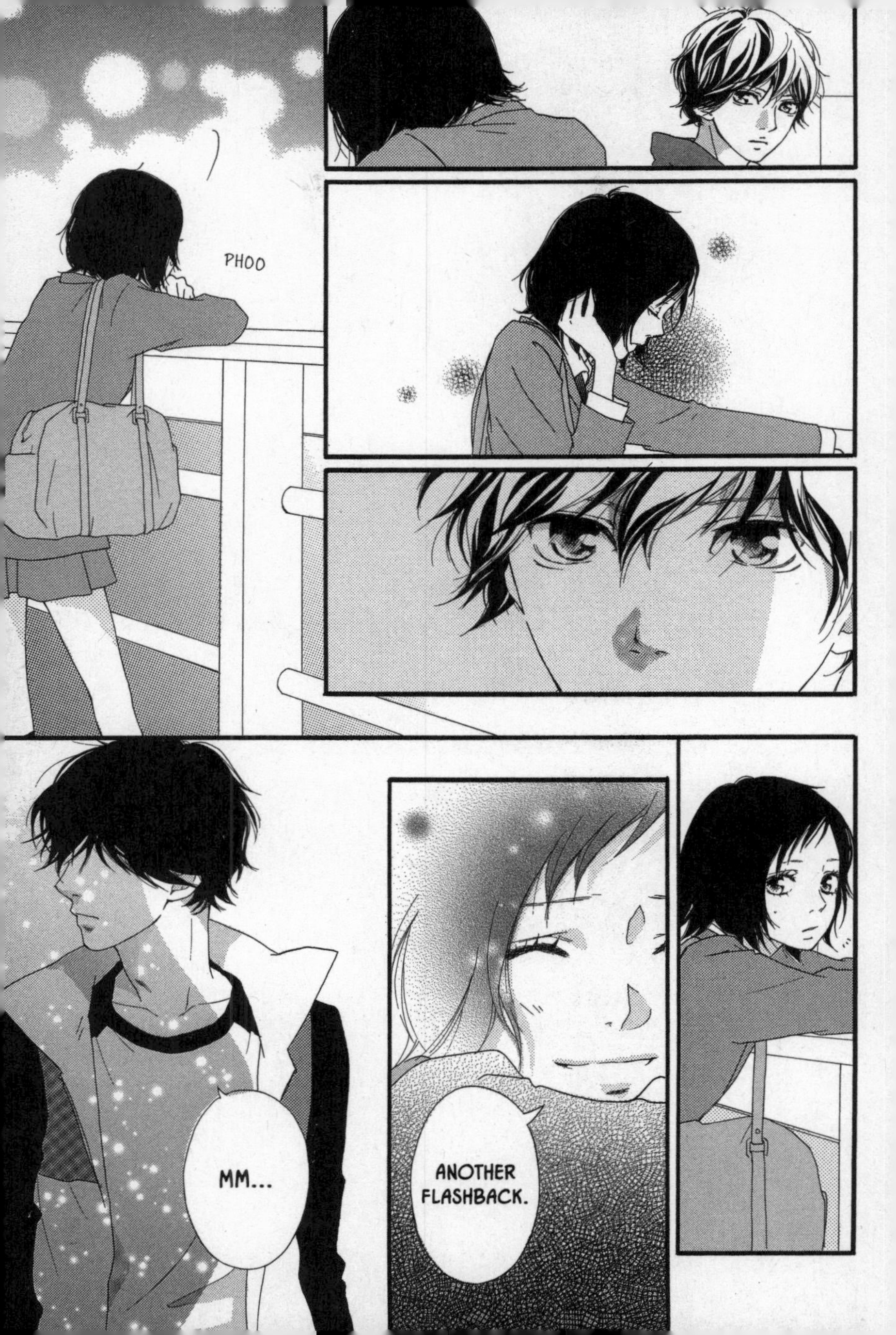
PHOO
ANOTHER FLASHBACK.
MM...

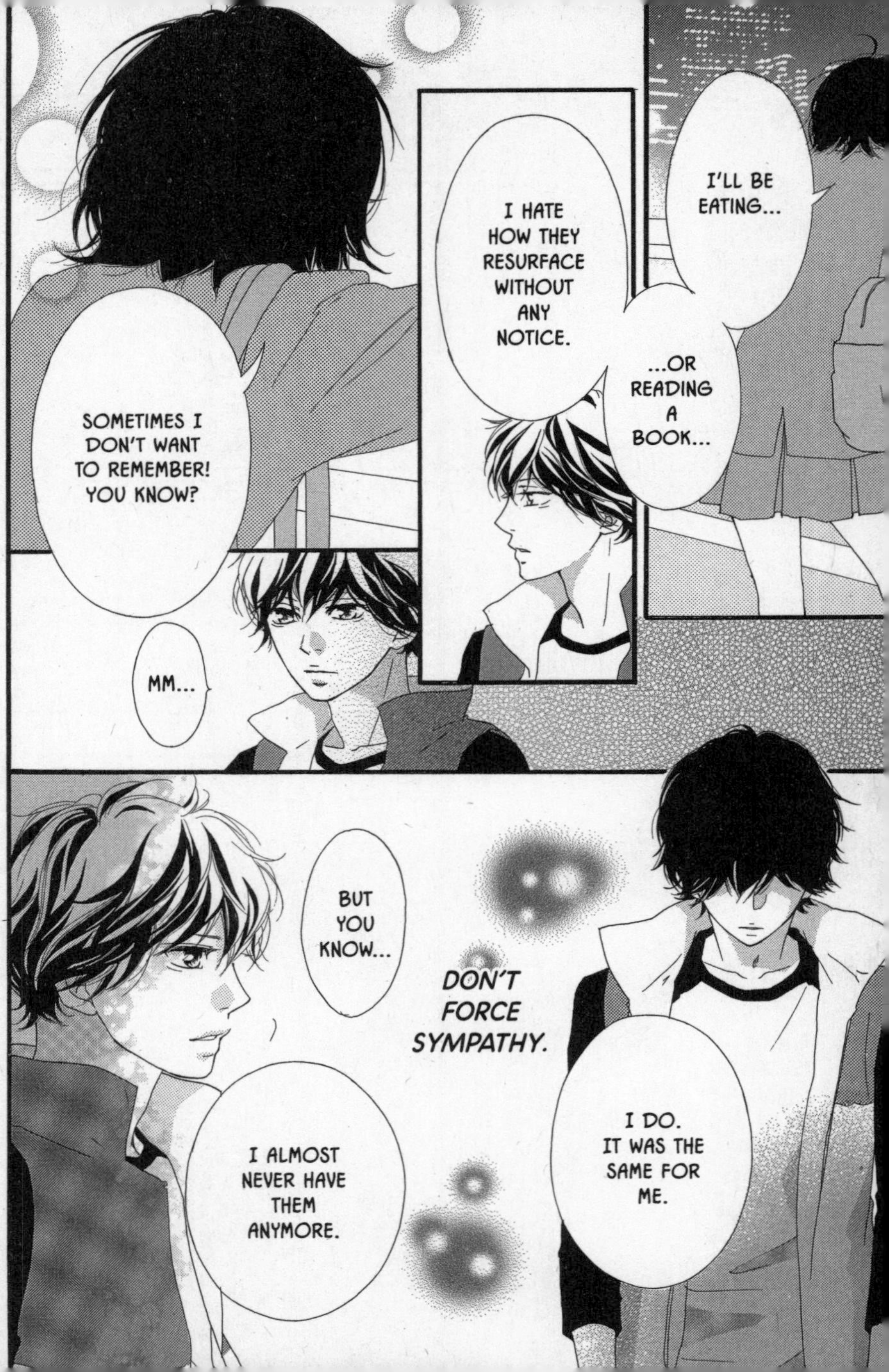
I'LL BE EATING...
...OR READING A BOOK...
I HATE HOW THEY RESURFACE WITHOUT ANY NOTICE.
SOMETIMES I DON'T WANT TO REMEMBER! YOU KNOW?
MM...
BUT YOU KNOW...
DON'T FORCE SYMPATHY.
I DO. IT WAS THE SAME FOR ME.
I ALMOST NEVER HAVE THEM ANYMORE.

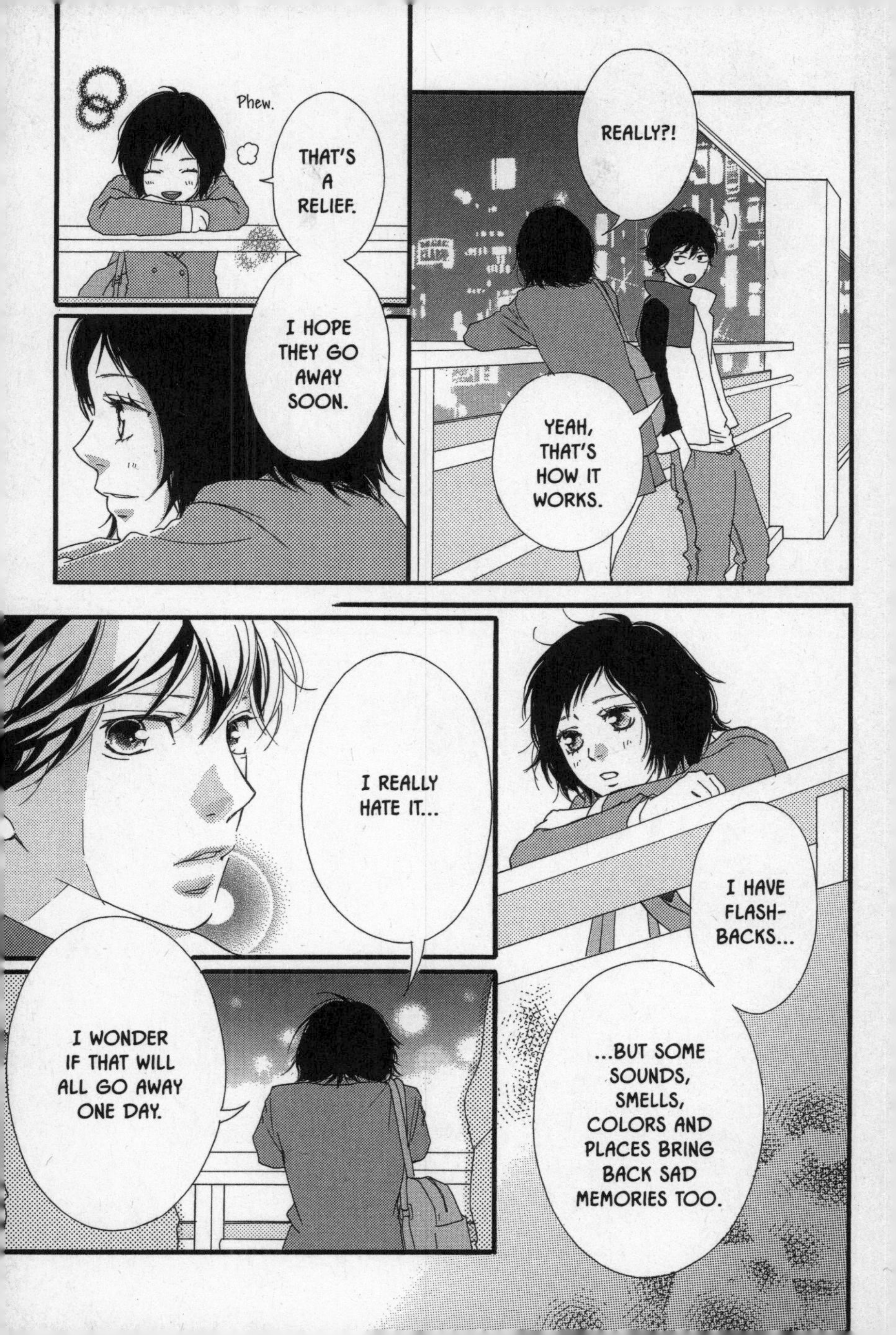
REALLY?!
YEAH, THAT'S HOW IT WORKS.
Phew.
THAT'S A RELIEF.
I HOPE THEY GO AWAY SOON.
I HAVE FLASH-BACKS...
...BUT SOME SOUNDS, SMELLS, COLORS AND PLACES BRING BACK SAD MEMORIES TOO.
I REALLY HATE IT...
I WONDER IF THAT WILL ALL GO AWAY ONE DAY.

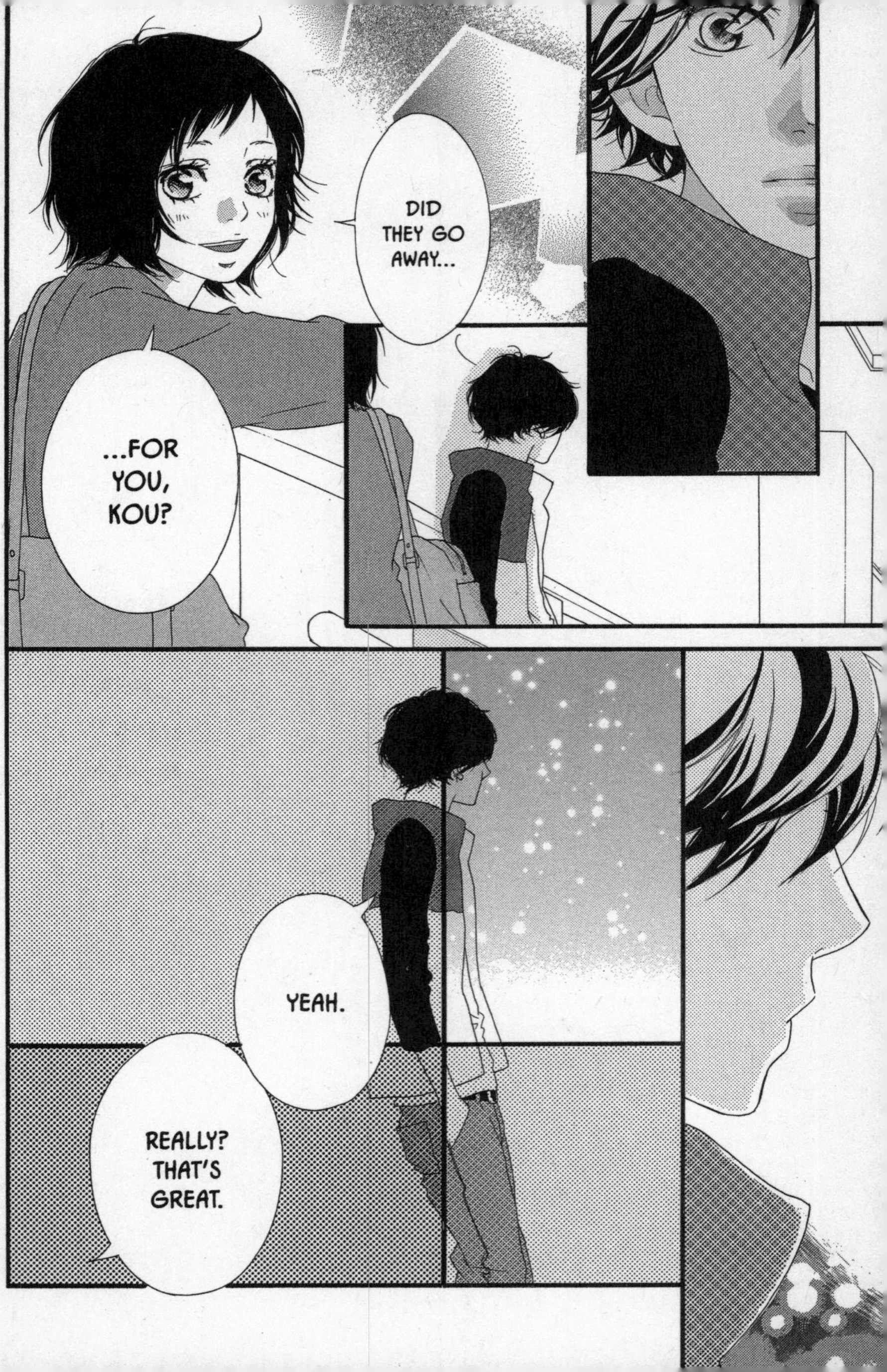
DID THEY GO AWAY...
...FOR YOU, KOU?
YEAH.
REALLY? THAT'S GREAT.

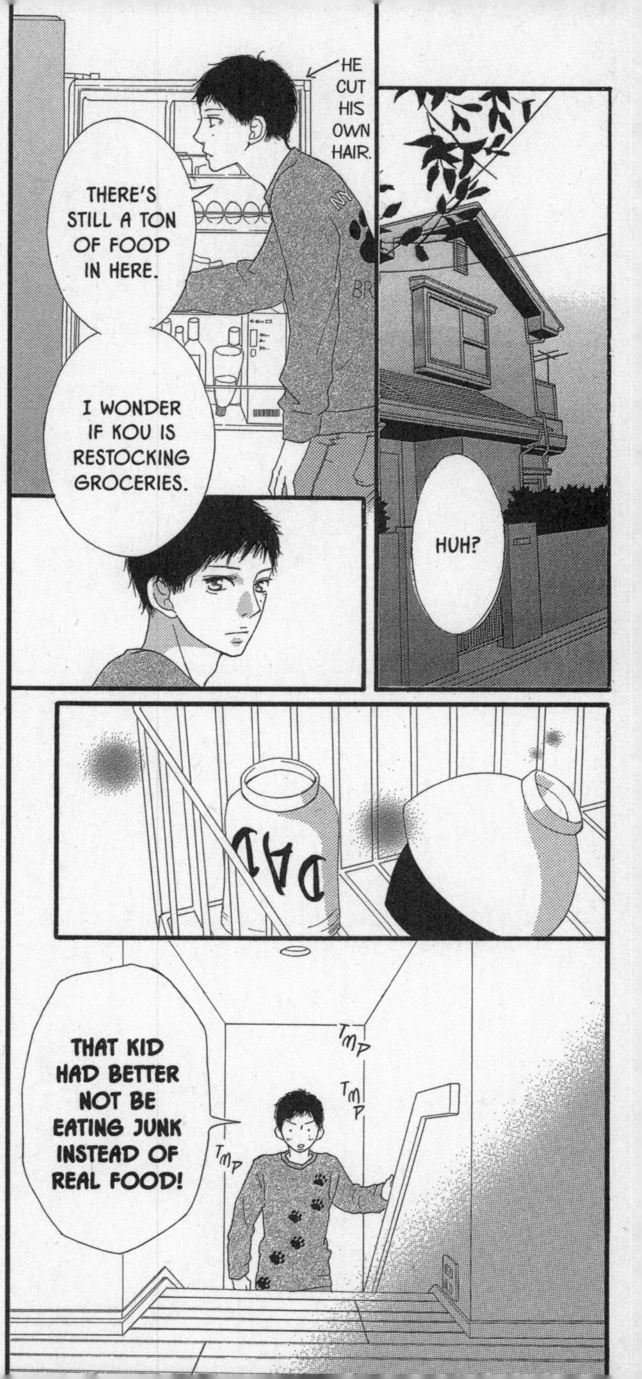
HUH?
HE CUT HIS OWN HAIR.
THERE'S STILL A TON OF FOOD IN HERE.
I WONDER IF KOU IS RESTOCKING GROCERIES.
DAD
TMP
TMP
TMP
THAT KID HAD BETTER NOT BE EATING JUNK INSTEAD OF REAL FOOD!

I love sleeping. I wasn't always this way, but if given the choice right now I would sleep. When I get stuck working on storyboards, I fall asleep gracefully... until I oversleep and then hate myself. The other day an interviewer asked me how I deal with stress and how I reward myself. I replied the same to both questions: "Sleep!" It made me realize just how much I love sleeping. Of course there are times when I'm working and don't get to sleep much for a few days in a row, which is all the more reason why I make sure to sleep when I can. I couldn't be happier than when I finish a manuscript and can go to sleep without setting my alarm clock! I'll wake up and wonder what day and time it is, looking at the clock with excitement. Recently I slept for 19 hours straight. I was so impressed with myself that I want to do that again.

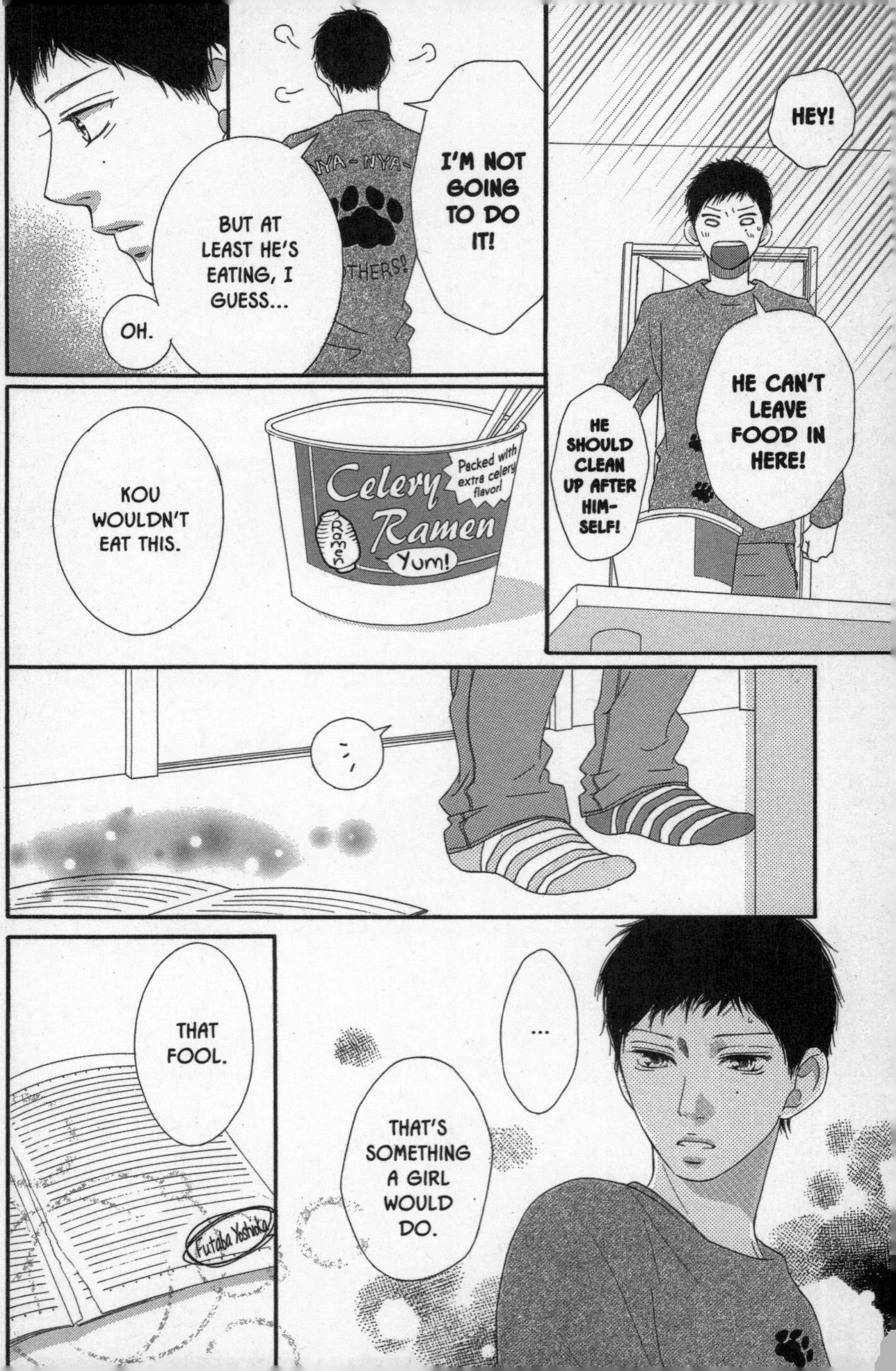
HEY!
HE CAN'T LEAVE FOOD IN HERE!
HE SHOULD CLEAN UP AFTER HIM-SELF!
I'M NOT GOING TO DO IT!
BUT AT LEAST HE'S EATING, I GUESS...
OH.
Celery Ramen
Packed with extra celery flavor!
Ramen
Yum!
KOU WOULDN'T EAT THIS.
...
THAT'S SOMETHING A GIRL WOULD DO.
THAT FOOL.
Futaba Yoshioka

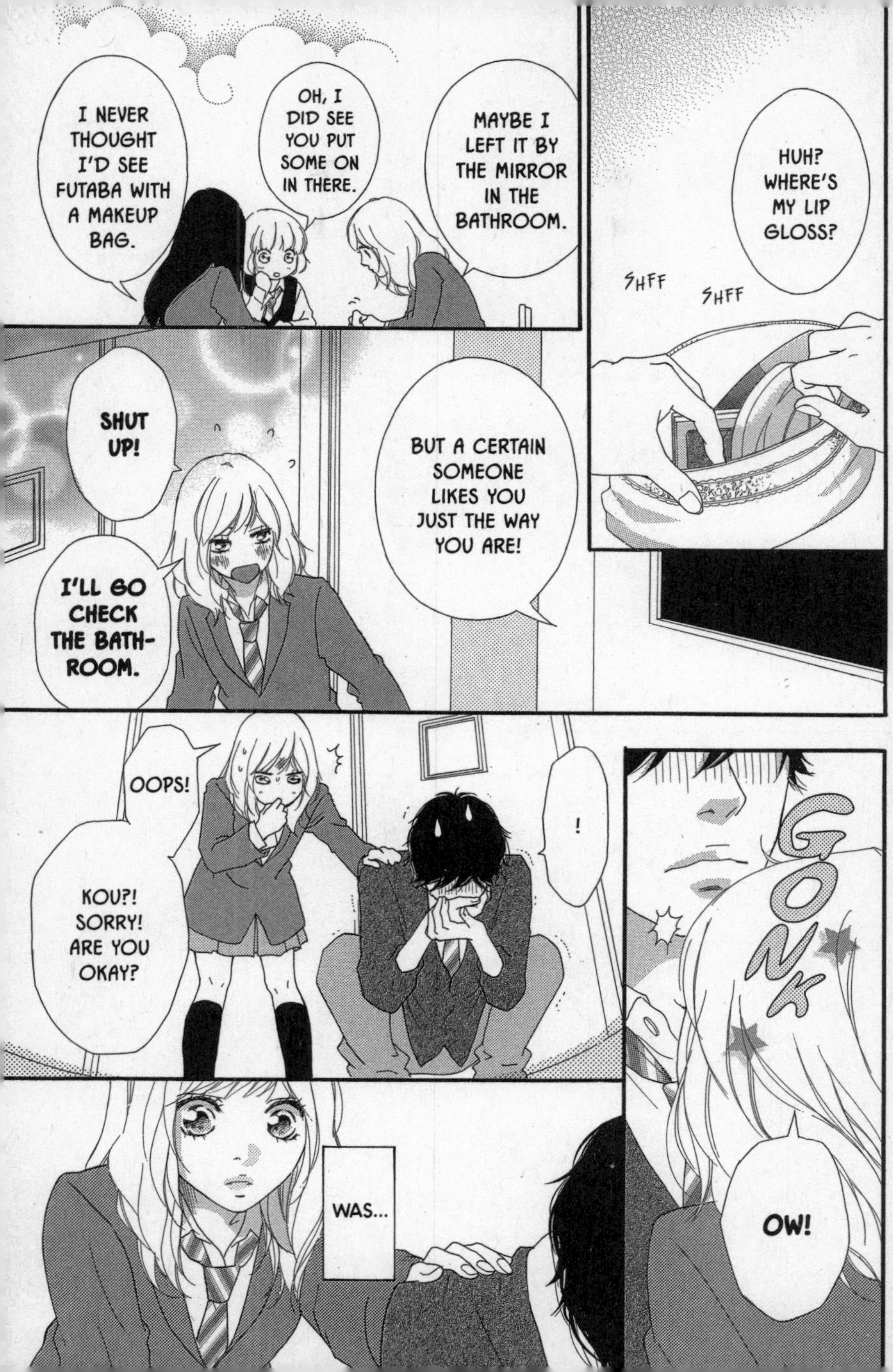
HUH? WHERE'S MY LIP GLOSS?
SHFF
SHFF
MAYBE I LEFT IT BY THE MIRROR IN THE BATHROOM.
OH, I DID SEE YOU PUT SOME ON IN THERE.
I NEVER THOUGHT I'D SEE FUTABA WITH A MAKEUP BAG.
BUT A CERTAIN SOMEONE LIKES YOU JUST THE WAY YOU ARE!
SHUT UP!
I'LL GO CHECK THE BATH-ROOM.
GONK
OW!
!
OOPS!
KOU?! SORRY! ARE YOU OKAY?
WAS...

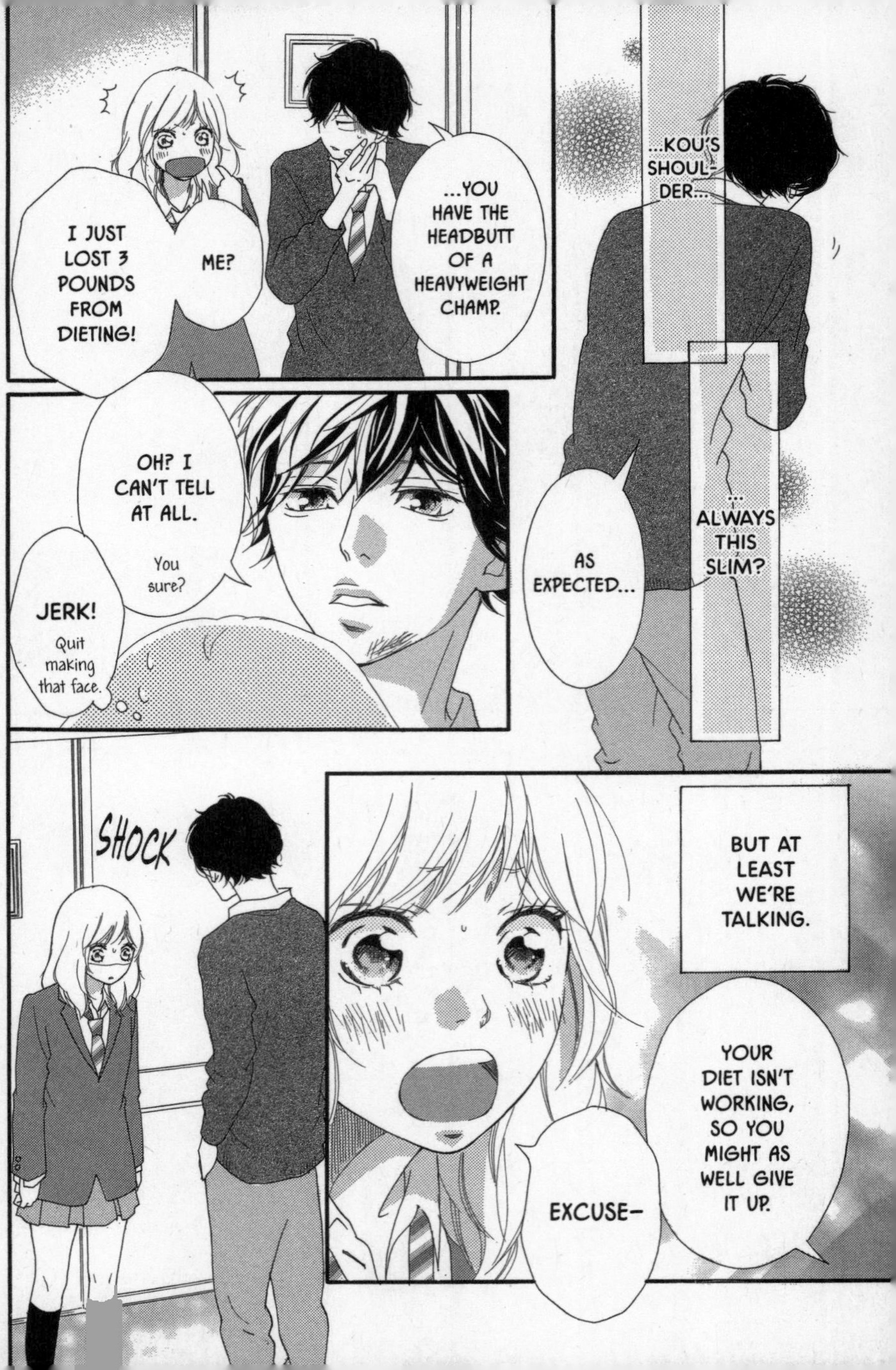
...KOU'S SHOULDER...
... ALWAYS THIS SLIM?
AS EXPECTED...
...YOU HAVE THE HEADBUTT OF A HEAVYWEIGHT CHAMP.
ME?
I JUST LOST 3 POUNDS FROM DIETING!
OH? I CAN'T TELL AT ALL.
You sure?
JERK!
Quit making that face.
BUT AT LEAST WE'RE TALKING.
YOUR DIET ISN'T WORKING, SO YOU MIGHT AS WELL GIVE IT UP.
EXCUSE–
SHOCK

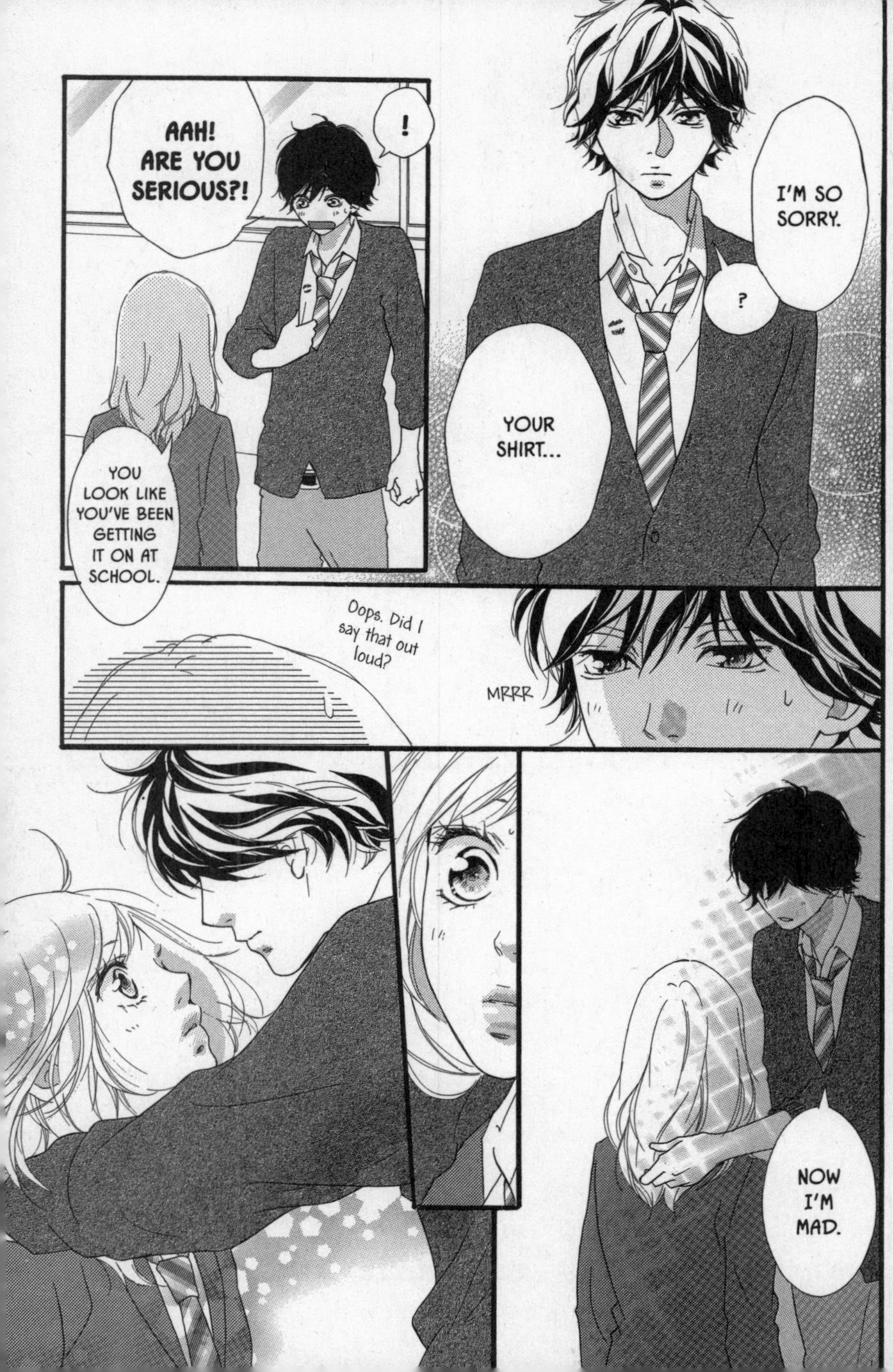
I'M SO SORRY.
?
YOUR SHIRT...
!
AAH! ARE YOU SERIOUS?!
YOU LOOK LIKE YOU'VE BEEN GETTING IT ON AT SCHOOL.
MRRR
Oops. Did I say that out loud?
NOW I'M MAD.

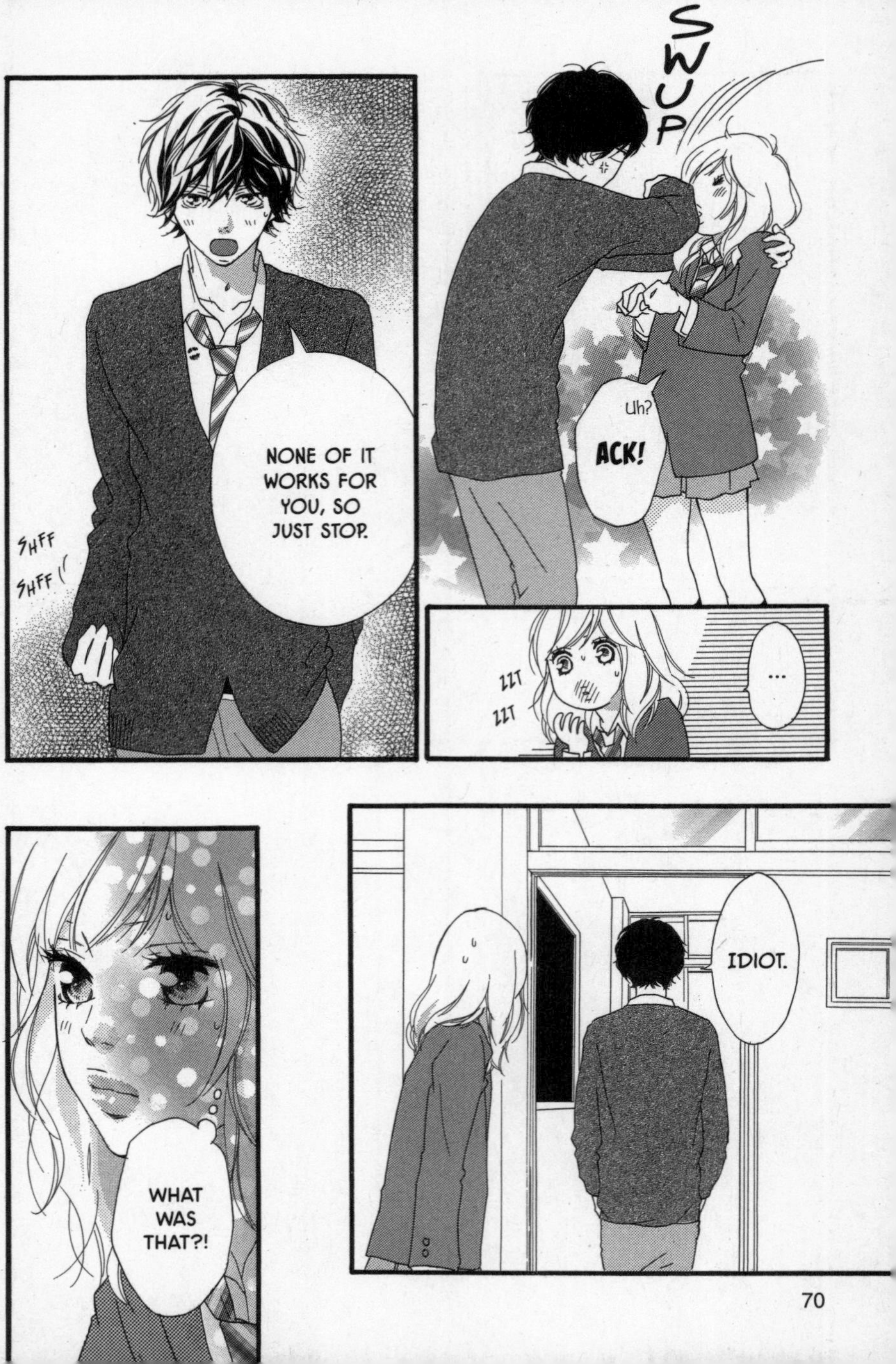
SWUP
Uh?
ACK!
...
ZZT
ZZT
NONE OF IT WORKS FOR YOU, SO JUST STOP.
SHFF
SHFF
IDIOT.
WHAT WAS THAT?!

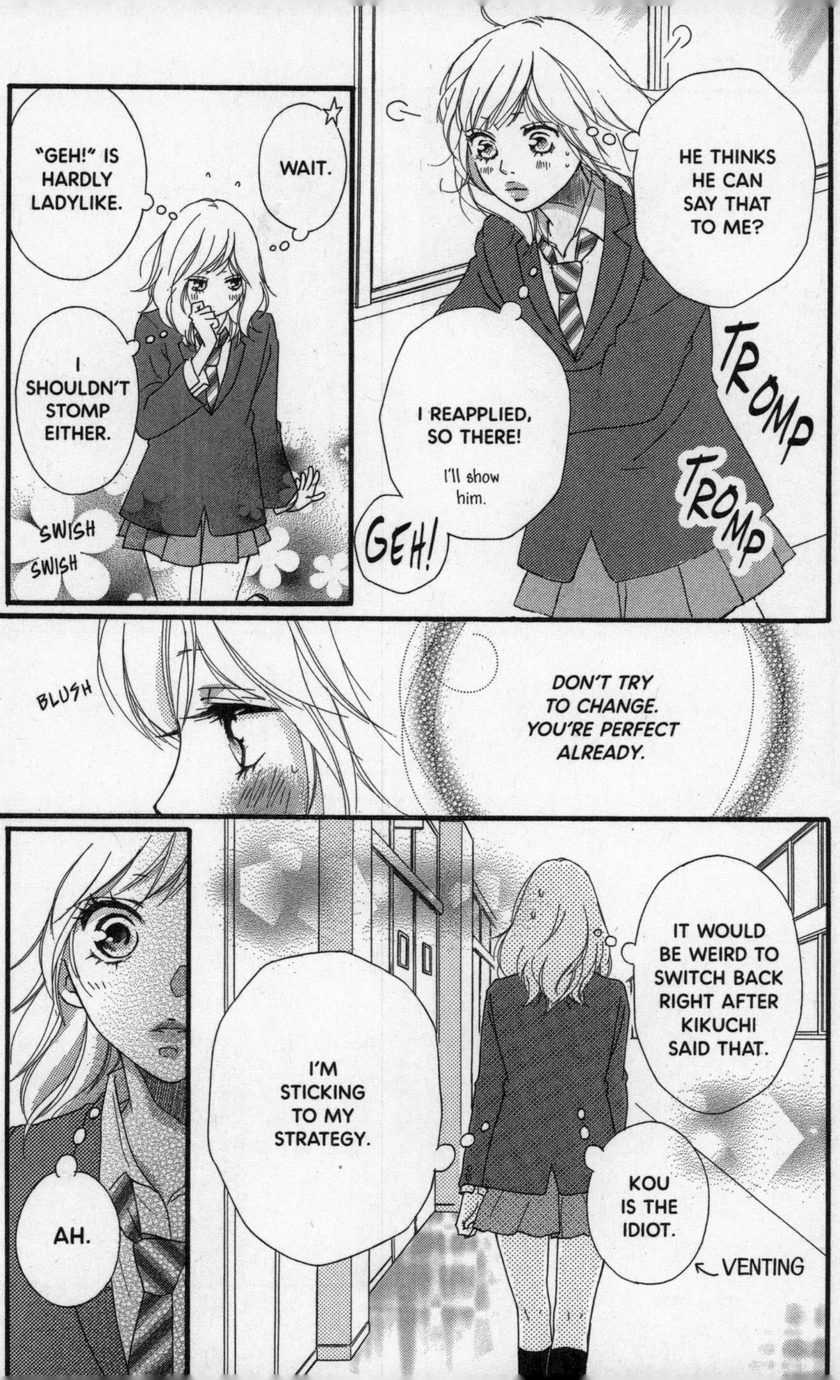
HE THINKS HE CAN SAY THAT TO ME?
TROMP
TROMP
I REAPPLIED, SO THERE!
I'll show him.
GEH!
WAIT.
"GEH!" IS HARDLY LADYLIKE.
I SHOULDN'T STOMP EITHER.
SWISH
SWISH
DON'T TRY TO CHANGE. YOU'RE PERFECT ALREADY.
BLUSH
IT WOULD BE WEIRD TO SWITCH BACK RIGHT AFTER KIKUCHI SAID THAT.
I'M STICKING TO MY STRATEGY.
KOU IS THE IDIOT.
VENTING
AH.

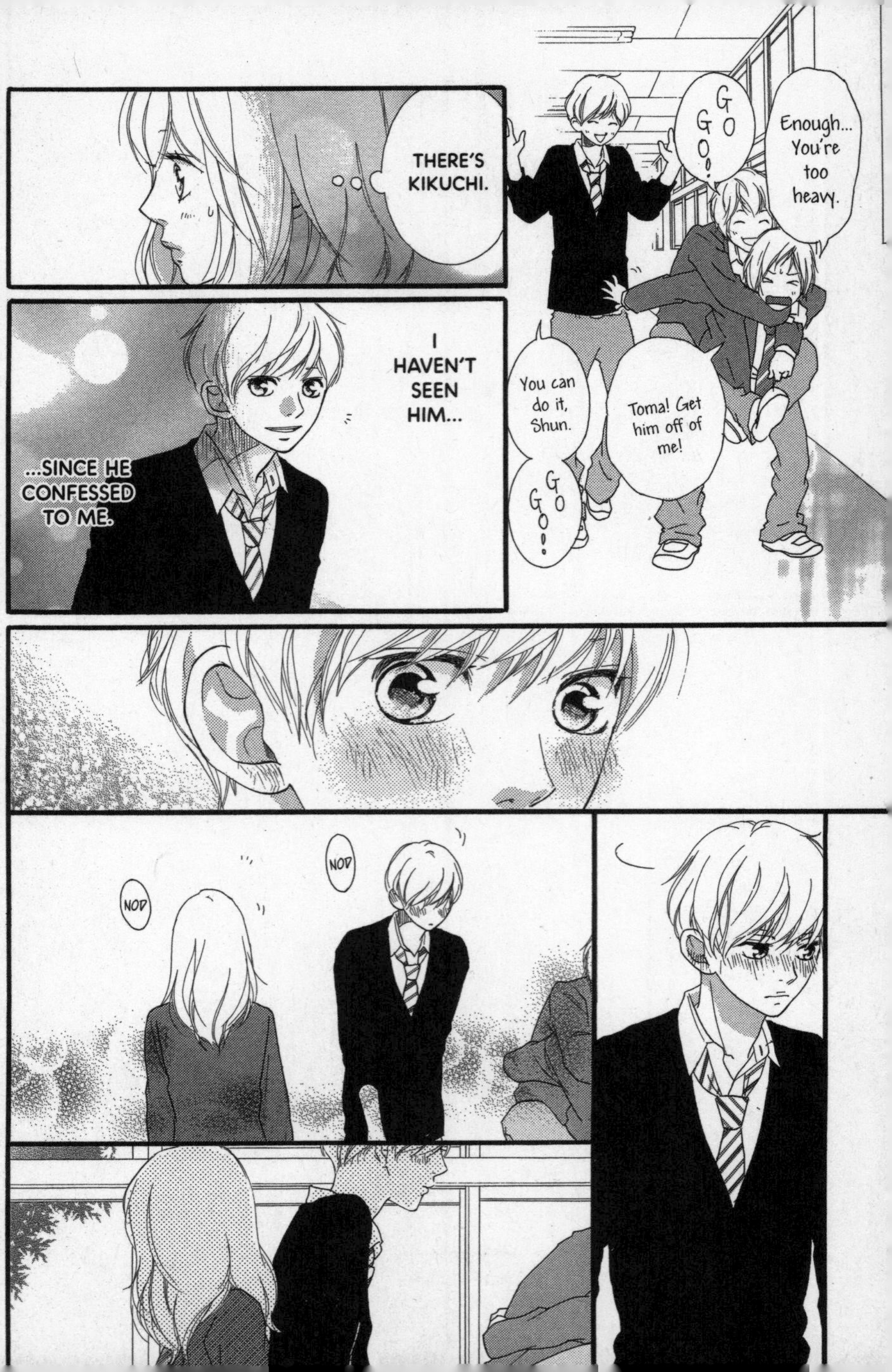
Enough... You're too heavy.
GO GO GO!
Toma! Get him off of me!
You can do it, Shun.
GO GO GO!
THERE'S KIKUCHI.
I HAVEN'T SEEN HIM...
...SINCE HE CONFESSED TO ME.
NOD
NOD

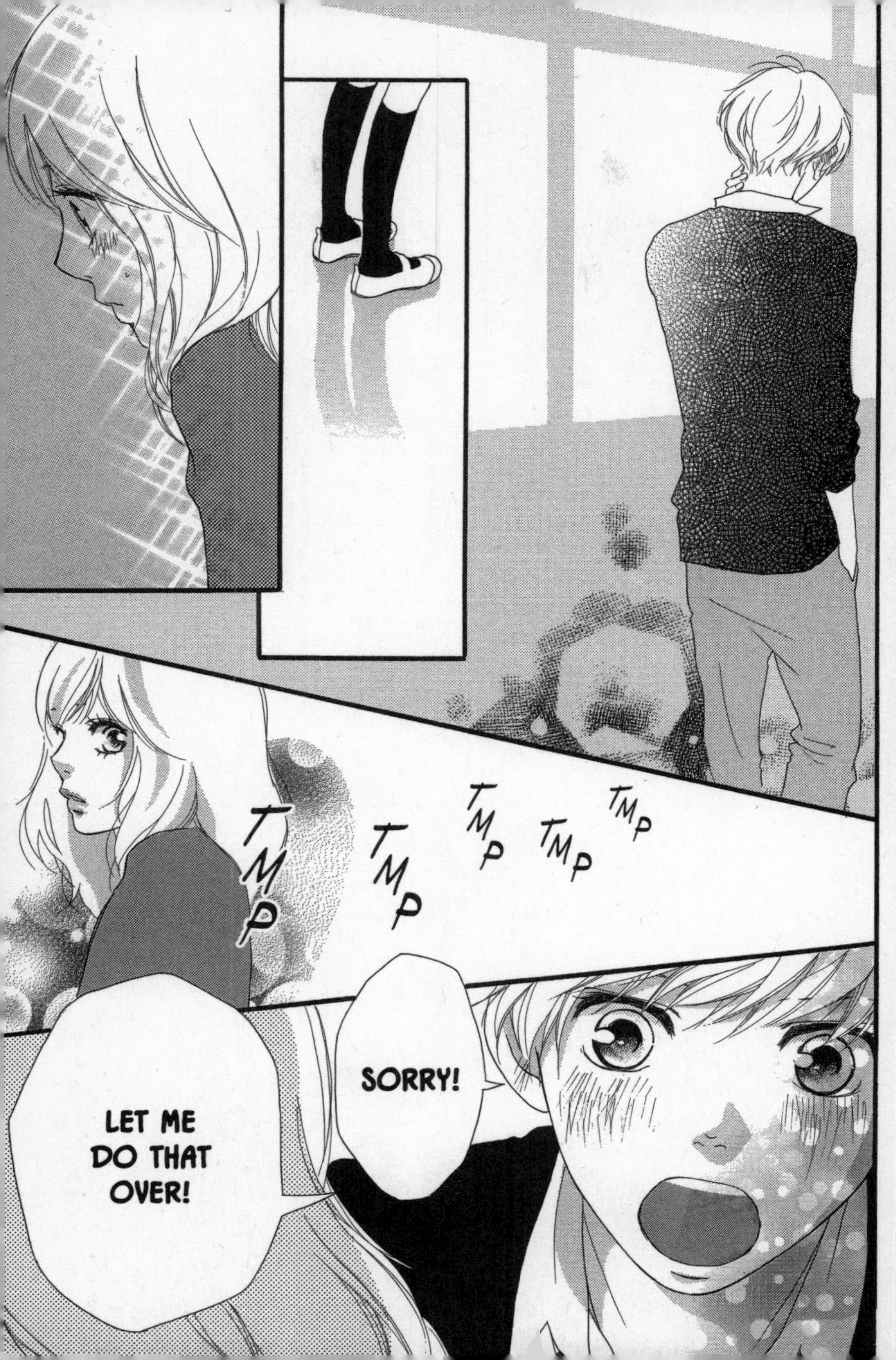
TMP
TMP
TMP
TMP
TMP
SORRY!
LET ME DO THAT OVER!

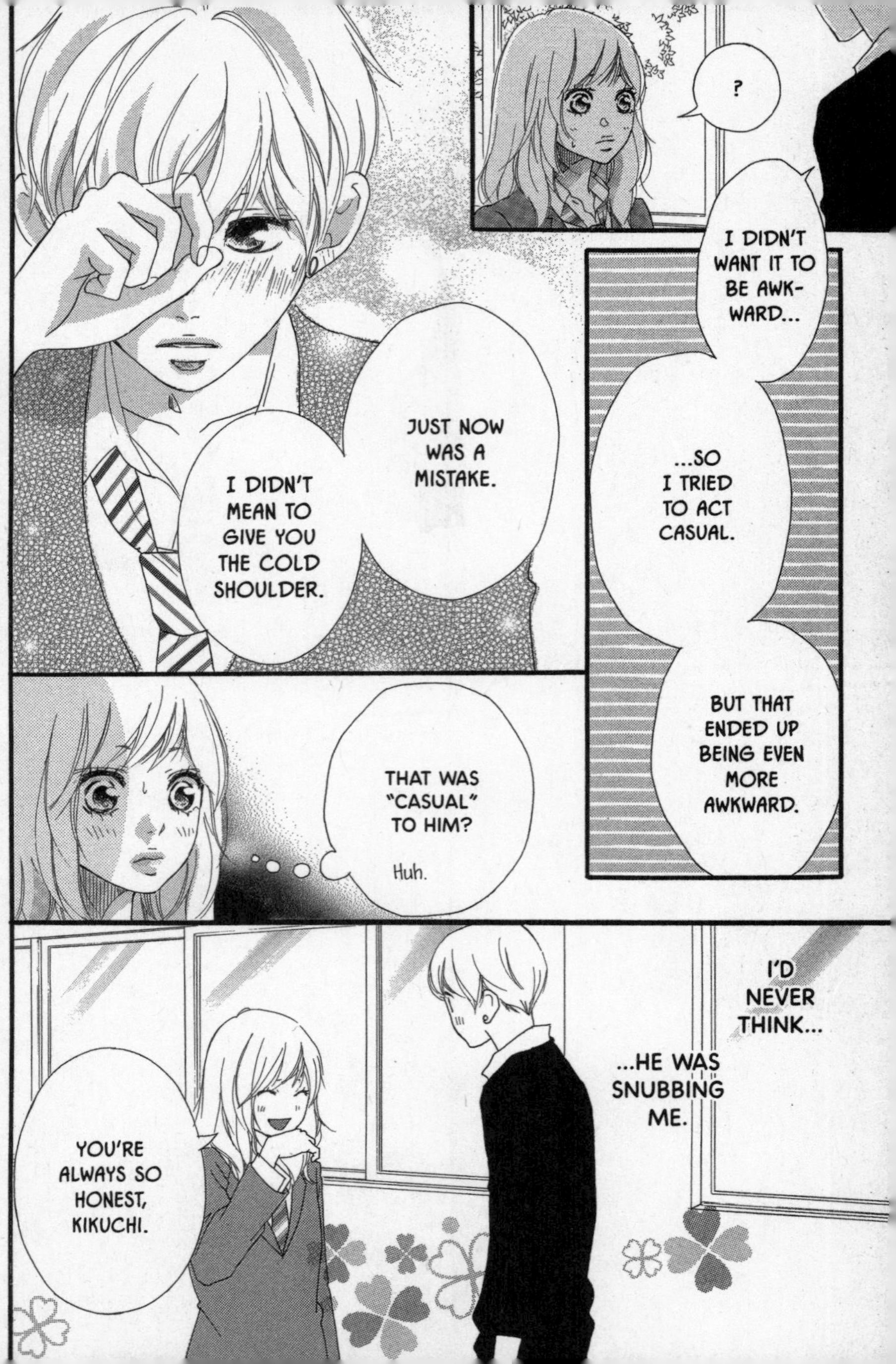
?
I DIDN'T WANT IT TO BE AWK-WARD...
...SO I TRIED TO ACT CASUAL.
BUT THAT ENDED UP BEING EVEN MORE AWKWARD.
JUST NOW WAS A MISTAKE.
I DIDN'T MEAN TO GIVE YOU THE COLD SHOULDER.
THAT WAS "CASUAL" TO HIM?
Huh.
I'D NEVER THINK...
...HE WAS SNUBBING ME.
YOU'RE ALWAYS SO HONEST, KIKUCHI.

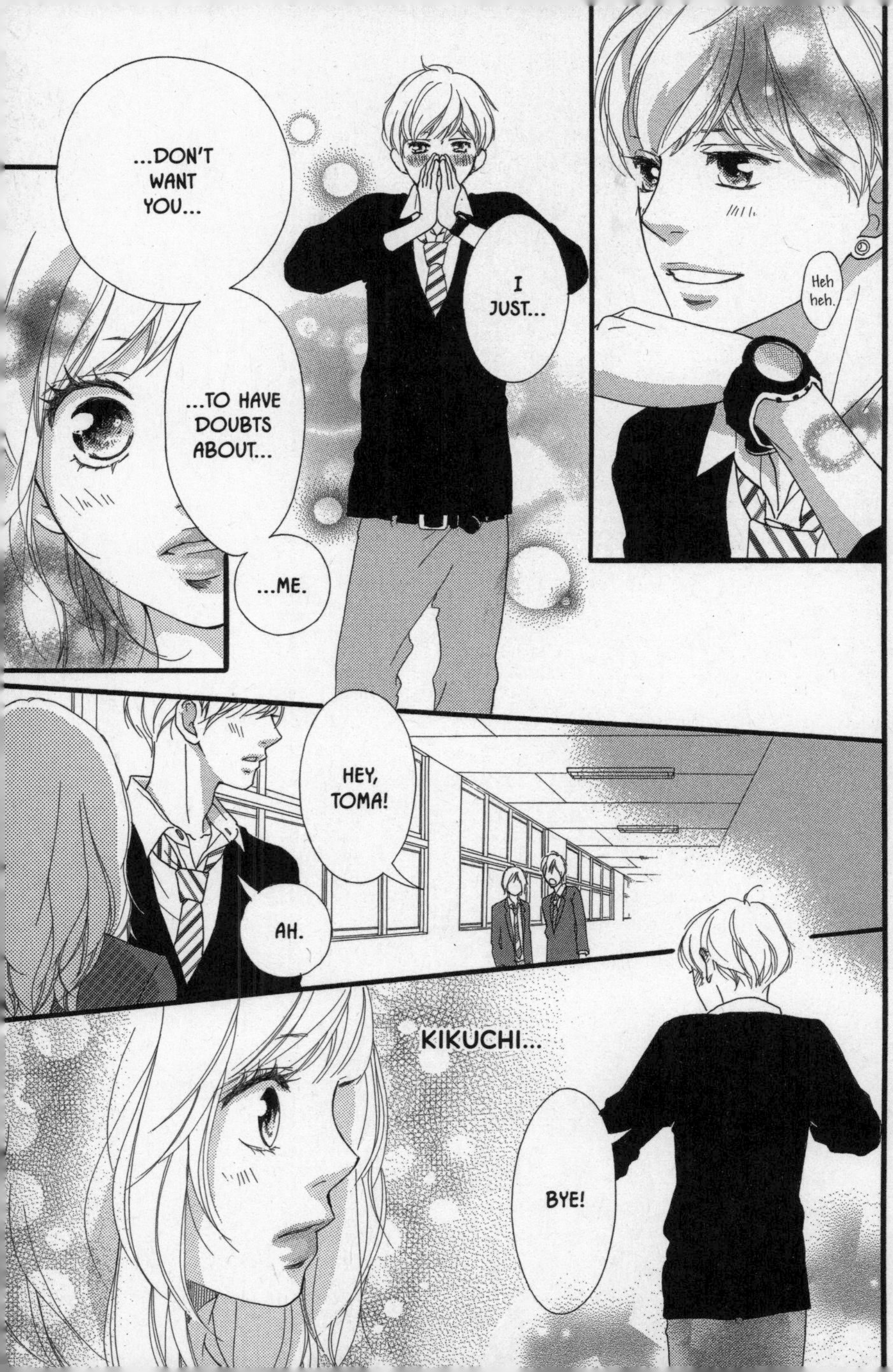
Heh heh.
I JUST...
...DON'T WANT YOU...
...TO HAVE DOUBTS ABOUT...
...ME.
HEY, TOMA!
AH.
KIKUCHI...
BYE!

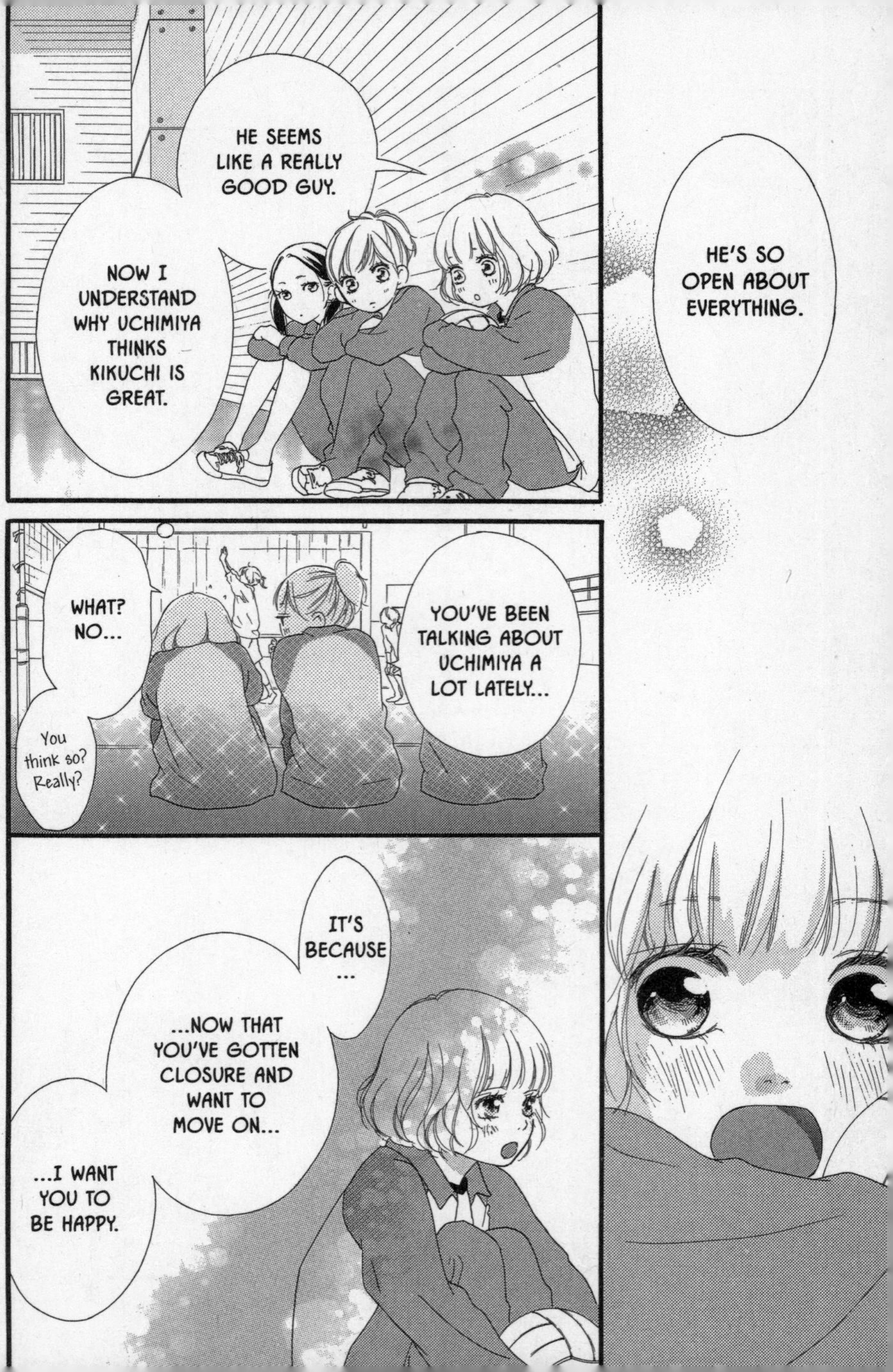
HE'S SO OPEN ABOUT EVERYTHING.
HE SEEMS LIKE A REALLY GOOD GUY.
NOW I UNDERSTAND WHY UCHIMIYA THINKS KIKUCHI IS GREAT.
YOU'VE BEEN TALKING ABOUT UCHIMIYA A LOT LATELY...
WHAT? NO...
You think so? Really?
IT'S BECAUSE...
...NOW THAT YOU'VE GOTTEN CLOSURE AND WANT TO MOVE ON...
...I WANT YOU TO BE HAPPY.

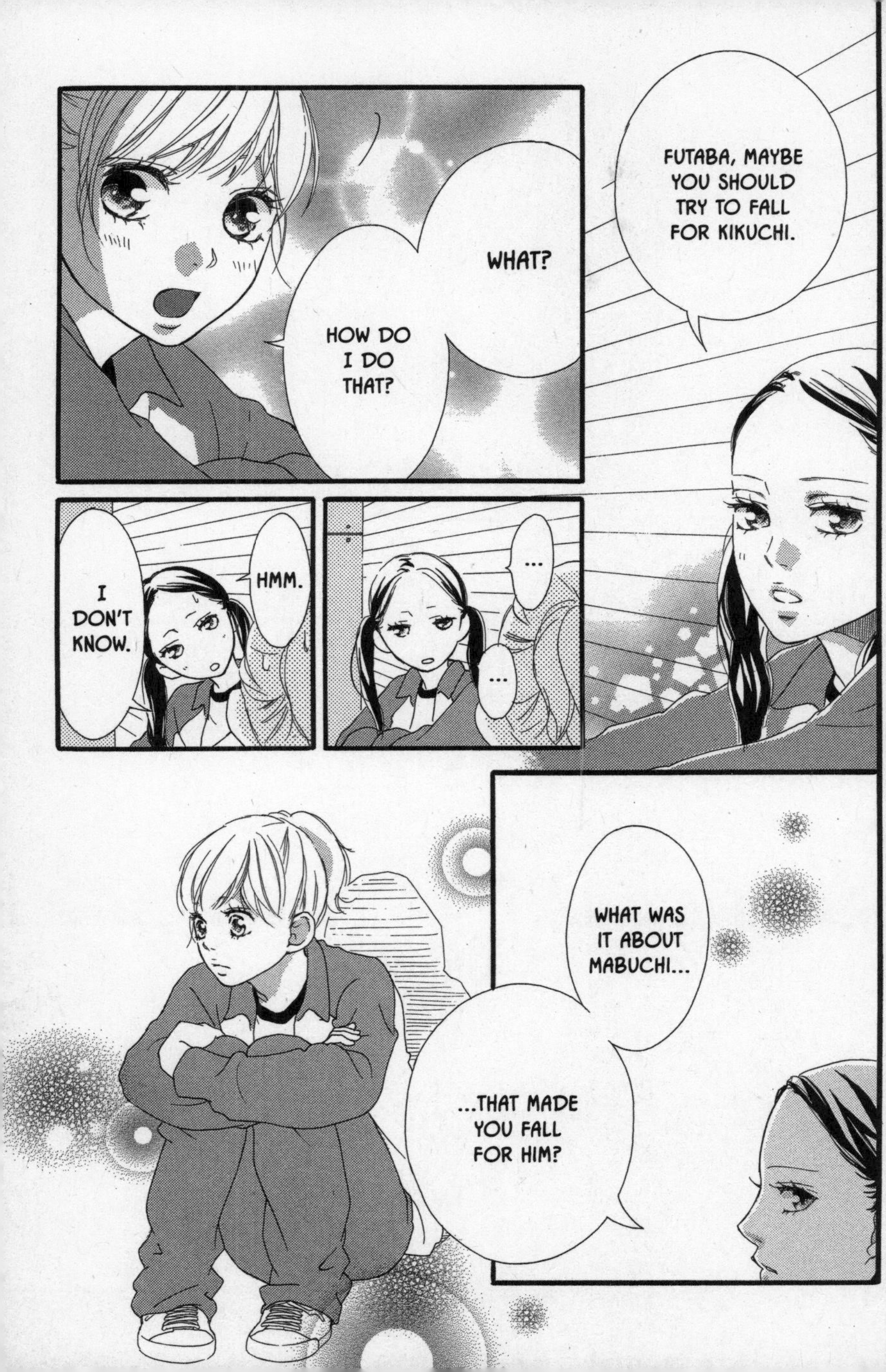
FUTABA, MAYBE YOU SHOULD TRY TO FALL FOR KIKUCHI.
WHAT?
HOW DO I DO THAT?
...
...
HMM.
I DON'T KNOW.
WHAT WAS IT ABOUT MABUCHI...
...THAT MADE YOU FALL FOR HIM?

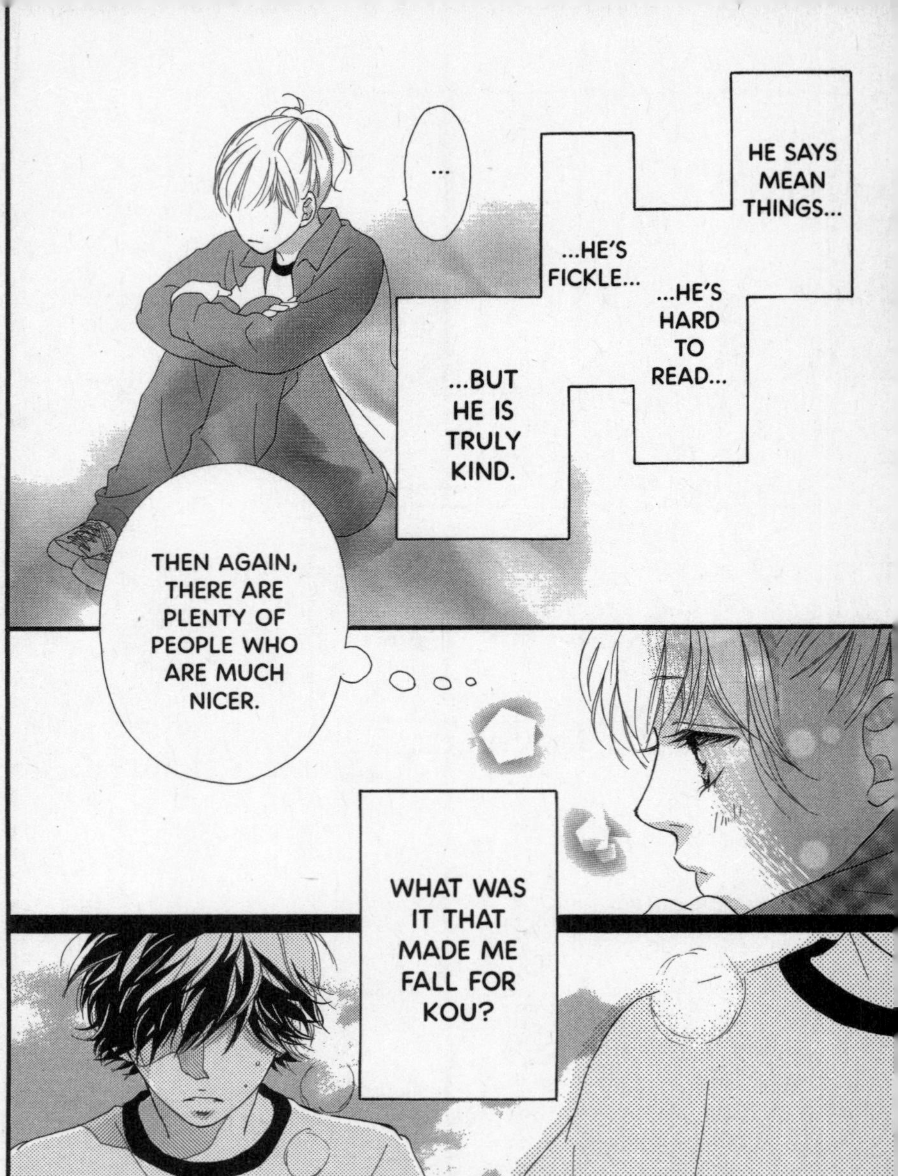
HE SAYS MEAN THINGS...
...HE'S FICKLE...
...HE'S HARD TO READ...
...BUT HE IS TRULY KIND.
...
THEN AGAIN, THERE ARE PLENTY OF PEOPLE WHO ARE MUCH NICER.
WHAT WAS IT THAT MADE ME FALL FOR KOU?

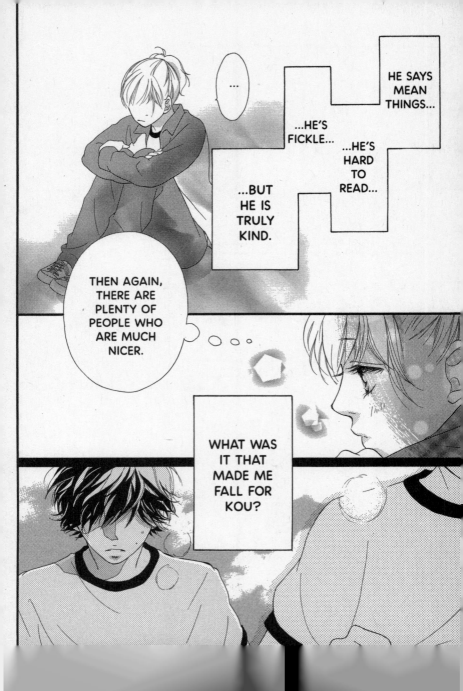

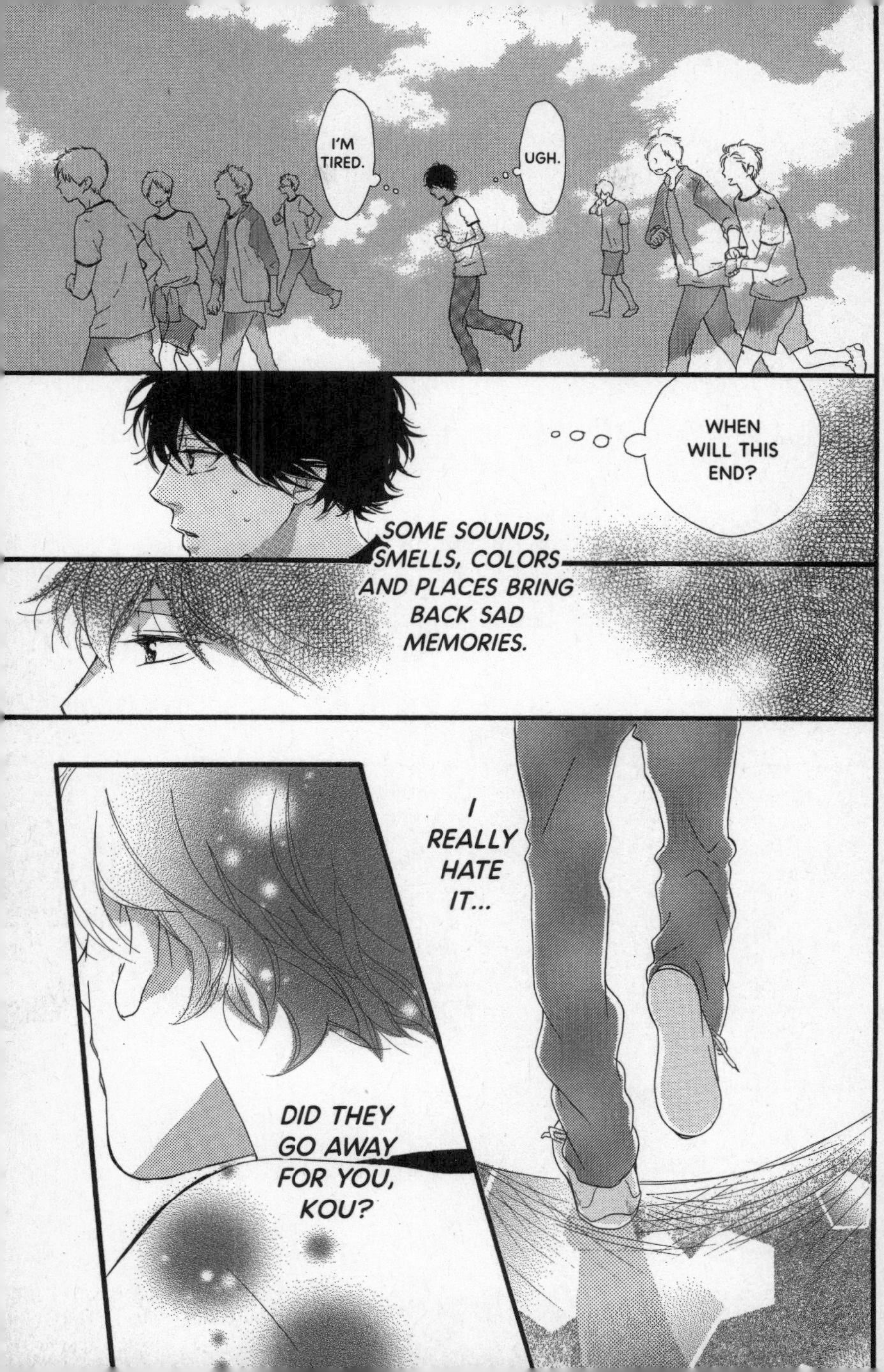
UGH.
I'M TIRED.
WHEN WILL THIS END?
SOME SOUNDS, SMELLS, COLORS AND PLACES BRING BACK SAD MEMORIES.
I REALLY HATE IT...
DID THEY GO AWAY FOR YOU, KOU?

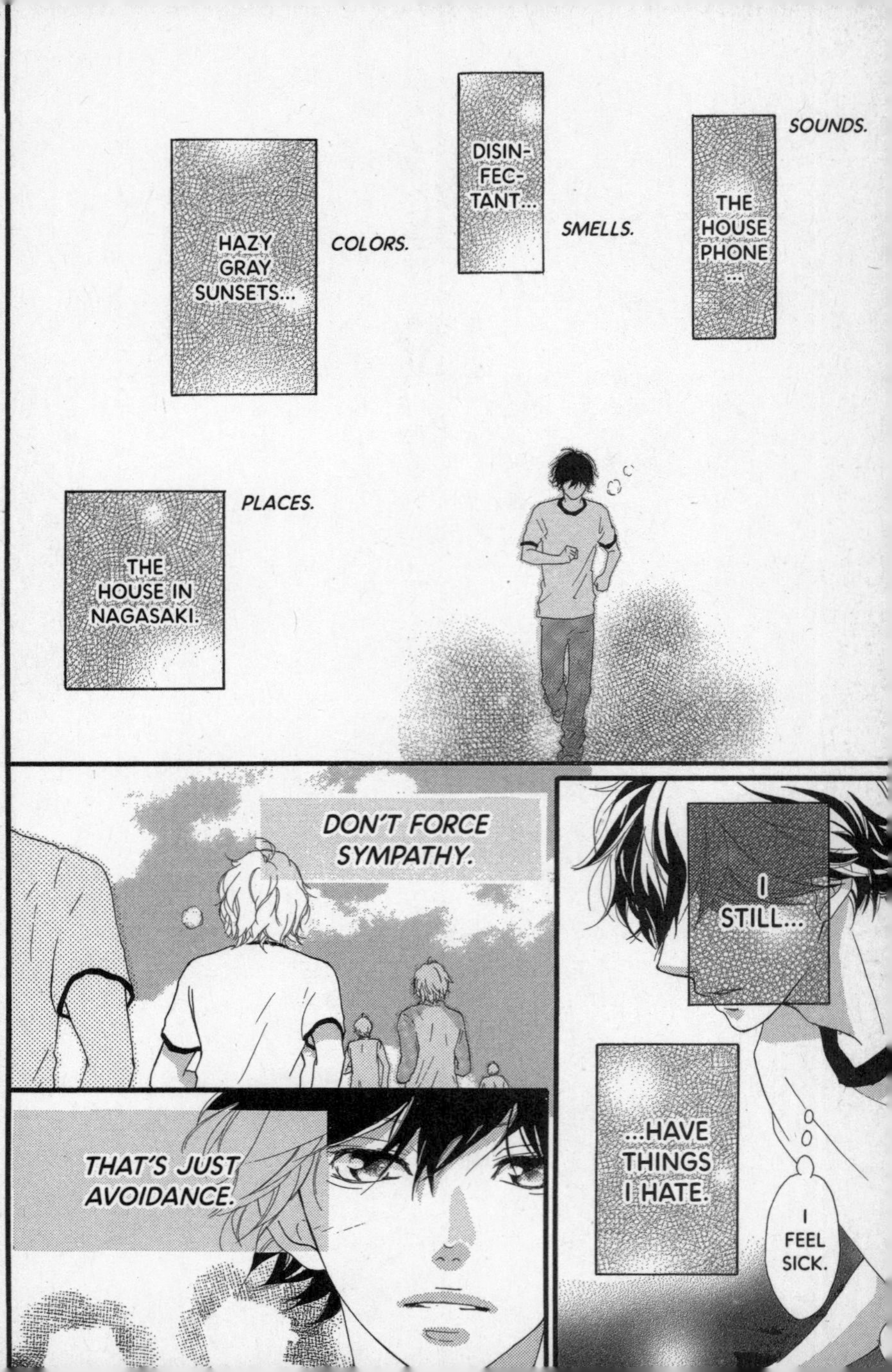
SOUNDS.
THE HOUSE PHONE ...
SMELLS.
DISIN-FEC-TANT...
COLORS.
HAZY GRAY SUNSETS...
PLACES.
THE HOUSE IN NAGASAKI.
I STILL...
...HAVE THINGS I HATE.
I FEEL SICK.
DON'T FORCE SYMPATHY.
THAT'S JUST AVOIDANCE.

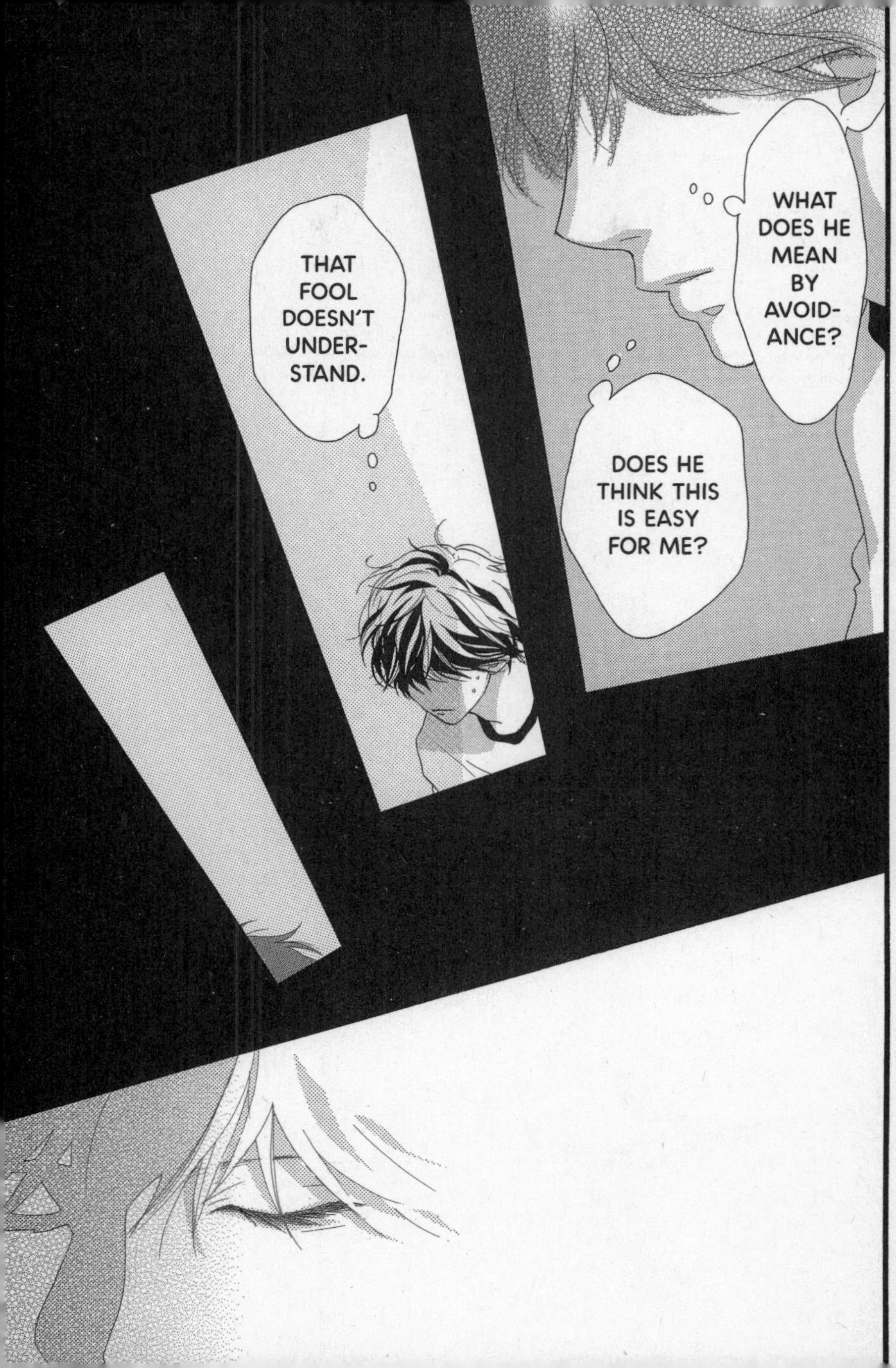
WHAT DOES HE MEAN BY AVOID-ANCE?
DOES HE THINK THIS IS EASY FOR ME?
THAT FOOL DOESN'T UNDER-STAND.

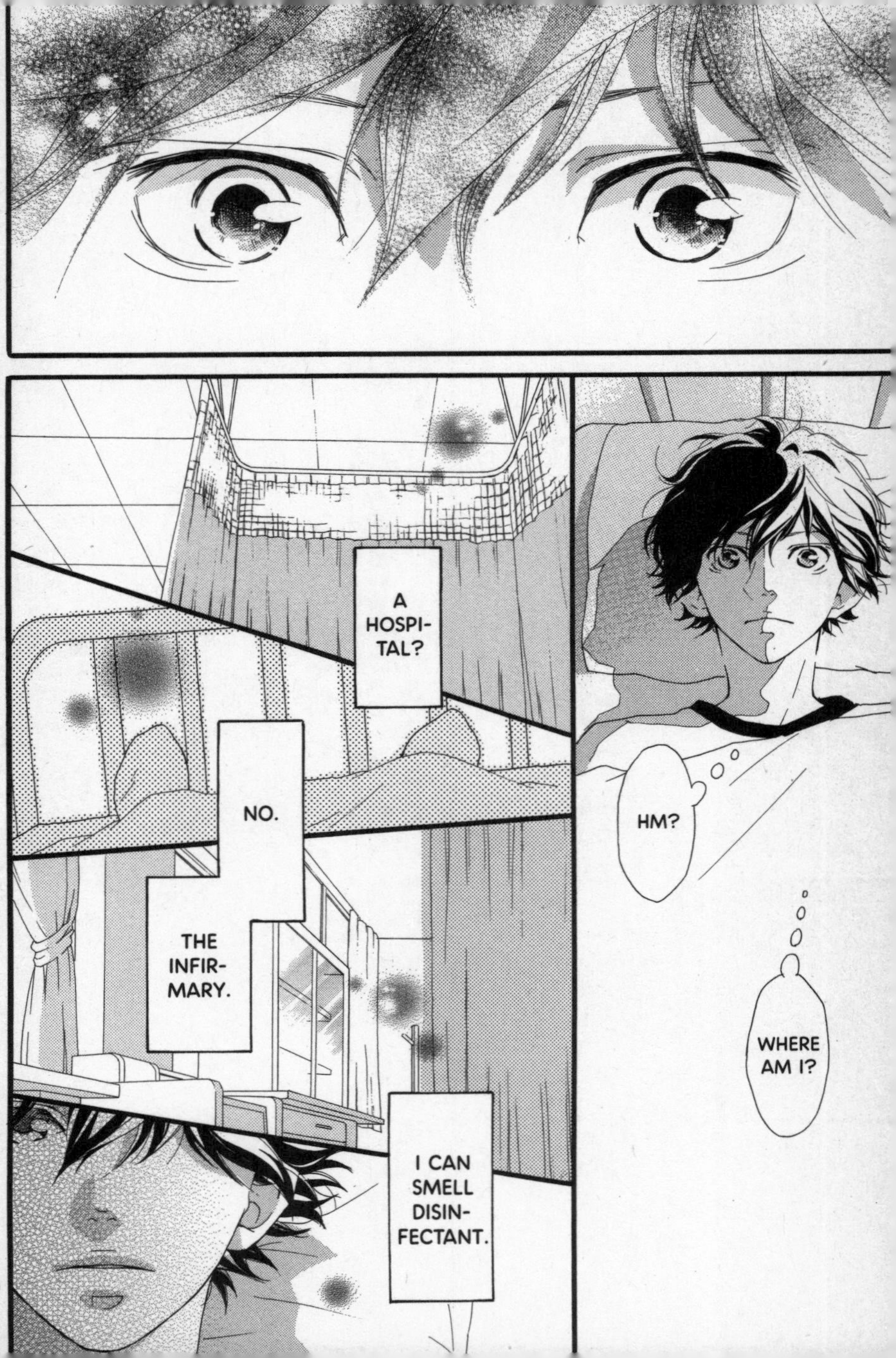
HM?
WHERE AM I?
A HOSPITAL?
NO.
THE INFIRMARY.
I CAN SMELL DISINFECTANT.

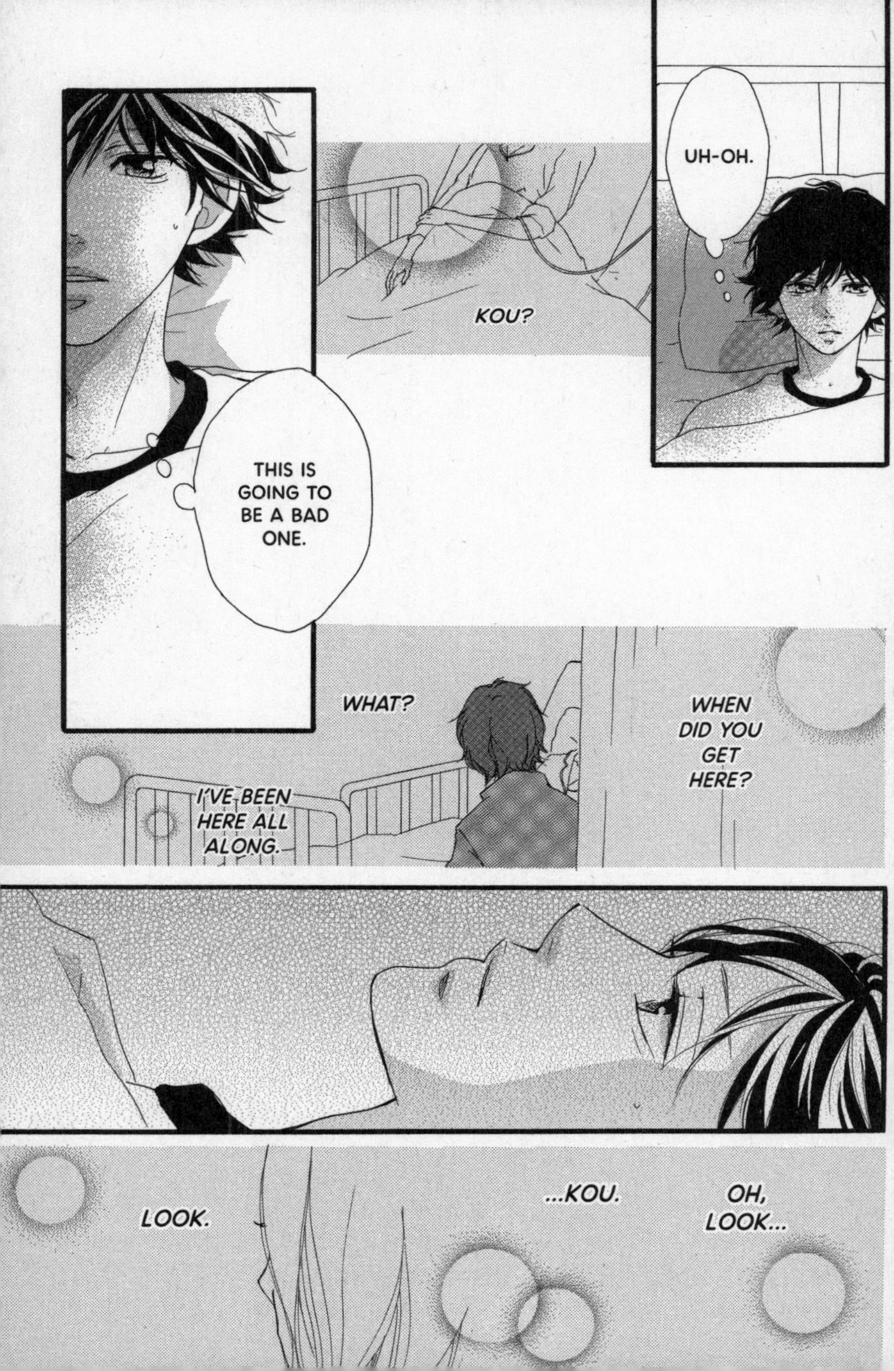
UH-OH.
KOU?
THIS IS GOING TO BE A BAD ONE.
WHEN DID YOU GET HERE?
WHAT?
I'VE BEEN HERE ALL ALONG.
OH, LOOK...
...KOU.
LOOK.

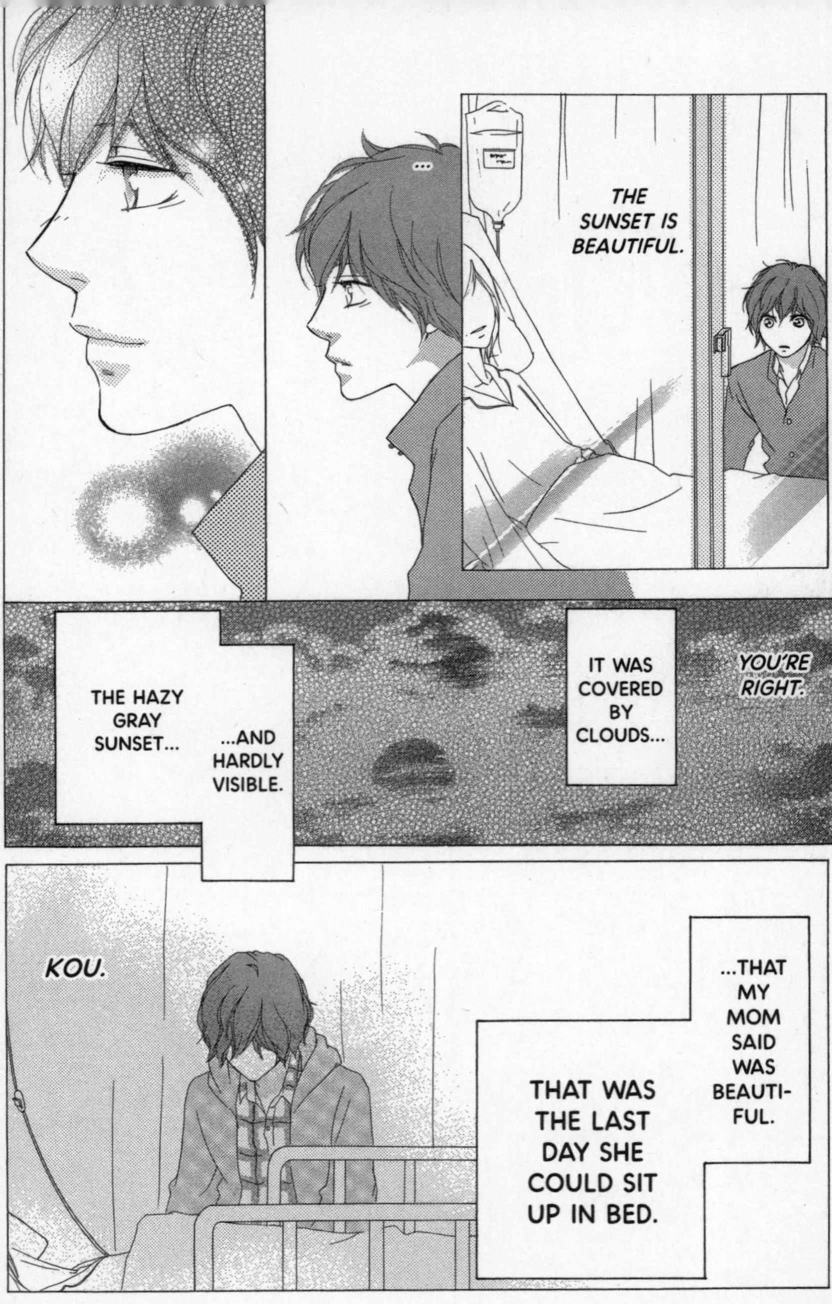
THE SUNSET IS BEAUTIFUL.
YOU'RE RIGHT.
IT WAS COVERED BY CLOUDS...
THE HAZY GRAY SUNSET...
...AND HARDLY VISIBLE.
...THAT MY MOM SAID WAS BEAUTI-FUL.
THAT WAS THE LAST DAY SHE COULD SIT UP IN BED.
KOU.

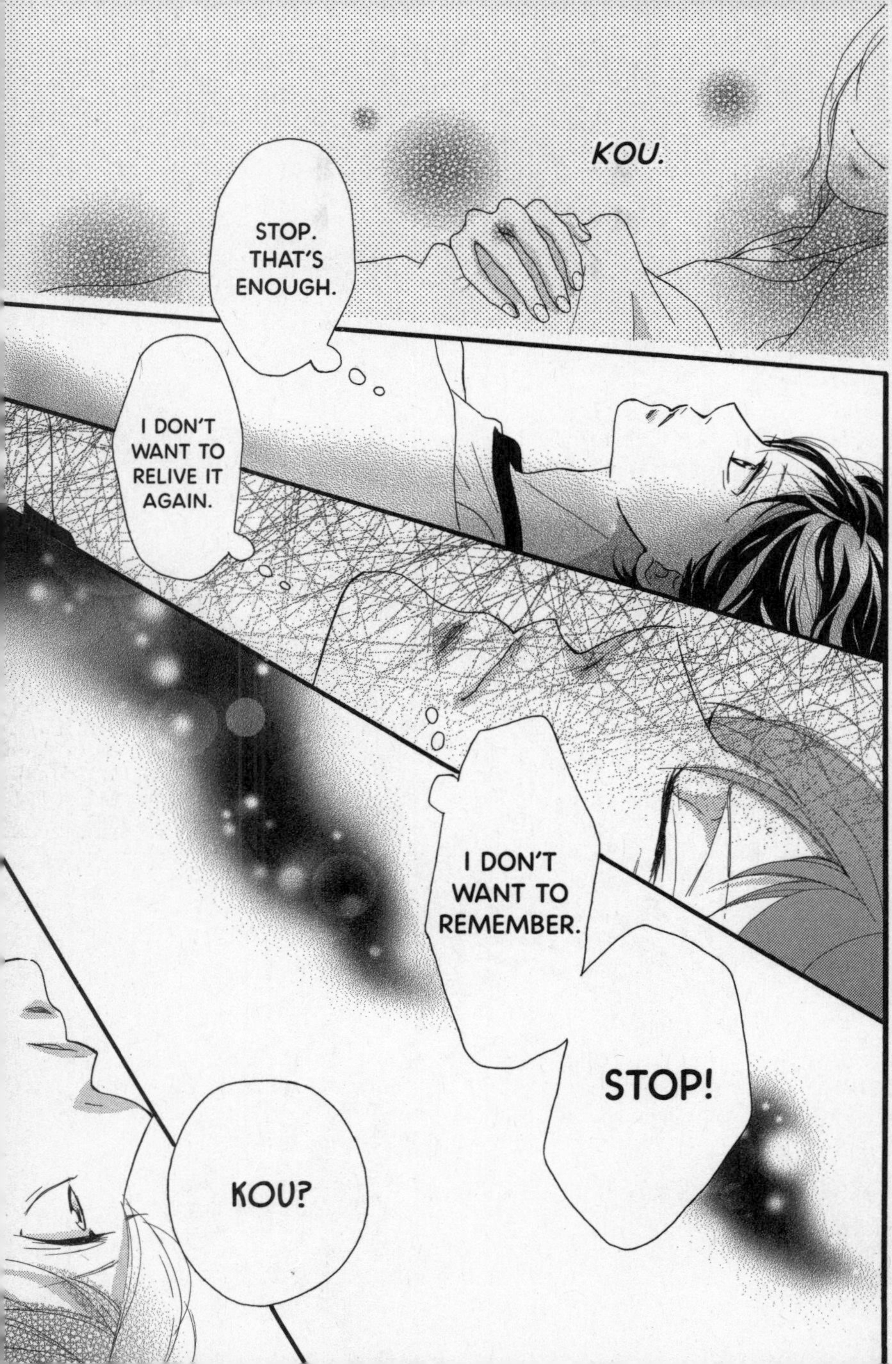
KOU.
STOP. THAT'S ENOUGH.
I DON'T WANT TO RELIVE IT AGAIN.
I DON'T WANT TO REMEMBER.
STOP!
KOU?

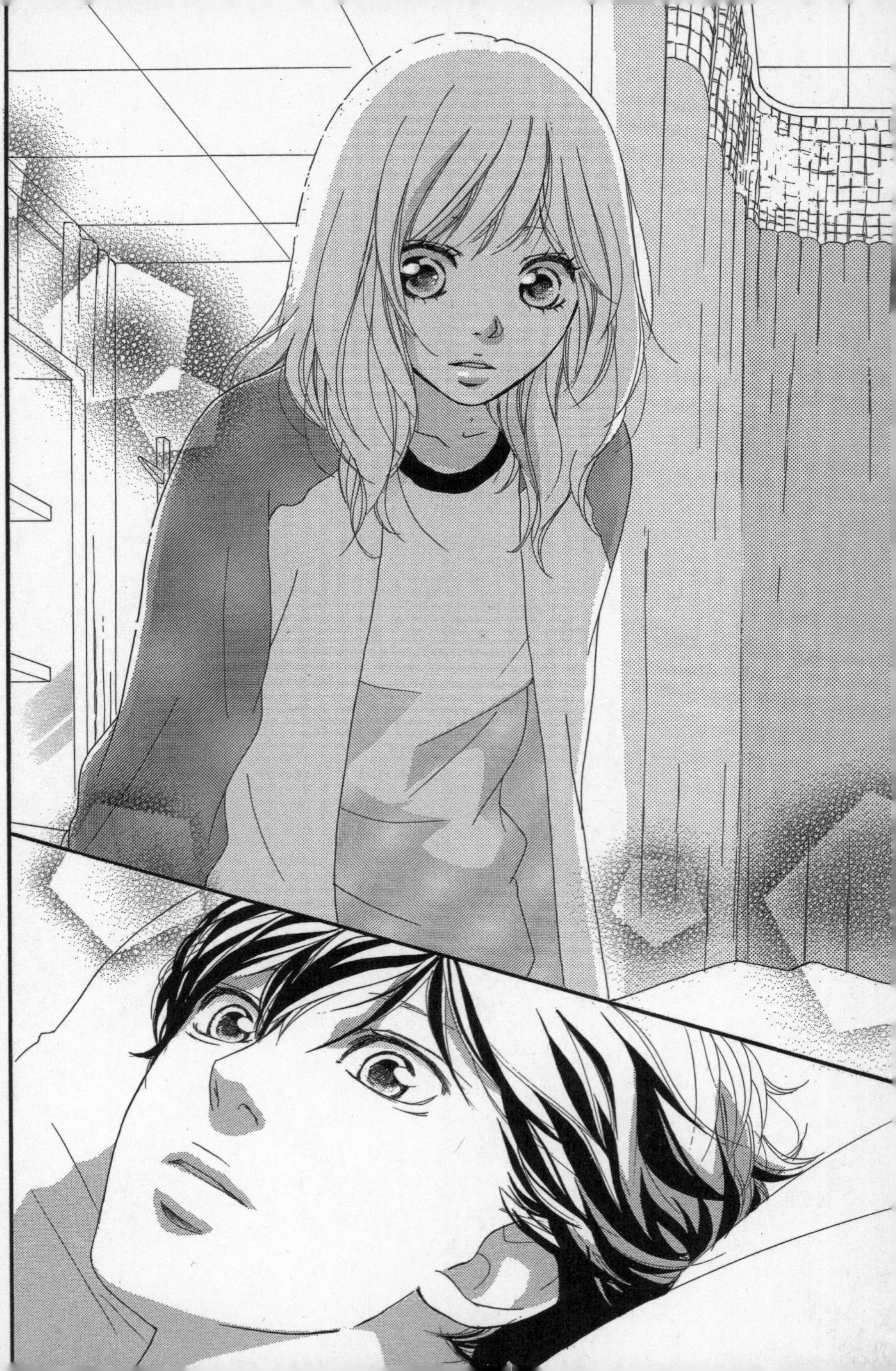

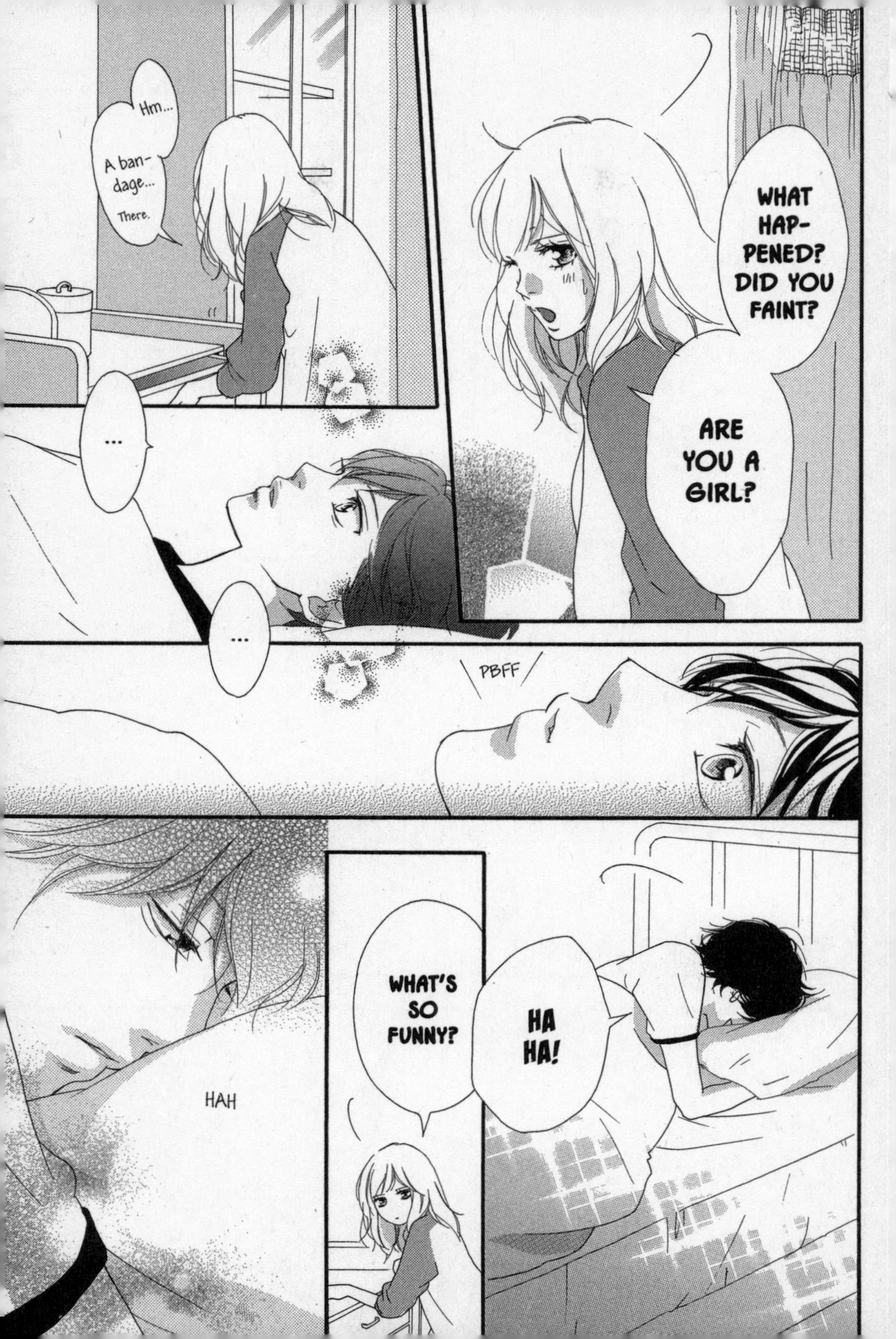
WHAT HAP-PENED? DID YOU FAINT?
ARE YOU A GIRL?
Hm...
A ban-dage...
There.
...
...
PBFF
HA HA!
WHAT'S SO FUNNY?
HAH

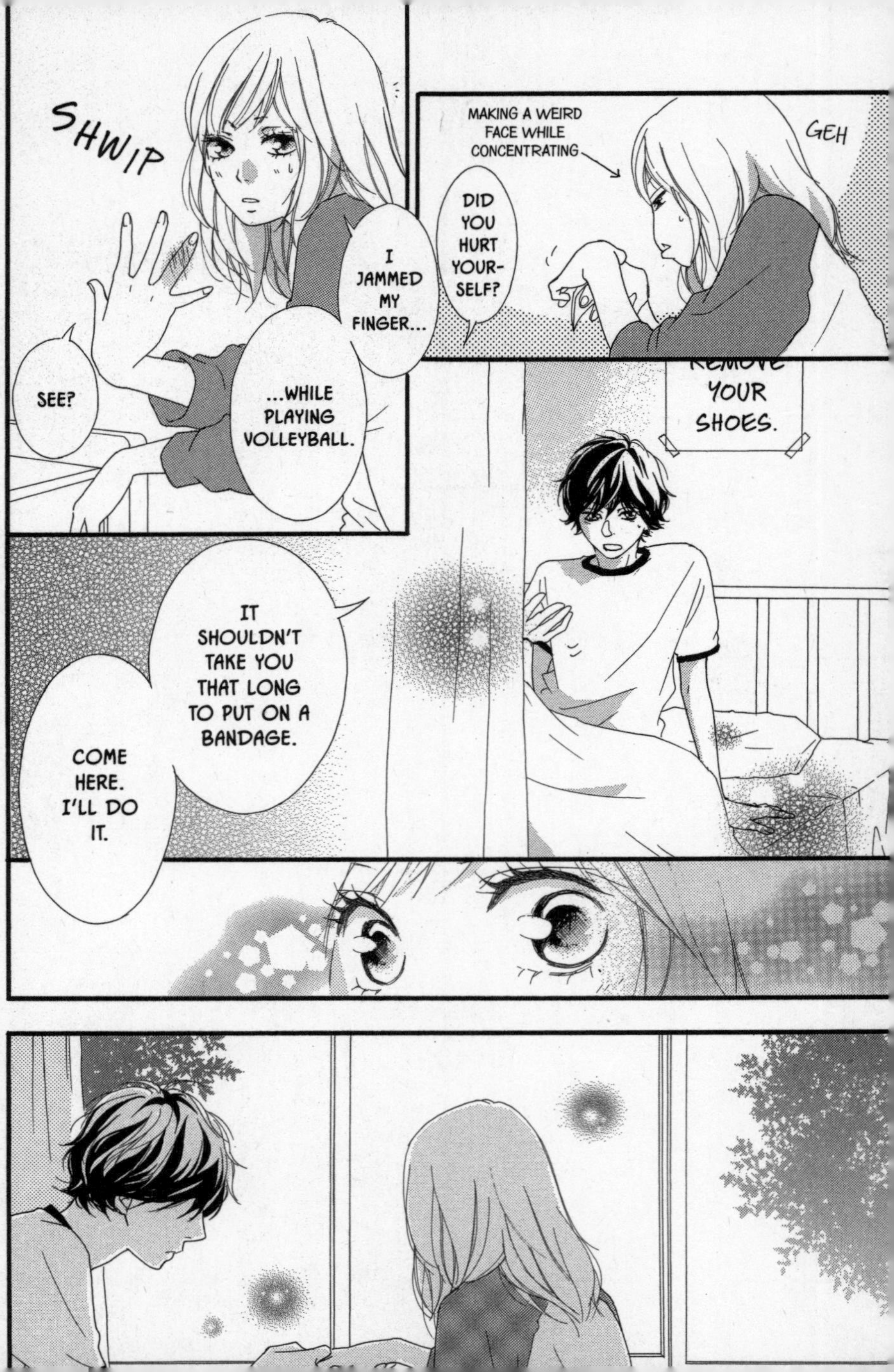
MAKING A WEIRD FACE WHILE CONCENTRATING
GEH
DID YOU HURT YOURSELF?
SHWIP
I JAMMED MY FINGER...
...WHILE PLAYING VOLLEYBALL.
SEE?
YOUR SHOES.
IT SHOULDN'T TAKE YOU THAT LONG TO PUT ON A BANDAGE.
COME HERE. I'LL DO IT.

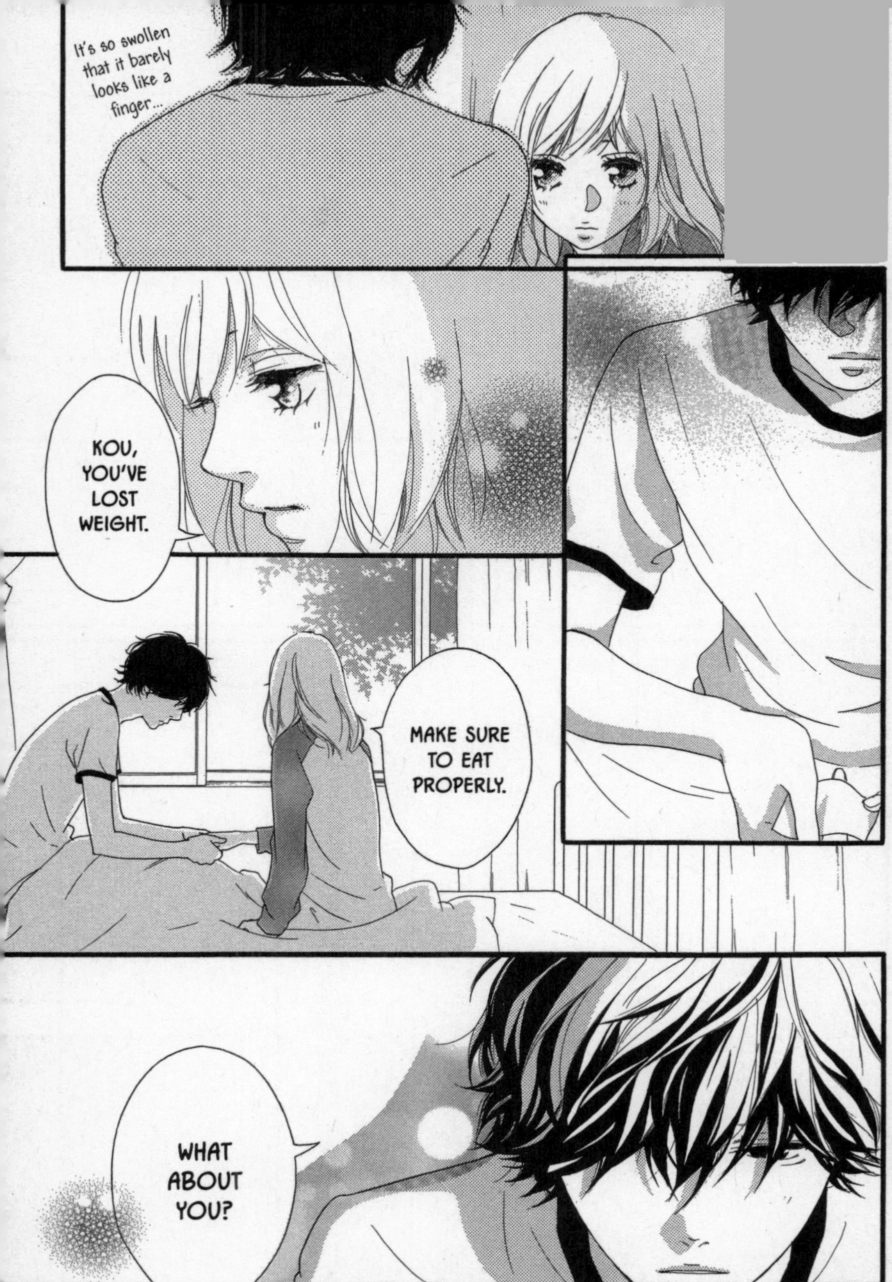
It's so swollen that it barely looks like a finger...
KOU, YOU'VE LOST WEIGHT.
MAKE SURE TO EAT PROPERLY.
WHAT ABOUT YOU?

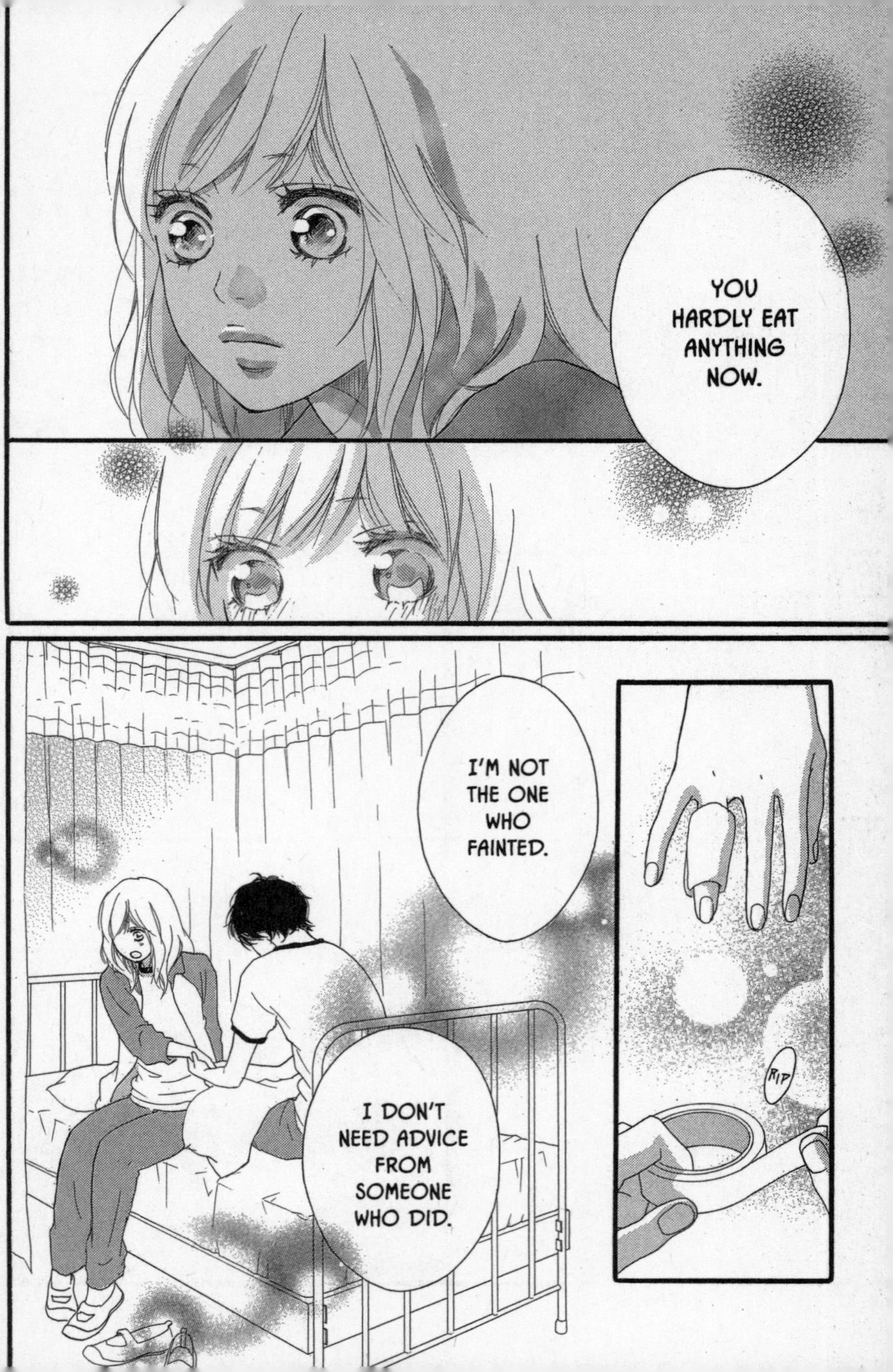
YOU HARDLY EAT ANYTHING NOW.
RIP
I'M NOT THE ONE WHO FAINTED.
I DON'T NEED ADVICE FROM SOMEONE WHO DID.

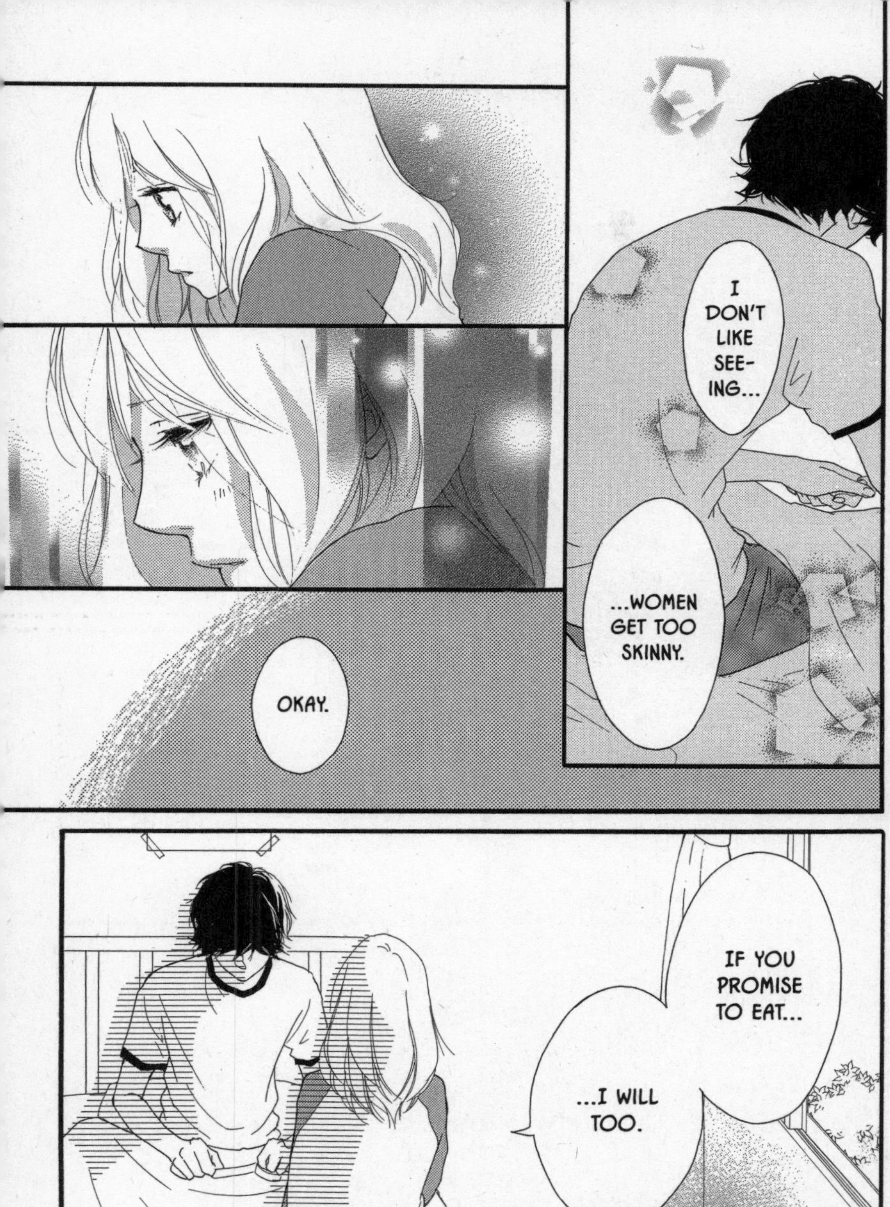
I DON'T LIKE SEE-ING...
...WOMEN GET TOO SKINNY.
OKAY.
IF YOU PROMISE TO EAT...
...I WILL TOO.

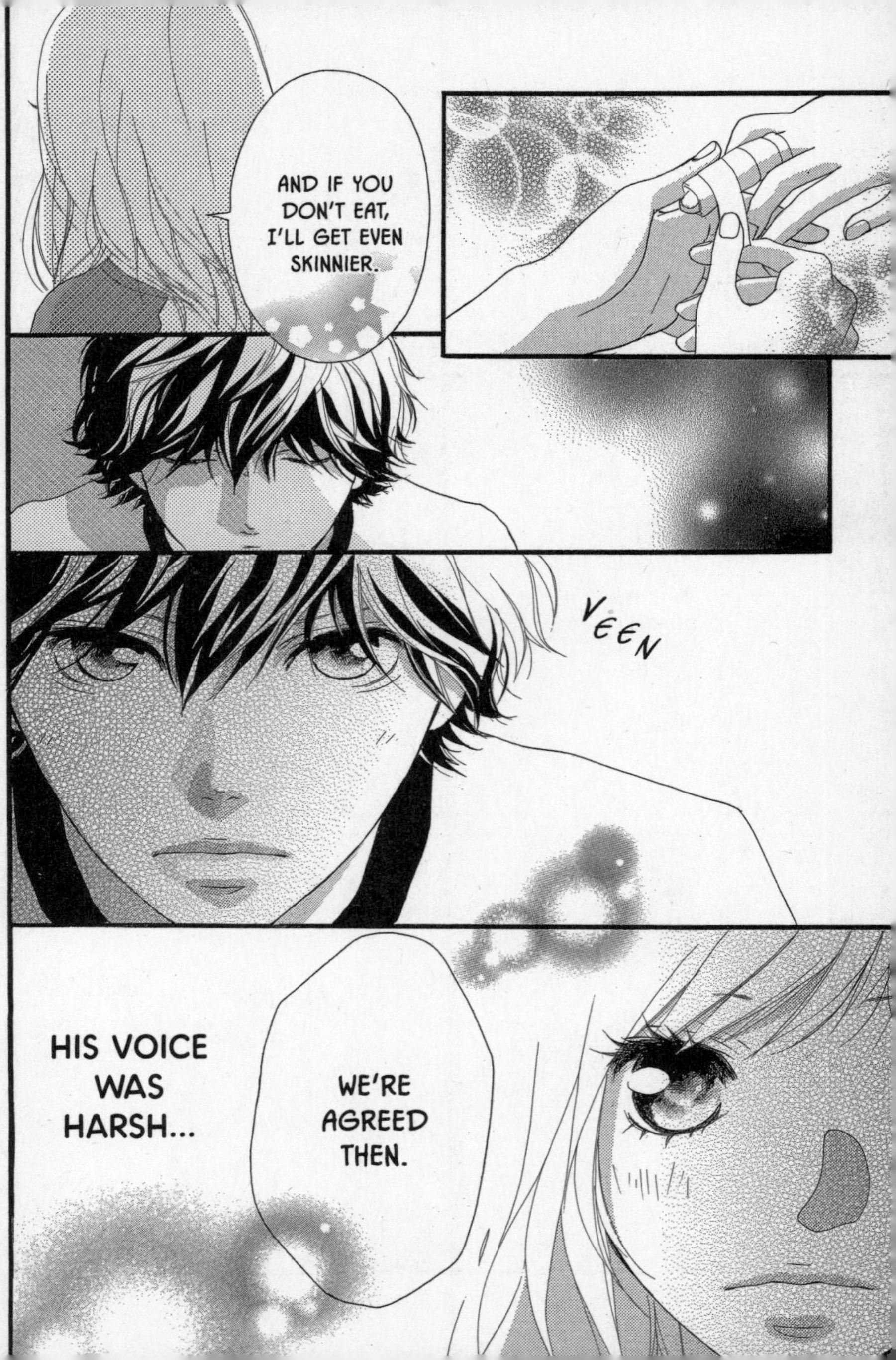
AND IF YOU DON'T EAT, I'LL GET EVEN SKINNIER.
VEEN
WE'RE AGREED THEN.
HIS VOICE WAS HARSH...

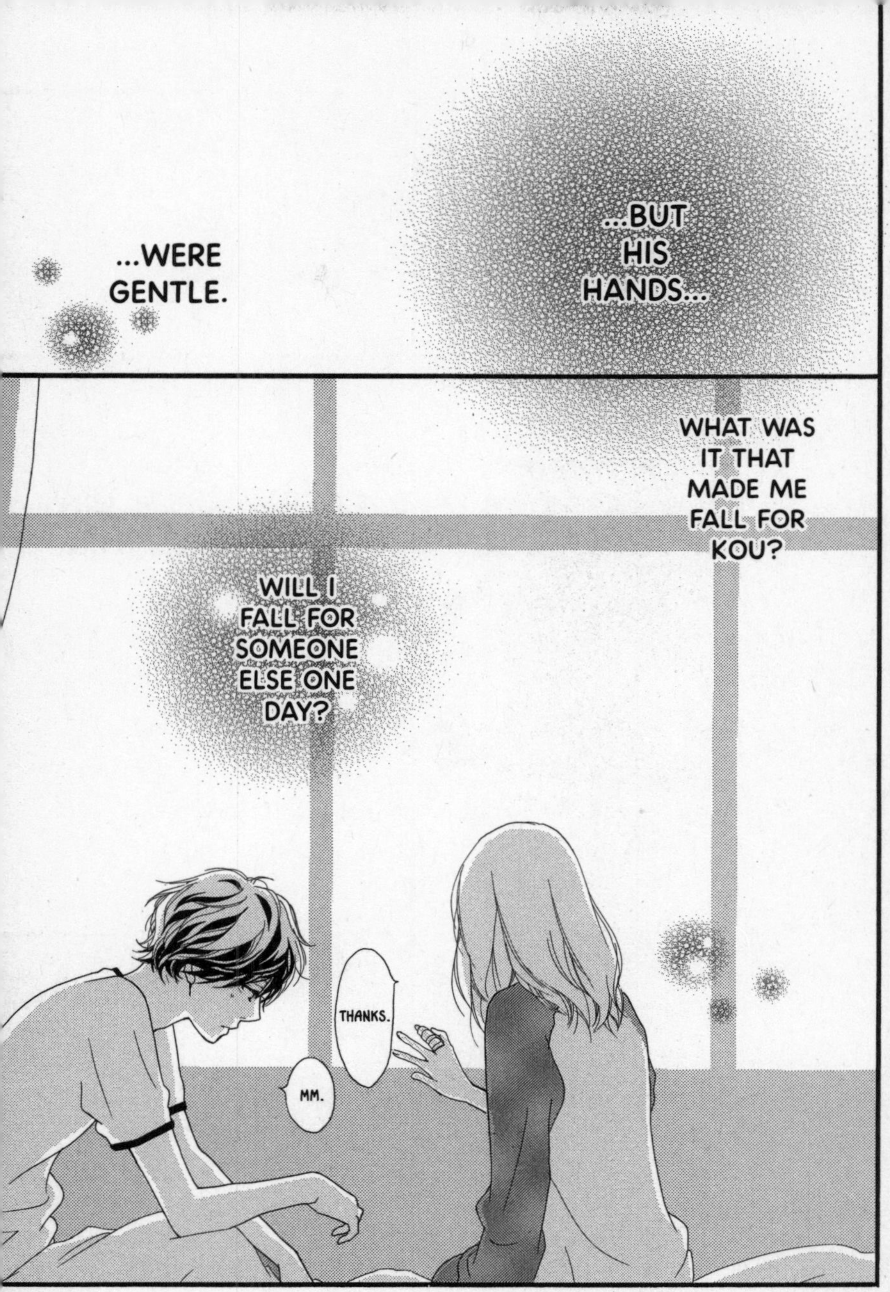
...BUT HIS HANDS...
...WERE GENTLE.
WHAT WAS IT THAT MADE ME FALL FOR KOU?
WILL I FALL FOR SOMEONE ELSE ONE DAY?
THANKS.
MM.

Q & A Page!

It's been a while since I answered your questions. It's going to be brief, but here goes!

Q : Do you model your characters off anything?

A : I sometimes borrow hairstyles or names from others, but I don't really use any character models. When I first debuted as a manga artist, I tried using a model at my editor's suggestion. While working on the story, I completely lost interest in the model, which made me lose interest in drawing as well. I realized that method doesn't work for me.

Q : Is "Io Sakisaka" your real name?

A : It's a pen name. I wanted a surname that started with *Sa*, and I ended up with this one. There isn't really any meaning behind the name, but I found out that the kanji stroke count is pretty auspicious, which makes me happy.

Q : Are you a woman? A man?

A : I'm a woman.

Q : Can you see dwarves or fairies?

A : Unfortunately I cannot. Maybe my heart is not pure enough...

I picked the questions that were the most fun. Perhaps I'll do another one of these pages when I have another stack of fun questions. In the meantime, please keep sending them in. ♡

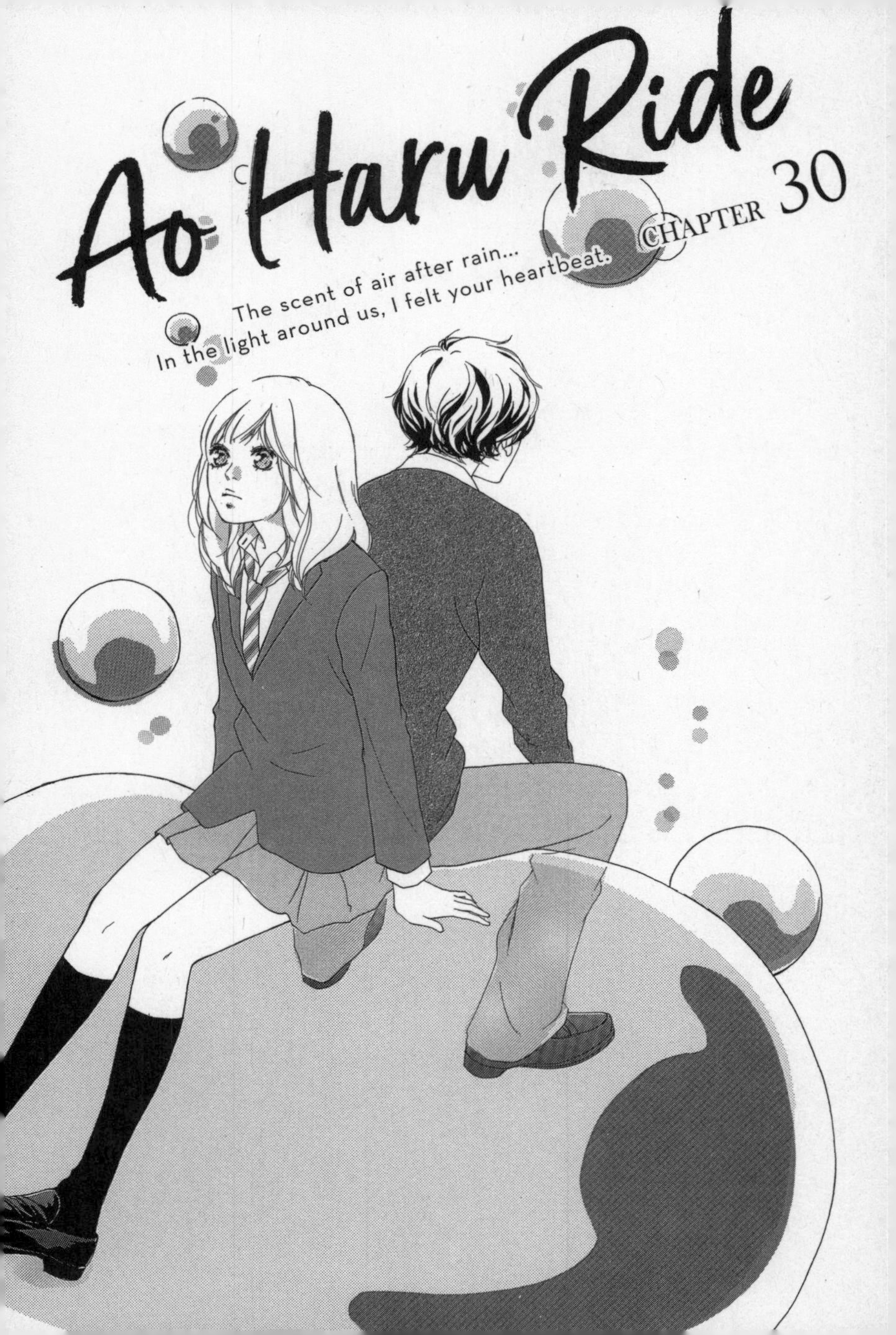
Ao Haru Ride
CHAPTER 30
The scent of air after rain...
In the light around us, I felt your heartbeat.

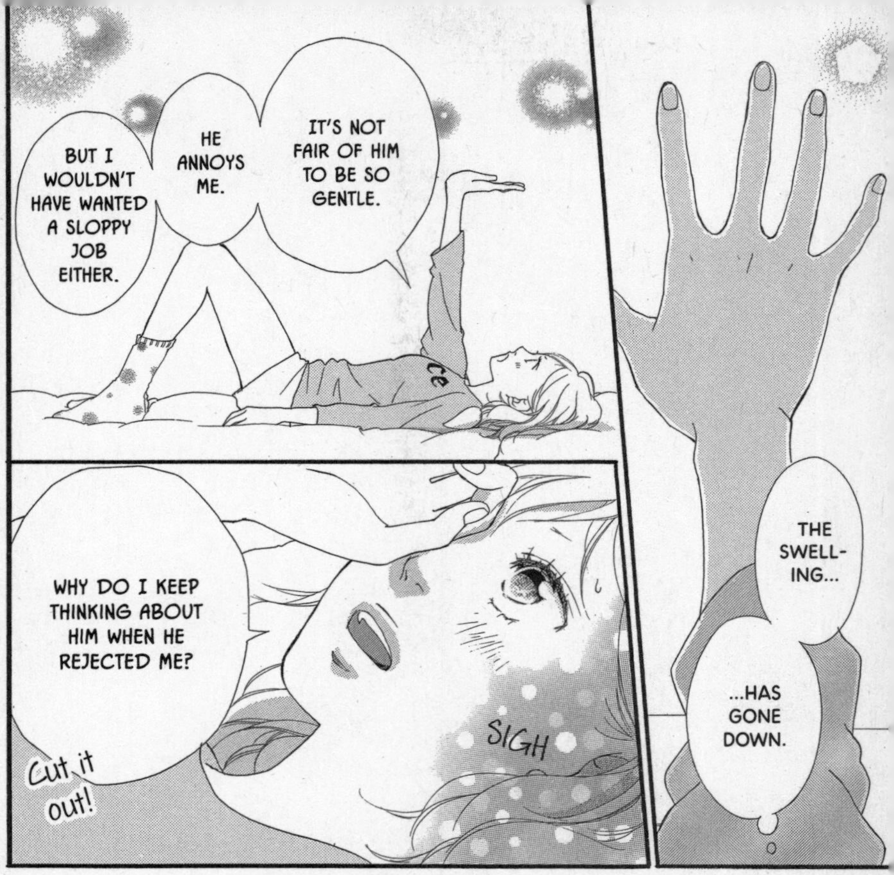
THE SWELLING...
...HAS GONE DOWN.
IT'S NOT FAIR OF HIM TO BE SO GENTLE.
HE ANNOYS ME.
BUT I WOULDN'T HAVE WANTED A SLOPPY JOB EITHER.
WHY DO I KEEP THINKING ABOUT HIM WHEN HE REJECTED ME?
SIGH
Cut it out!

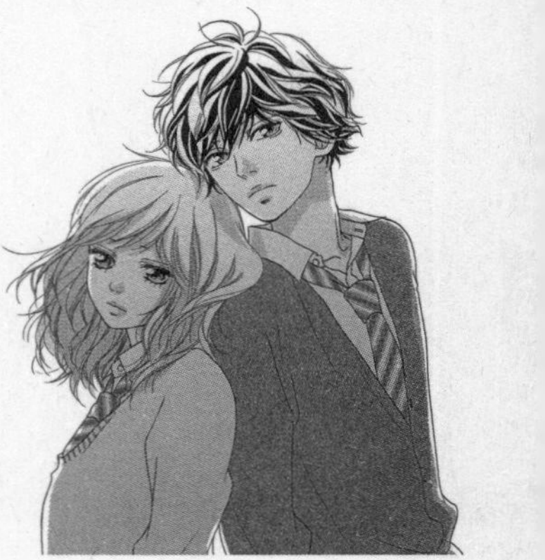

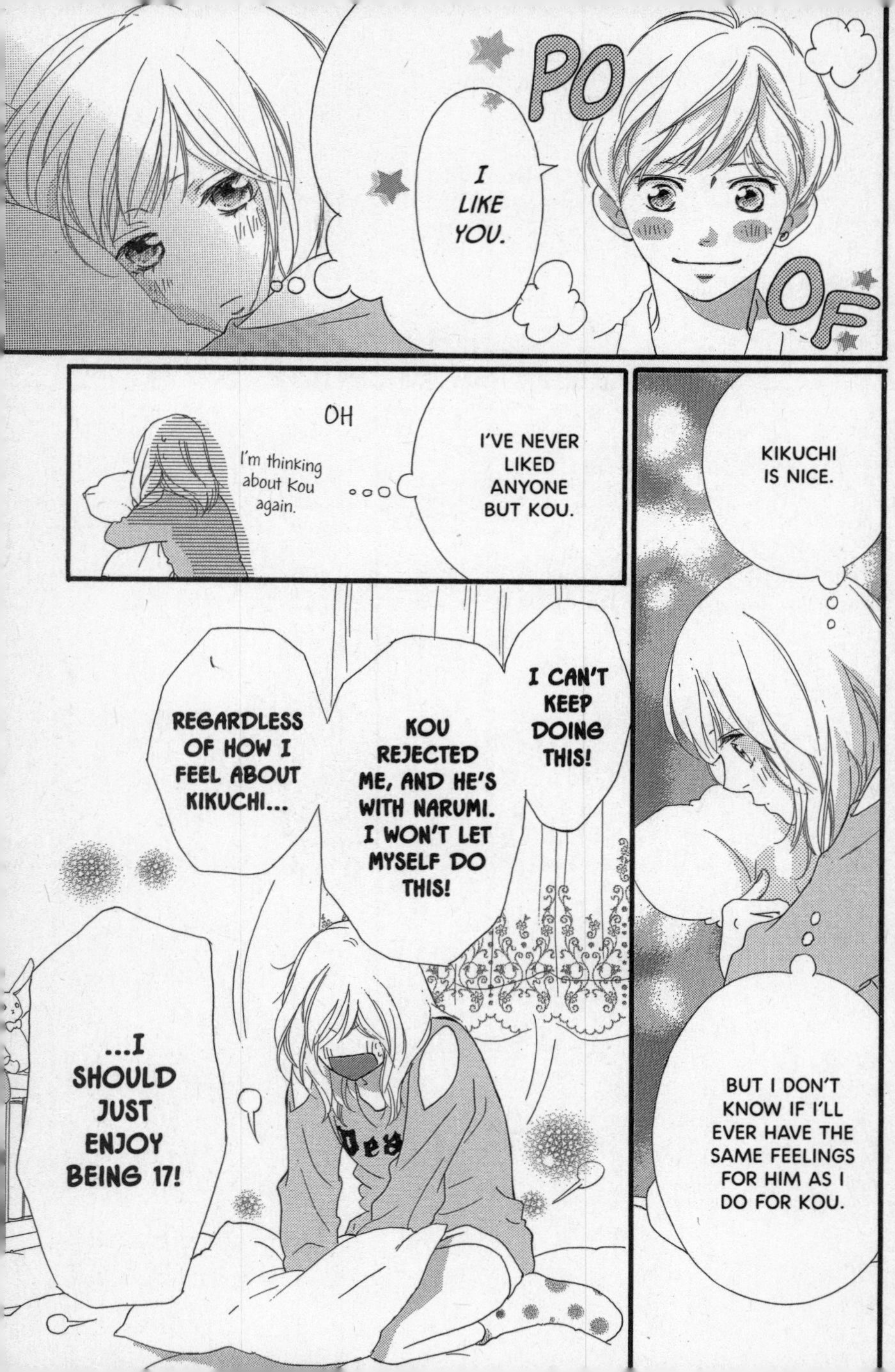
POOF
I LIKE YOU.
KIKUCHI IS NICE.
BUT I DON'T KNOW IF I'LL EVER HAVE THE SAME FEELINGS FOR HIM AS I DO FOR KOU.
I'VE NEVER LIKED ANYONE BUT KOU.
OH
I'm thinking about Kou again.
I CAN'T KEEP DOING THIS!
KOU REJECTED ME, AND HE'S WITH NARUMI. I WON'T LET MYSELF DO THIS!
REGARDLESS OF HOW I FEEL ABOUT KIKUCHI...
...I SHOULD JUST ENJOY BEING 17!

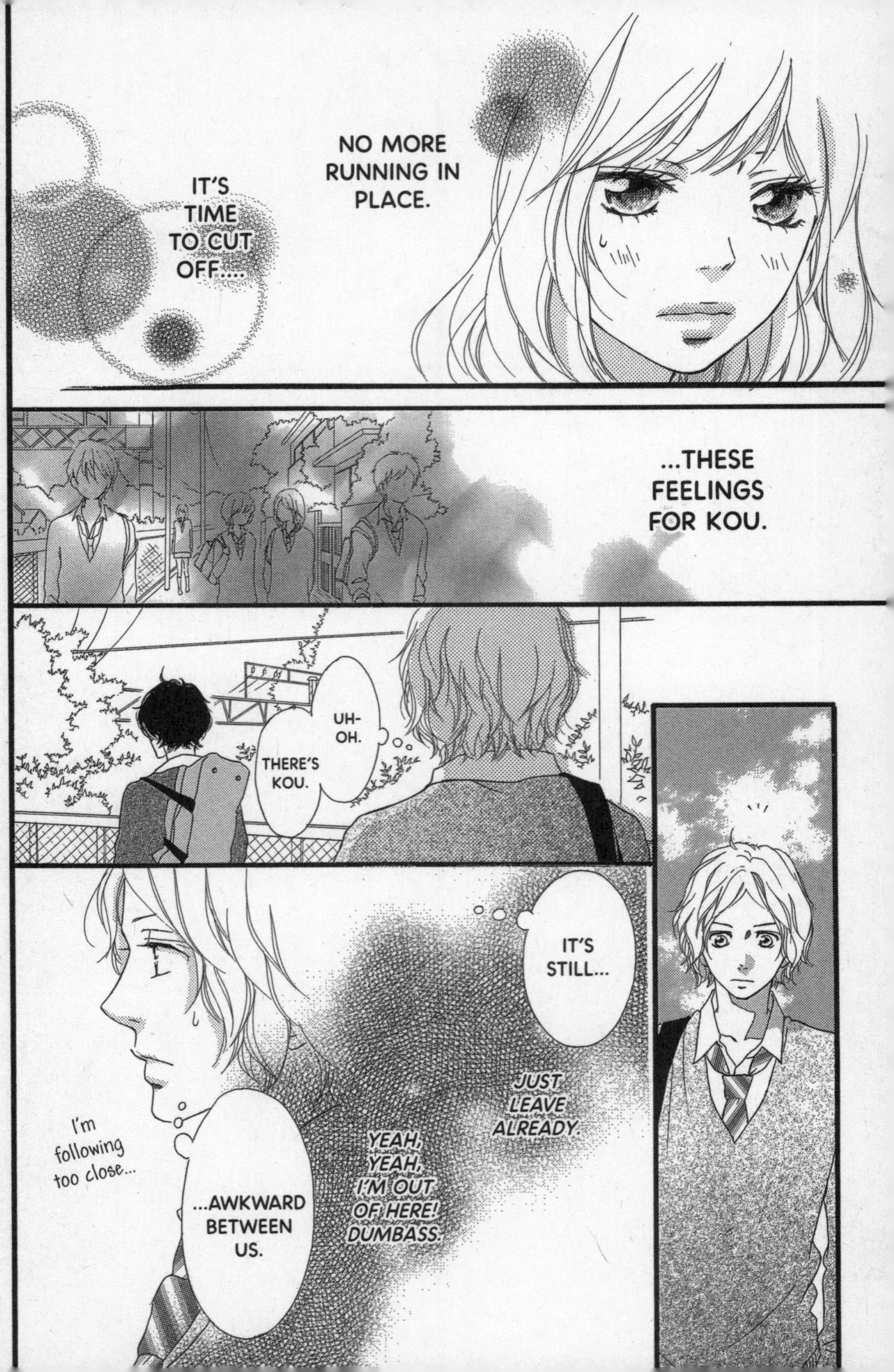
NO MORE RUNNING IN PLACE.
IT'S TIME TO CUT OFF....
...THESE FEELINGS FOR KOU.
UH-OH.
THERE'S KOU.
IT'S STILL...
...AWKWARD BETWEEN US.
JUST LEAVE ALREADY.
YEAH, YEAH, I'M OUT OF HERE! DUMBASS.
I'm following too close...

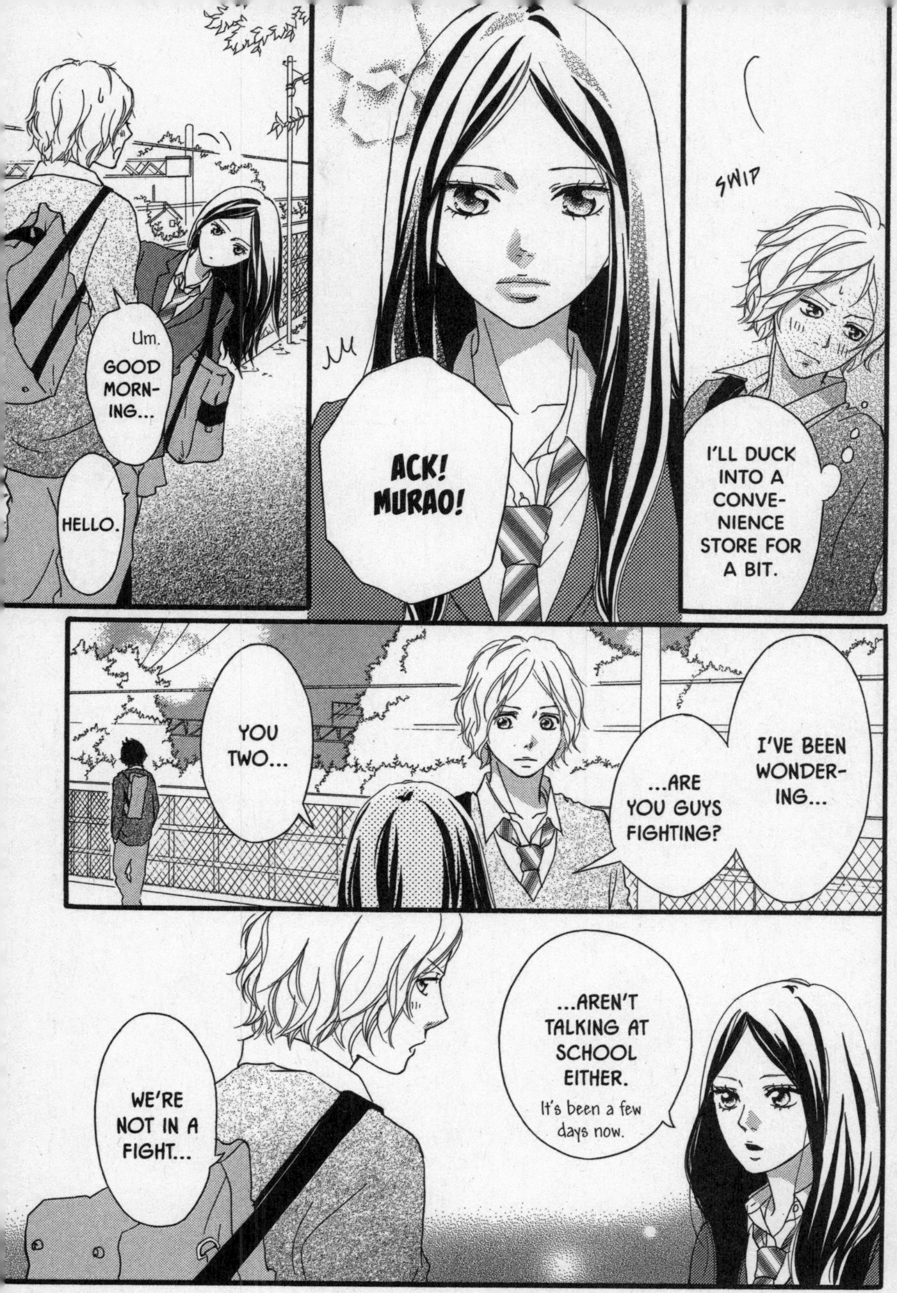
SWIP
I'LL DUCK INTO A CONVENIENCE STORE FOR A BIT.
ACK! MURAO!
Um. GOOD MORNING...
HELLO.
I'VE BEEN WONDERING...
...ARE YOU GUYS FIGHTING?
YOU TWO...
...AREN'T TALKING AT SCHOOL EITHER. It's been a few days now.
WE'RE NOT IN A FIGHT...

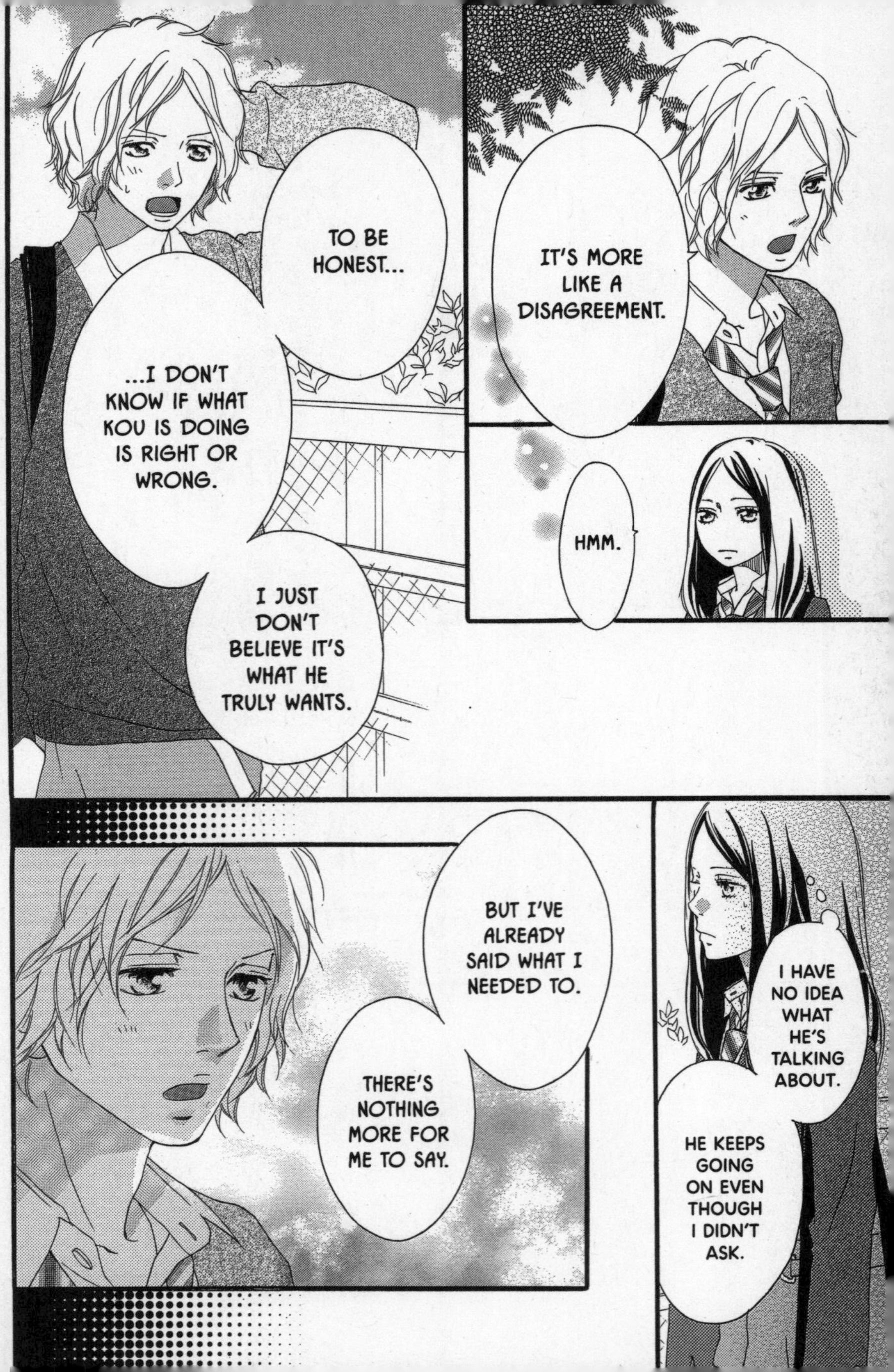
IT'S MORE LIKE A DISAGREEMENT.
HMM.
TO BE HONEST...
...I DON'T KNOW IF WHAT KOU IS DOING IS RIGHT OR WRONG.
I JUST DON'T BELIEVE IT'S WHAT HE TRULY WANTS.
I HAVE NO IDEA WHAT HE'S TALKING ABOUT.
HE KEEPS GOING ON EVEN THOUGH I DIDN'T ASK.
BUT I'VE ALREADY SAID WHAT I NEEDED TO.
THERE'S NOTHING MORE FOR ME TO SAY.

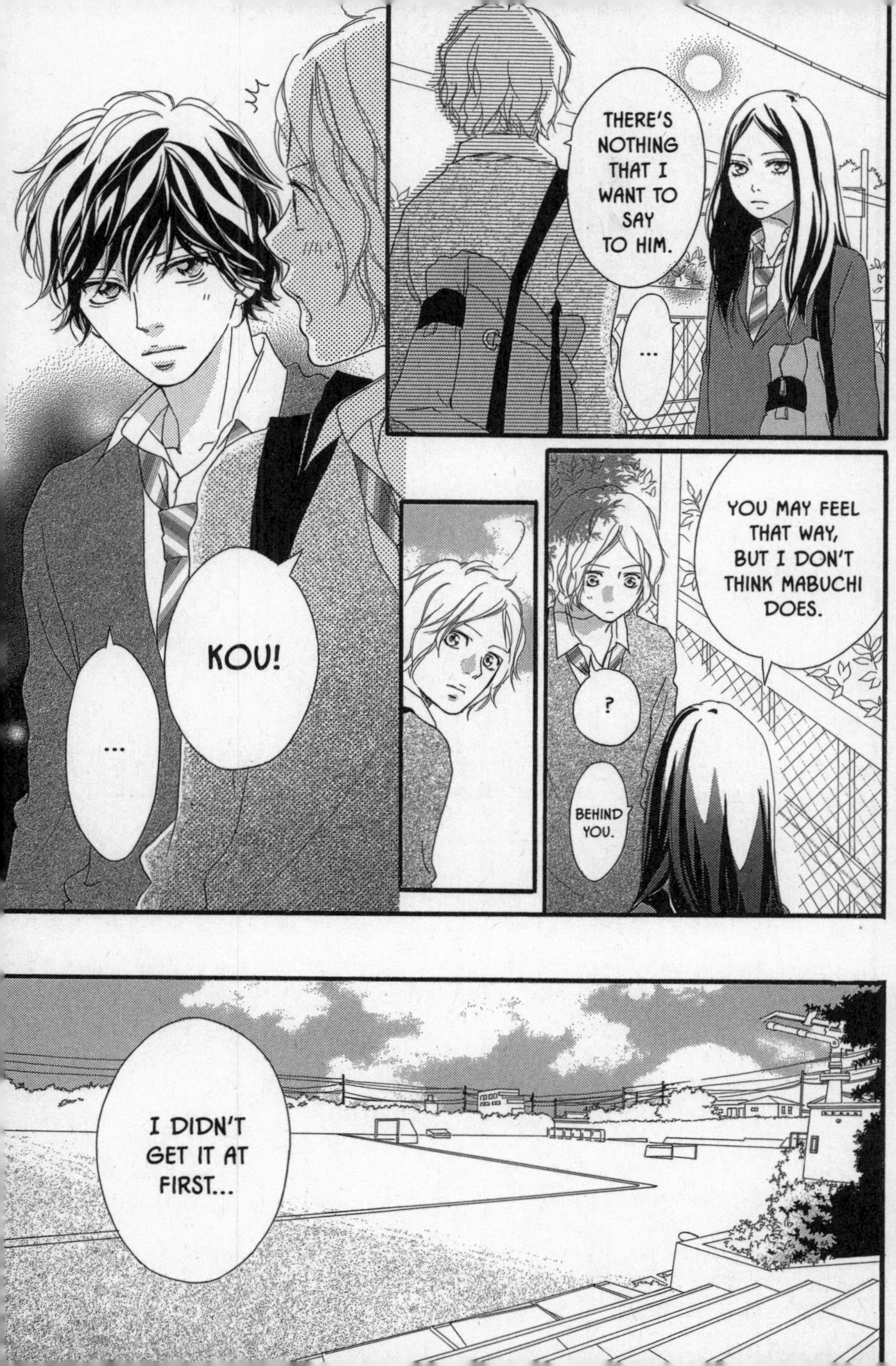
THERE'S NOTHING THAT I WANT TO SAY TO HIM.
...
YOU MAY FEEL THAT WAY, BUT I DON'T THINK MABUCHI DOES.
?
BEHIND YOU.
KOU!
...
I DIDN'T GET IT AT FIRST...

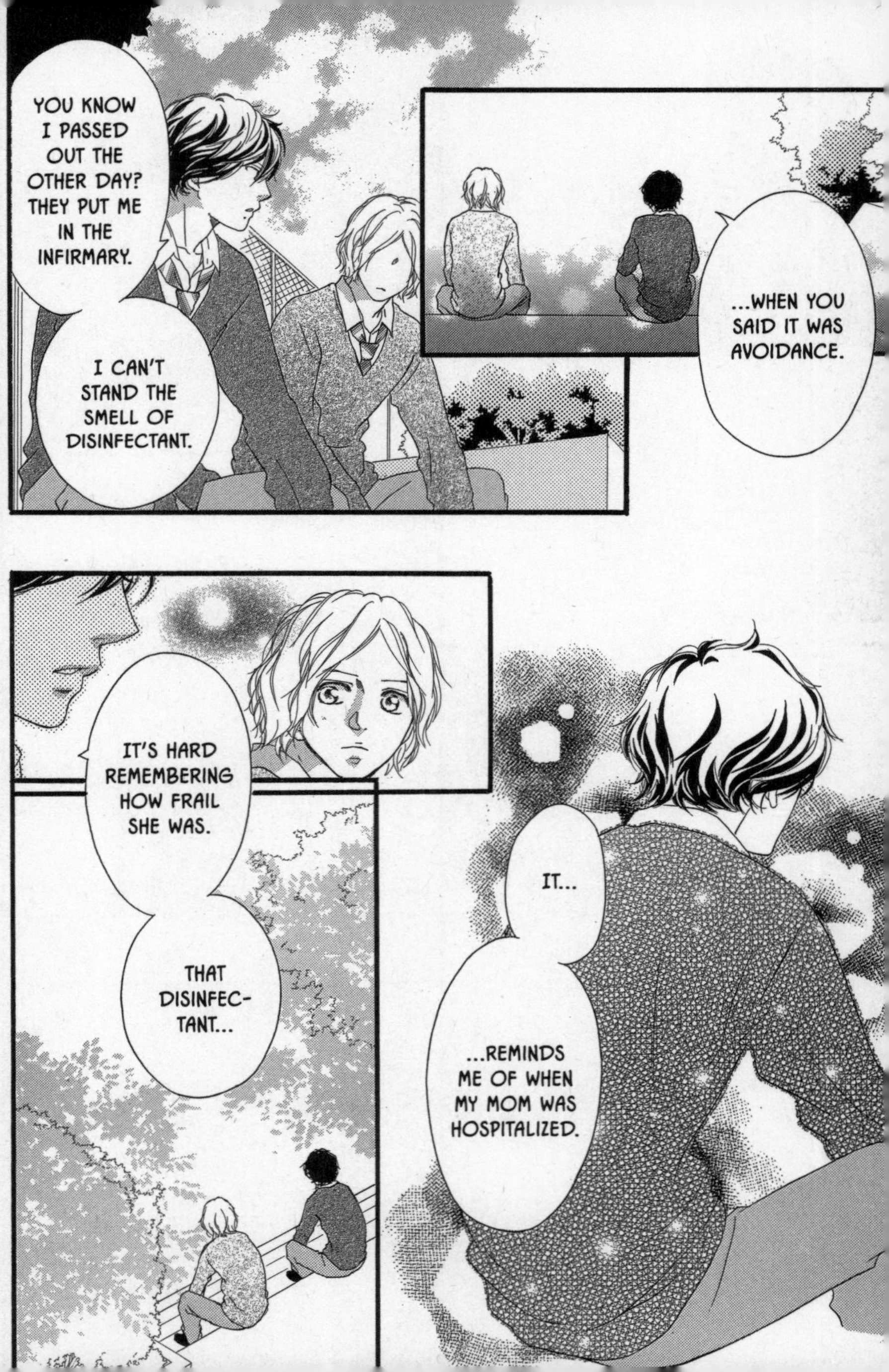
...WHEN YOU SAID IT WAS AVOIDANCE.
YOU KNOW I PASSED OUT THE OTHER DAY? THEY PUT ME IN THE INFIRMARY.
I CAN'T STAND THE SMELL OF DISINFECTANT.
IT...
...REMINDS ME OF WHEN MY MOM WAS HOSPITALIZED.
IT'S HARD REMEMBERING HOW FRAIL SHE WAS.
THAT DISINFEC-TANT...

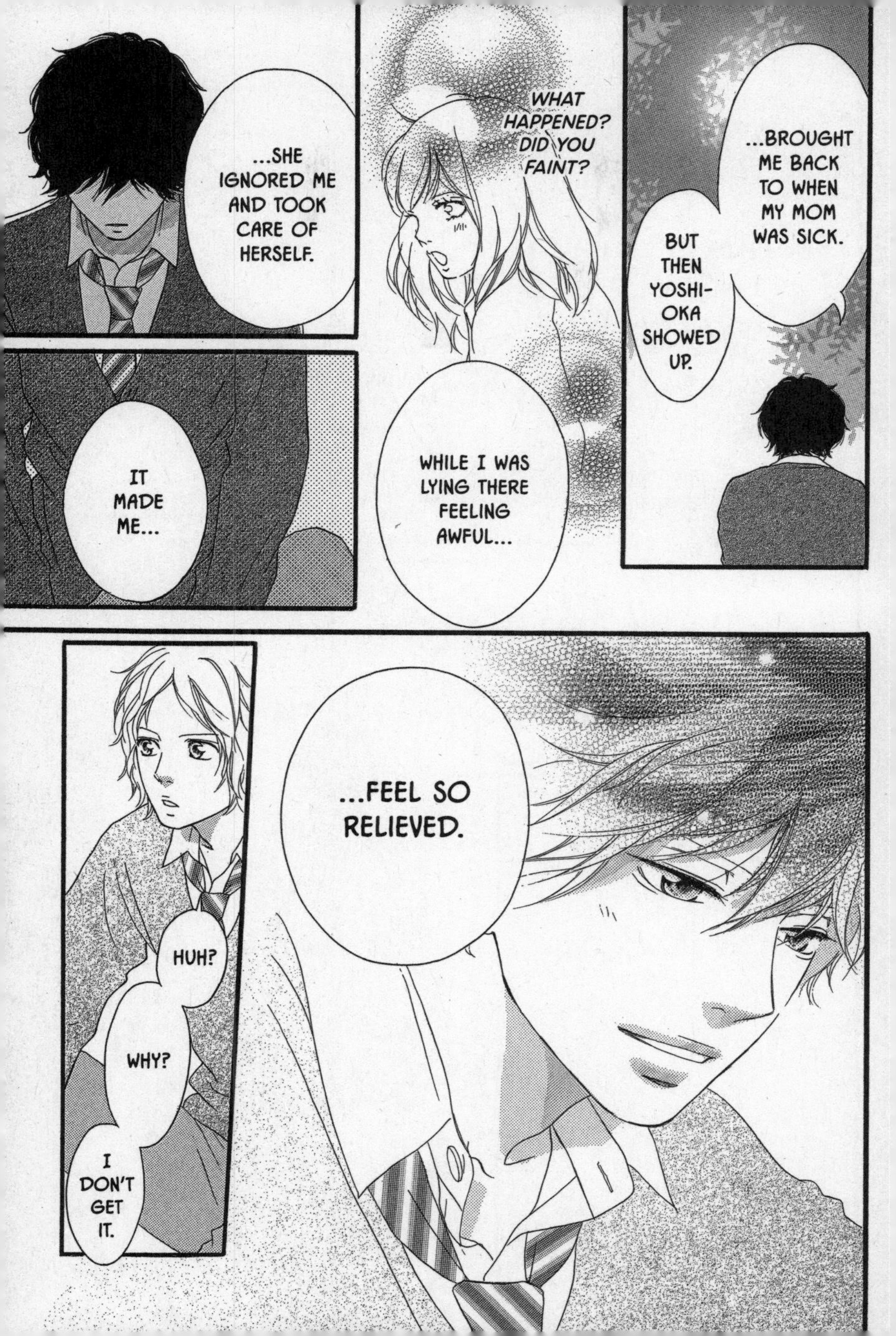
...BROUGHT ME BACK TO WHEN MY MOM WAS SICK.
BUT THEN YOSHI-OKA SHOWED UP.
WHAT HAPPENED? DID YOU FAINT?
WHILE I WAS LYING THERE FEELING AWFUL...
...SHE IGNORED ME AND TOOK CARE OF HERSELF.
IT MADE ME...
...FEEL SO RELIEVED.
HUH?
WHY?
I DON'T GET IT.

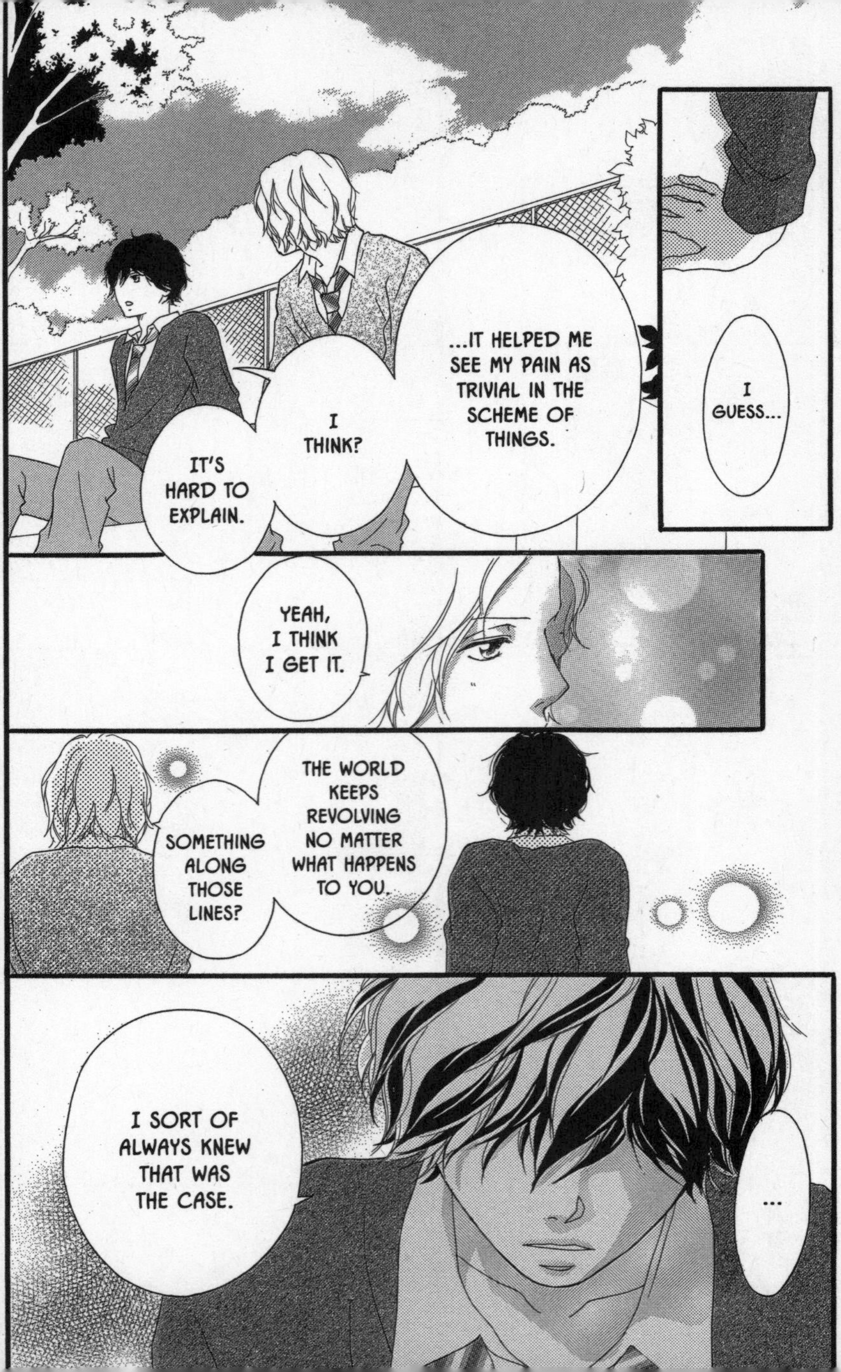
I GUESS...
...IT HELPED ME SEE MY PAIN AS TRIVIAL IN THE SCHEME OF THINGS.
I THINK?
IT'S HARD TO EXPLAIN.
YEAH, I THINK I GET IT.
THE WORLD KEEPS REVOLVING NO MATTER WHAT HAPPENS TO YOU.
SOMETHING ALONG THOSE LINES?
...
I SORT OF ALWAYS KNEW THAT WAS THE CASE.

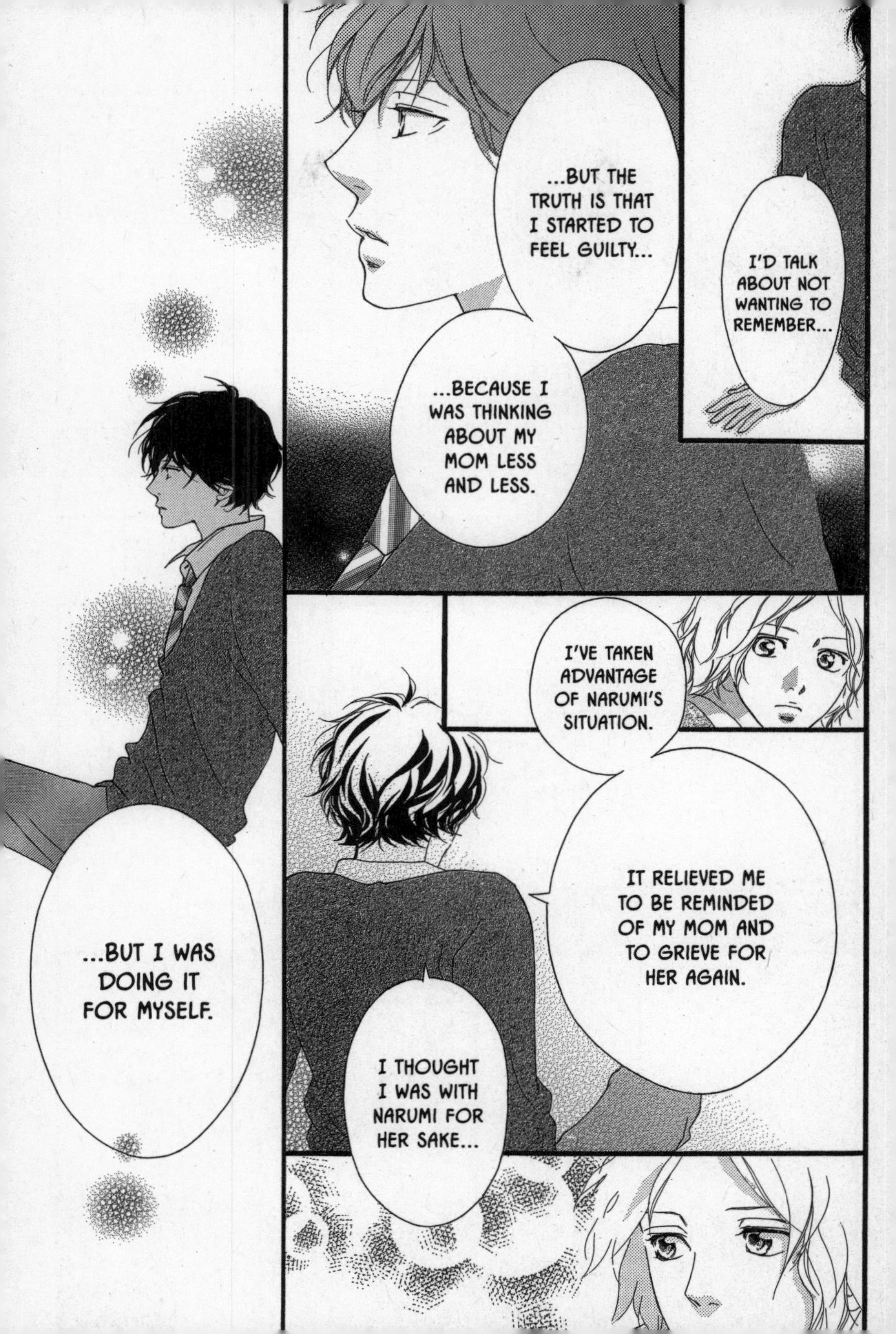

I'D TALK ABOUT NOT WANTING TO REMEMBER...
...BUT THE TRUTH IS THAT I STARTED TO FEEL GUILTY...
...BECAUSE I WAS THINKING ABOUT MY MOM LESS AND LESS.
I'VE TAKEN ADVANTAGE OF NARUMI'S SITUATION.
IT RELIEVED ME TO BE REMINDED OF MY MOM AND TO GRIEVE FOR HER AGAIN.
I THOUGHT I WAS WITH NARUMI FOR HER SAKE...
...BUT I WAS DOING IT FOR MYSELF.

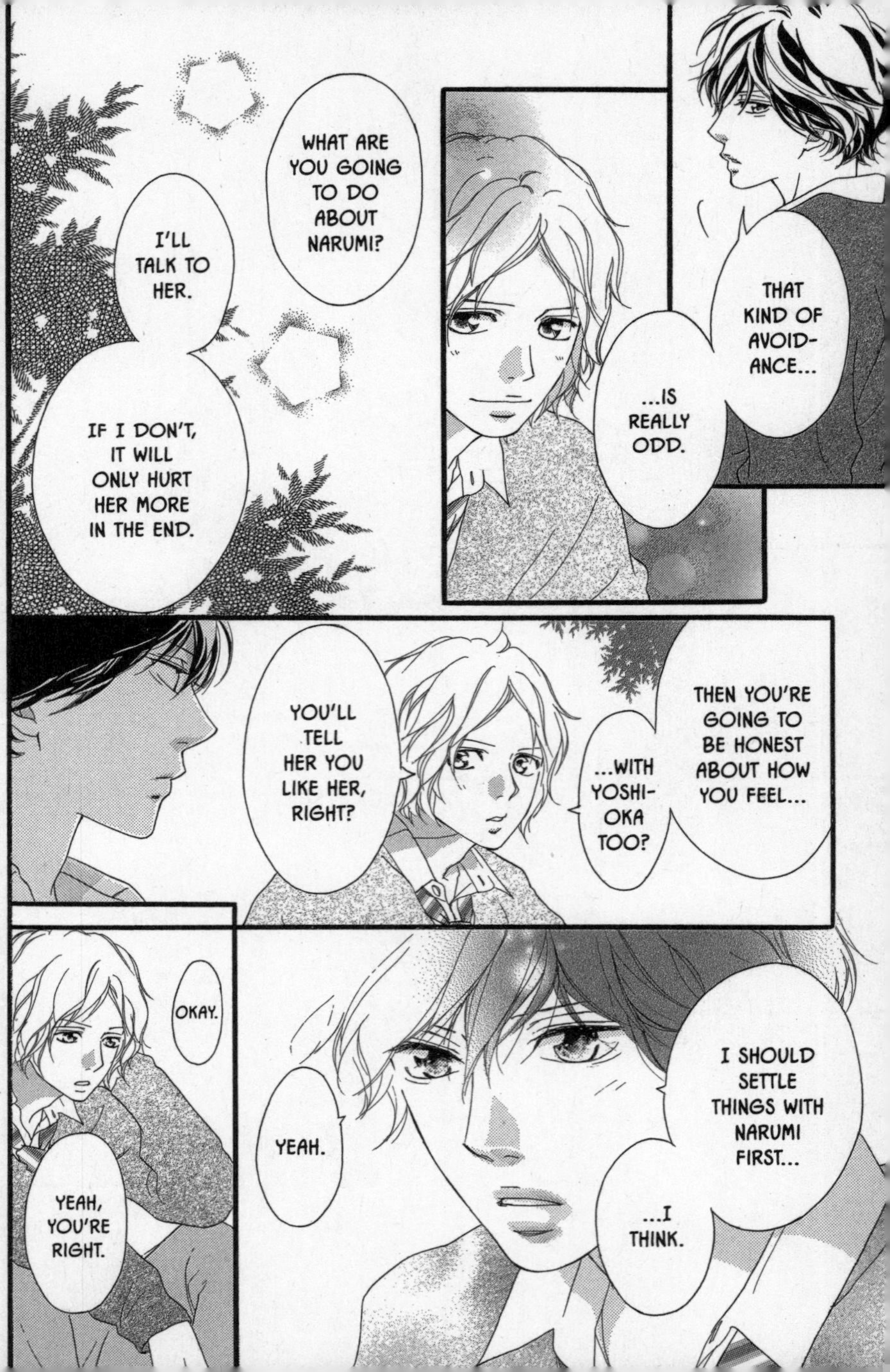
THAT KIND OF AVOID-ANCE...
...IS REALLY ODD.
WHAT ARE YOU GOING TO DO ABOUT NARUMI?
I'LL TALK TO HER.
IF I DON'T, IT WILL ONLY HURT HER MORE IN THE END.
THEN YOU'RE GOING TO BE HONEST ABOUT HOW YOU FEEL...
...WITH YOSHI-OKA TOO?
YOU'LL TELL HER YOU LIKE HER, RIGHT?
I SHOULD SETTLE THINGS WITH NARUMI FIRST...
...I THINK.
YEAH.
OKAY.
YEAH, YOU'RE RIGHT.

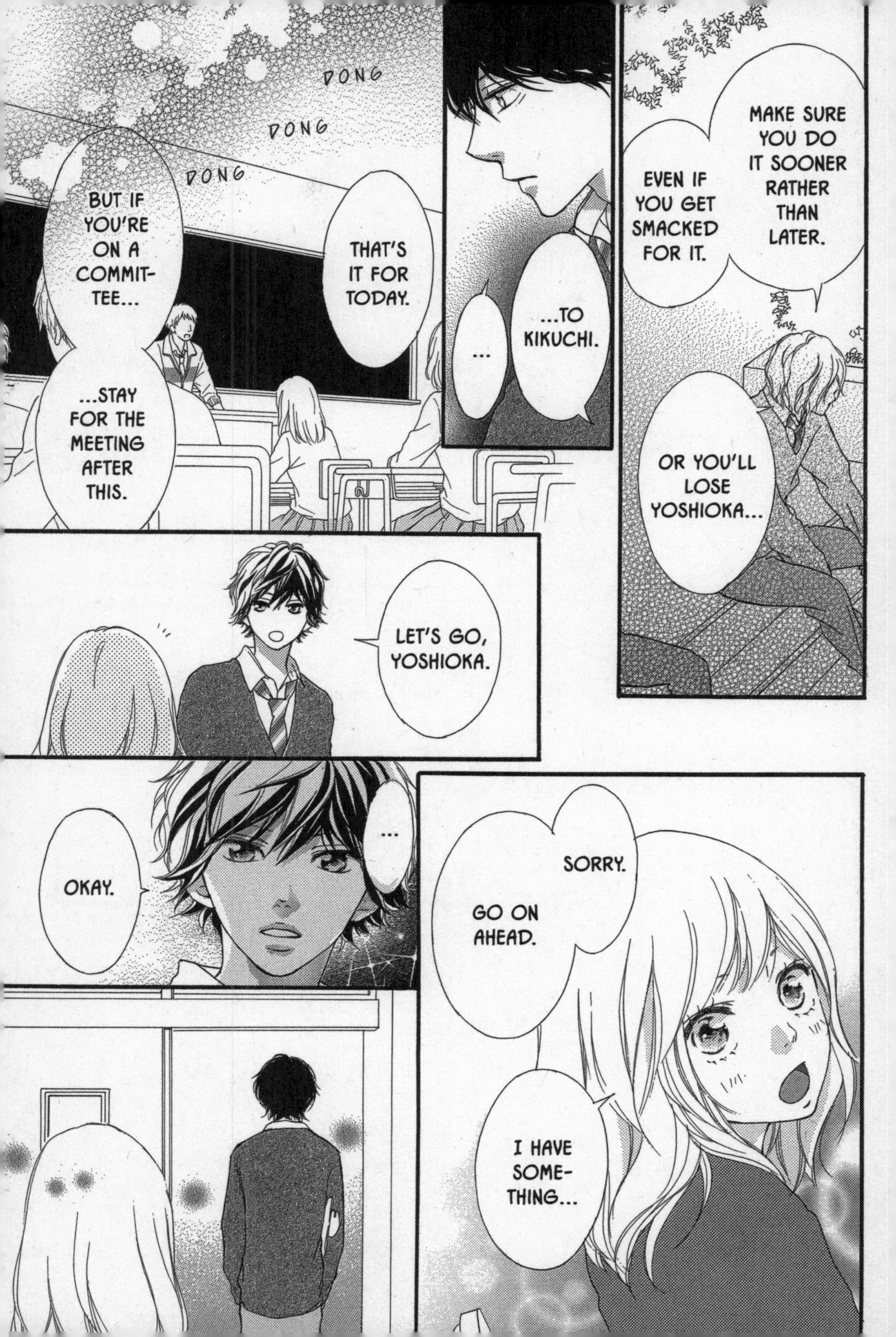
MAKE SURE YOU DO IT SOONER RATHER THAN LATER.
EVEN IF YOU GET SMACKED FOR IT.
OR YOU'LL LOSE YOSHIOKA...
...TO KIKUCHI.
...
DONG
DONG
DONG
THAT'S IT FOR TODAY.
BUT IF YOU'RE ON A COMMITTEE...
...STAY FOR THE MEETING AFTER THIS.
LET'S GO, YOSHIOKA.
SORRY.
GO ON AHEAD.
I HAVE SOMETHING...
...
OKAY.

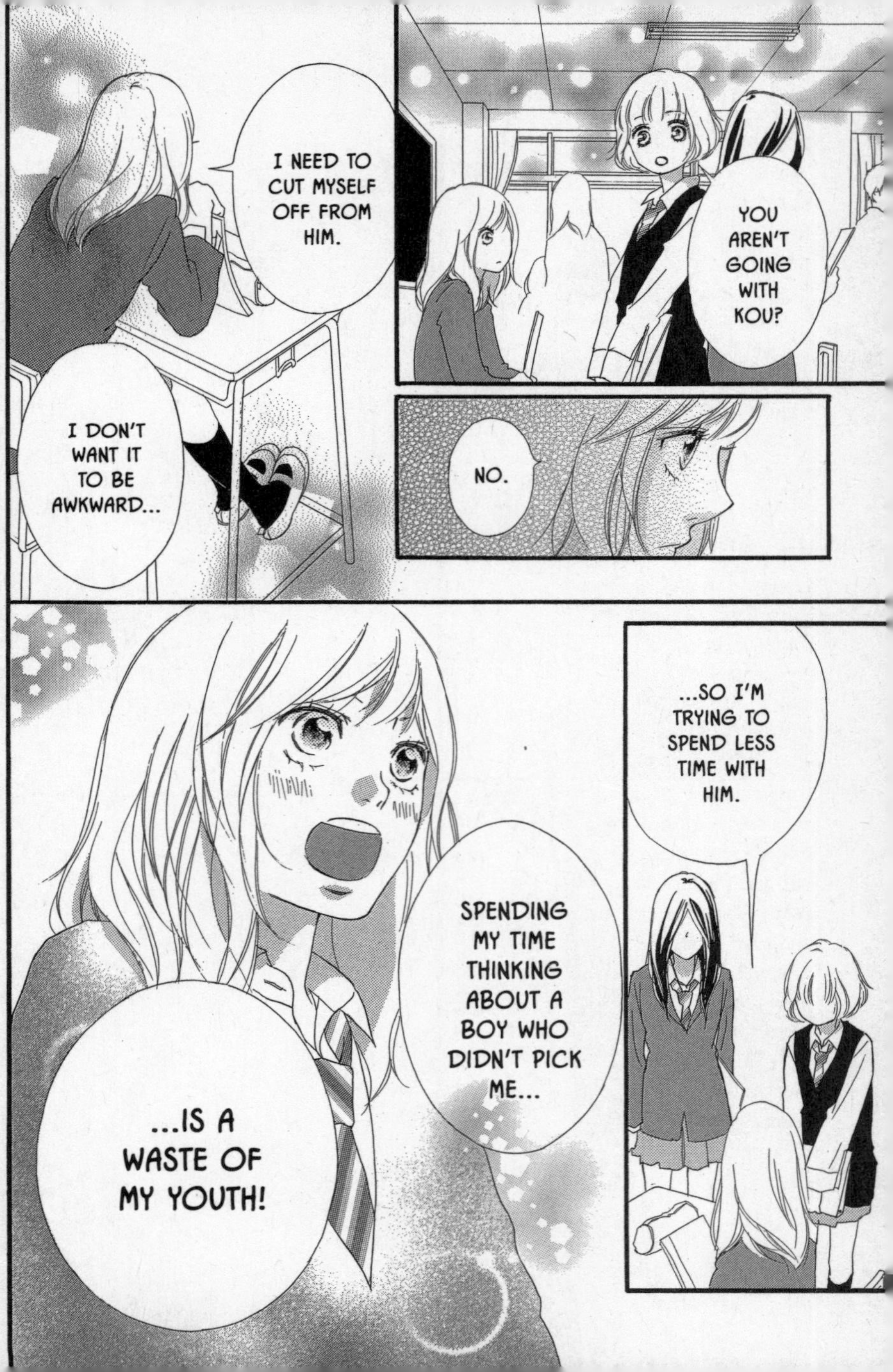
YOU AREN'T GOING WITH KOU?
NO.
I NEED TO CUT MYSELF OFF FROM HIM.
I DON'T WANT IT TO BE AWKWARD...
...SO I'M TRYING TO SPEND LESS TIME WITH HIM.
SPENDING MY TIME THINKING ABOUT A BOY WHO DIDN'T PICK ME...
...IS A WASTE OF MY YOUTH!

Thank you all for your letters and Twitter replies. I get so much motivation from my fans! On my last birthday, I was grateful to receive lovely drawings and shikishi from many people. And the other day, I received an especially long letter—the longest I had ever received. It was the kind of letter that you can't stop reading once you've started (the writer shared a story from her own school days), and as I read it, I felt like I was experiencing the delicate, nuanced emotions in the letter. The back of my throat grew hot, and I wanted to keep reading for ever and ever! It was such a beautiful letter. I think it could make a great manga bonus story. I'm pretty sure I was making strange noises while reading it. Thank you very much. ♡

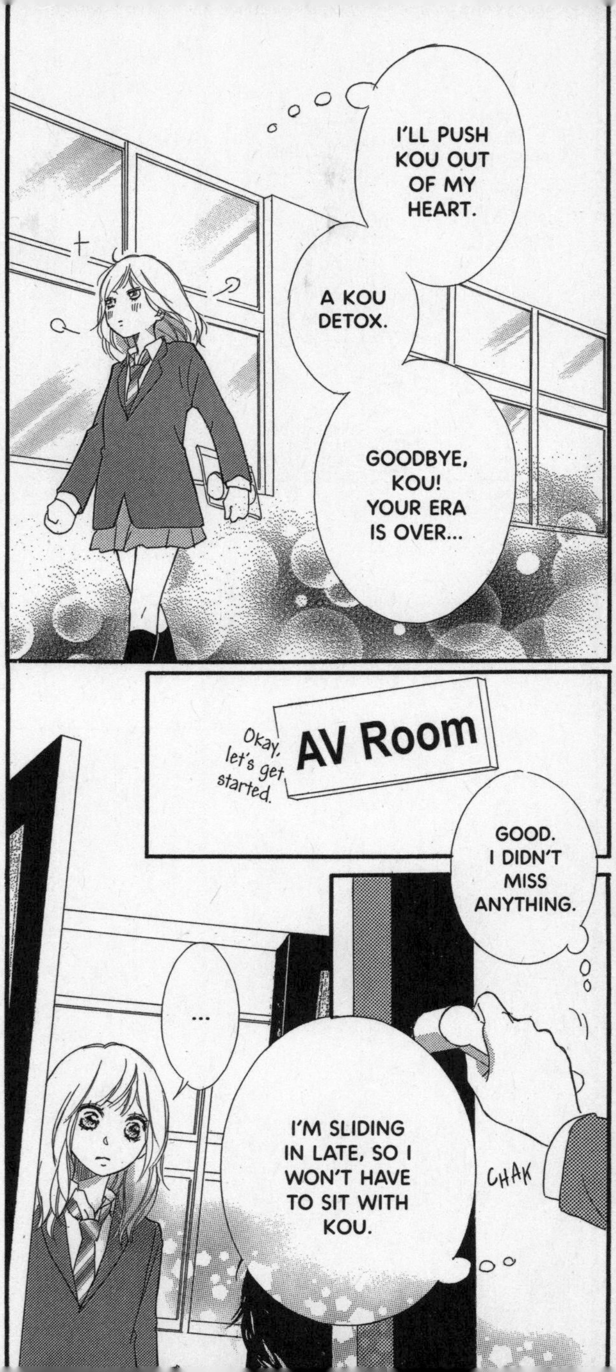

I'LL PUSH KOU OUT OF MY HEART.
A KOU DETOX.
GOODBYE, KOU! YOUR ERA IS OVER...
AV Room
Okay, let's get started.
GOOD. I DIDN'T MISS ANYTHING.
I'M SLIDING IN LATE, SO I WON'T HAVE TO SIT WITH KOU.
CHAK
...

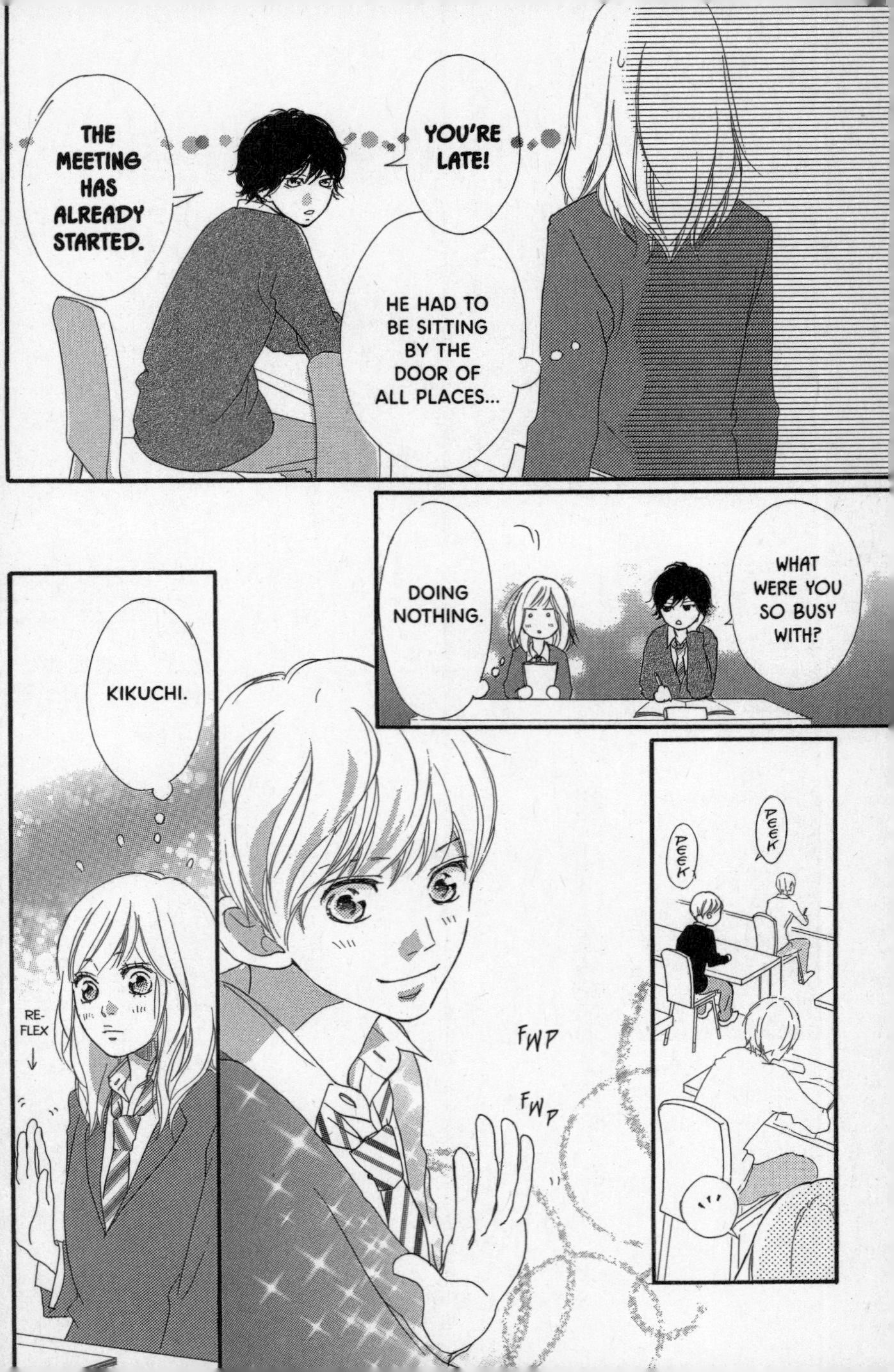
YOU'RE LATE!
THE MEETING HAS ALREADY STARTED.
HE HAD TO BE SITTING BY THE DOOR OF ALL PLACES...
WHAT WERE YOU SO BUSY WITH?
DOING NOTHING.
PEEK
PEEK
FWP
FWP
KIKUCHI.
RE-FLEX

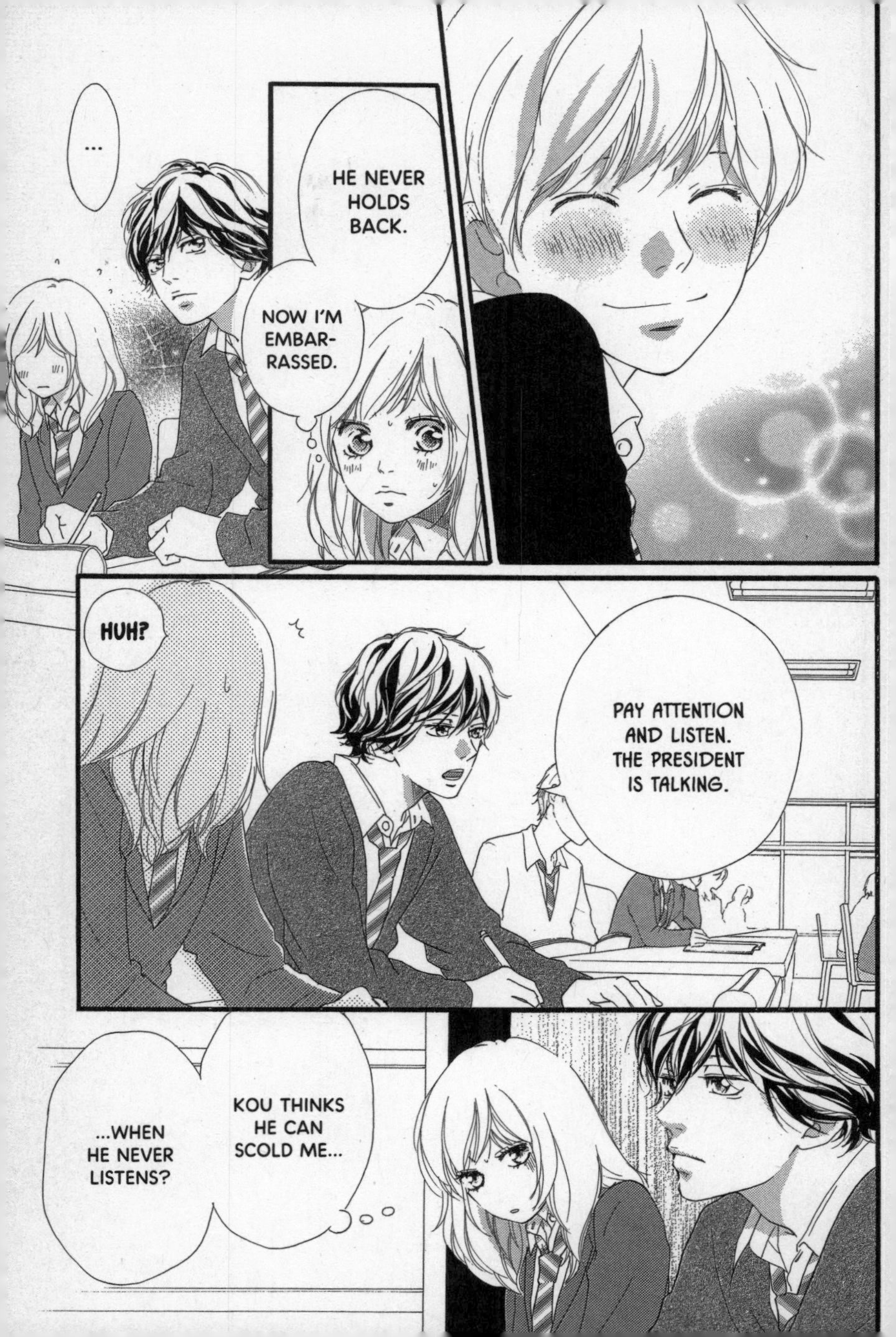
HE NEVER HOLDS BACK.
NOW I'M EMBARRASSED.
...
PAY ATTENTION AND LISTEN. THE PRESIDENT IS TALKING.
HUH?
KOU THINKS HE CAN SCOLD ME...
...WHEN HE NEVER LISTENS?

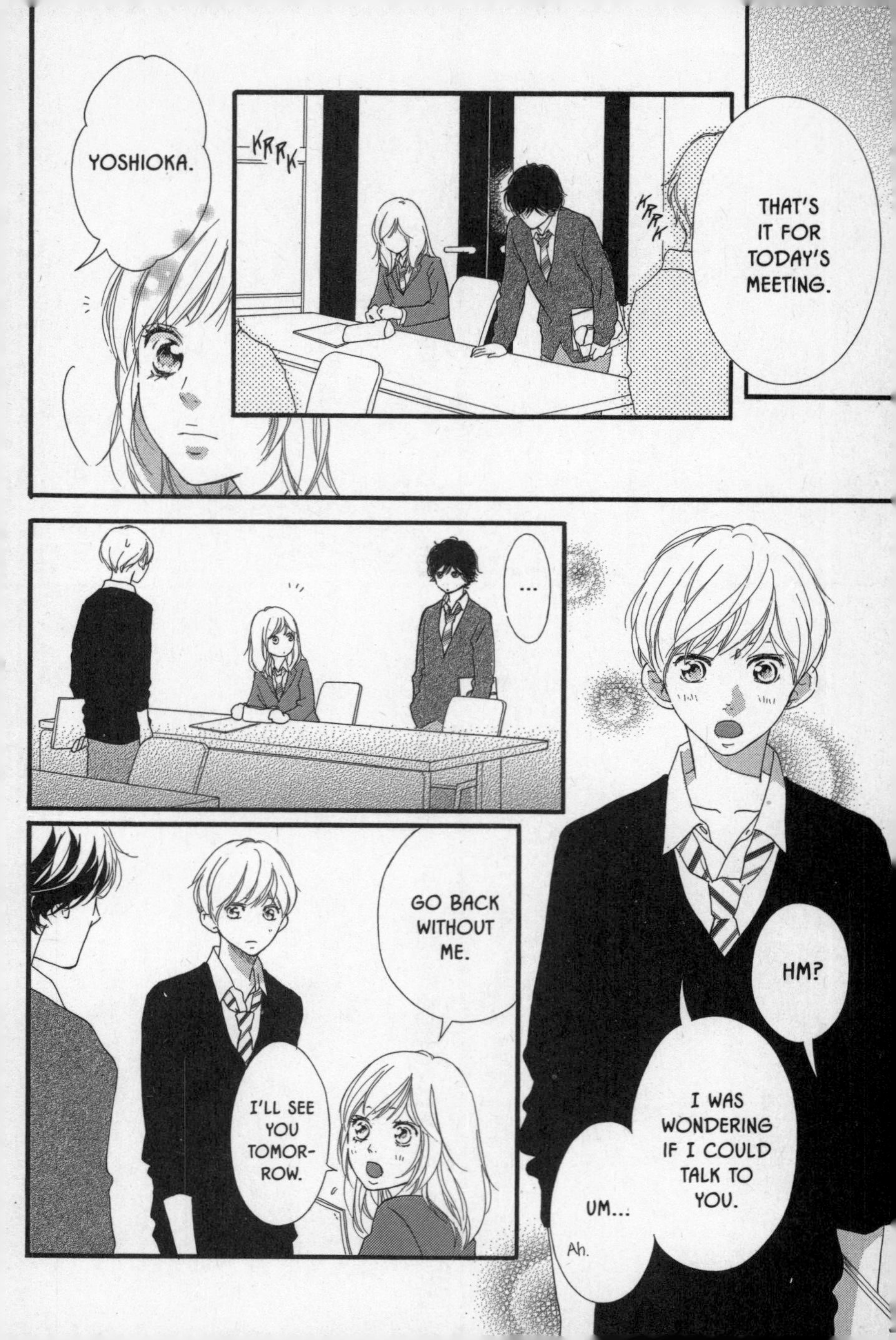
THAT'S IT FOR TODAY'S MEETING.
KRRK
KRRK
YOSHIOKA.
HM?
I WAS WONDERING IF I COULD TALK TO YOU.
UM...
Ah.
...
GO BACK WITHOUT ME.
I'LL SEE YOU TOMOR-ROW.

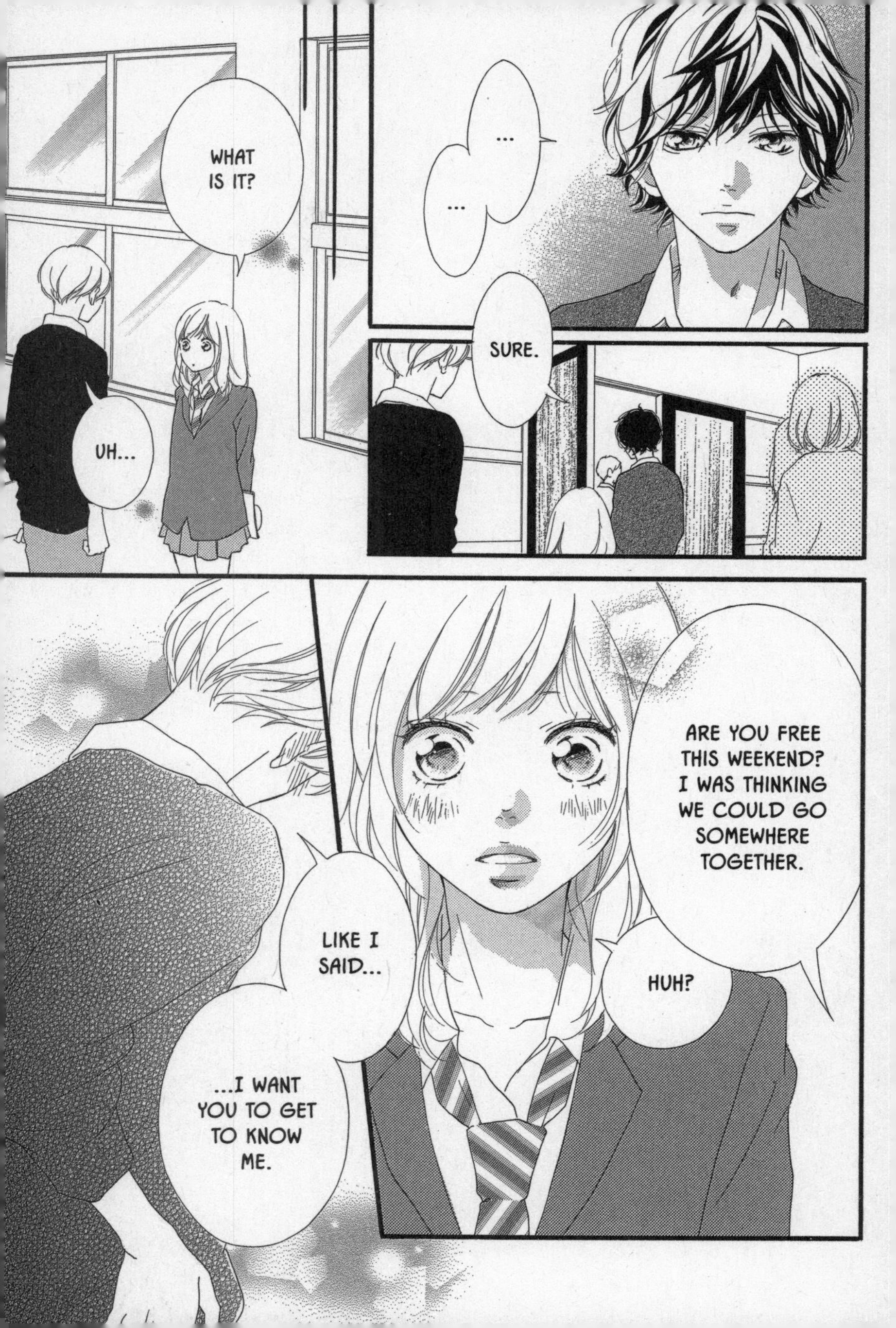
...
...
SURE.
WHAT IS IT?
UH...
ARE YOU FREE THIS WEEKEND? I WAS THINKING WE COULD GO SOMEWHERE TOGETHER.
HUH?
LIKE I SAID...
...I WANT YOU TO GET TO KNOW ME.

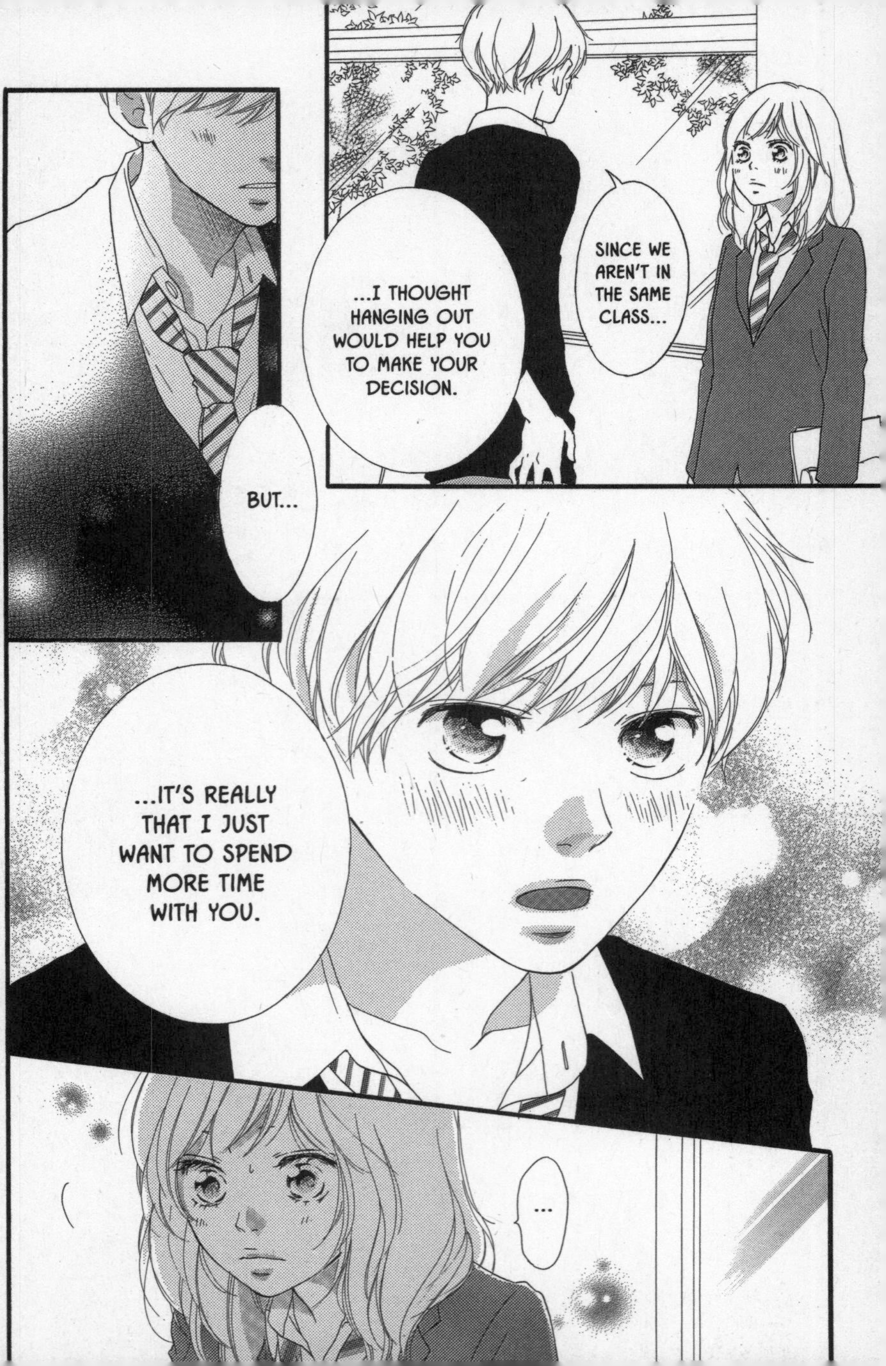
SINCE WE AREN'T IN THE SAME CLASS...
...I THOUGHT HANGING OUT WOULD HELP YOU TO MAKE YOUR DECISION.
BUT...
...IT'S REALLY THAT I JUST WANT TO SPEND MORE TIME WITH YOU.
...

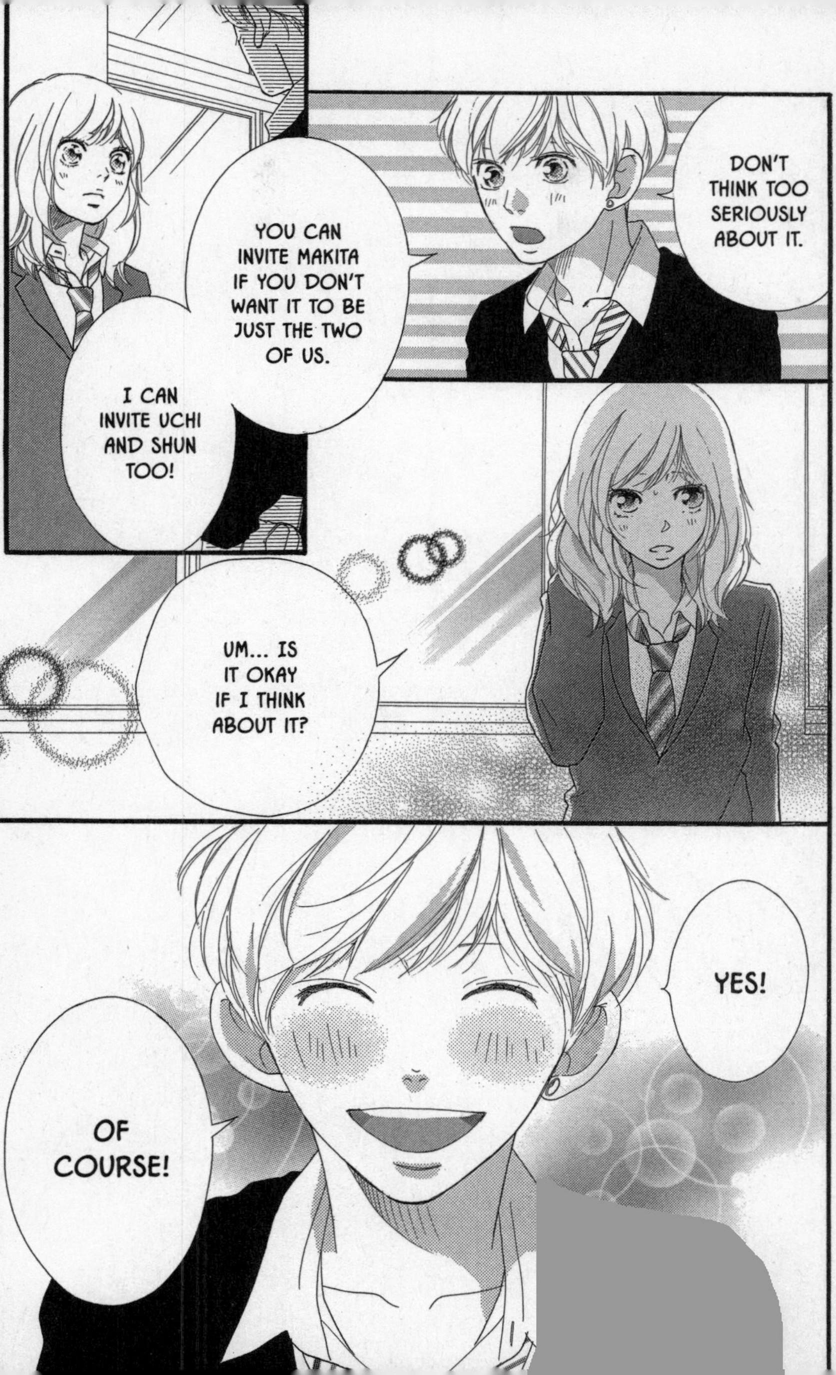
DON'T THINK TOO SERIOUSLY ABOUT IT.
YOU CAN INVITE MAKITA IF YOU DON'T WANT IT TO BE JUST THE TWO OF US.
I CAN INVITE UCHI AND SHUN TOO!
UM... IS IT OKAY IF I THINK ABOUT IT?
YES!
OF COURSE!

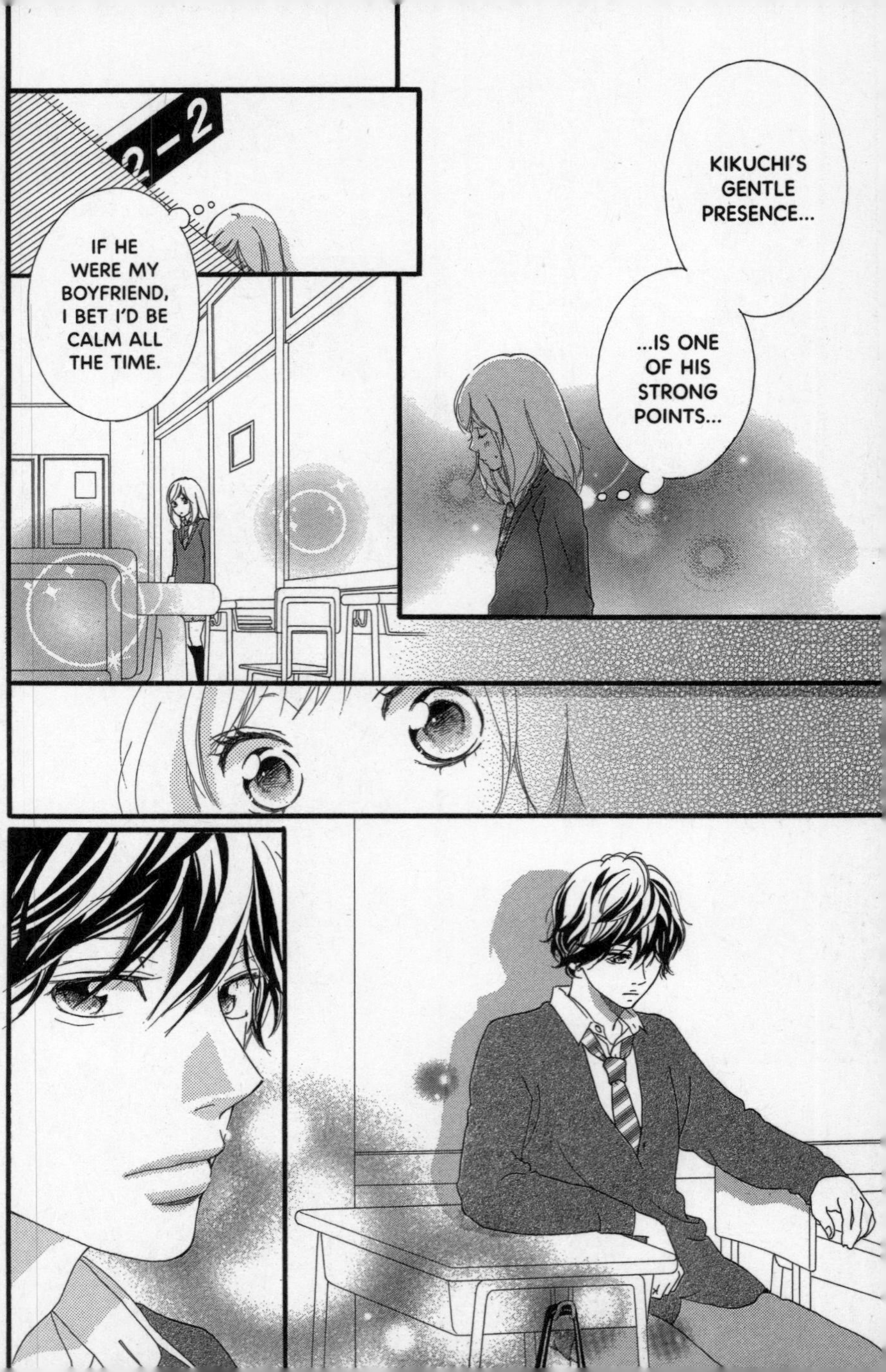
KIKUCHI'S GENTLE PRESENCE...
...IS ONE OF HIS STRONG POINTS...
2-2
IF HE WERE MY BOYFRIEND, I BET I'D BE CALM ALL THE TIME.

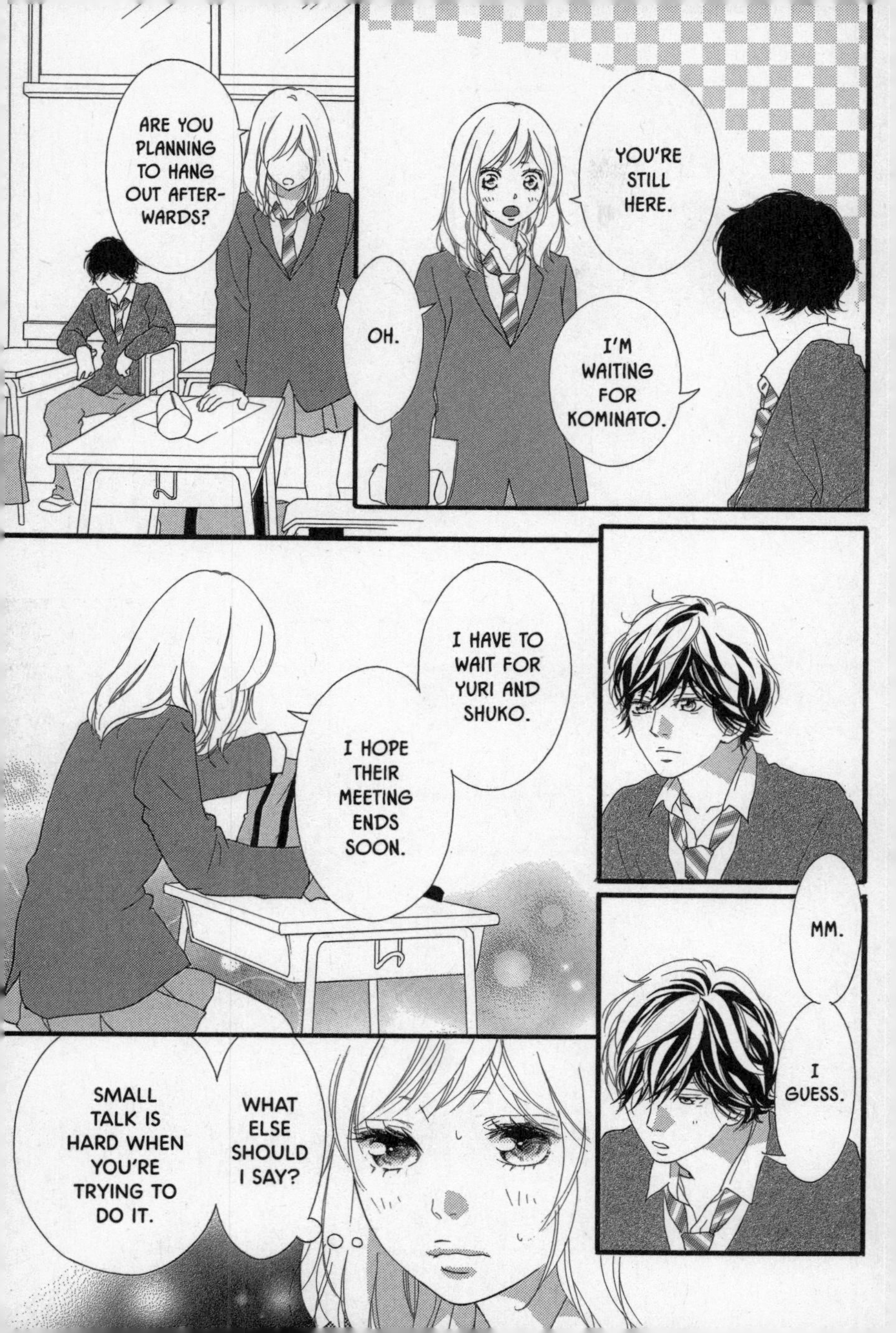
YOU'RE STILL HERE.
I'M WAITING FOR KOMINATO.
OH.
ARE YOU PLANNING TO HANG OUT AFTER-WARDS?
I HAVE TO WAIT FOR YURI AND SHUKO.
I HOPE THEIR MEETING ENDS SOON.
MM.
I GUESS.
WHAT ELSE SHOULD I SAY?
SMALL TALK IS HARD WHEN YOU'RE TRYING TO DO IT.

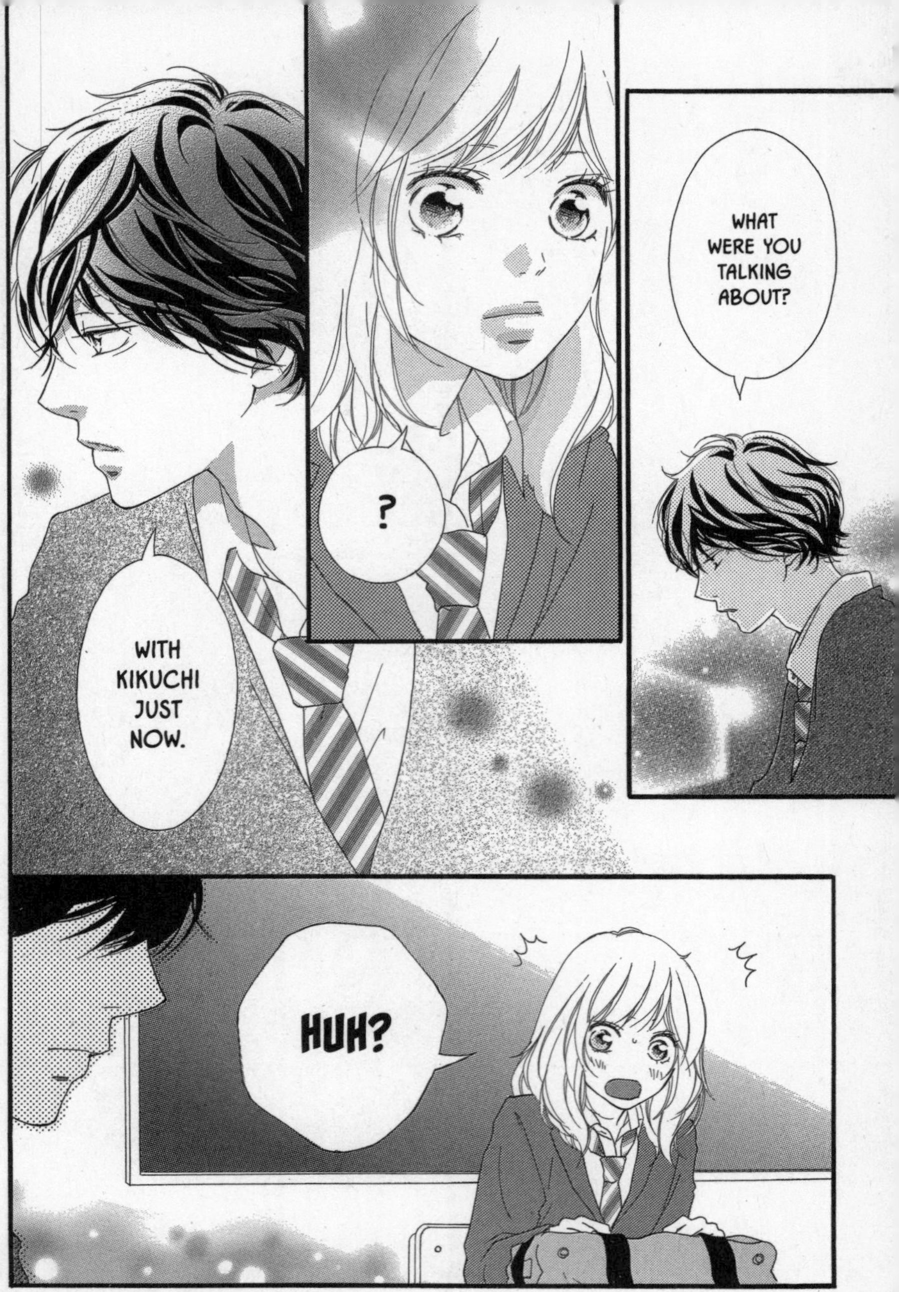
WHAT WERE YOU TALKING ABOUT?
?
WITH KIKUCHI JUST NOW.
HUH?

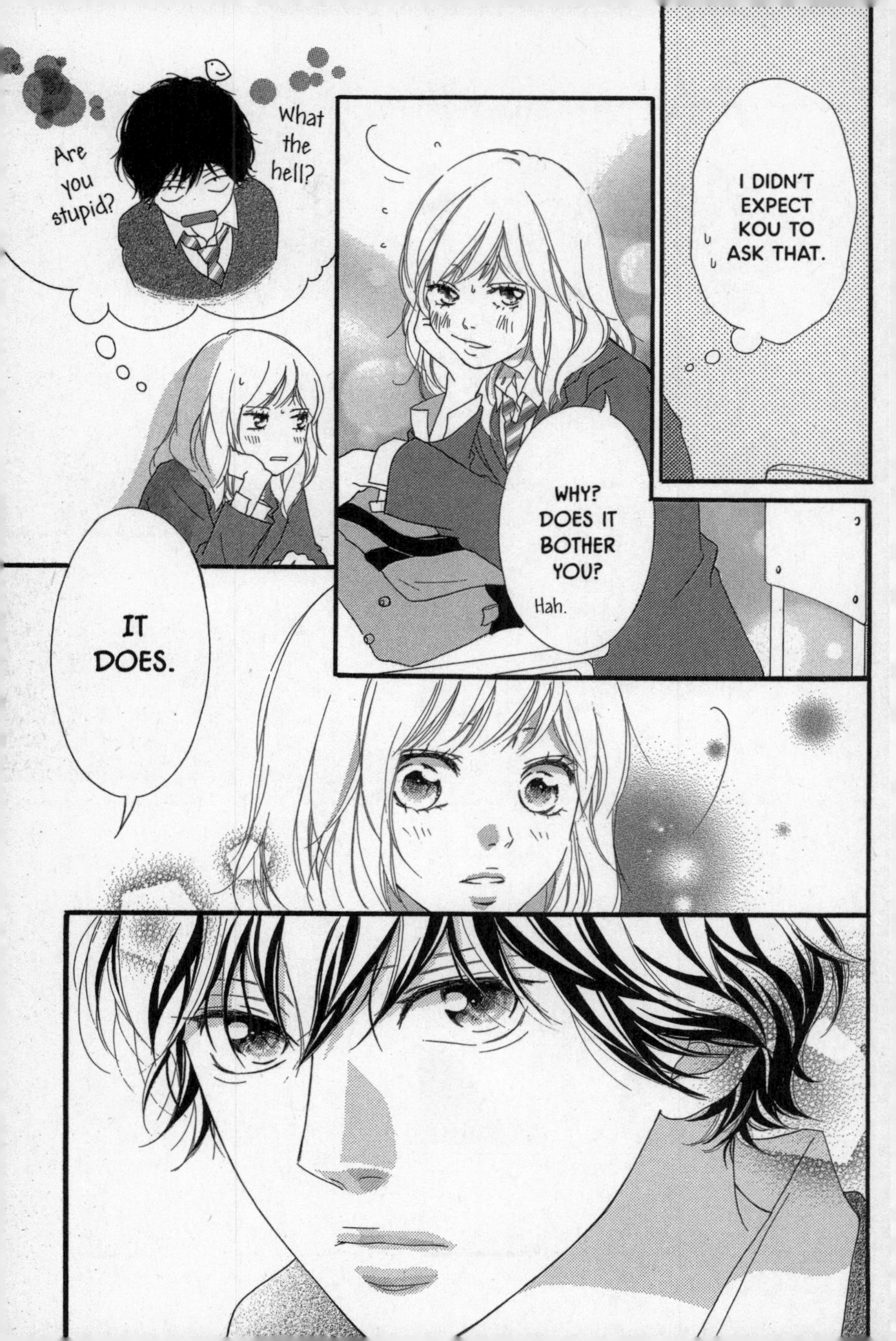
I DIDN'T EXPECT KOU TO ASK THAT.
WHY? DOES IT BOTHER YOU?
Hah.
What the hell?
Are you stupid?
IT DOES.

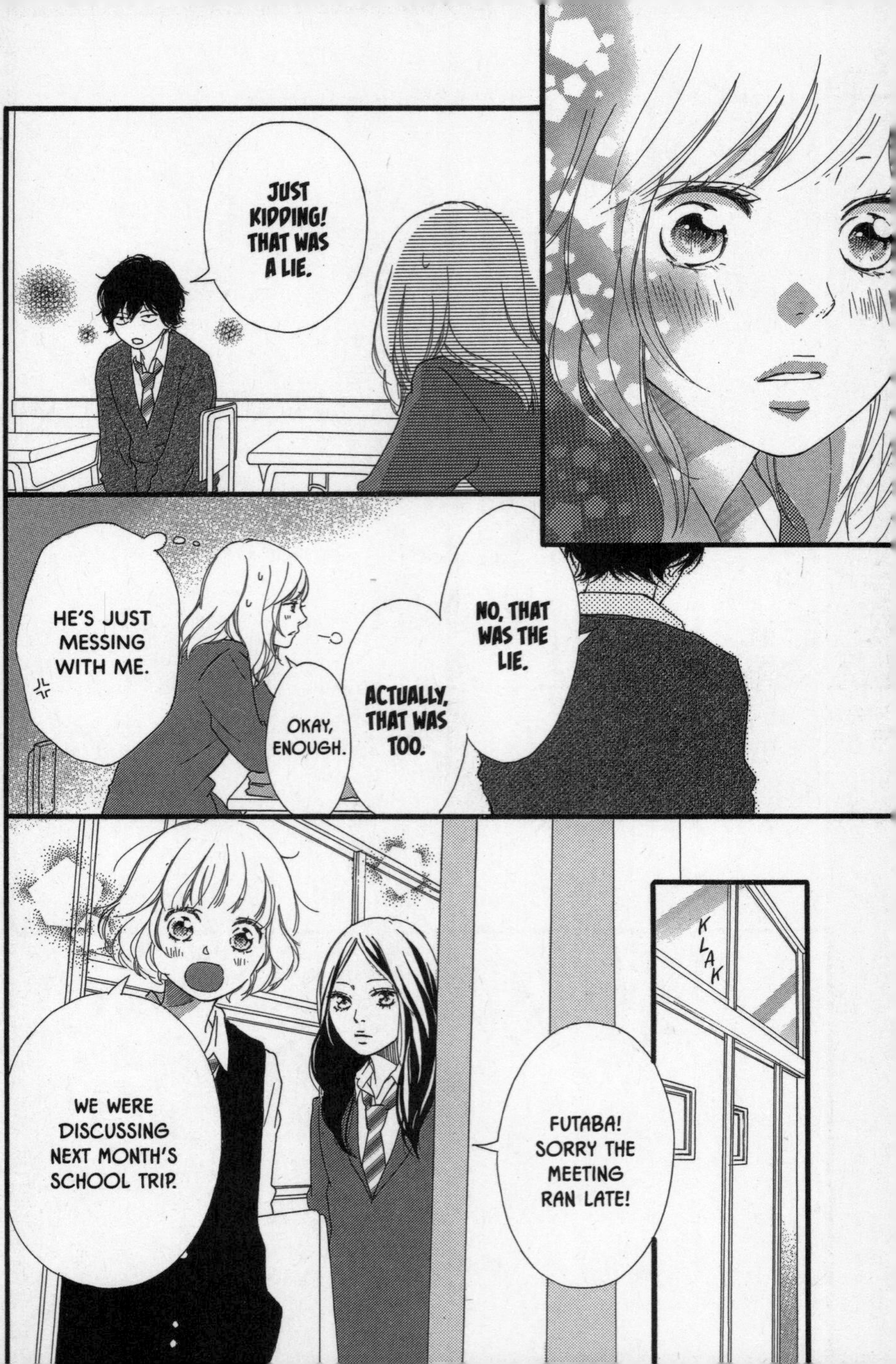
JUST KIDDING! THAT WAS A LIE.
NO, THAT WAS THE LIE.
ACTUALLY, THAT WAS TOO.
OKAY, ENOUGH.
HE'S JUST MESSING WITH ME.
KLAK
FUTABA! SORRY THE MEETING RAN LATE!
WE WERE DISCUSSING NEXT MONTH'S SCHOOL TRIP.

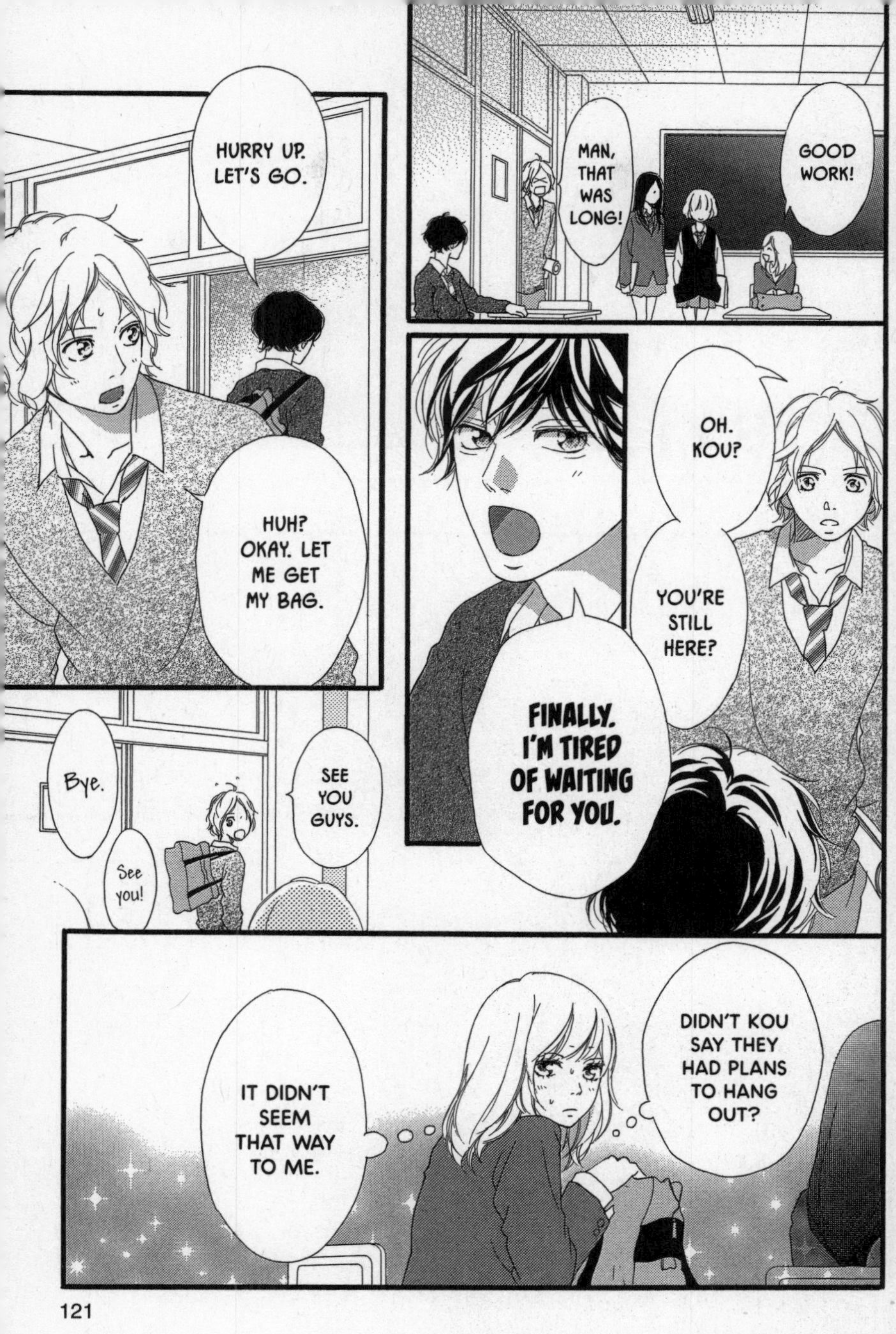
GOOD WORK!
MAN, THAT WAS LONG!
OH. KOU?
YOU'RE STILL HERE?
FINALLY. I'M TIRED OF WAITING FOR YOU.
HURRY UP. LET'S GO.
HUH? OKAY. LET ME GET MY BAG.
SEE YOU GUYS.
Bye.
See you!
DIDN'T KOU SAY THEY HAD PLANS TO HANG OUT?
IT DIDN'T SEEM THAT WAY TO ME.

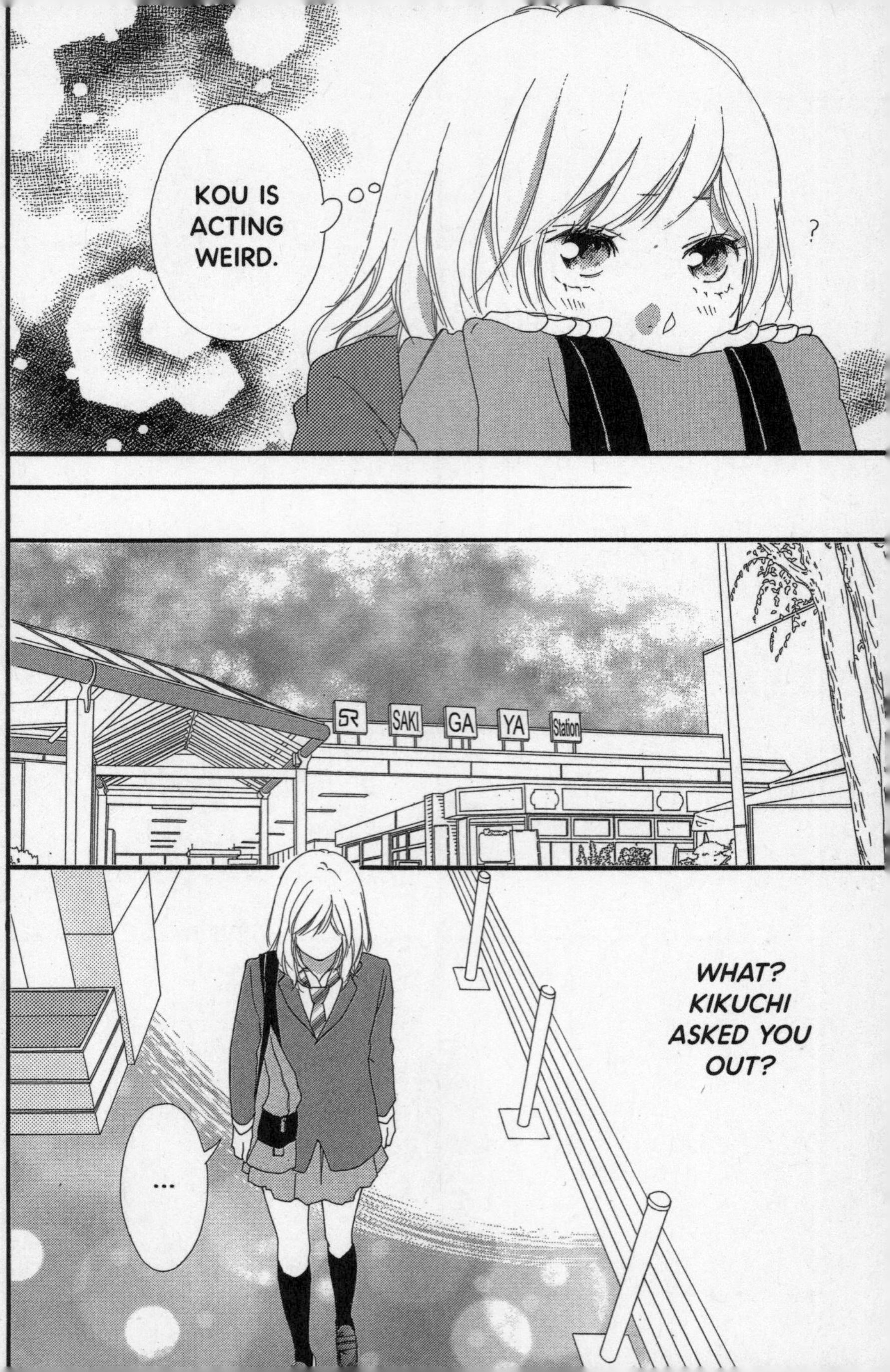
KOU IS ACTING WEIRD.
?
SR SAKI GA YA Station
WHAT? KIKUCHI ASKED YOU OUT?
...

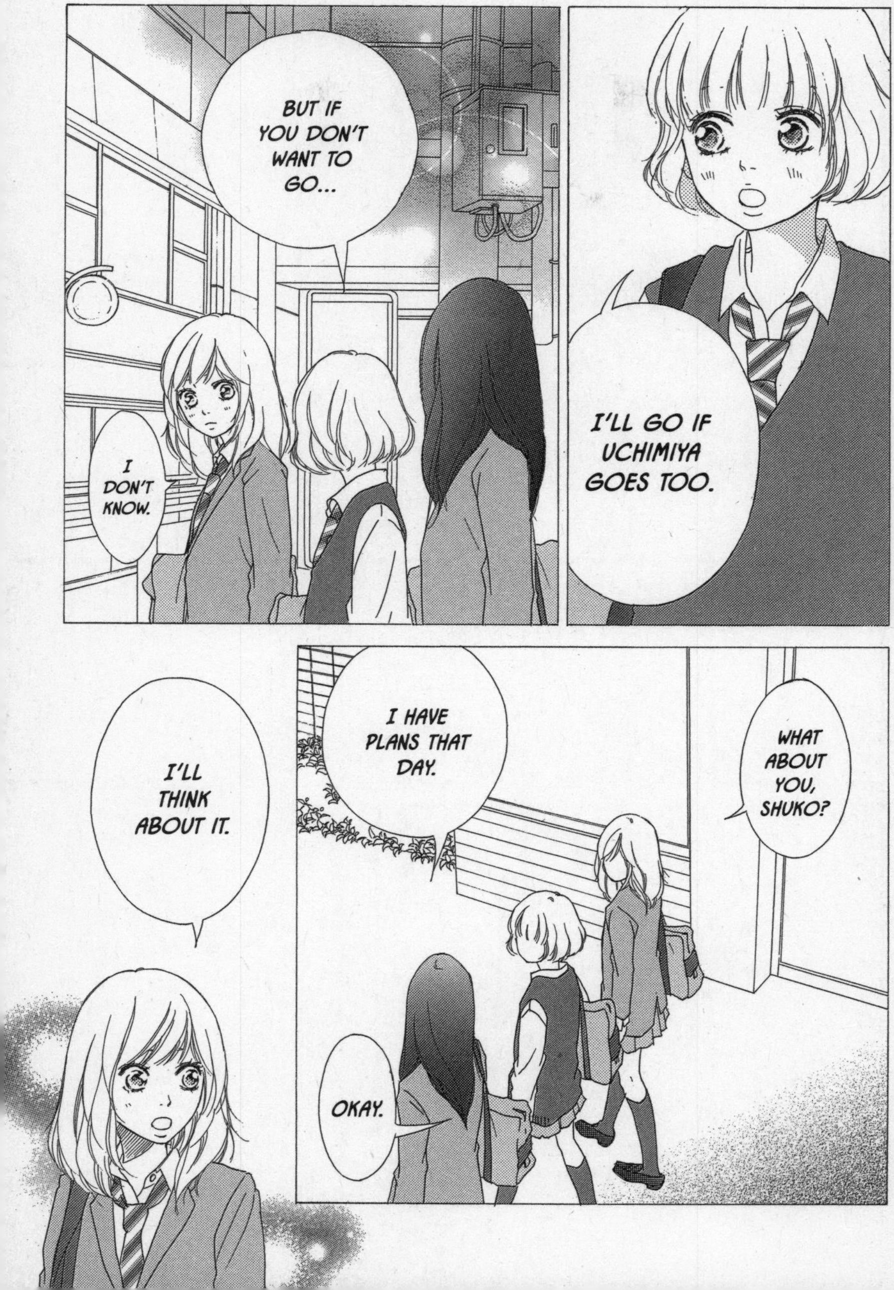
I'LL GO IF UCHIMIYA GOES TOO.
BUT IF YOU DON'T WANT TO GO...
I DON'T KNOW.
WHAT ABOUT YOU, SHUKO?
I HAVE PLANS THAT DAY.
OKAY.
I'LL THINK ABOUT IT.

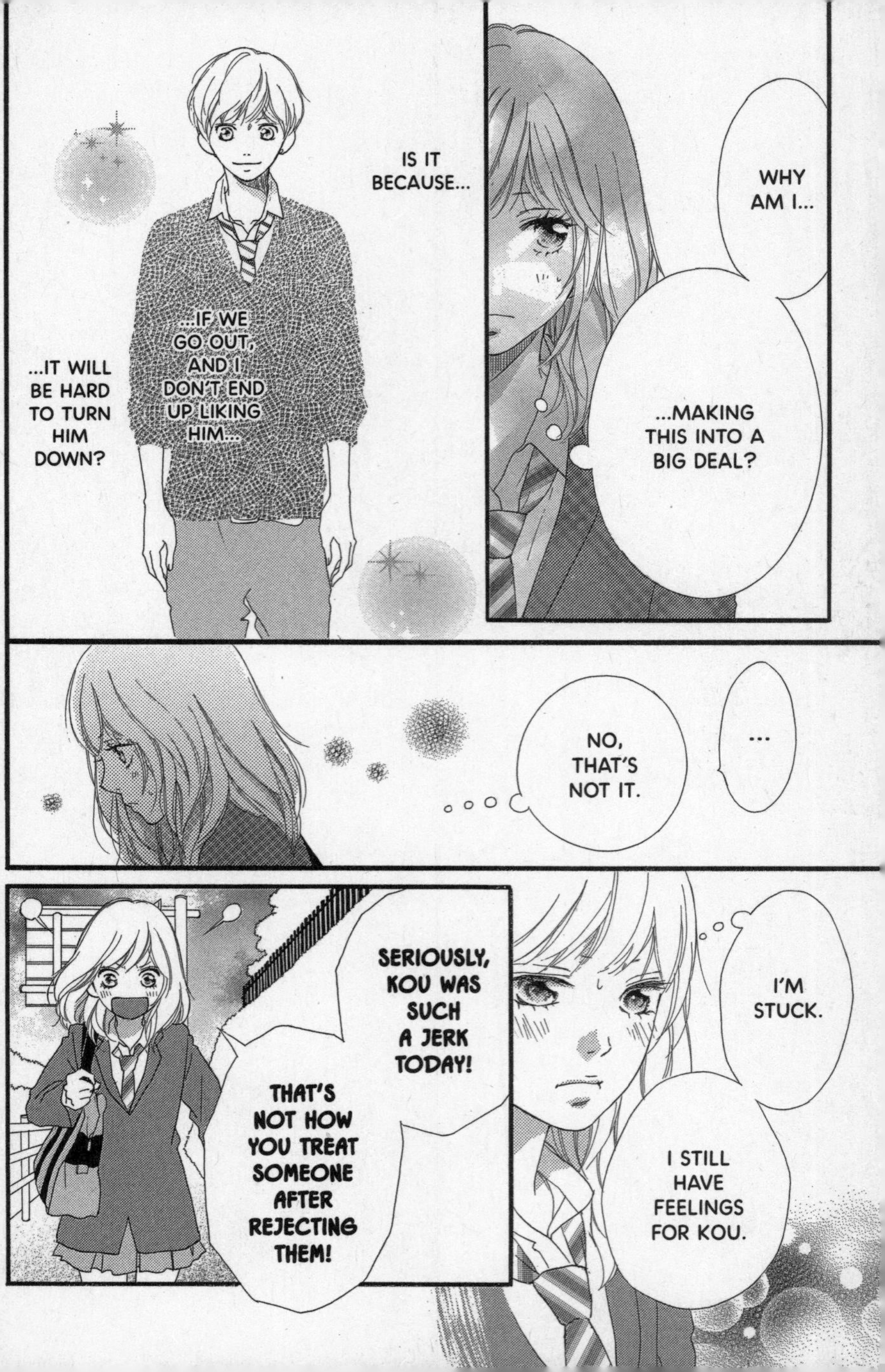
WHY AM I...
...MAKING THIS INTO A BIG DEAL?
IS IT BECAUSE...
...IF WE GO OUT, AND I DON'T END UP LIKING HIM...
...IT WILL BE HARD TO TURN HIM DOWN?
...
NO, THAT'S NOT IT.
I'M STUCK.
I STILL HAVE FEELINGS FOR KOU.
SERIOUSLY, KOU WAS SUCH A JERK TODAY!
THAT'S NOT HOW YOU TREAT SOMEONE AFTER REJECTING THEM!

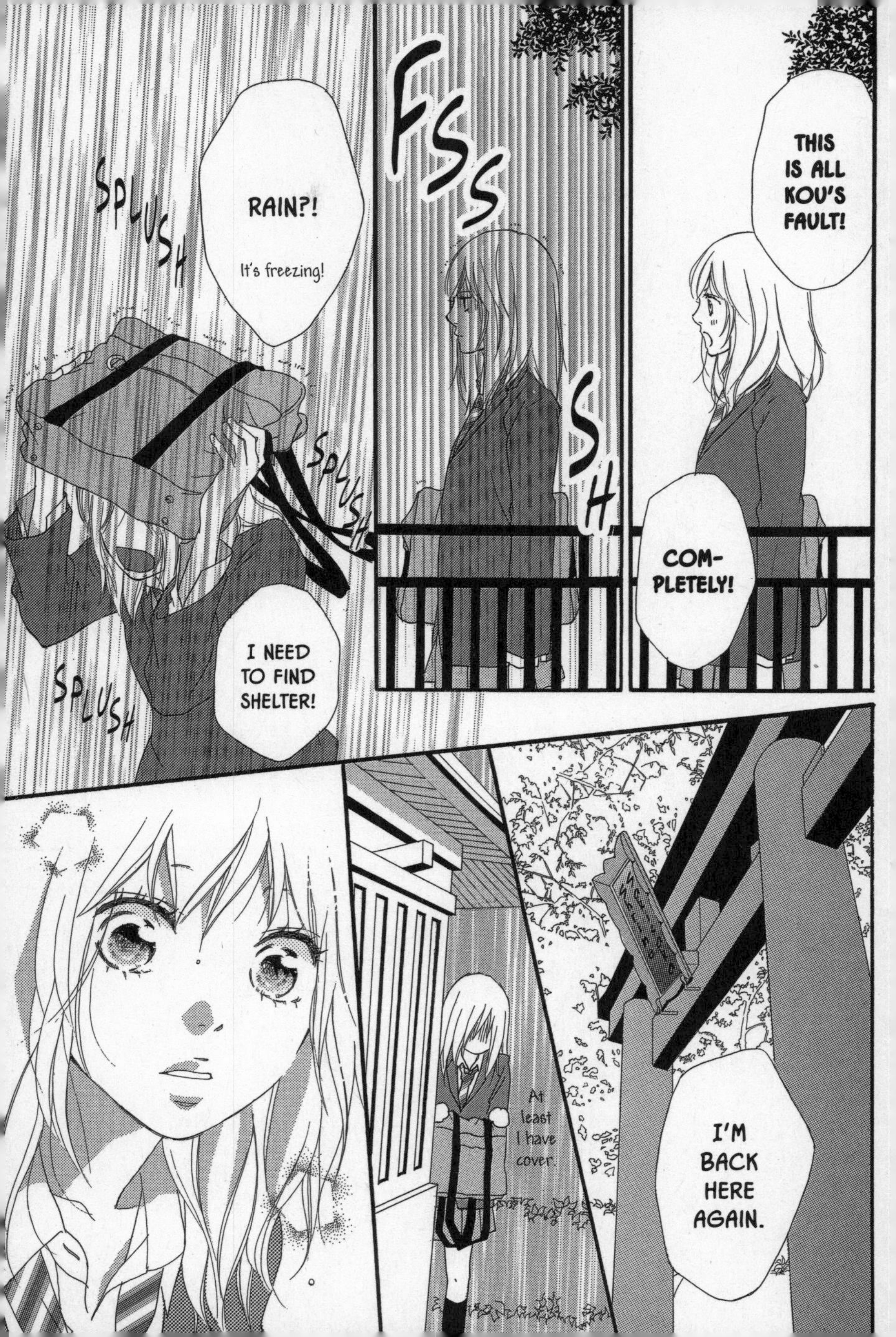
THIS IS ALL KOU'S FAULT!
COM-PLETELY!
FSS
SH
RAIN?!
It's freezing!
SPLUSH
SPLUSH
I NEED TO FIND SHELTER!
SPLUSH
I'M BACK HERE AGAIN.
At least I have cover.

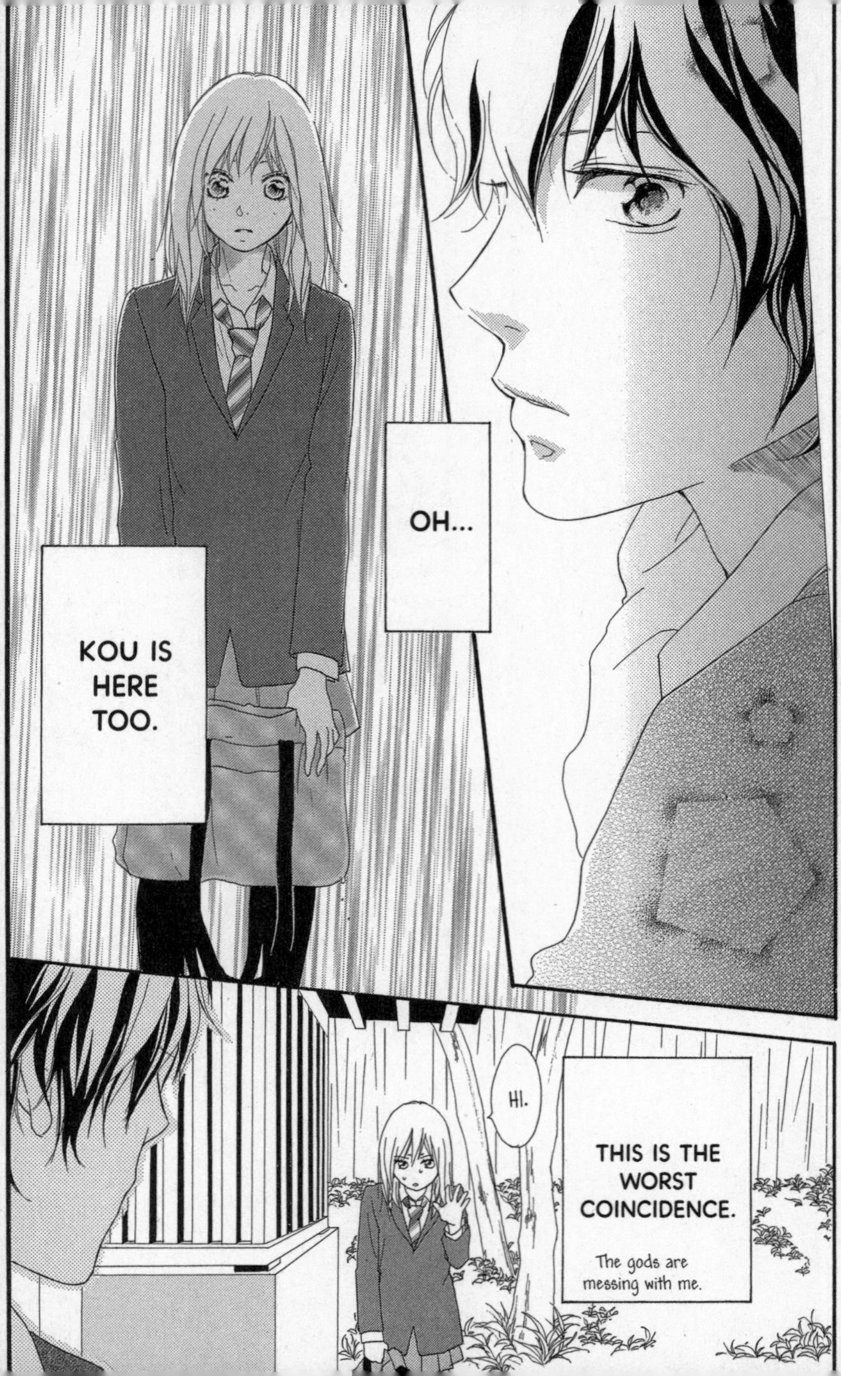
OH...
KOU IS HERE TOO.
THIS IS THE WORST COINCIDENCE.
The gods are messing with me.
HI.

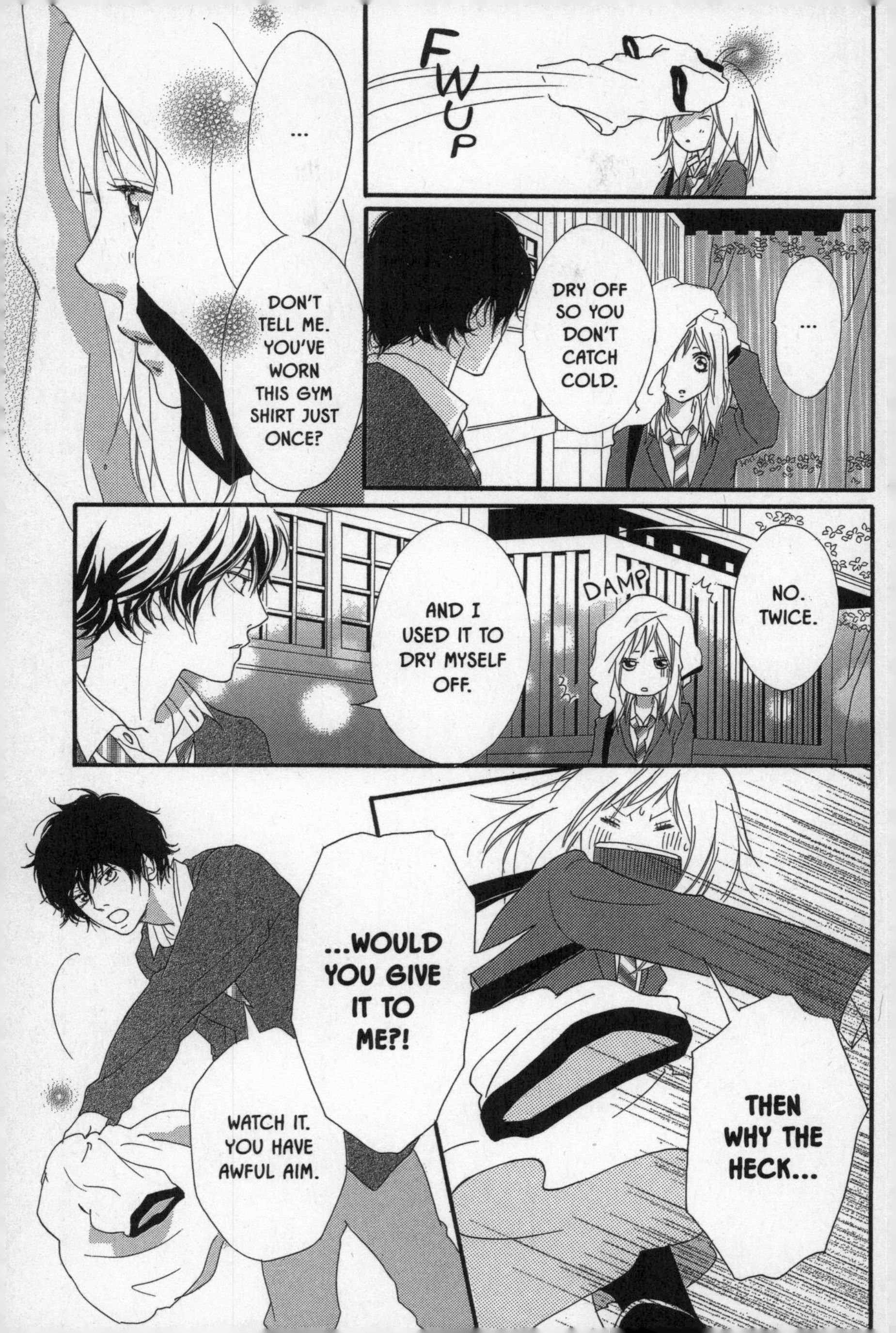
FWUP
DRY OFF SO YOU DON'T CATCH COLD.
...
...
DON'T TELL ME. YOU'VE WORN THIS GYM SHIRT JUST ONCE?
NO. TWICE.
DAMP
AND I USED IT TO DRY MYSELF OFF.
THEN WHY THE HECK...
...WOULD YOU GIVE IT TO ME?!
WATCH IT. YOU HAVE AWFUL AIM.

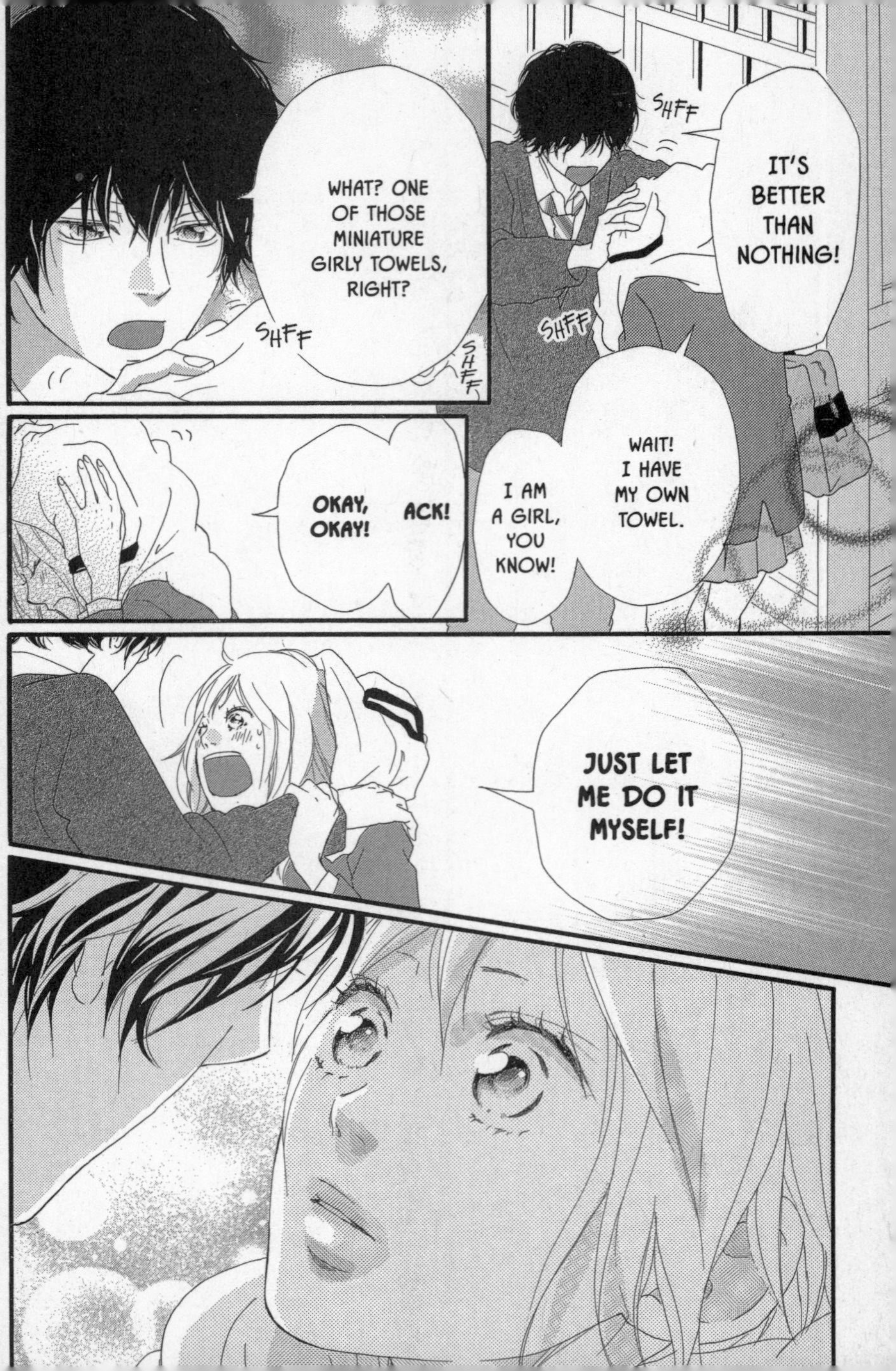
SHFF
IT'S BETTER THAN NOTHING!
SHFF
WAIT! I HAVE MY OWN TOWEL.
I AM A GIRL, YOU KNOW!
WHAT? ONE OF THOSE MINIATURE GIRLY TOWELS, RIGHT?
SHFF
SHFF
ACK!
OKAY, OKAY!
JUST LET ME DO IT MYSELF!

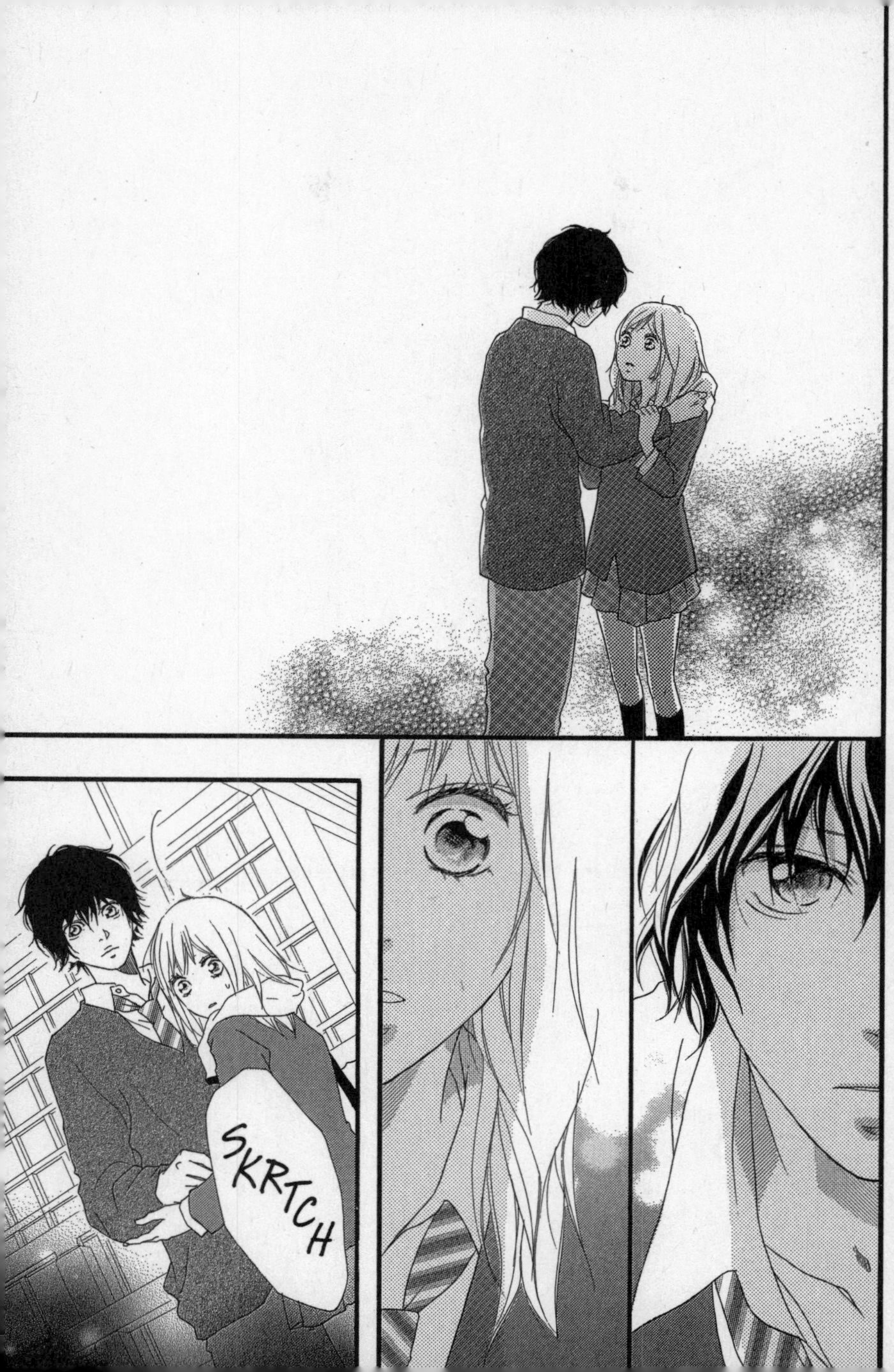
SKRTCH

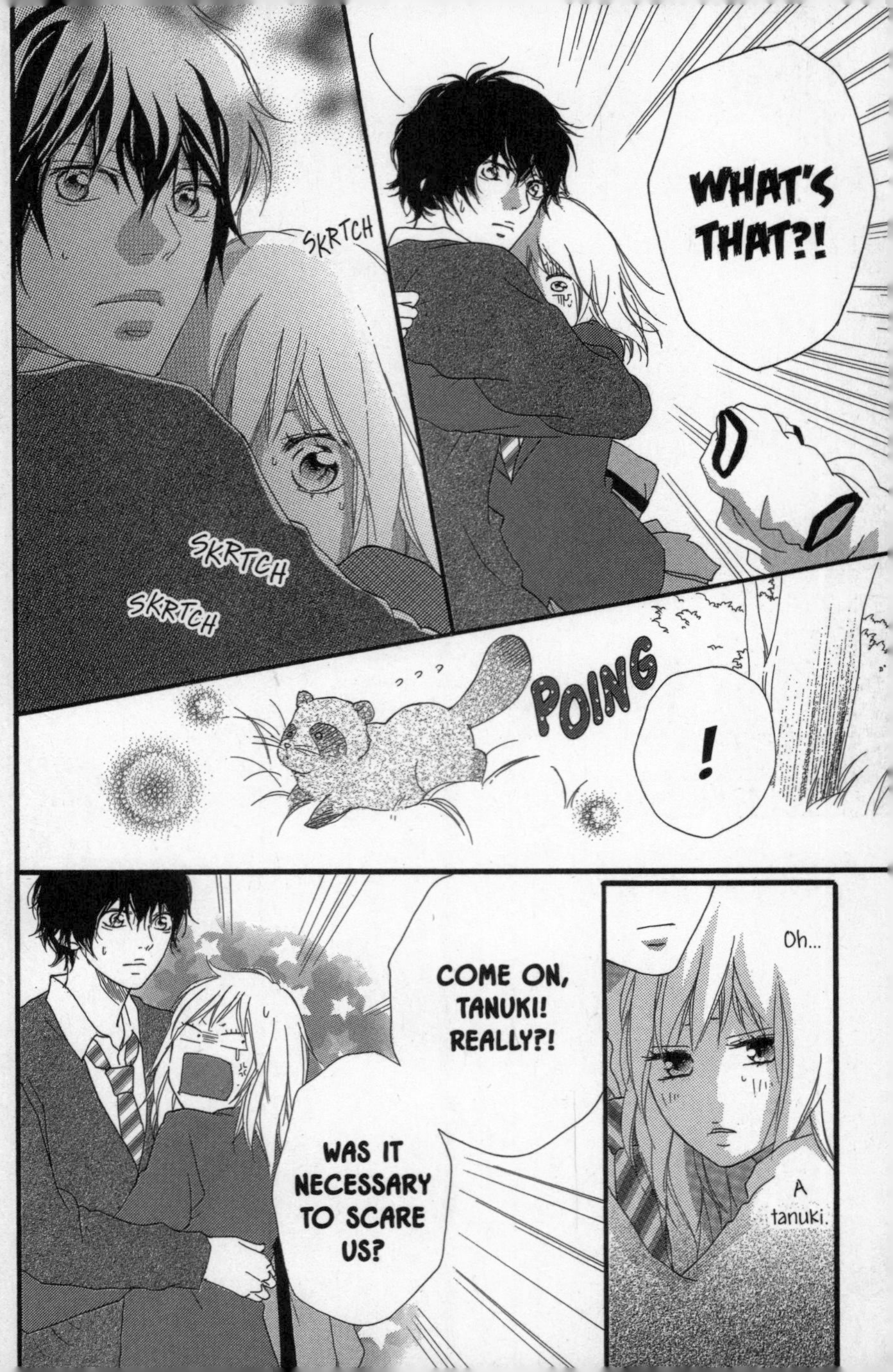
WHAT'S THAT?!
SKRTCH
SKRTCH
SKRTCH
POING
!
Oh...
A tanuki.
COME ON, TANUKI! REALLY?!
WAS IT NECESSARY TO SCARE US?

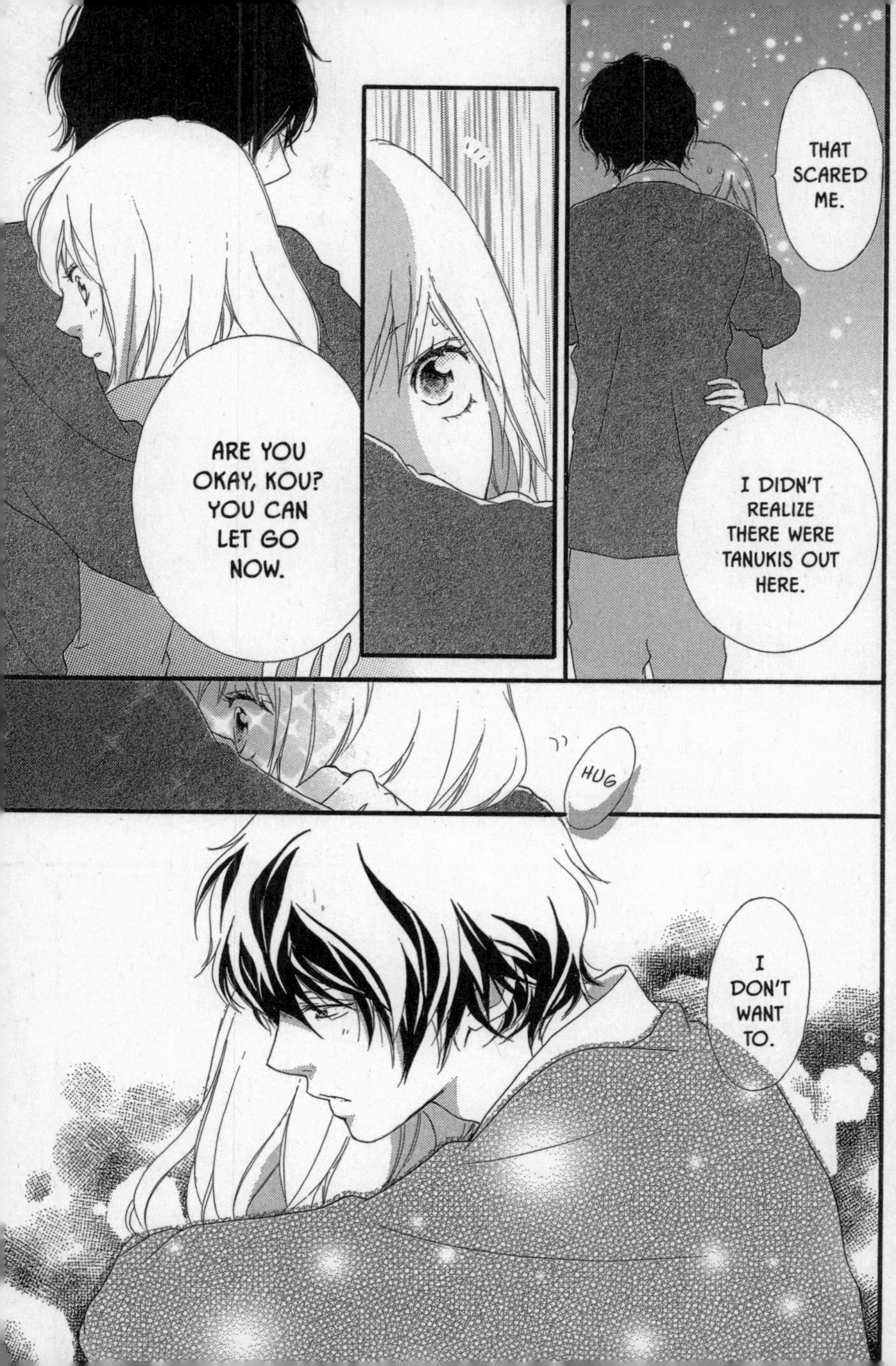
THAT SCARED ME.
I DIDN'T REALIZE THERE WERE TANUKIS OUT HERE.
ARE YOU OKAY, KOU? YOU CAN LET GO NOW.
HUG
I DON'T WANT TO.

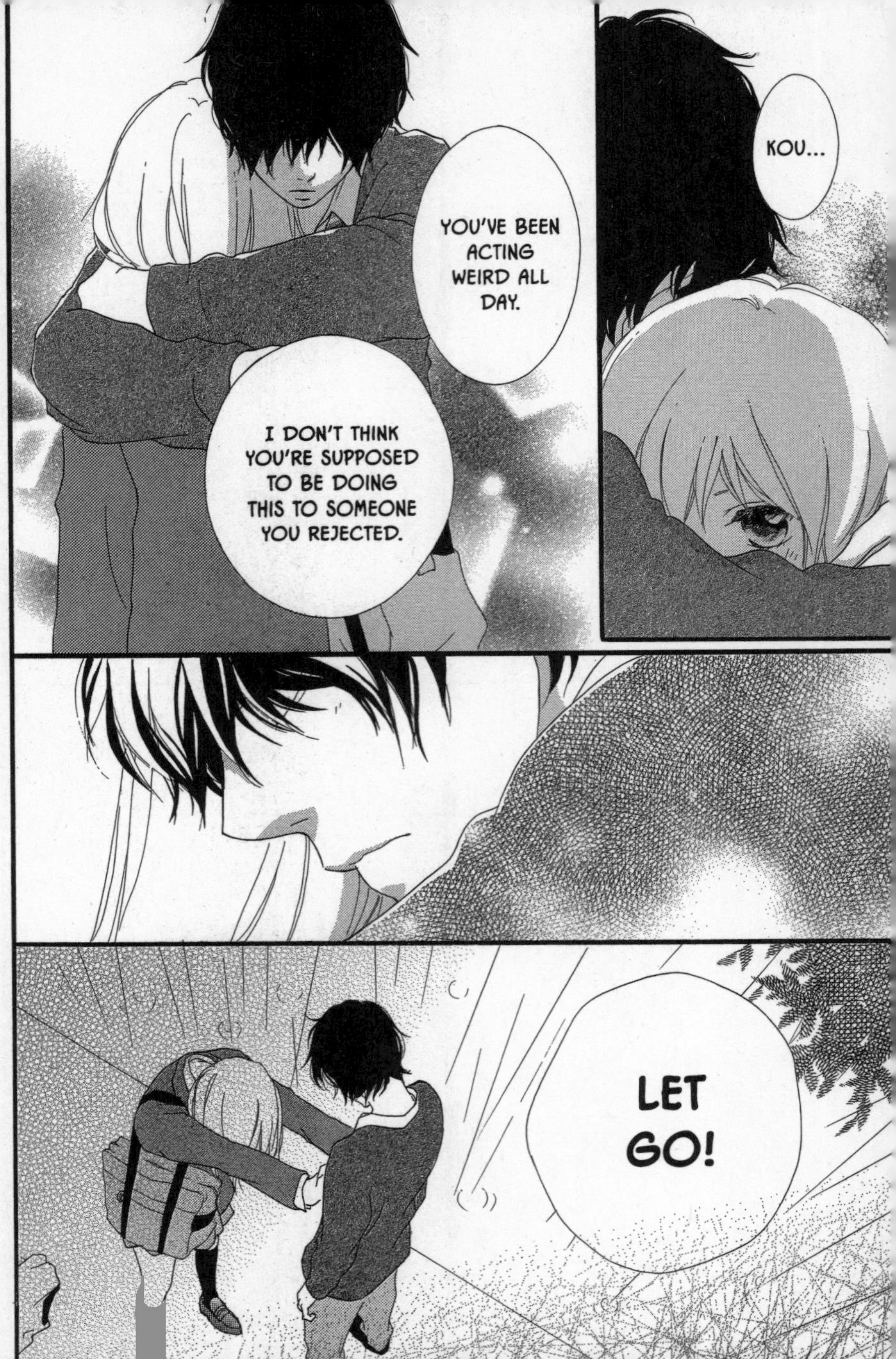
KOU...
YOU'VE BEEN ACTING WEIRD ALL DAY.
I DON'T THINK YOU'RE SUPPOSED TO BE DOING THIS TO SOMEONE YOU REJECTED.
LET GO!

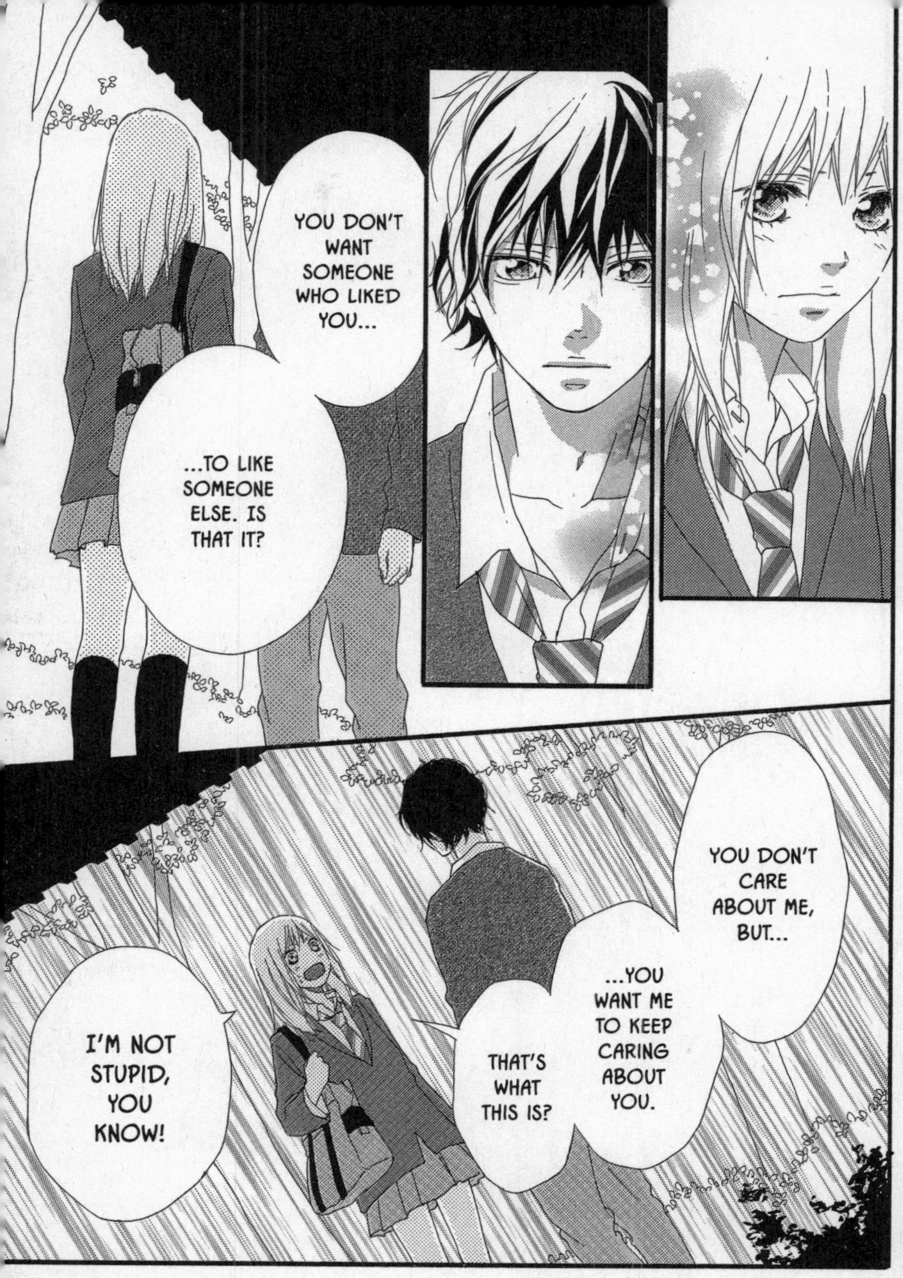
YOU DON'T WANT SOMEONE WHO LIKED YOU...
...TO LIKE SOMEONE ELSE. IS THAT IT?
YOU DON'T CARE ABOUT ME, BUT...
...YOU WANT ME TO KEEP CARING ABOUT YOU.
THAT'S WHAT THIS IS?
I'M NOT STUPID, YOU KNOW!

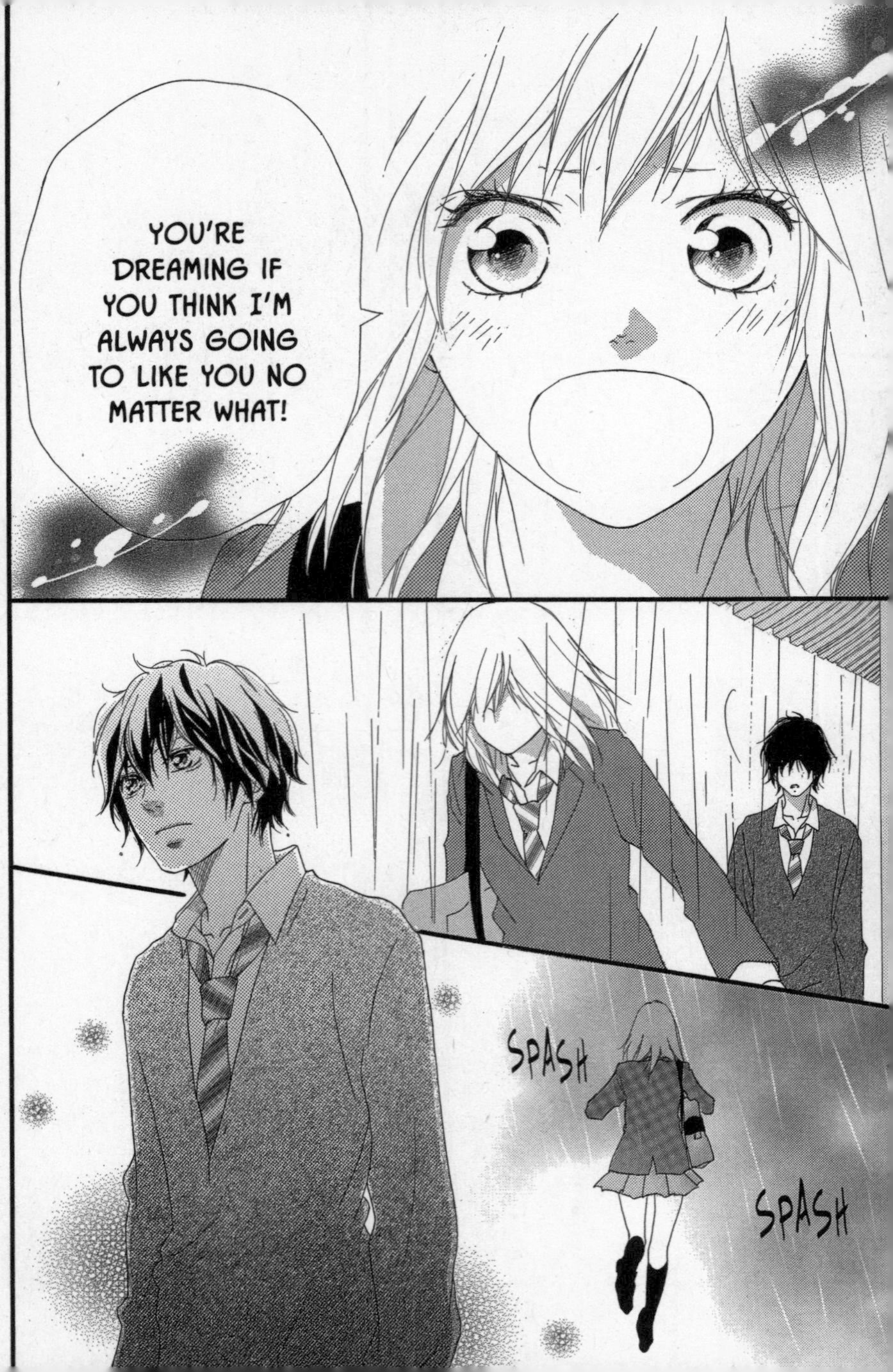
YOU'RE DREAMING IF YOU THINK I'M ALWAYS GOING TO LIKE YOU NO MATTER WHAT!
SPASH
SPASH

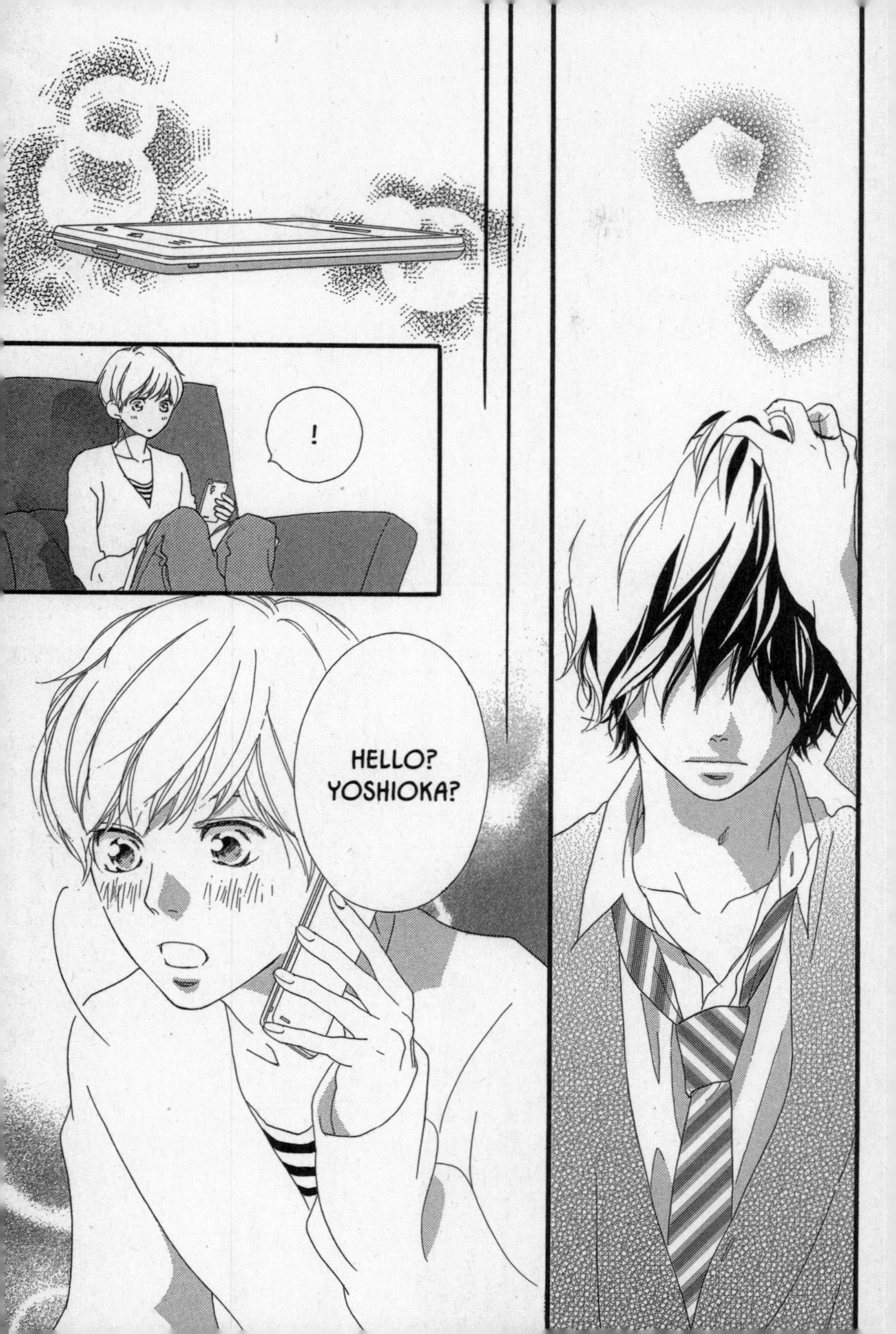
!
HELLO? YOSHIOKA?

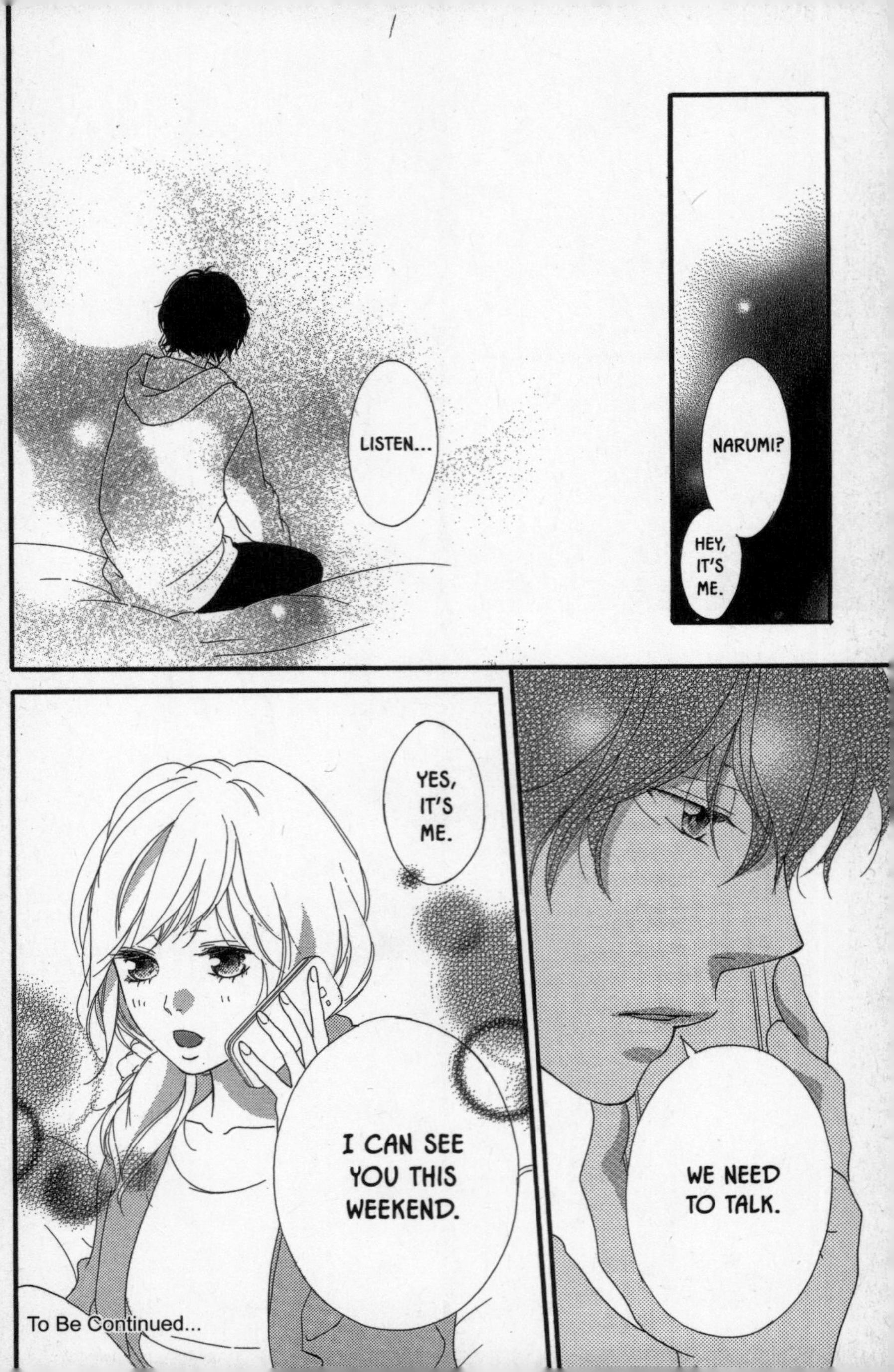
NARUMI?
HEY, IT'S ME.
LISTEN...
WE NEED TO TALK.
YES, IT'S ME.
I CAN SEE YOU THIS WEEKEND.
To Be Continued...

AO HARU RIDE CHARACTERS 9

Haruhiko Uchimiya

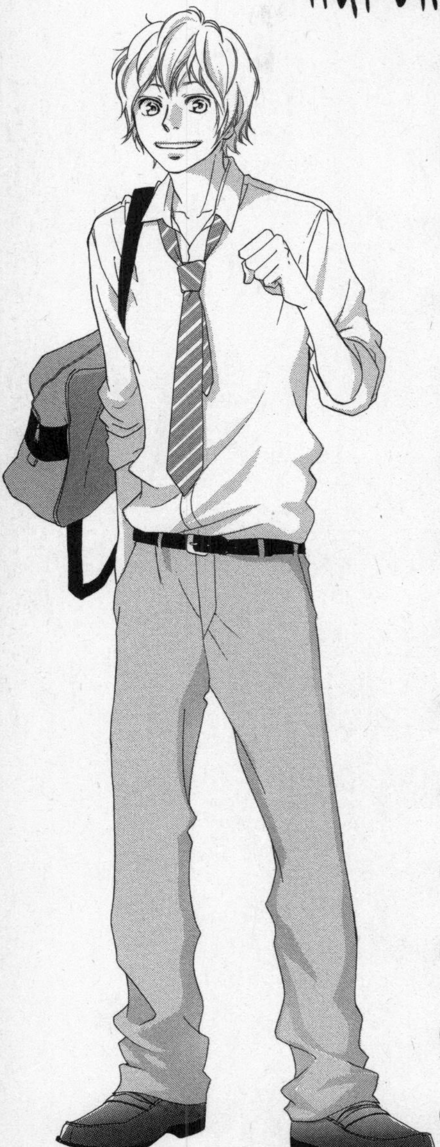

- **Birthday:**
  April 22nd
- **Astrological Sign, Blood Type:**
  Taurus, type A
- **Height, Weight:**
  5'9", 130 lbs.
- **Favorite Subject:**
  Science
- **Least Favorite Subject:**
  Art
- **Favorite Food:**
  Pizza toast
- **Least Favorite Food:**
  Fish skin
- **Favorite Music:**
  Saito Kazuyoshi
- **Siblings:**
  Older brother
- **Age When First Crush Happened:**
  Fourth grade
- **Fun Fact:**
  I have a nephew.
- **Favorite Snack:**
  Chococones
- **Favorite Drink:**
  NUDA Grapefruit
- **Favorite Color:**
  Both red and navy

AO HARU RIDE CHARACTERS 10

Shun Tachibanaki

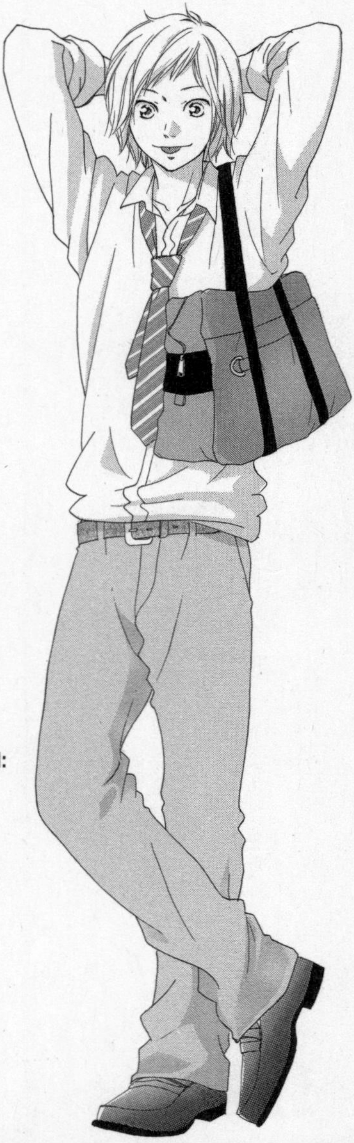

- **Birthday:**
  January 16th
- **Astrological Sign, Blood Type:**
  Capricorn, type AB
- **Height, Weight:**
  5'6", 121 lbs.
- **Favorite Subject:**
  Art
- **Least Favorite Subject:**
  Math
- **Favorite Food:**
  Tonkotsu ramen
- **Least Favorite Food:**
  Peas
- **Favorite Music:**
  Fujifabric
- **Siblings:**
  Younger sister
- **Age When First Crush Happened:**
  First year of junior high
- **Fun Fact:**
  I have 20/10 eyesight in both eyes.
- **Favorite Snack:**
  Chocorooms
- **Favorite Drink:**
  Dekavita
- **Favorite Color:**
  Black

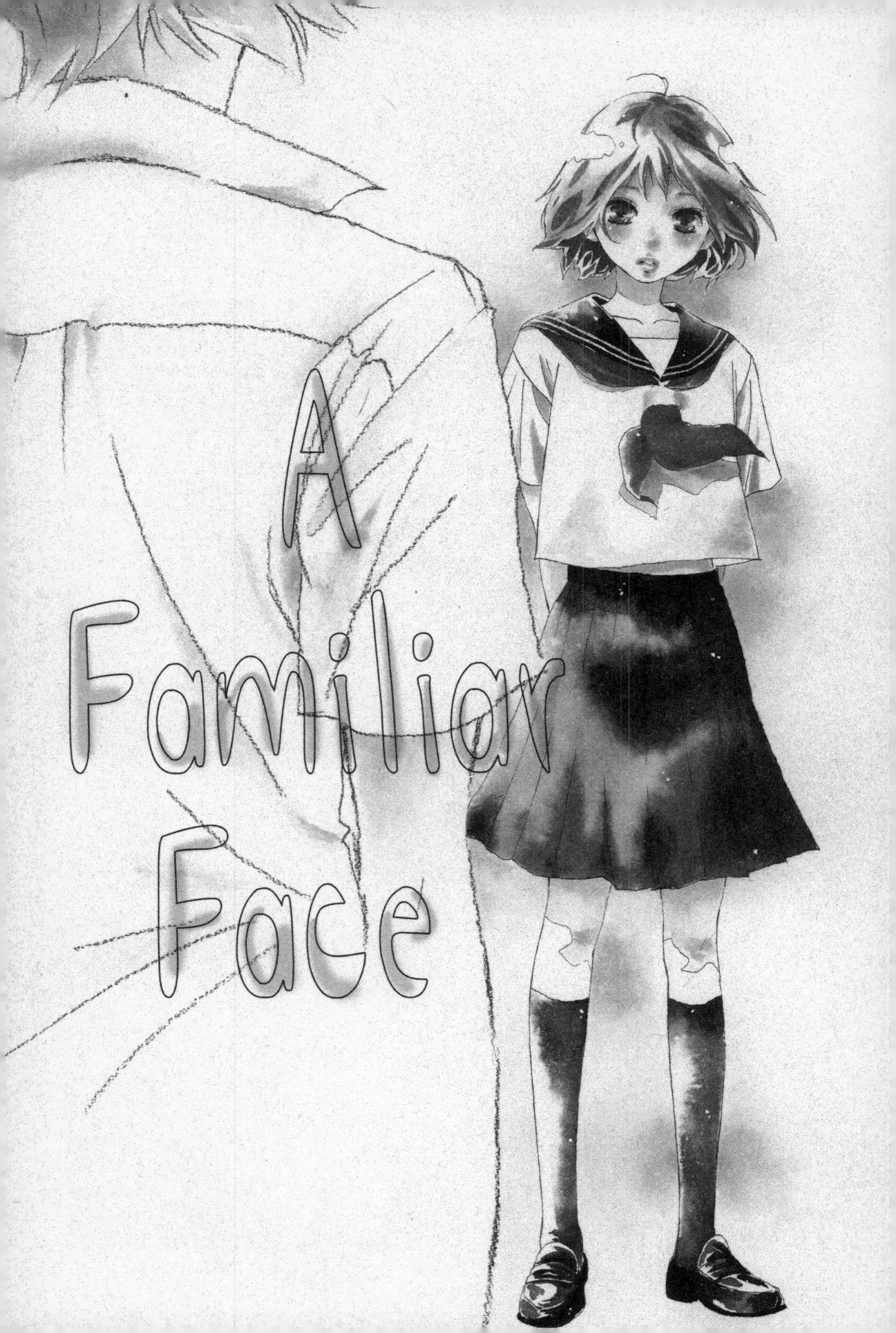
A Familiar Face

I wrote a one-shot for the first time in a long while!
Initially I thought I would write about 16 pages for it. As time
passed the story grew in my mind, and eventually it couldn't be
contained within 16 pages. I am grateful to be given the full
40 pages to tell this story. But the truth is I had to shave off a
few scenes here and there to make it fit. Since I hadn't written
a one-shot for some time, I had to stop and think about how to
proceed. I have to say that plotting it out took a really long time,
but it was really fun to work on! The only regret I have is that I
wanted to draw the boys in their traditional uniforms, but it was
published in the summer magazine issue, so they ended up in
summer uniforms. One side note: There is a scene with a train
in this story, and just as I was thinking that I tend to draw a lot
of trains and stations in my stories, my editor called me out on
it. But you know, I'm okay with being known as the mangaka who
draws trains.

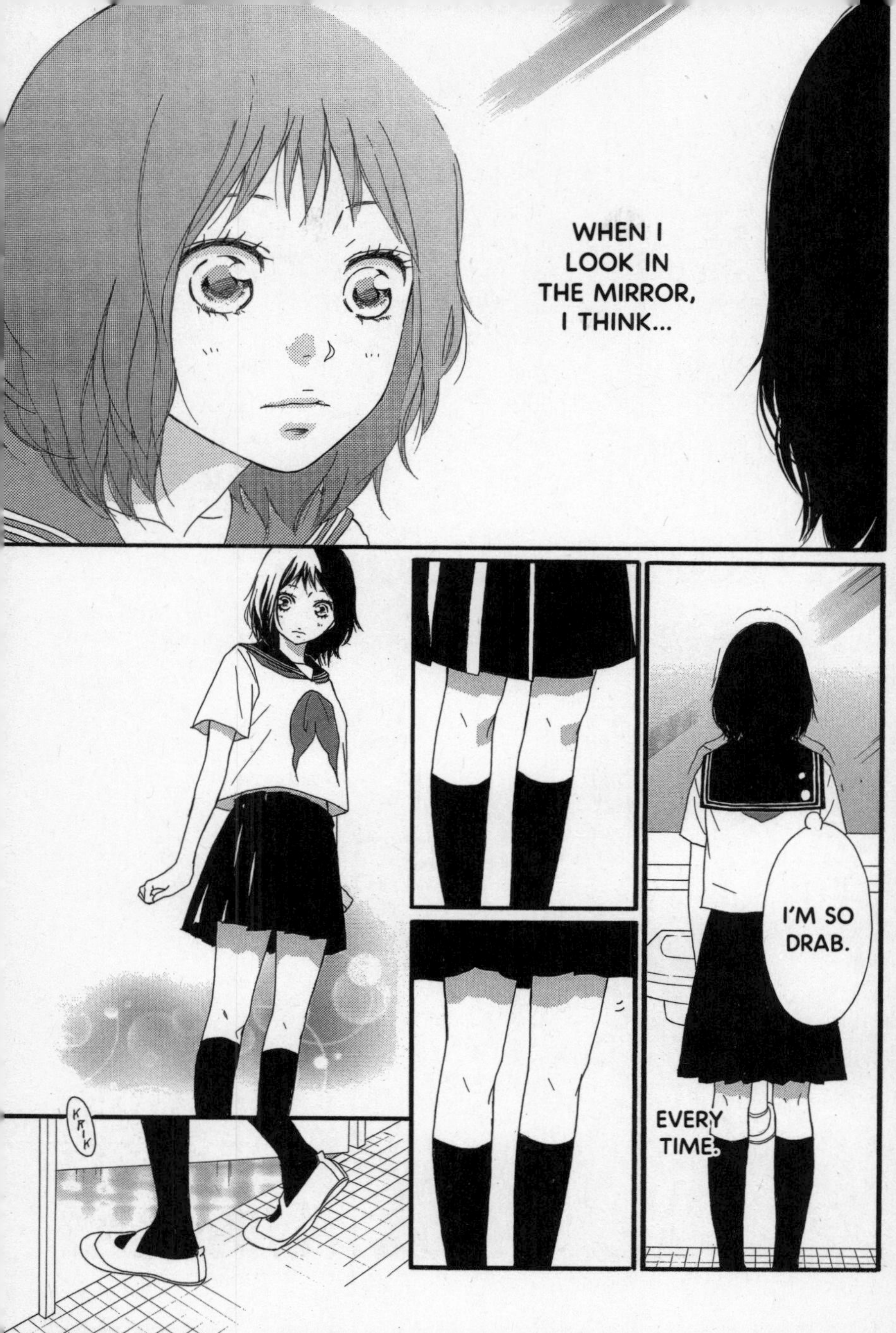
WHEN I LOOK IN THE MIRROR, I THINK...
I'M SO DRAB.
EVERY TIME.
KRIK

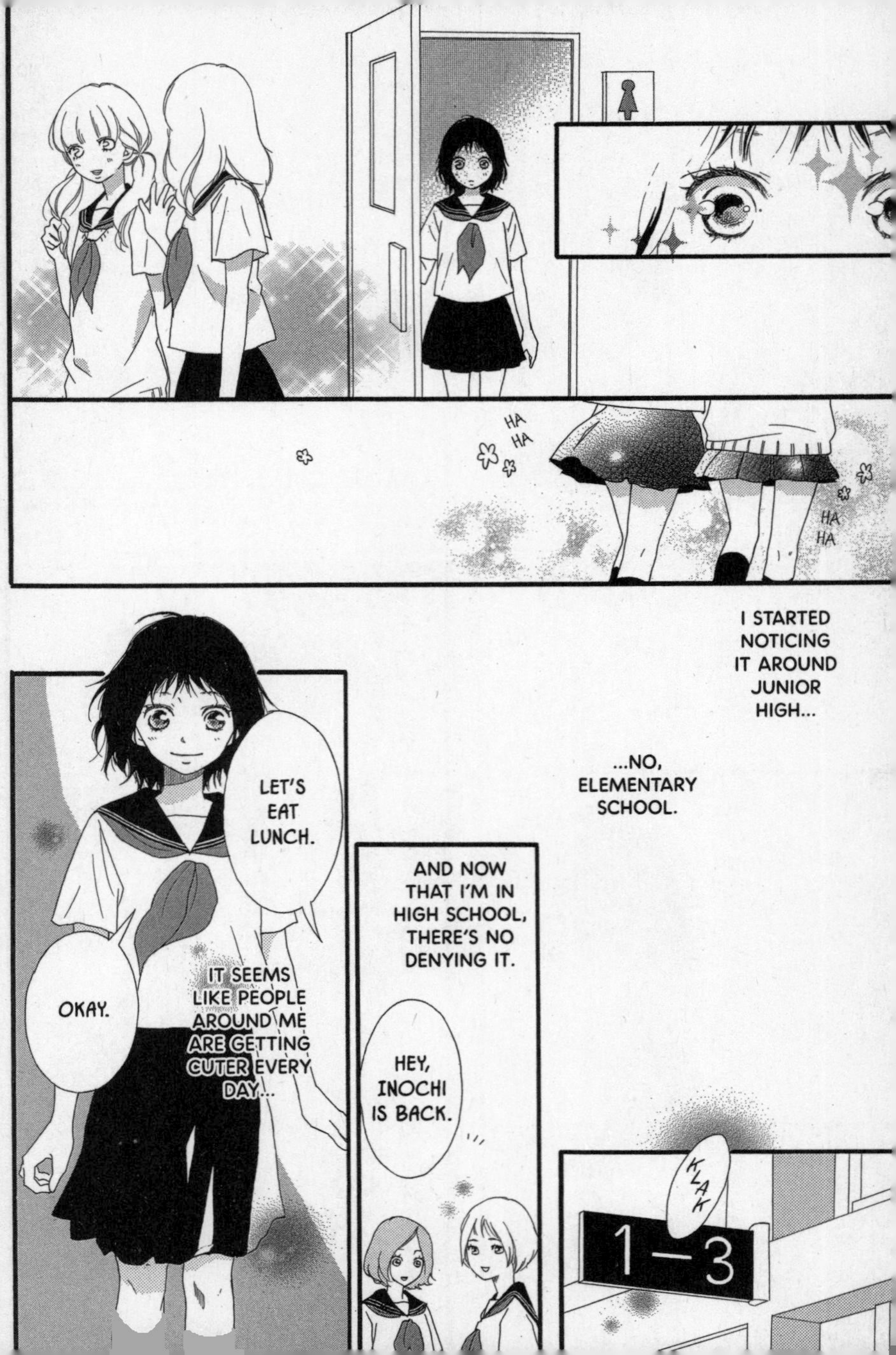
HA
HA
HA
HA
I STARTED NOTICING IT AROUND JUNIOR HIGH...
...NO, ELEMENTARY SCHOOL.
KLAK
1—3
AND NOW THAT I'M IN HIGH SCHOOL, THERE'S NO DENYING IT.
HEY, INOCHI IS BACK.
LET'S EAT LUNCH.
OKAY.
IT SEEMS LIKE PEOPLE AROUND ME ARE GETTING CUTER EVERY DAY...

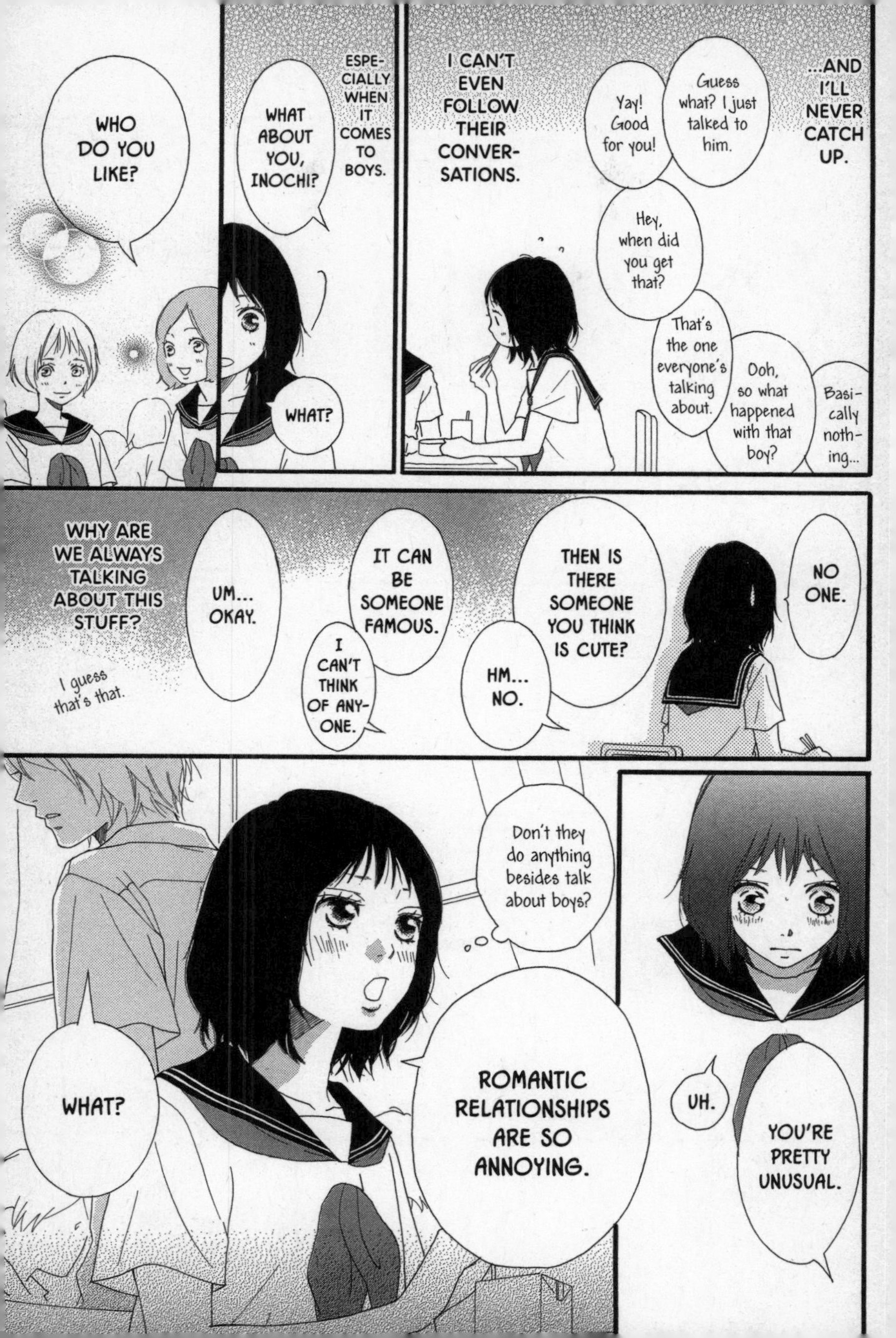
...AND I'LL NEVER CATCH UP.
Guess what? I just talked to him.
Yay! Good for you!
I CAN'T EVEN FOLLOW THEIR CONVER- SATIONS.
Hey, when did you get that?
Basi- cally noth- ing...
Ooh, so what happened with that boy?
That's the one everyone's talking about.
ESPE- CIALLY WHEN IT COMES TO BOYS.
WHAT ABOUT YOU, INOCHI?
WHAT?
WHO DO YOU LIKE?
NO ONE.
THEN IS THERE SOMEONE YOU THINK IS CUTE?
HM... NO.
IT CAN BE SOMEONE FAMOUS.
I CAN'T THINK OF ANY- ONE.
UM... OKAY.
WHY ARE WE ALWAYS TALKING ABOUT THIS STUFF?
I guess that's that.
UH.
YOU'RE PRETTY UNUSUAL.
Don't they do anything besides talk about boys?
ROMANTIC RELATIONSHIPS ARE SO ANNOYING.
WHAT?

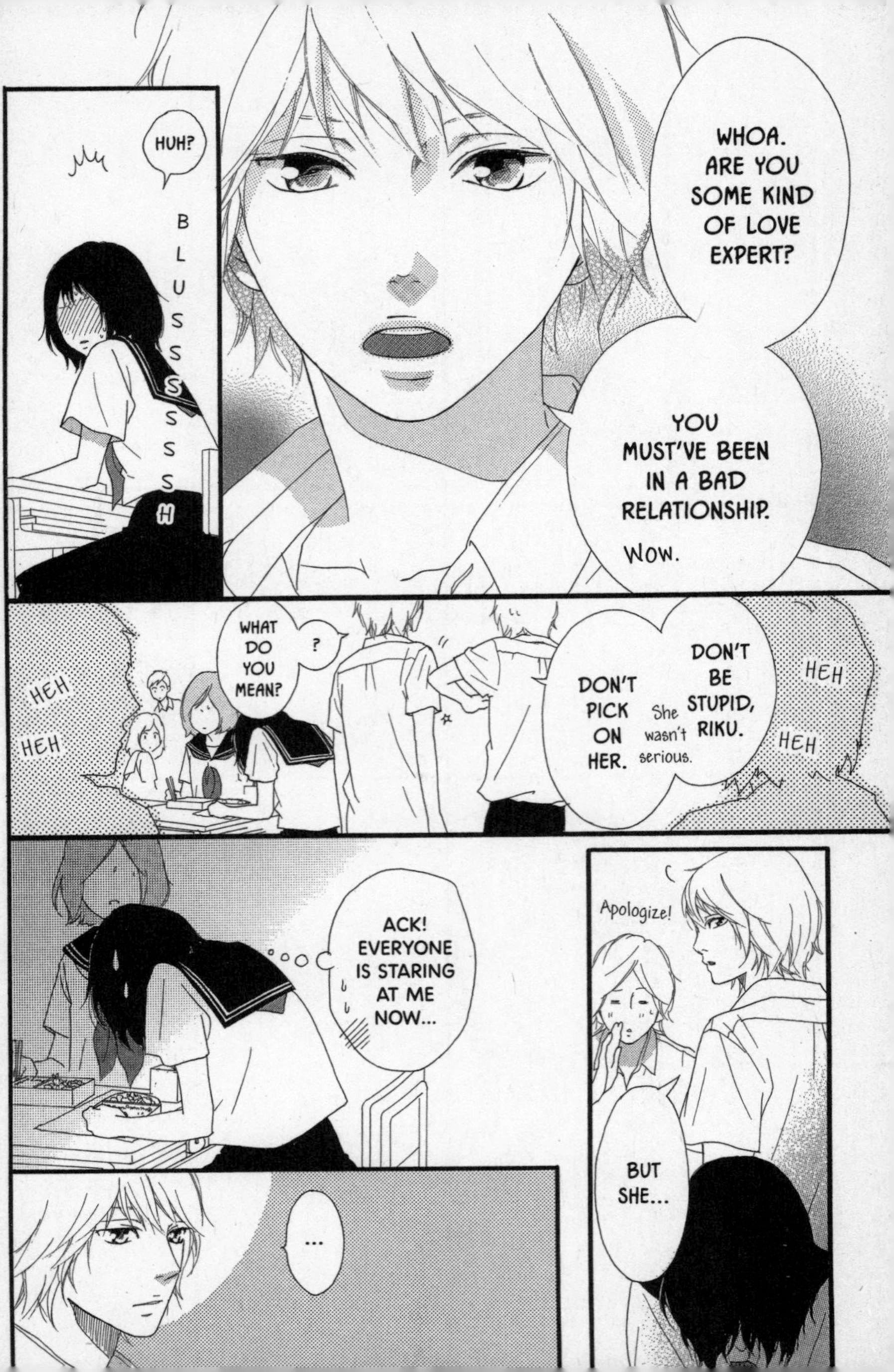
WHOA. ARE YOU SOME KIND OF LOVE EXPERT?
YOU MUST'VE BEEN IN A BAD RELATIONSHIP. WOW.
HUH?
BLUSSSSSSH
DON'T BE STUPID, RIKU.
She wasn't serious.
DON'T PICK ON HER.
HEH
HEH
?
WHAT DO YOU MEAN?
HEH
HEH
Apologize!
BUT SHE...
ACK! EVERYONE IS STARING AT ME NOW...
...

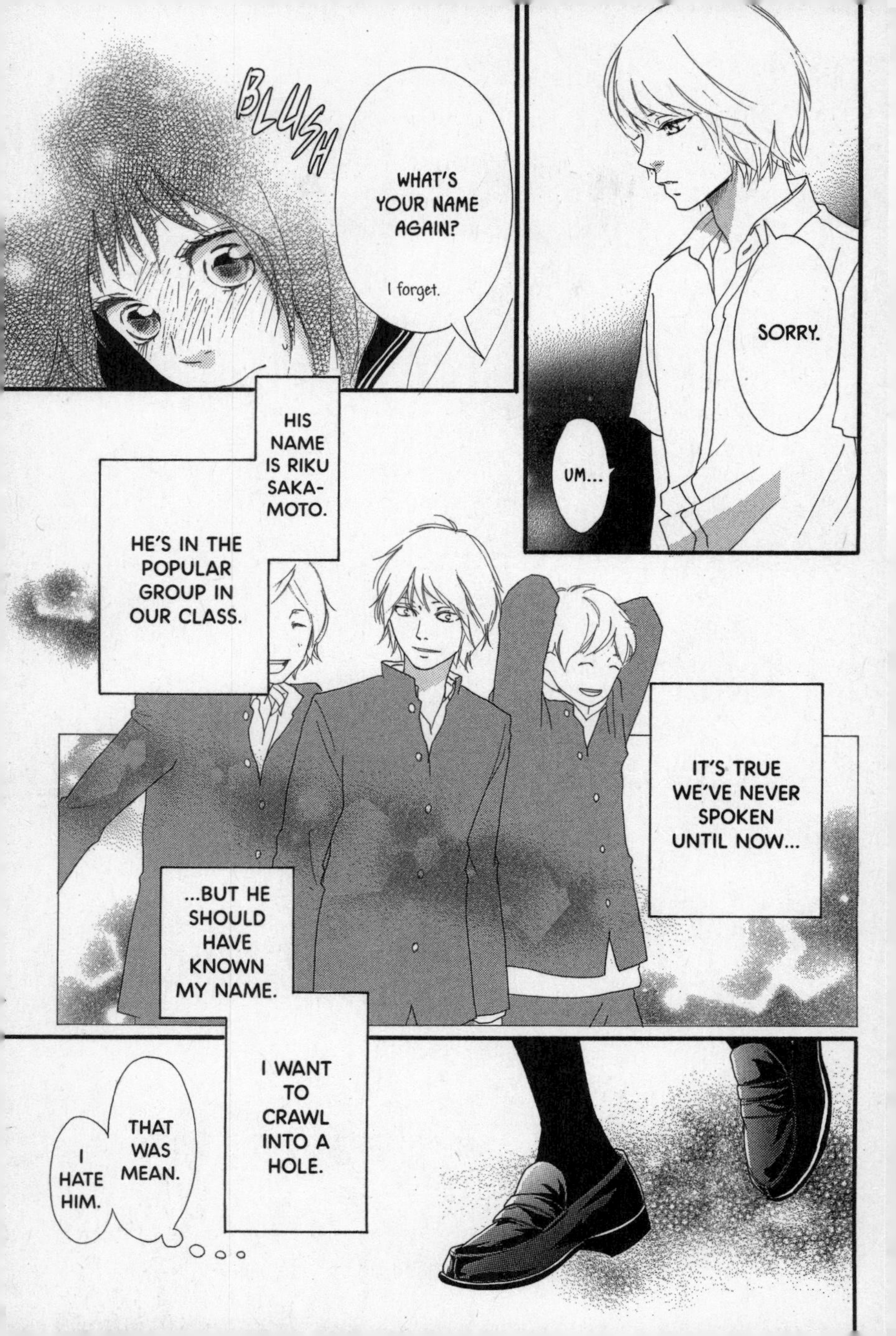
SORRY.
UM...
BLUSH
WHAT'S YOUR NAME AGAIN?
I forget.
HIS NAME IS RIKU SAKA-MOTO.
HE'S IN THE POPULAR GROUP IN OUR CLASS.
IT'S TRUE WE'VE NEVER SPOKEN UNTIL NOW...
...BUT HE SHOULD HAVE KNOWN MY NAME.
I WANT TO CRAWL INTO A HOLE.
THAT WAS MEAN.
I HATE HIM.

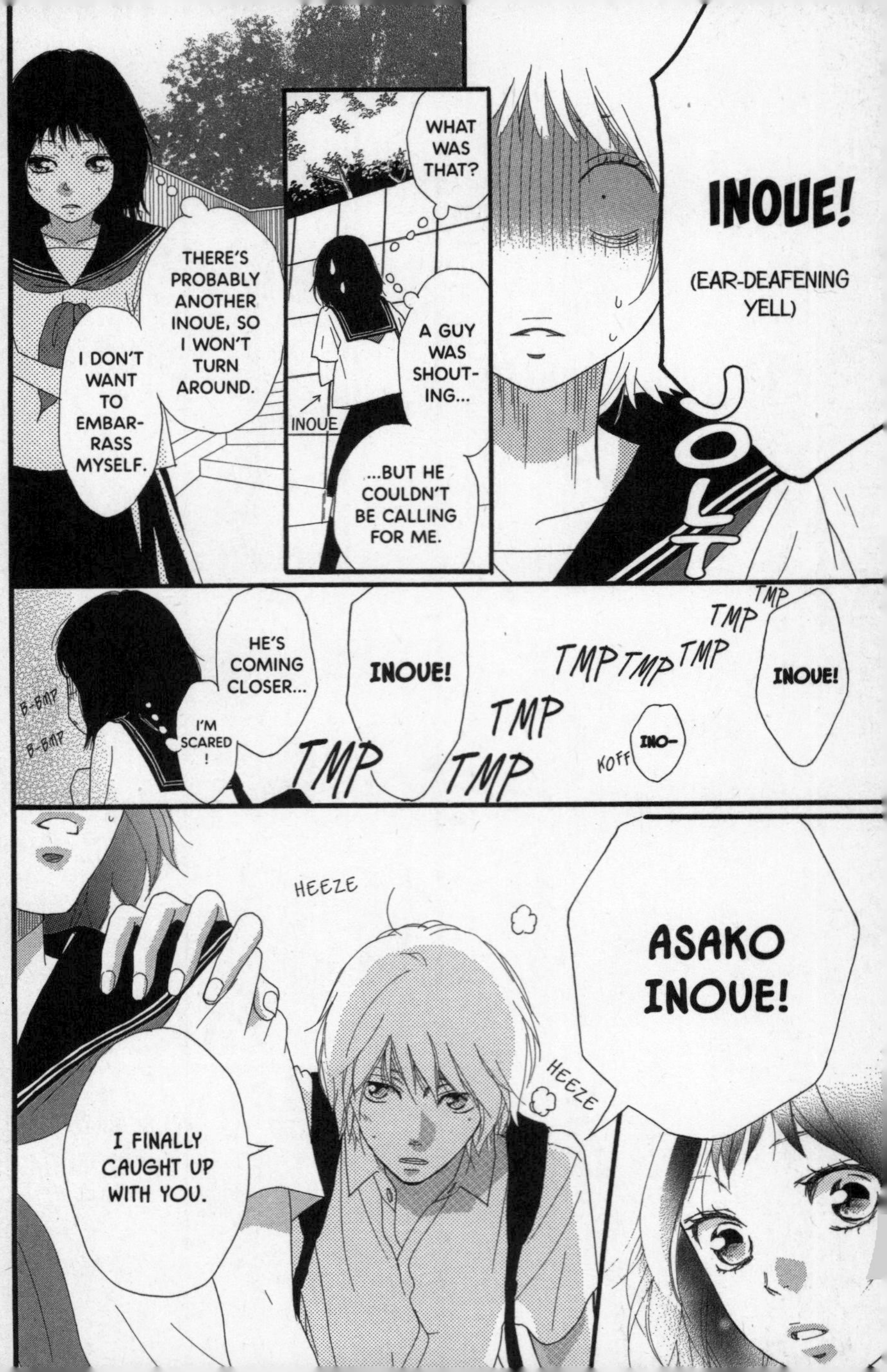
INOUE!
(EAR-DEAFENING YELL)
JOLT
WHAT WAS THAT?
A GUY WAS SHOUT-ING...
...BUT HE COULDN'T BE CALLING FOR ME.
INOUE
THERE'S PROBABLY ANOTHER INOUE, SO I WON'T TURN AROUND.
I DON'T WANT TO EMBAR-RASS MYSELF.
TMP TMP TMP
INOUE!
INO-
KOFF
TMP TMP TMP TMP TMP TMP
INOUE!
HE'S COMING CLOSER...
I'M SCARED!
B-BMP
B-BMP
ASAKO INOUE!
HEEZE
HEEZE
I FINALLY CAUGHT UP WITH YOU.

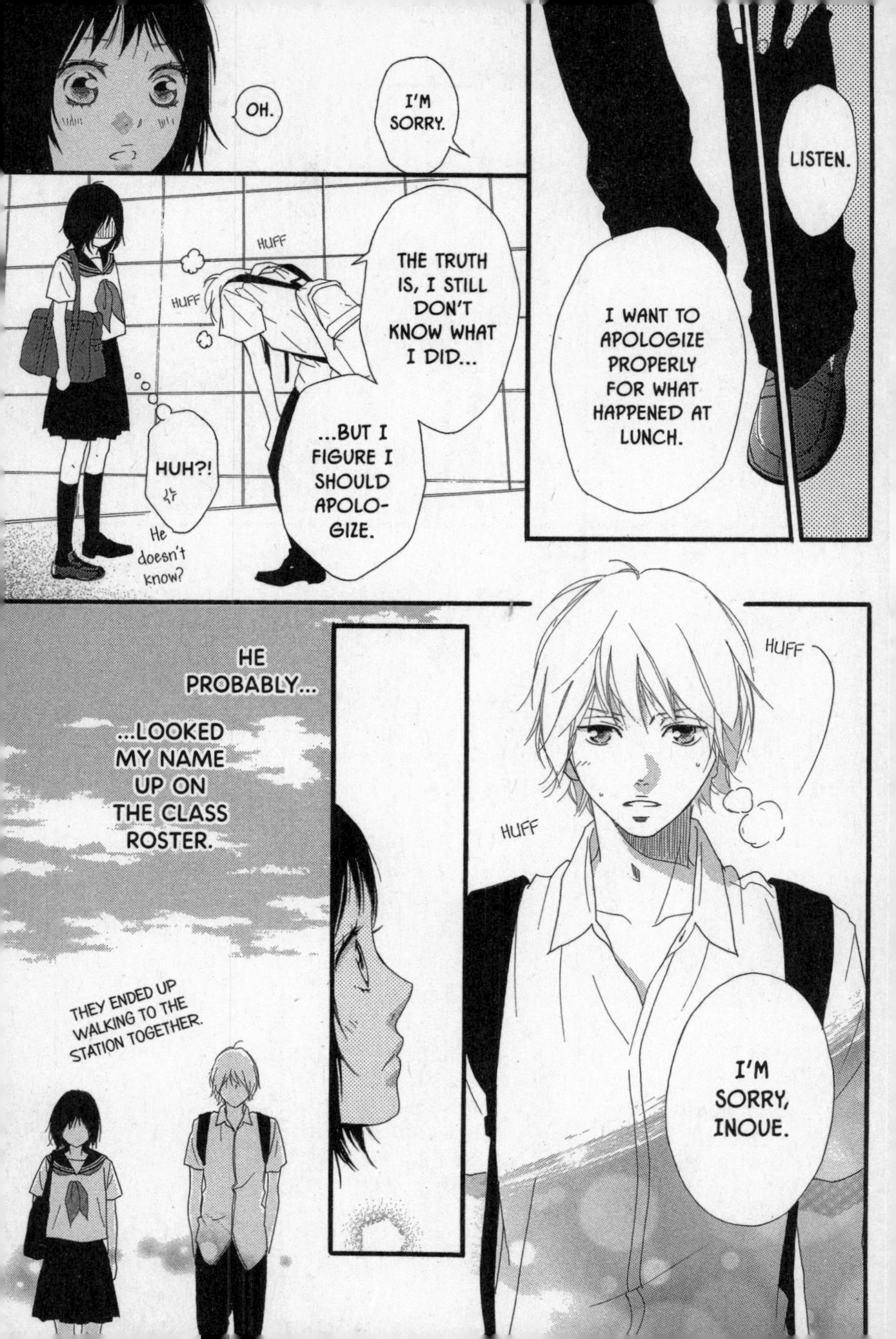
LISTEN.
I WANT TO APOLOGIZE PROPERLY FOR WHAT HAPPENED AT LUNCH.
I'M SORRY.
OH.
THE TRUTH IS, I STILL DON'T KNOW WHAT I DID...
...BUT I FIGURE I SHOULD APOLO-GIZE.
HUFF
HUFF
HUH?!
He doesn't know?
HUFF
HUFF
I'M SORRY, INOUE.
HE PROBABLY...
...LOOKED MY NAME UP ON THE CLASS ROSTER.
THEY ENDED UP WALKING TO THE STATION TOGETHER.

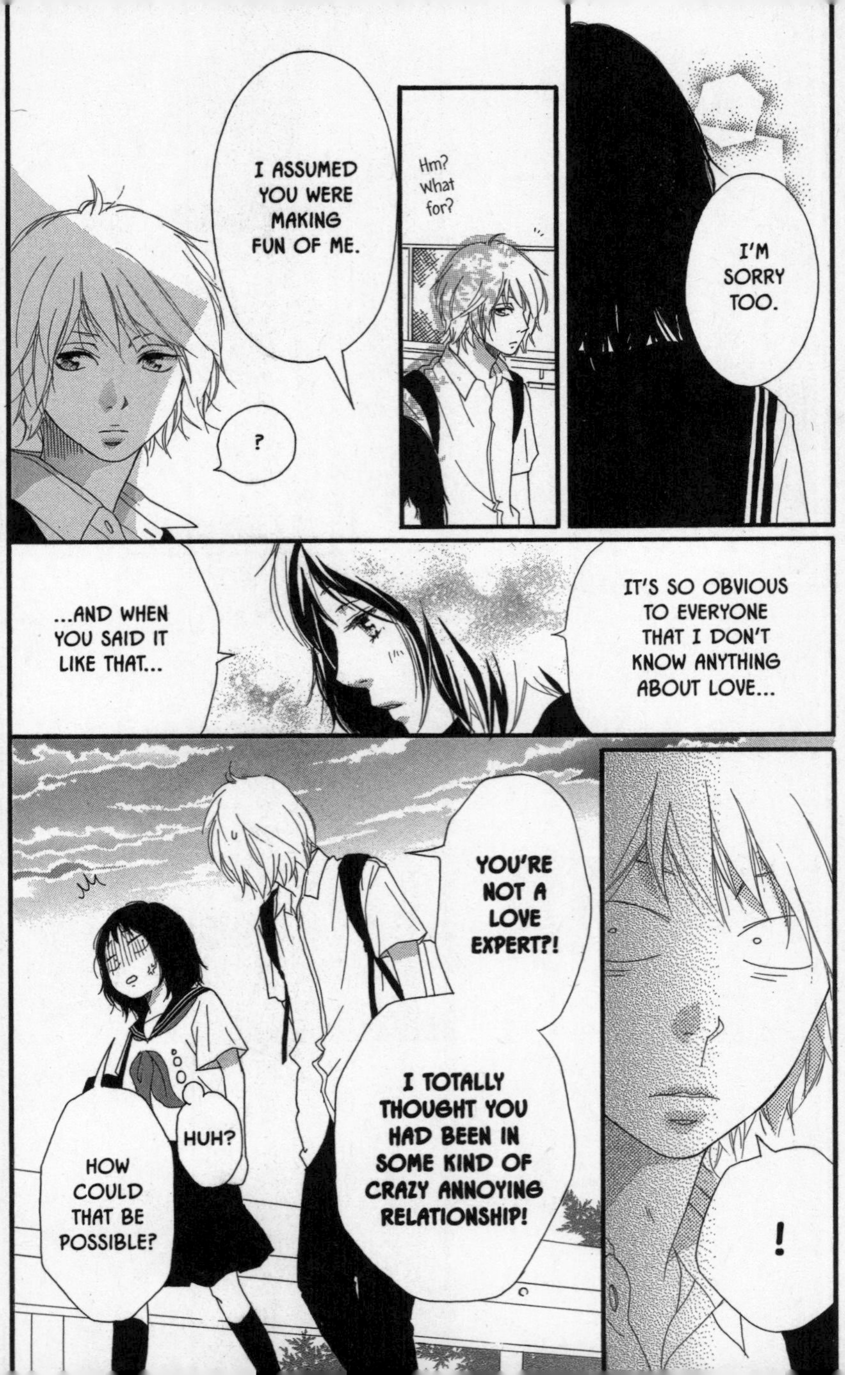
I'M SORRY TOO.
Hm? What for?
I ASSUMED YOU WERE MAKING FUN OF ME.
?
IT'S SO OBVIOUS TO EVERYONE THAT I DON'T KNOW ANYTHING ABOUT LOVE...
...AND WHEN YOU SAID IT LIKE THAT...
!
YOU'RE NOT A LOVE EXPERT?!
I TOTALLY THOUGHT YOU HAD BEEN IN SOME KIND OF CRAZY ANNOYING RELATIONSHIP!
HUH?
HOW COULD THAT BE POSSIBLE?

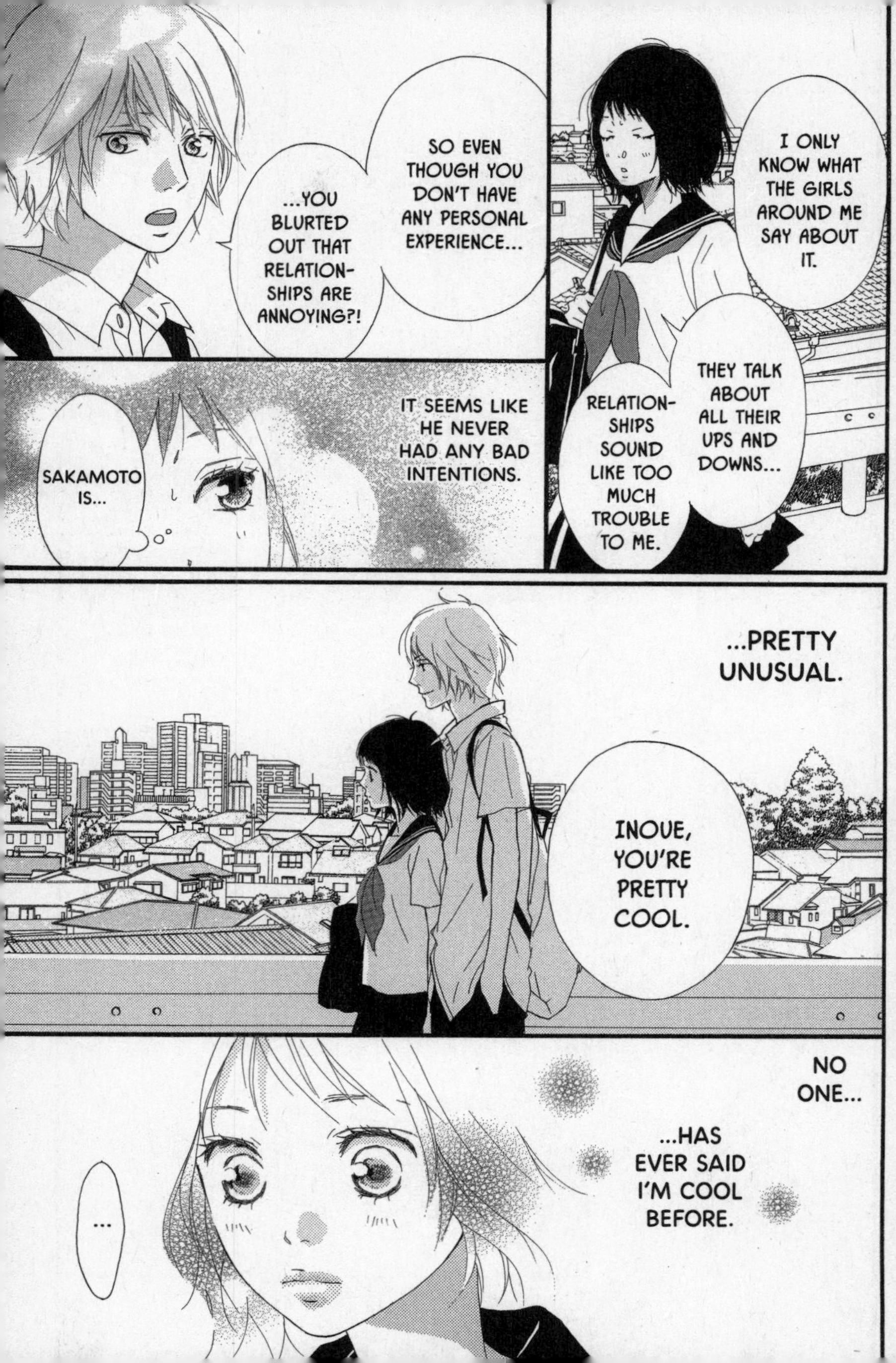
I ONLY KNOW WHAT THE GIRLS AROUND ME SAY ABOUT IT.
THEY TALK ABOUT ALL THEIR UPS AND DOWNS...
RELATIONSHIPS SOUND LIKE TOO MUCH TROUBLE TO ME.
SO EVEN THOUGH YOU DON'T HAVE ANY PERSONAL EXPERIENCE...
...YOU BLURTED OUT THAT RELATIONSHIPS ARE ANNOYING?!
IT SEEMS LIKE HE NEVER HAD ANY BAD INTENTIONS.
SAKAMOTO IS...
...PRETTY UNUSUAL.
INOUE, YOU'RE PRETTY COOL.
NO ONE...
...HAS EVER SAID I'M COOL BEFORE.
...

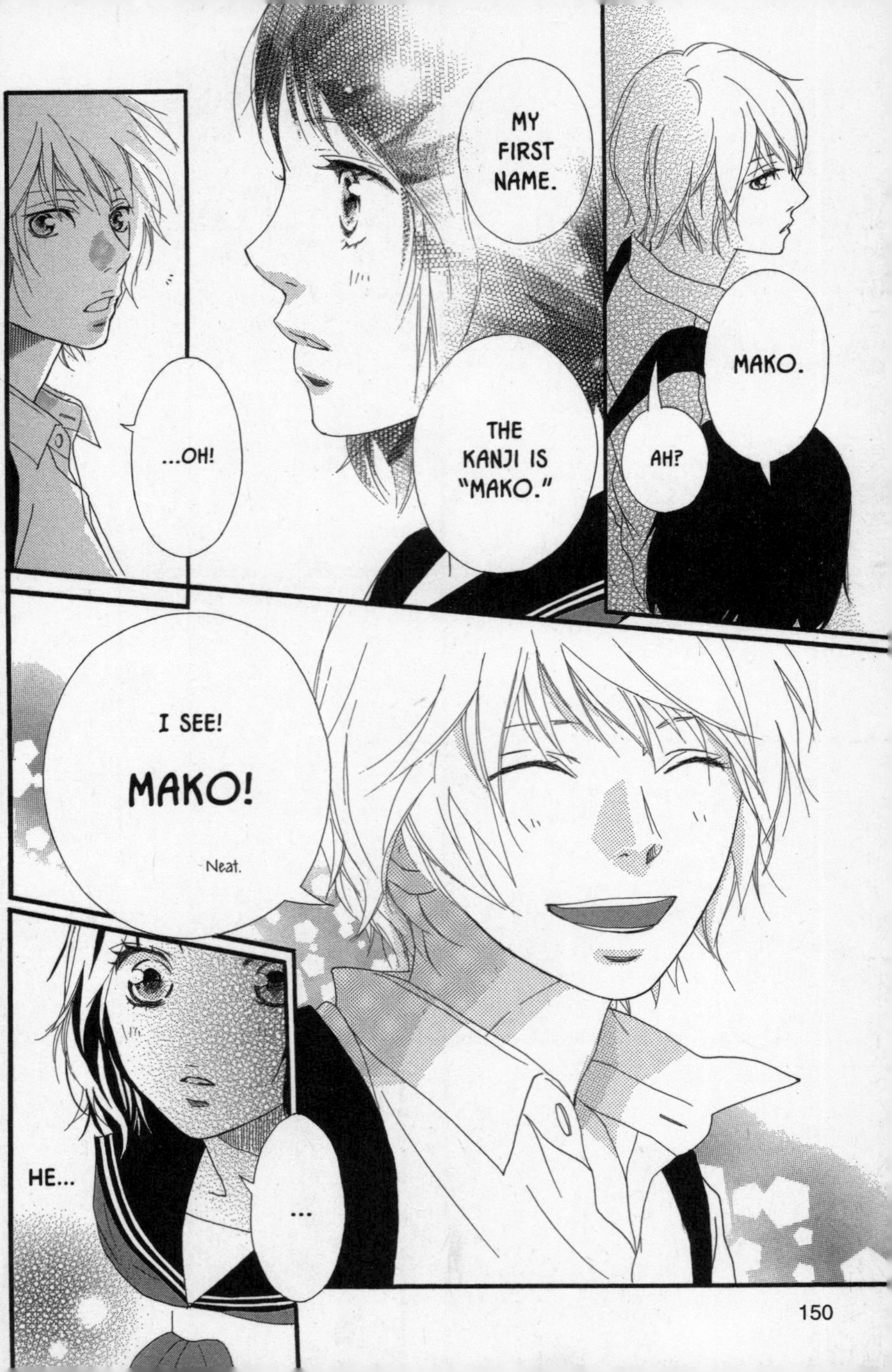
MAKO.
AH?
MY FIRST NAME.
THE KANJI IS "MAKO."
...OH!
I SEE! MAKO!
Neat.
...
HE...

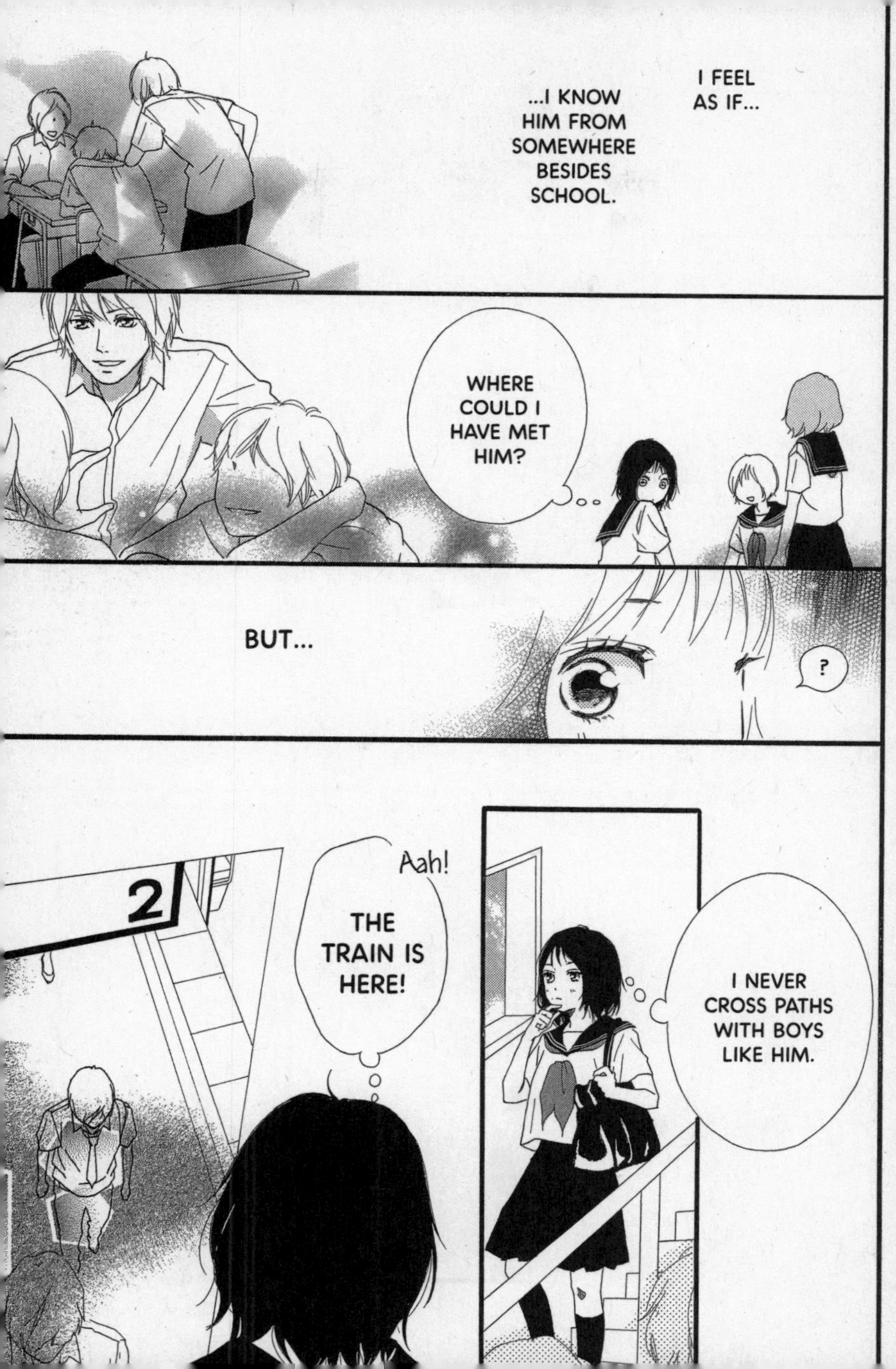
I FEEL AS IF...
...I KNOW HIM FROM SOMEWHERE BESIDES SCHOOL.
WHERE COULD I HAVE MET HIM?
?
BUT...
I NEVER CROSS PATHS WITH BOYS LIKE HIM.
Aah!
THE TRAIN IS HERE!
2

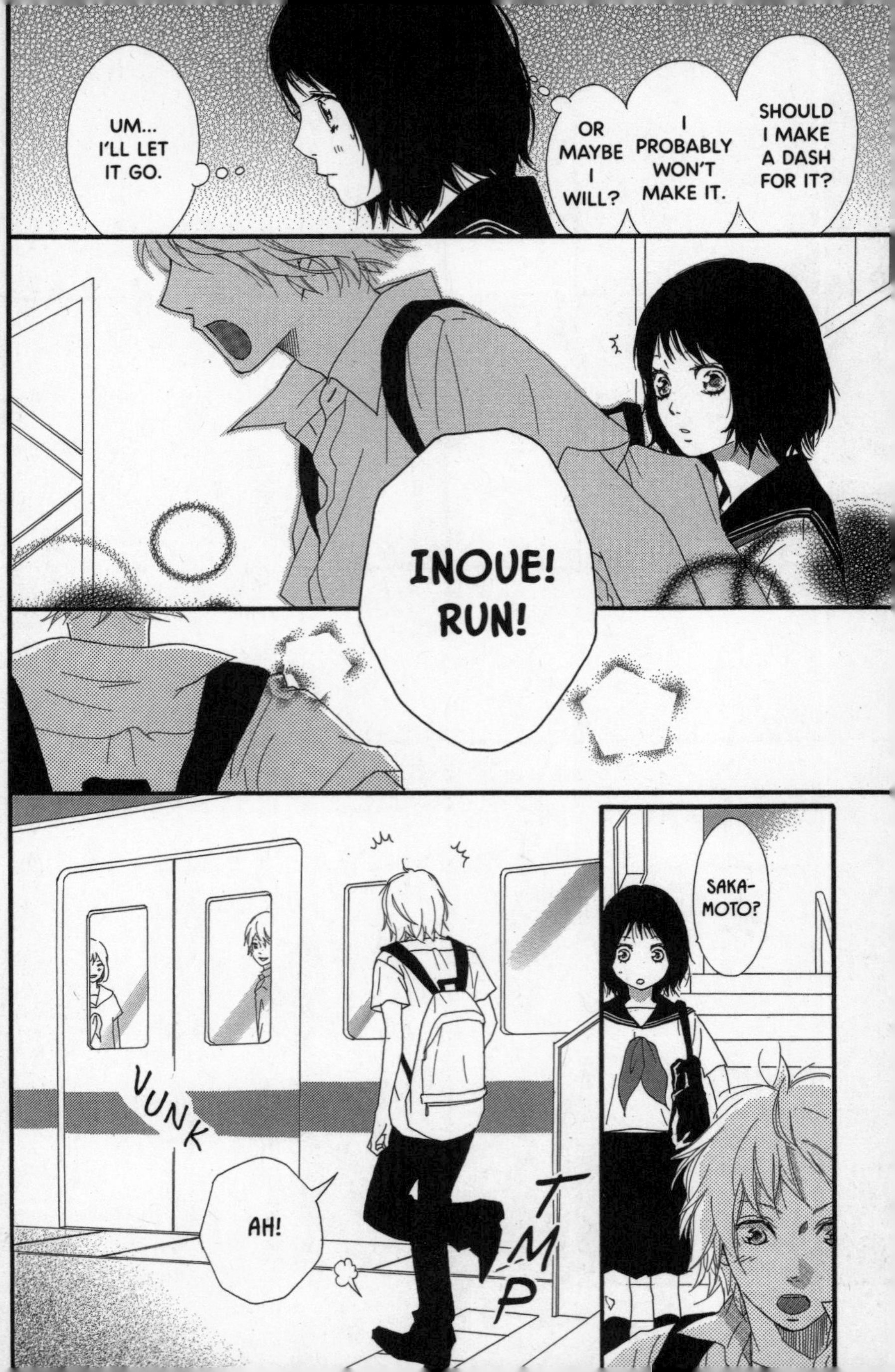
SHOULD I MAKE A DASH FOR IT?
I PROBABLY WON'T MAKE IT.
OR MAYBE I WILL?
UM... I'LL LET IT GO.
INOUE! RUN!
SAKA-MOTO?
VUNK
TMP
AH!

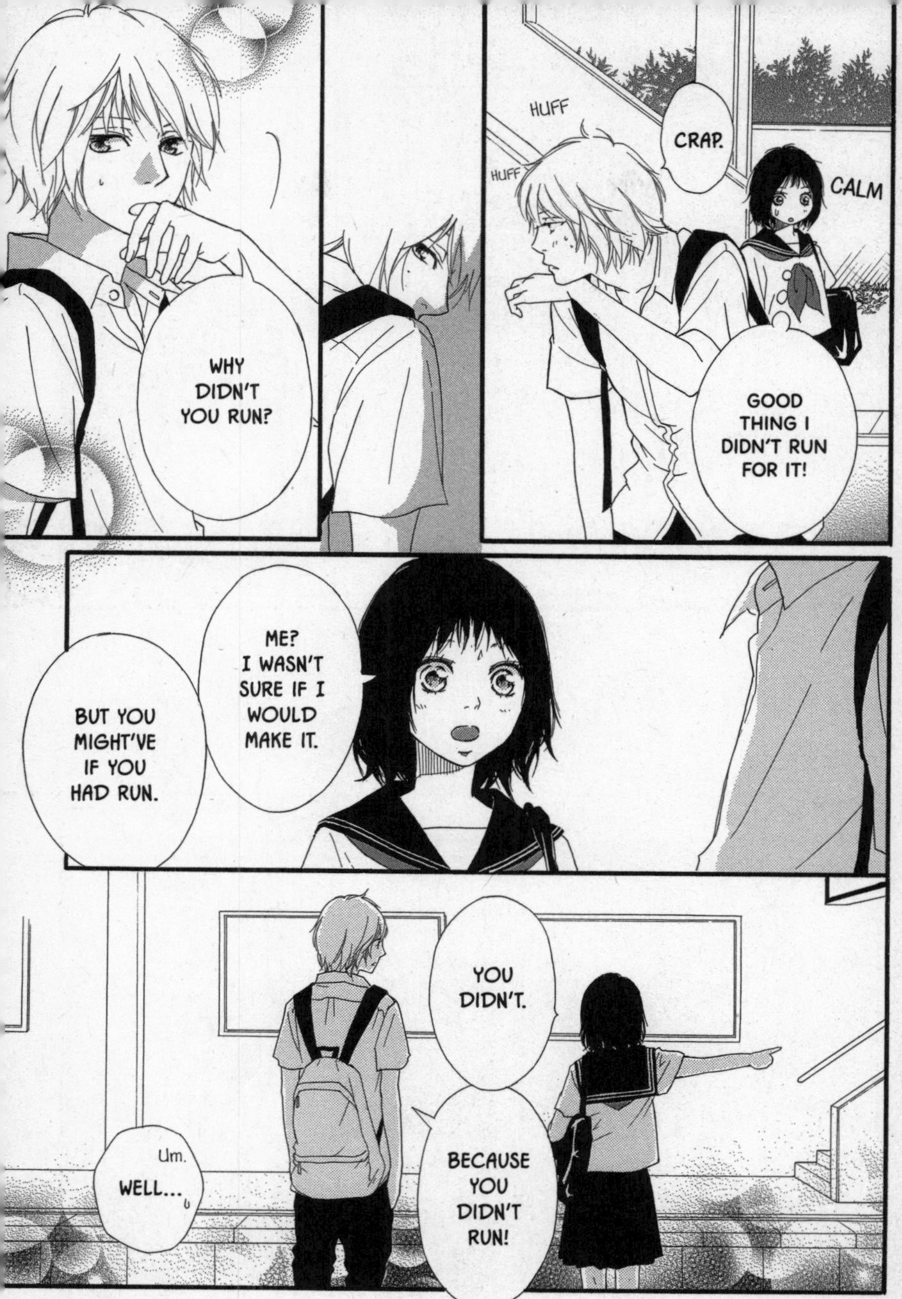

HUFF
HUFF
CRAP.
CALM
GOOD THING I DIDN'T RUN FOR IT!
WHY DIDN'T YOU RUN?
ME? I WASN'T SURE IF I WOULD MAKE IT.
BUT YOU MIGHT'VE IF YOU HAD RUN.
YOU DIDN'T.
BECAUSE YOU DIDN'T RUN!
Um.
WELL...

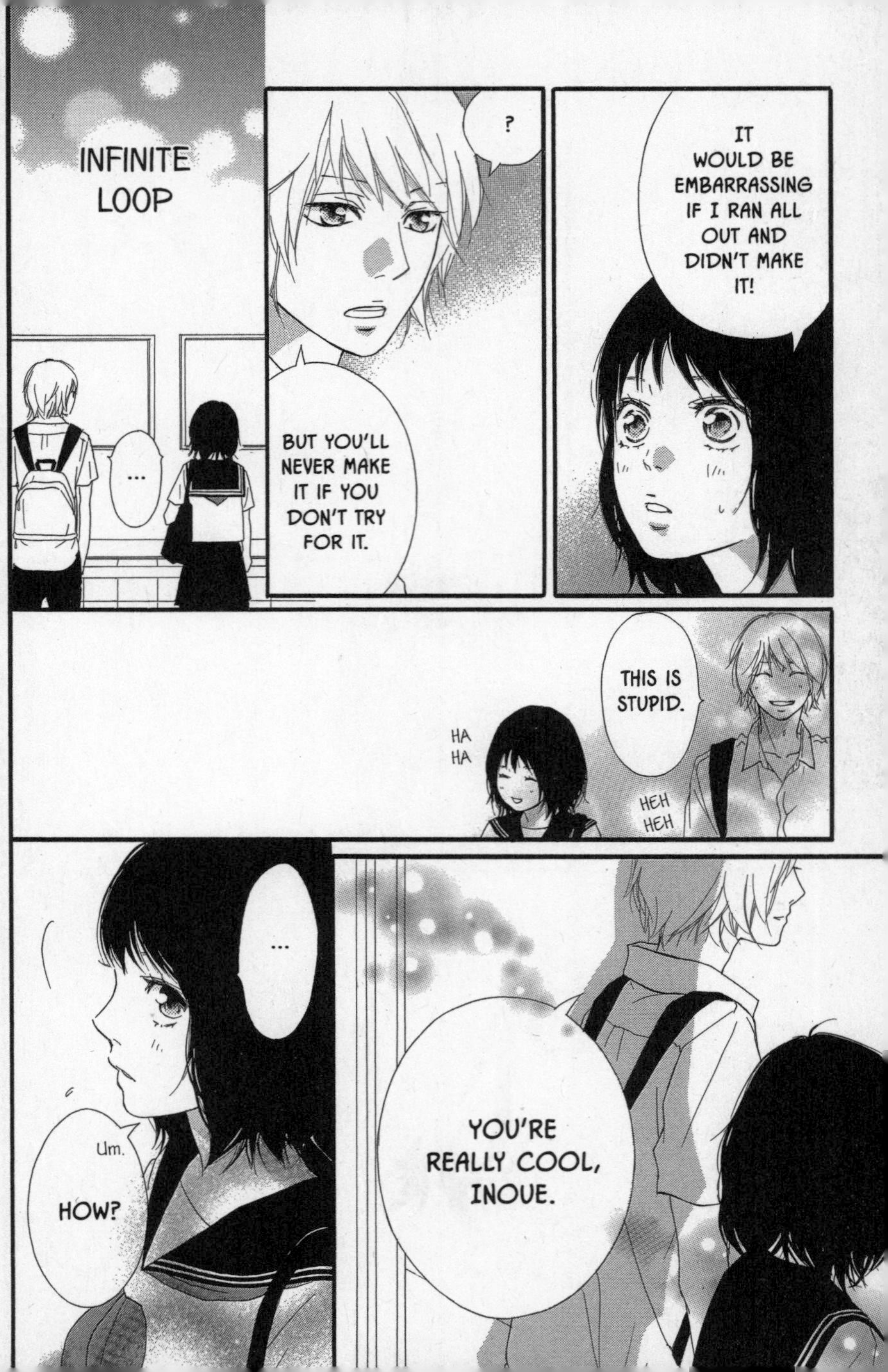
IT WOULD BE EMBARRASSING IF I RAN ALL OUT AND DIDN'T MAKE IT!
?
BUT YOU'LL NEVER MAKE IT IF YOU DON'T TRY FOR IT.
INFINITE LOOP
...
THIS IS STUPID.
HEH HEH
HA HA
YOU'RE REALLY COOL, INOUE.
...
Um.
HOW?

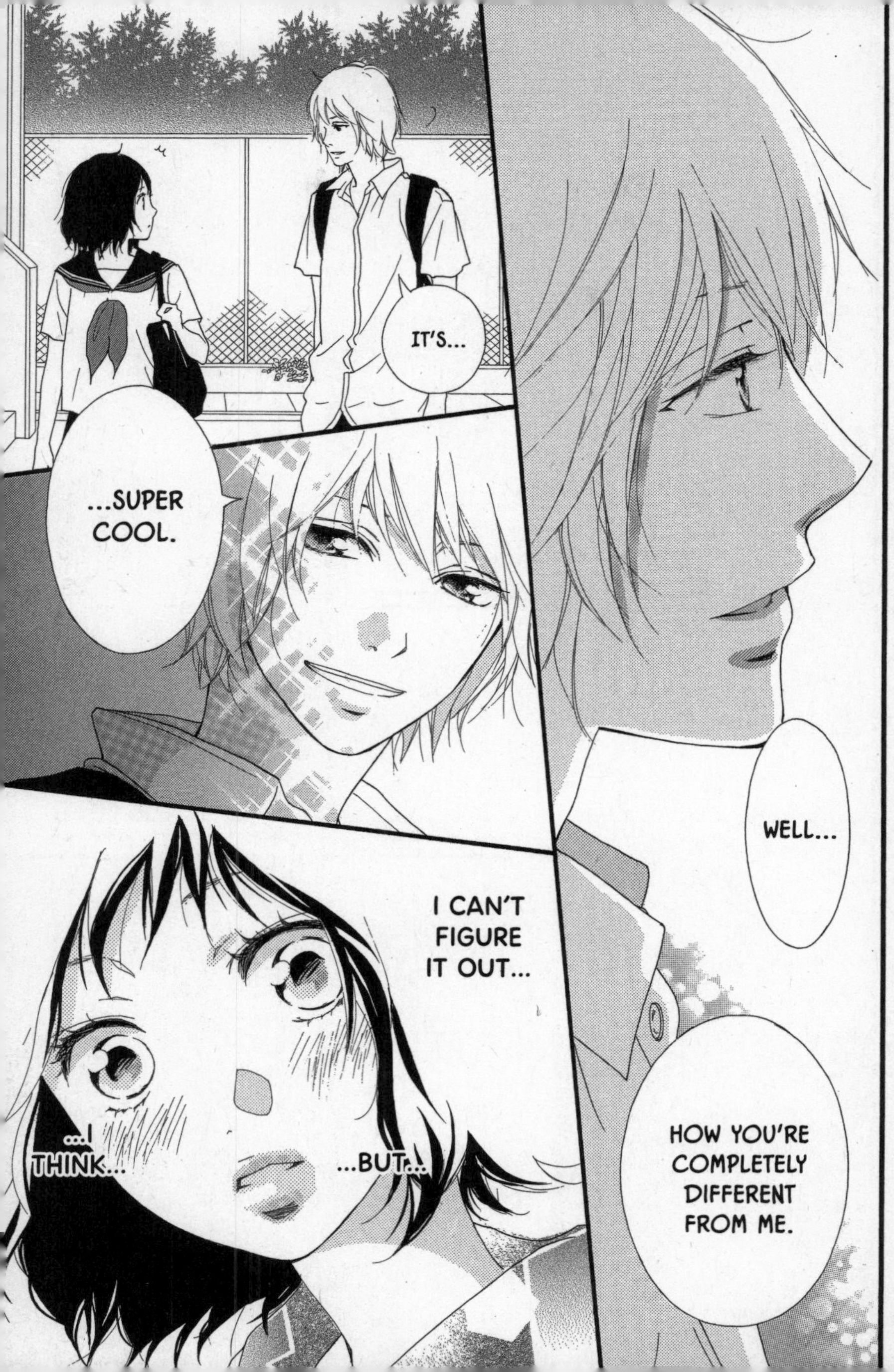
WELL...
HOW YOU'RE COMPLETELY DIFFERENT FROM ME.
IT'S...
...SUPER COOL.
I CAN'T FIGURE IT OUT...
...BUT...
...I THINK...

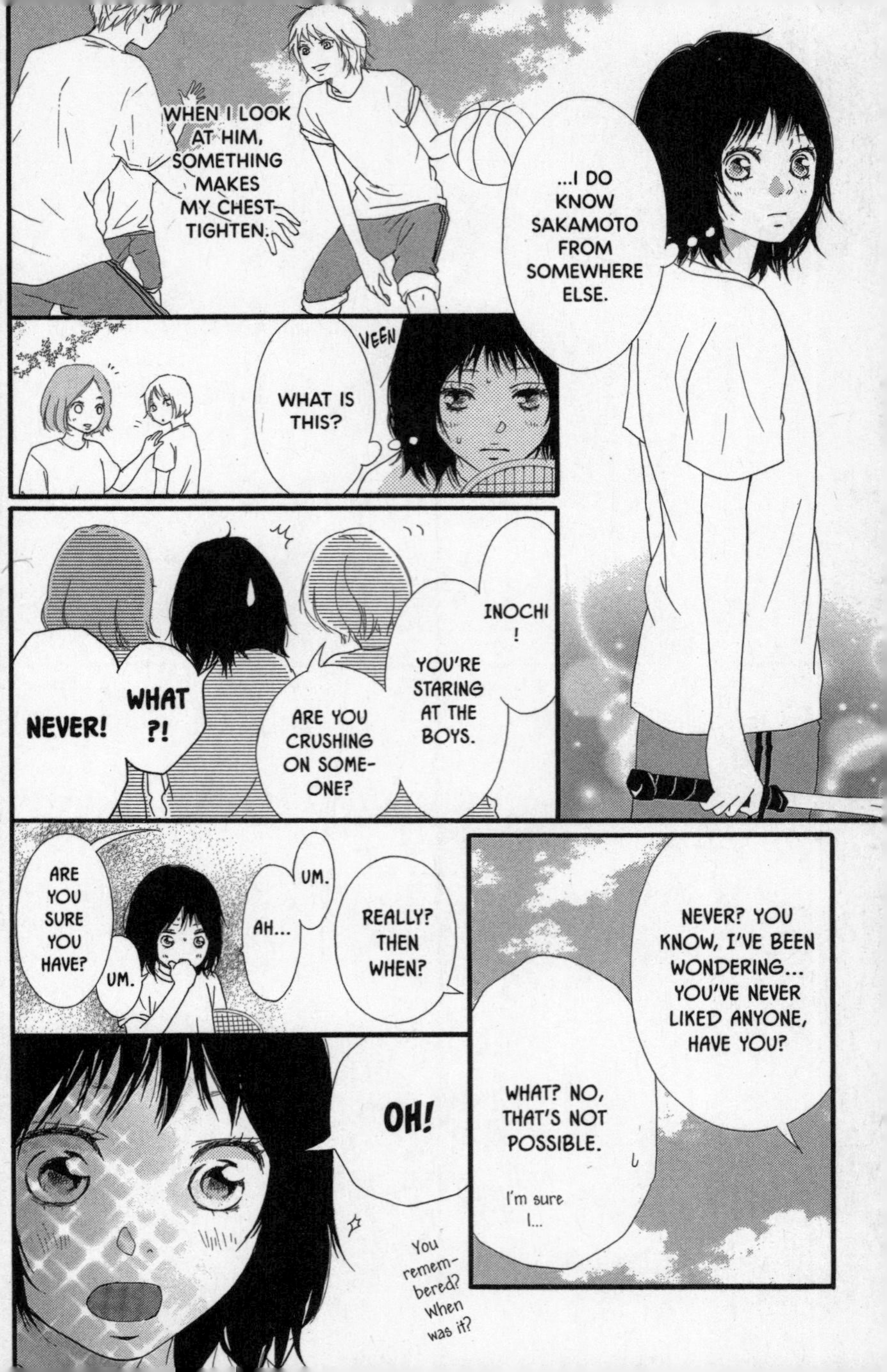
...I DO KNOW SAKAMOTO FROM SOMEWHERE ELSE.
WHEN I LOOK AT HIM, SOMETHING MAKES MY CHEST TIGHTEN.
VEEN
WHAT IS THIS?
INOCHI!
YOU'RE STARING AT THE BOYS.
ARE YOU CRUSHING ON SOME-ONE?
WHAT?!
NEVER!
NEVER? YOU KNOW, I'VE BEEN WONDERING... YOU'VE NEVER LIKED ANYONE, HAVE YOU?
WHAT? NO, THAT'S NOT POSSIBLE.
I'm sure I...
UM.
REALLY? THEN WHEN?
AH...
ARE YOU SURE YOU HAVE?
UM.
OH!
You remem-bered? When was it?

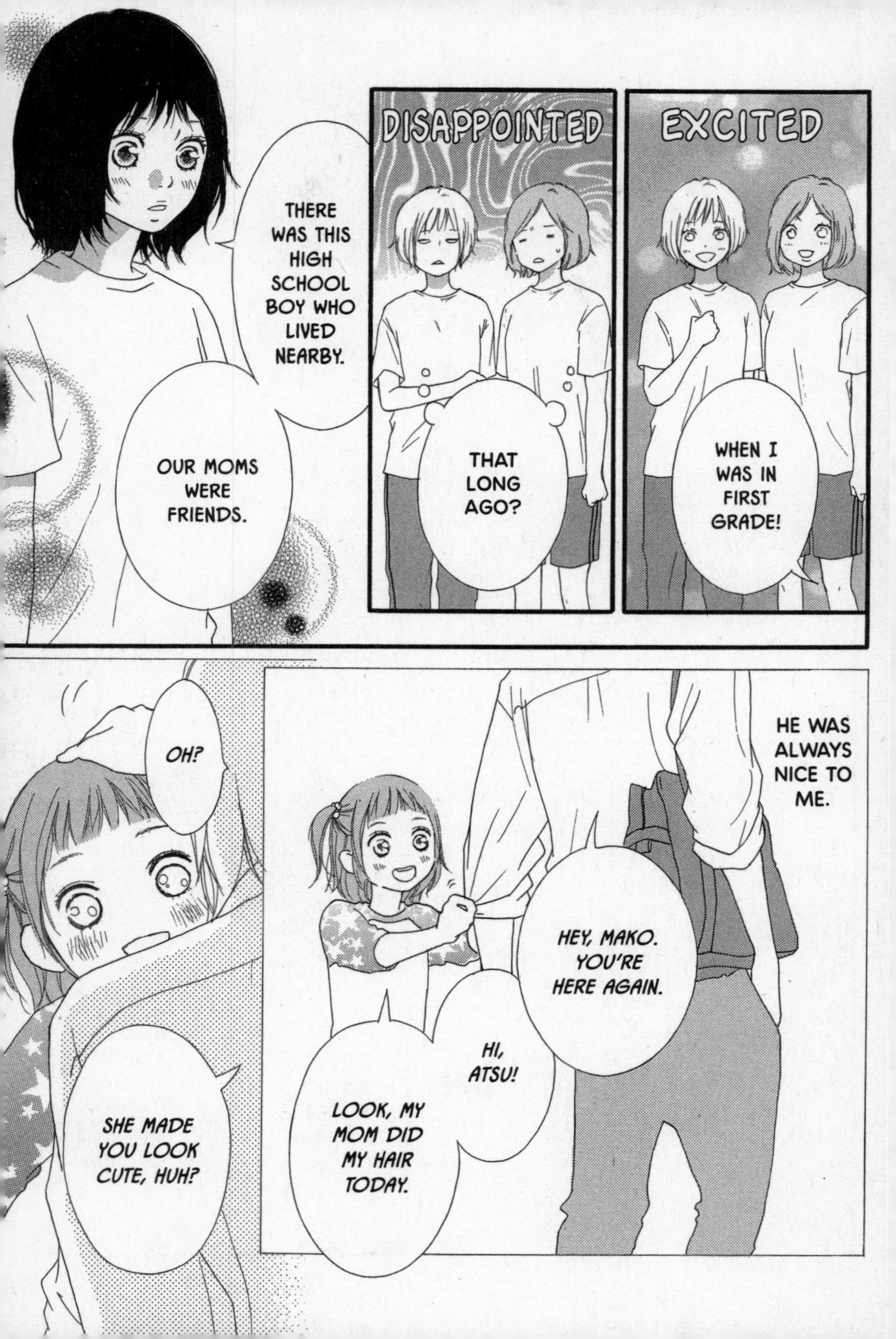
EXCITED
WHEN I WAS IN FIRST GRADE!
DISAPPOINTED
THAT LONG AGO?
THERE WAS THIS HIGH SCHOOL BOY WHO LIVED NEARBY.
OUR MOMS WERE FRIENDS.
HE WAS ALWAYS NICE TO ME.
HEY, MAKO. YOU'RE HERE AGAIN.
HI, ATSU!
LOOK, MY MOM DID MY HAIR TODAY.
OH?
SHE MADE YOU LOOK CUTE, HUH?

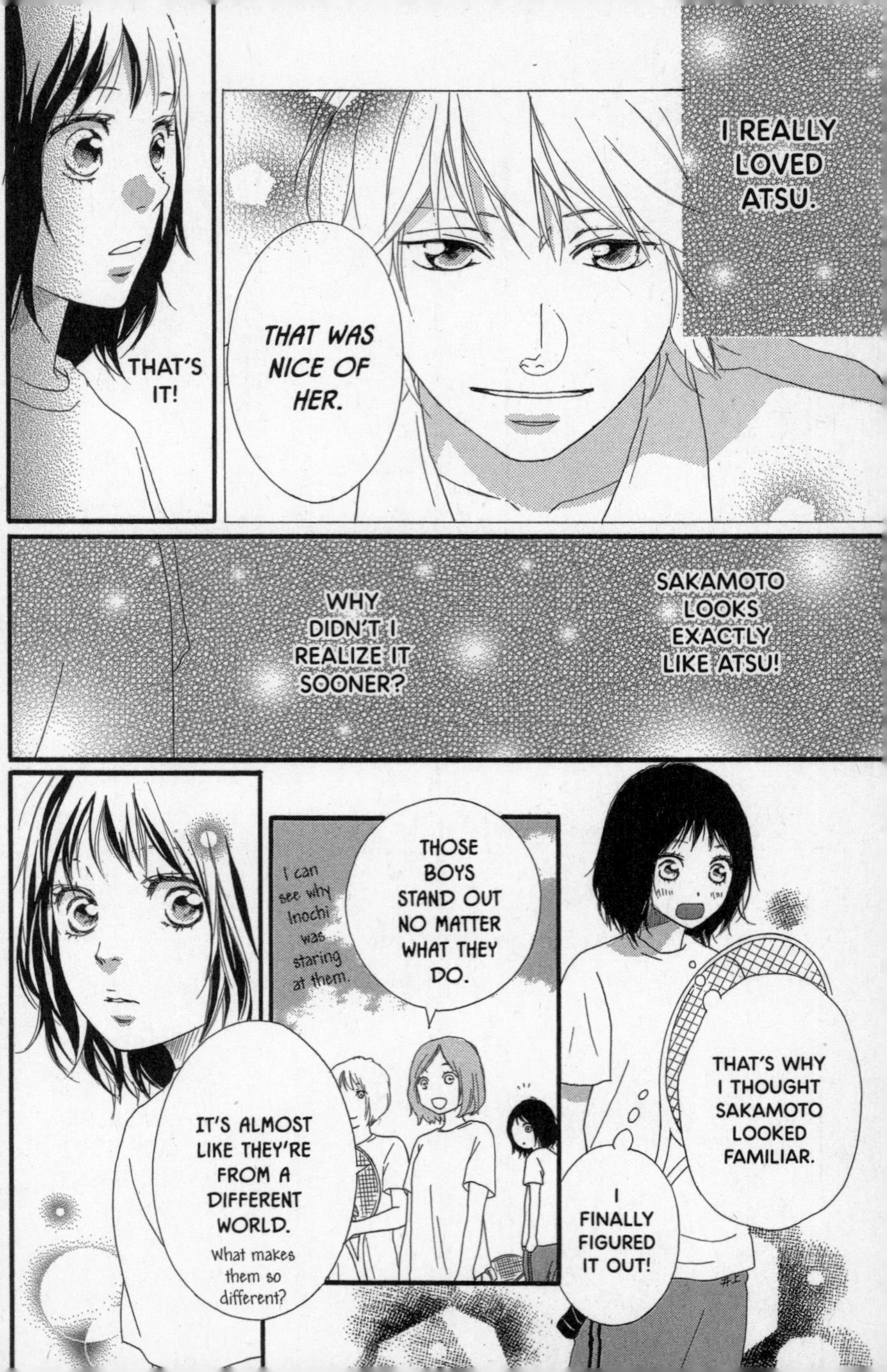
I REALLY LOVED ATSU.
THAT WAS NICE OF HER.
THAT'S IT!
SAKAMOTO LOOKS EXACTLY LIKE ATSU!
WHY DIDN'T I REALIZE IT SOONER?
THAT'S WHY I THOUGHT SAKAMOTO LOOKED FAMILIAR.
I FINALLY FIGURED IT OUT!
THOSE BOYS STAND OUT NO MATTER WHAT THEY DO.
I can see why Inochi was staring at them.
IT'S ALMOST LIKE THEY'RE FROM A DIFFERENT WORLD.
What makes them so different?

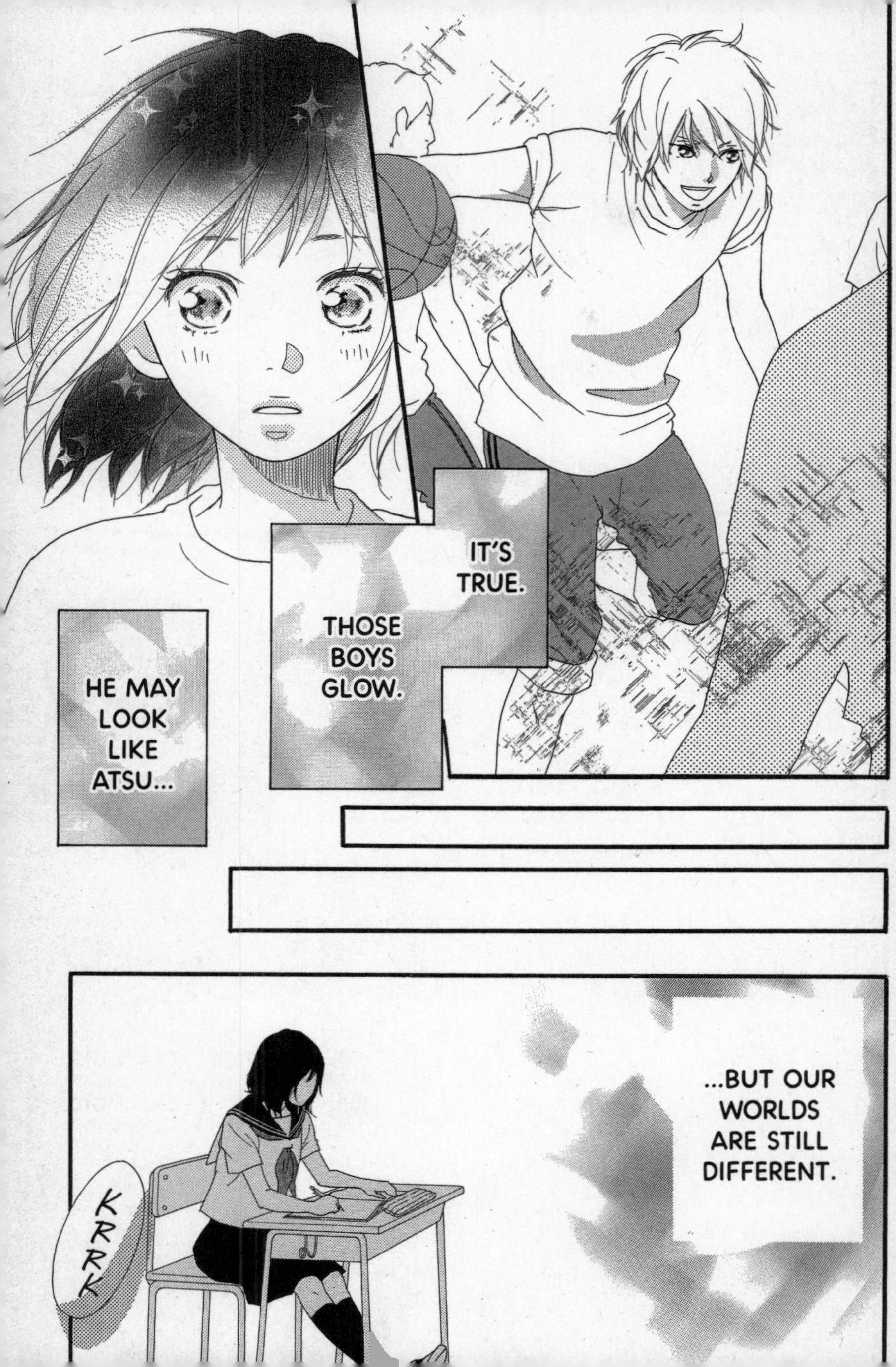
IT'S TRUE.
THOSE BOYS GLOW.
HE MAY LOOK LIKE ATSU...
...BUT OUR WORLDS ARE STILL DIFFERENT.
KRRK

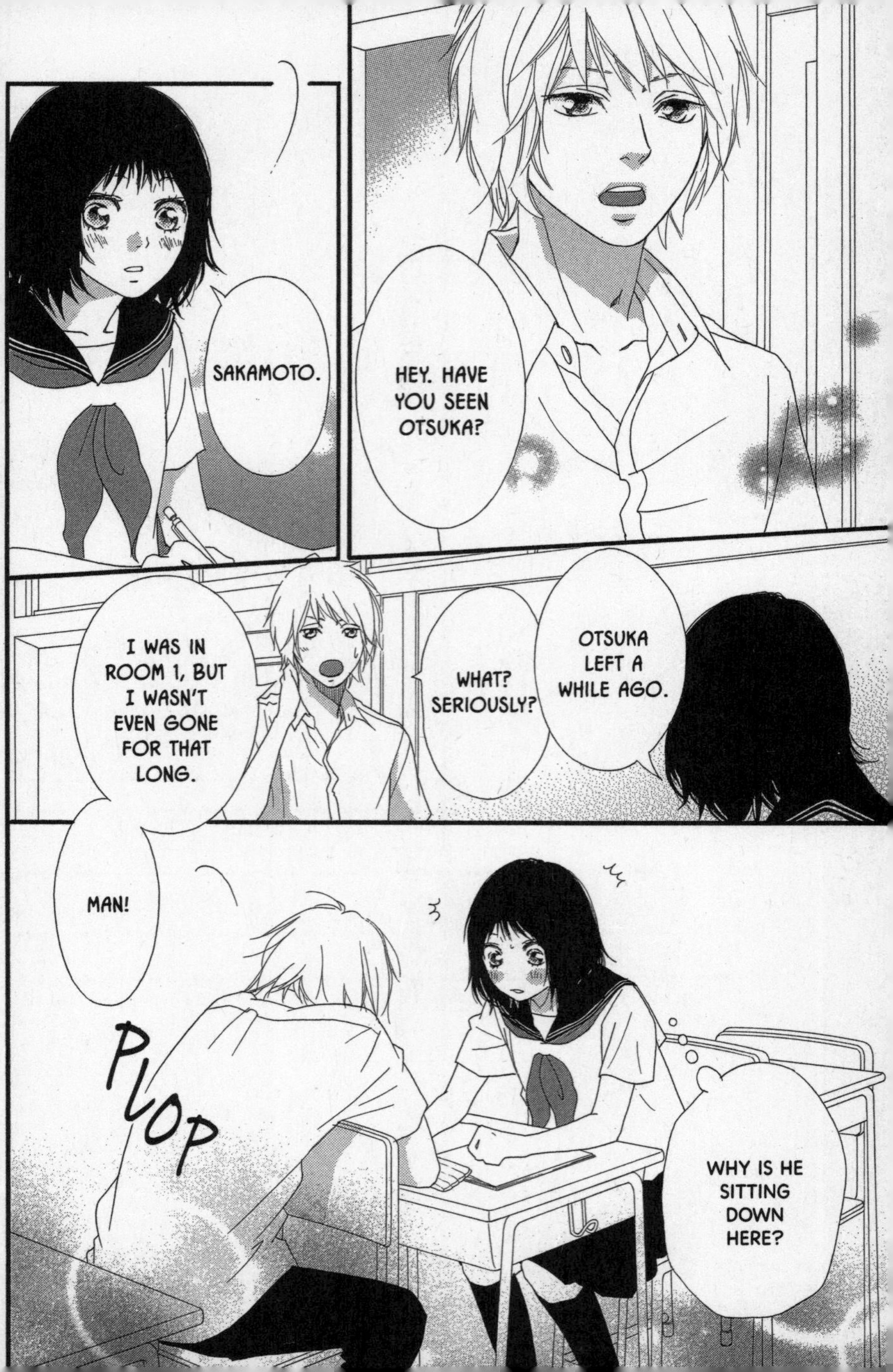
HEY. HAVE YOU SEEN OTSUKA?
SAKAMOTO.
OTSUKA LEFT A WHILE AGO.
WHAT? SERIOUSLY?
I WAS IN ROOM 1, BUT I WASN'T EVEN GONE FOR THAT LONG.
MAN!
PLOP
WHY IS HE SITTING DOWN HERE?

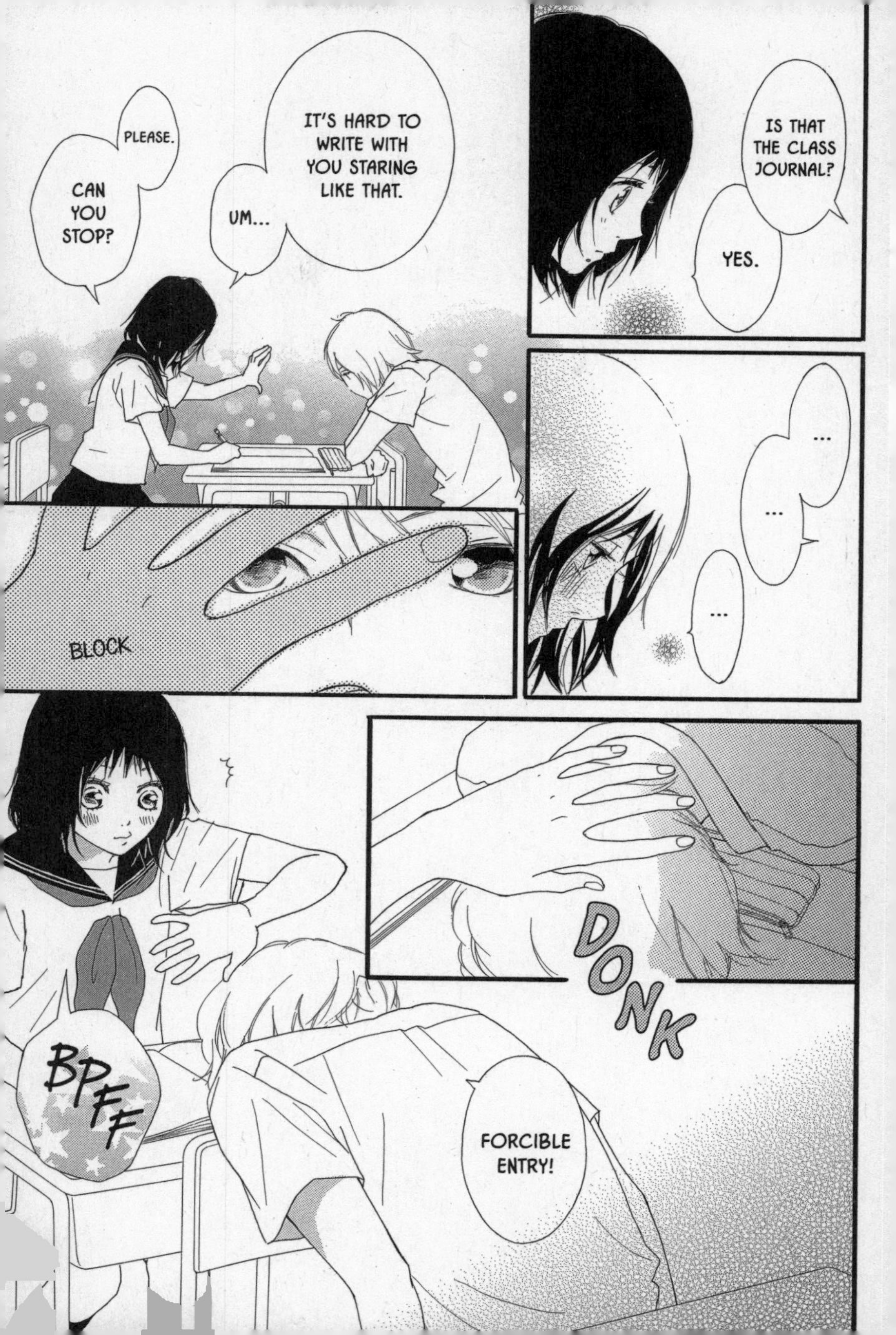
IS THAT THE CLASS JOURNAL?
YES.
UM...
IT'S HARD TO WRITE WITH YOU STARING LIKE THAT.
PLEASE.
CAN YOU STOP?
...
...
...
BLOCK
DONK
FORCIBLE ENTRY!
BPFF

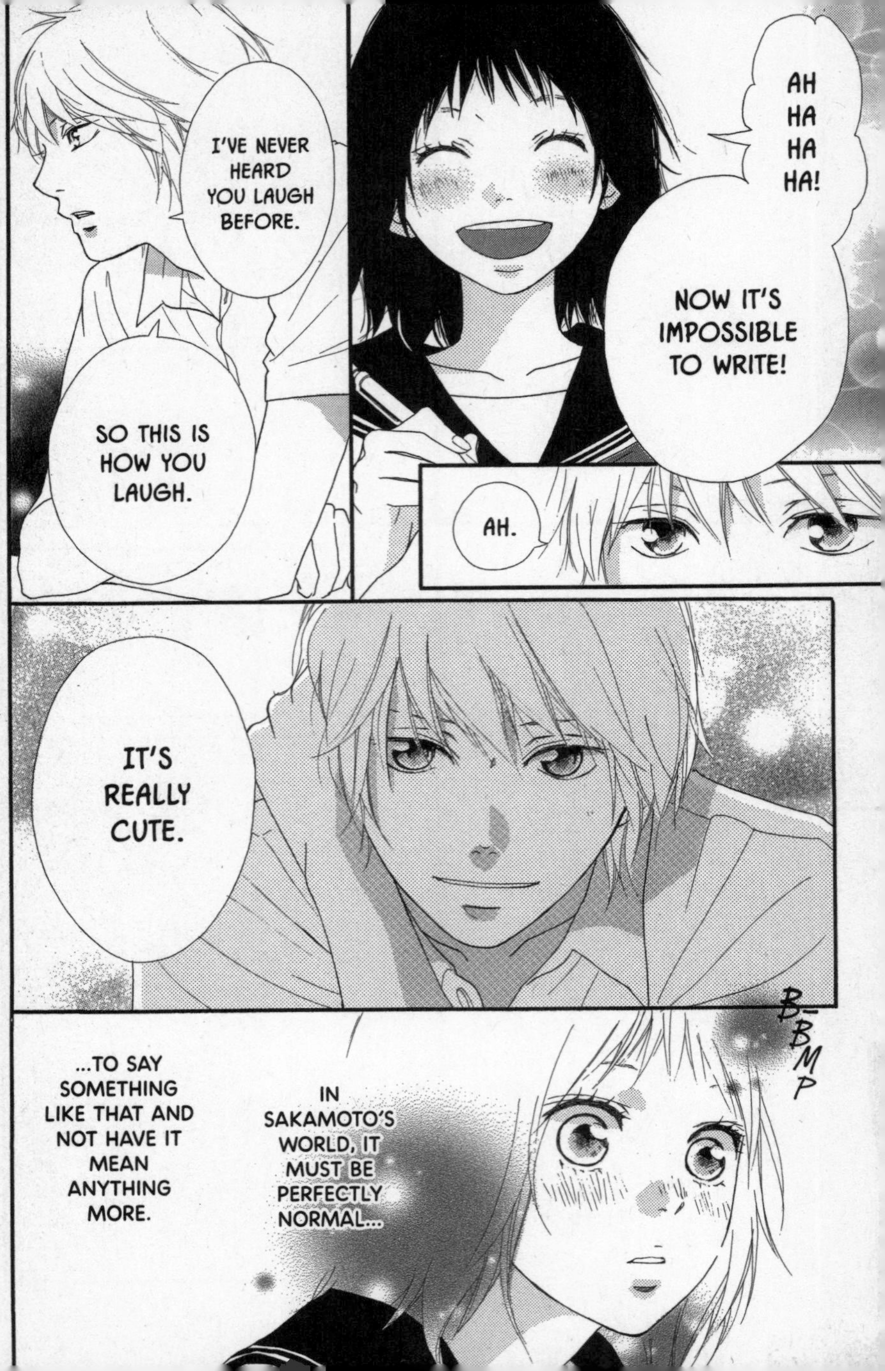
AH HA HA HA!
NOW IT'S IMPOSSIBLE TO WRITE!
AH.
I'VE NEVER HEARD YOU LAUGH BEFORE.
SO THIS IS HOW YOU LAUGH.
IT'S REALLY CUTE.
B-BMP
IN SAKAMOTO'S WORLD, IT MUST BE PERFECTLY NORMAL...
...TO SAY SOMETHING LIKE THAT AND NOT HAVE IT MEAN ANYTHING MORE.

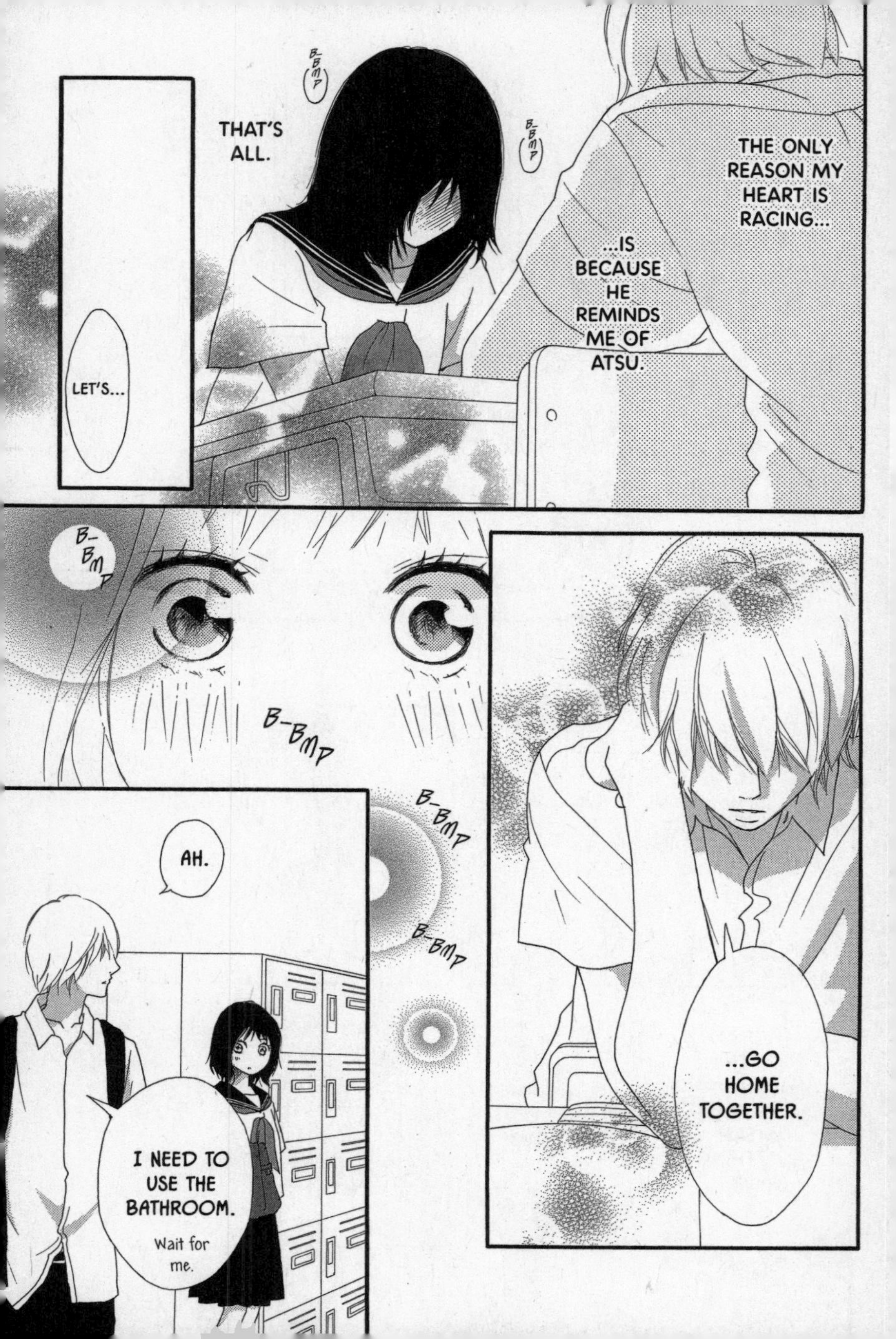
THE ONLY REASON MY HEART IS RACING...
...IS BECAUSE HE REMINDS ME OF ATSU.
B-BMP
THAT'S ALL.
B-BMP
LET'S...
...GO HOME TOGETHER.
B-BMP
B-BMP
B-BMP
B-BMP
AH.
I NEED TO USE THE BATHROOM.
Wait for me.

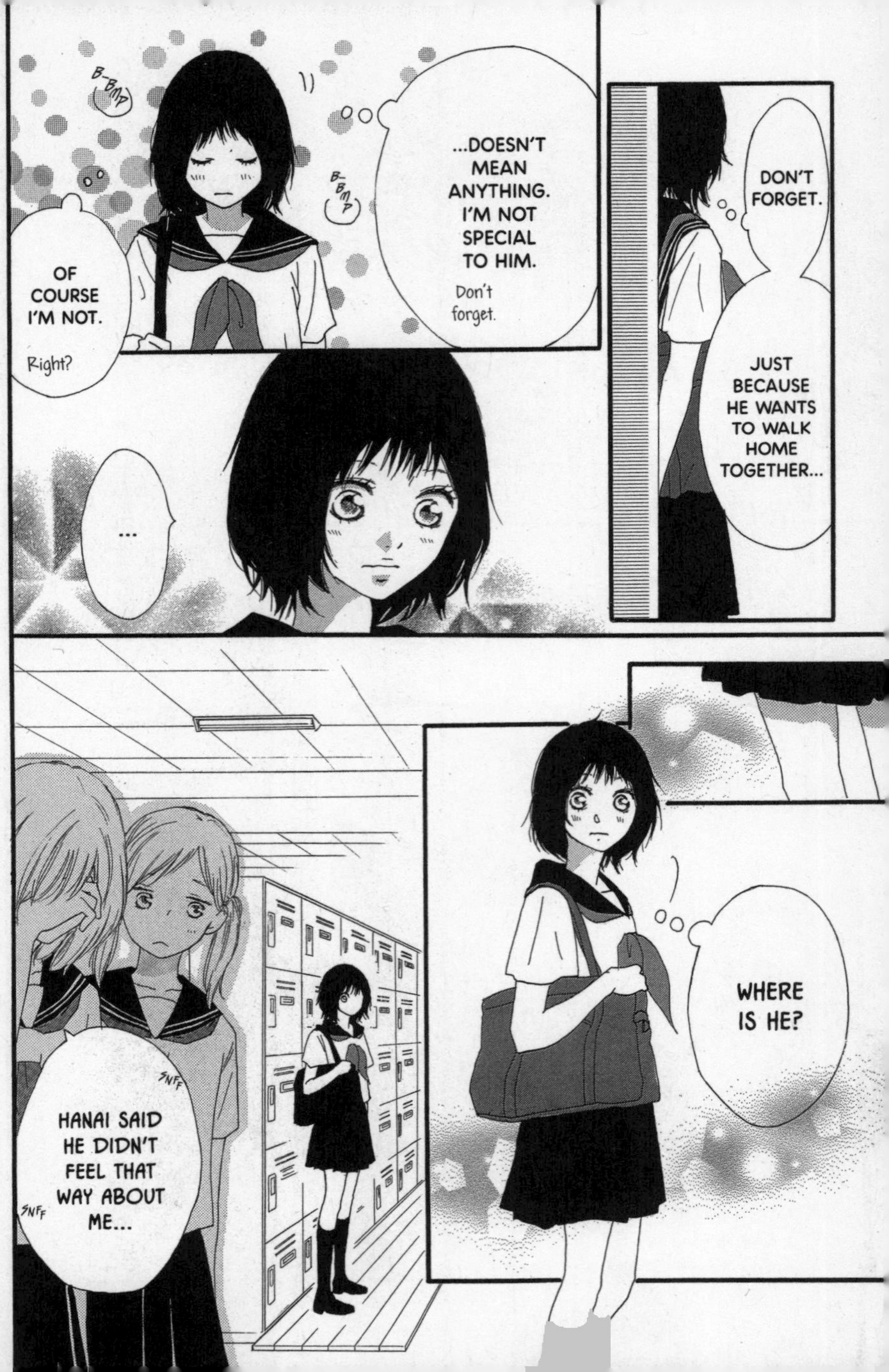
DON'T FORGET.
JUST BECAUSE HE WANTS TO WALK HOME TOGETHER...
B-BMP
B-BMP
...DOESN'T MEAN ANYTHING. I'M NOT SPECIAL TO HIM.
Don't forget.
OF COURSE I'M NOT.
Right?
...
WHERE IS HE?
SNFF
HANAI SAID HE DIDN'T FEEL THAT WAY ABOUT ME...
SNFF

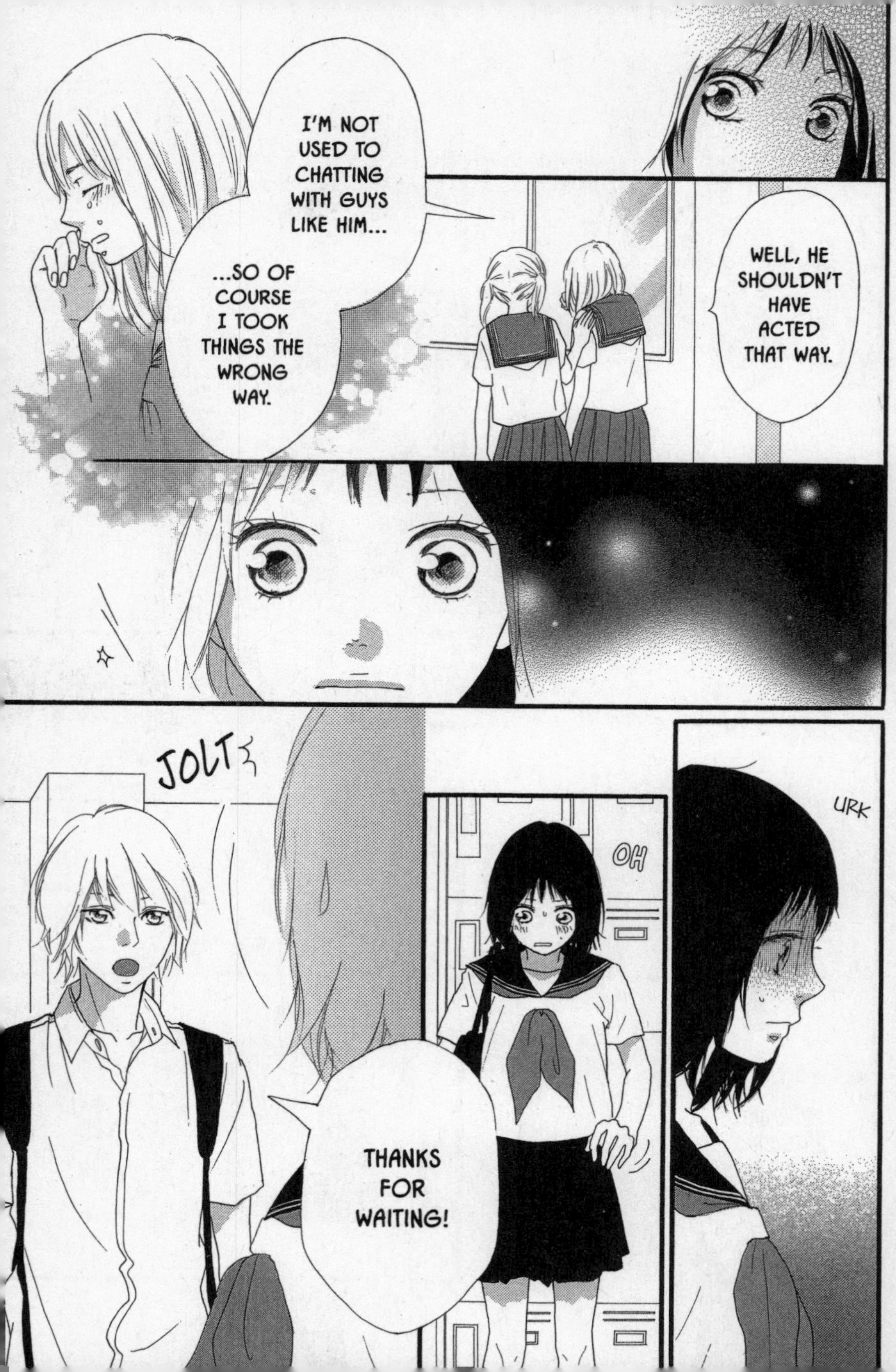
WELL, HE SHOULDN'T HAVE ACTED THAT WAY.
I'M NOT USED TO CHATTING WITH GUYS LIKE HIM...
...SO OF COURSE I TOOK THINGS THE WRONG WAY.
URK
OH
JOLT
THANKS FOR WAITING!

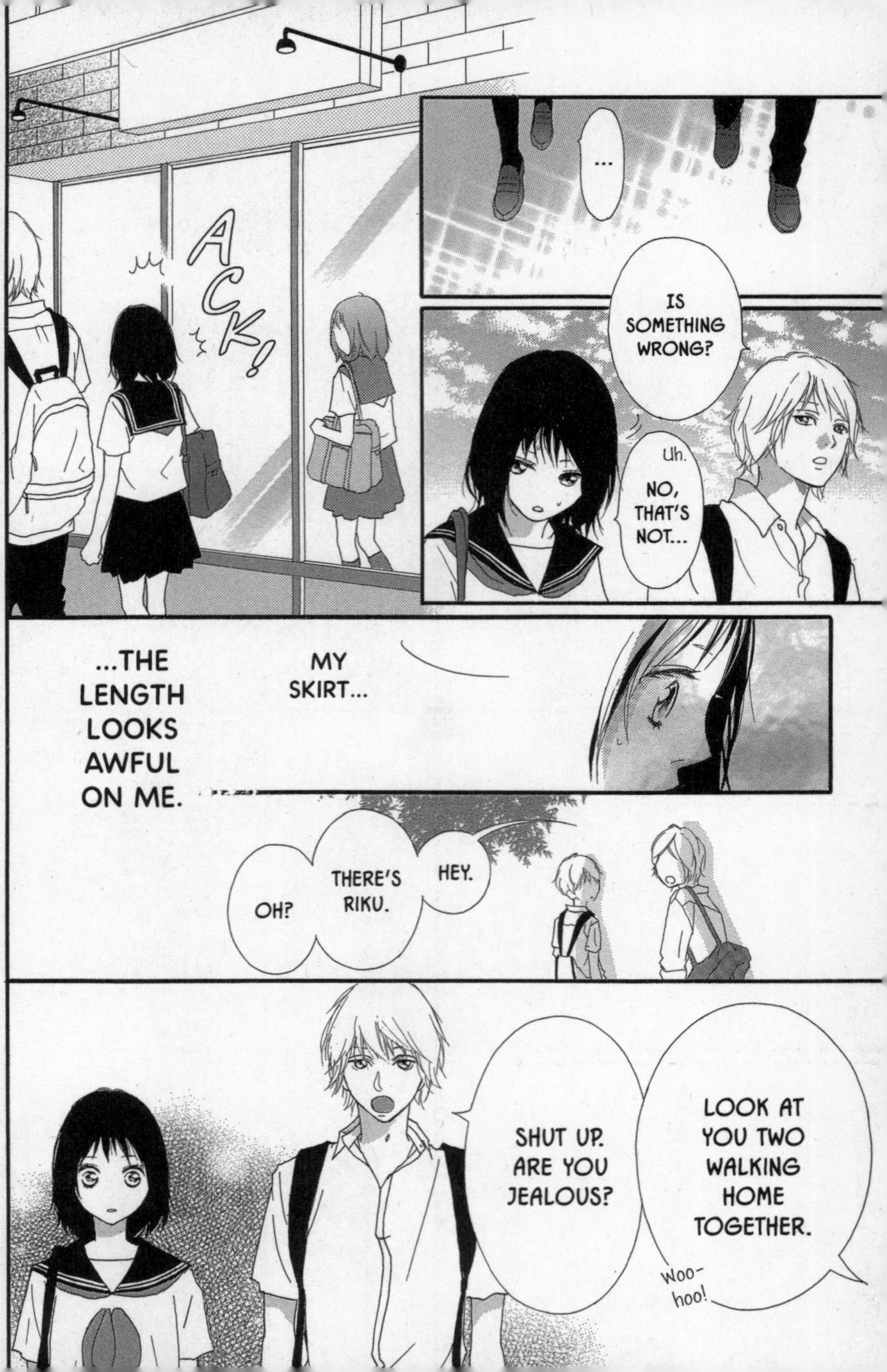
...
IS SOMETHING WRONG?
Uh.
NO, THAT'S NOT...
ACK!
MY SKIRT...
...THE LENGTH LOOKS AWFUL ON ME.
HEY.
THERE'S RIKU.
OH?
LOOK AT YOU TWO WALKING HOME TOGETHER.
Woo-hoo!
SHUT UP. ARE YOU JEALOUS?

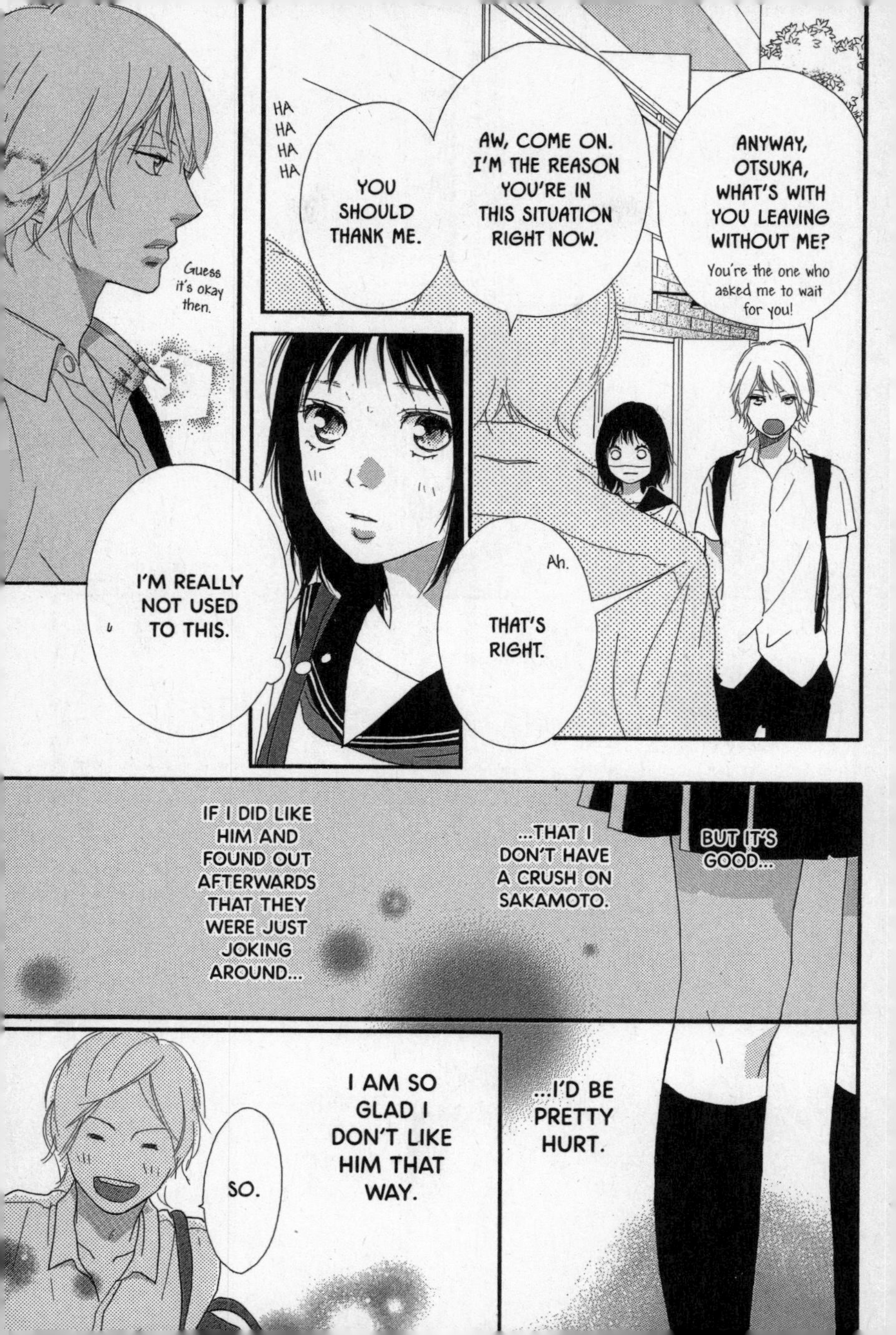
ANYWAY, OTSUKA, WHAT'S WITH YOU LEAVING WITHOUT ME?
You're the one who asked me to wait for you!
AW, COME ON. I'M THE REASON YOU'RE IN THIS SITUATION RIGHT NOW.
YOU SHOULD THANK ME.
HA HA HA HA
Guess it's okay then.
Ah.
THAT'S RIGHT.
I'M REALLY NOT USED TO THIS.
BUT IT'S GOOD...
...THAT I DON'T HAVE A CRUSH ON SAKAMOTO.
IF I DID LIKE HIM AND FOUND OUT AFTERWARDS THAT THEY WERE JUST JOKING AROUND...
...I'D BE PRETTY HURT.
I AM SO GLAD I DON'T LIKE HIM THAT WAY.
SO.

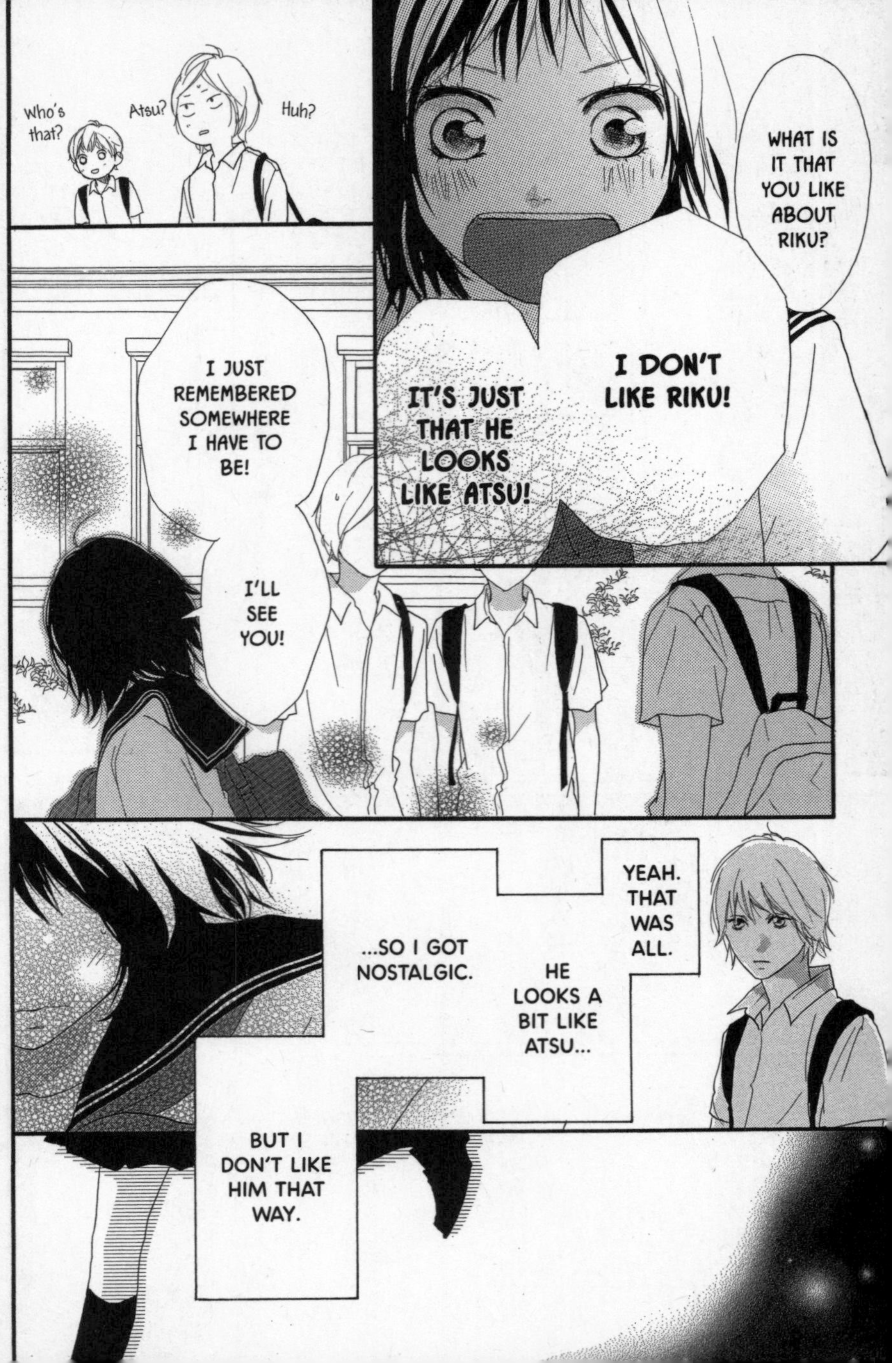
WHAT IS IT THAT YOU LIKE ABOUT RIKU?
I DON'T LIKE RIKU!
IT'S JUST THAT HE LOOKS LIKE ATSU!
Huh?
Atsu?
Who's that?
I JUST REMEMBERED SOMEWHERE I HAVE TO BE!
I'LL SEE YOU!
YEAH. THAT WAS ALL.
HE LOOKS A BIT LIKE ATSU...
...SO I GOT NOSTALGIC.
BUT I DON'T LIKE HIM THAT WAY.

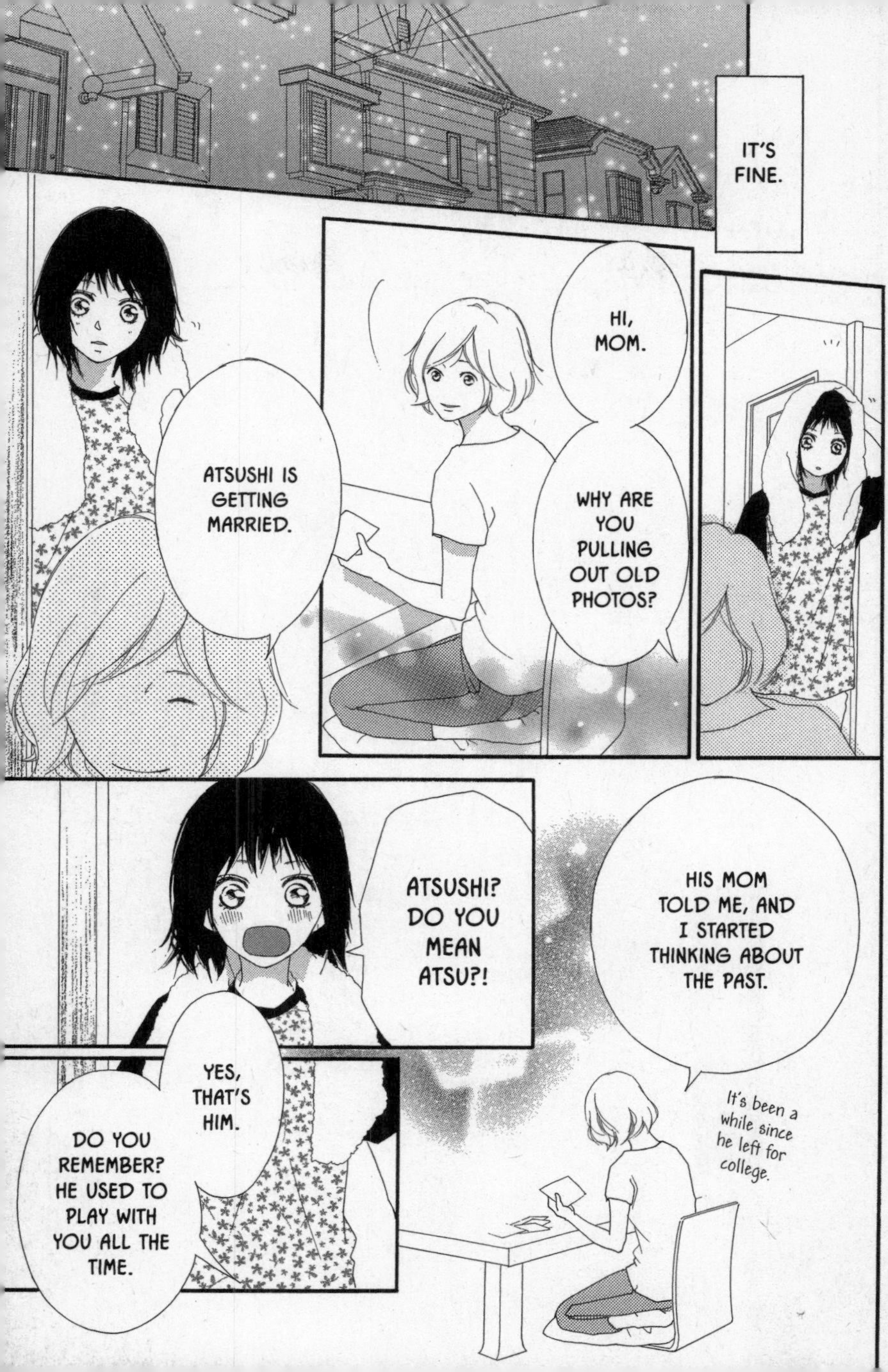
IT'S FINE.
HI, MOM.
WHY ARE YOU PULLING OUT OLD PHOTOS?
ATSUSHI IS GETTING MARRIED.
HIS MOM TOLD ME, AND I STARTED THINKING ABOUT THE PAST.
It's been a while since he left for college.
ATSUSHI? DO YOU MEAN ATSU?!
YES, THAT'S HIM.
DO YOU REMEMBER? HE USED TO PLAY WITH YOU ALL THE TIME.

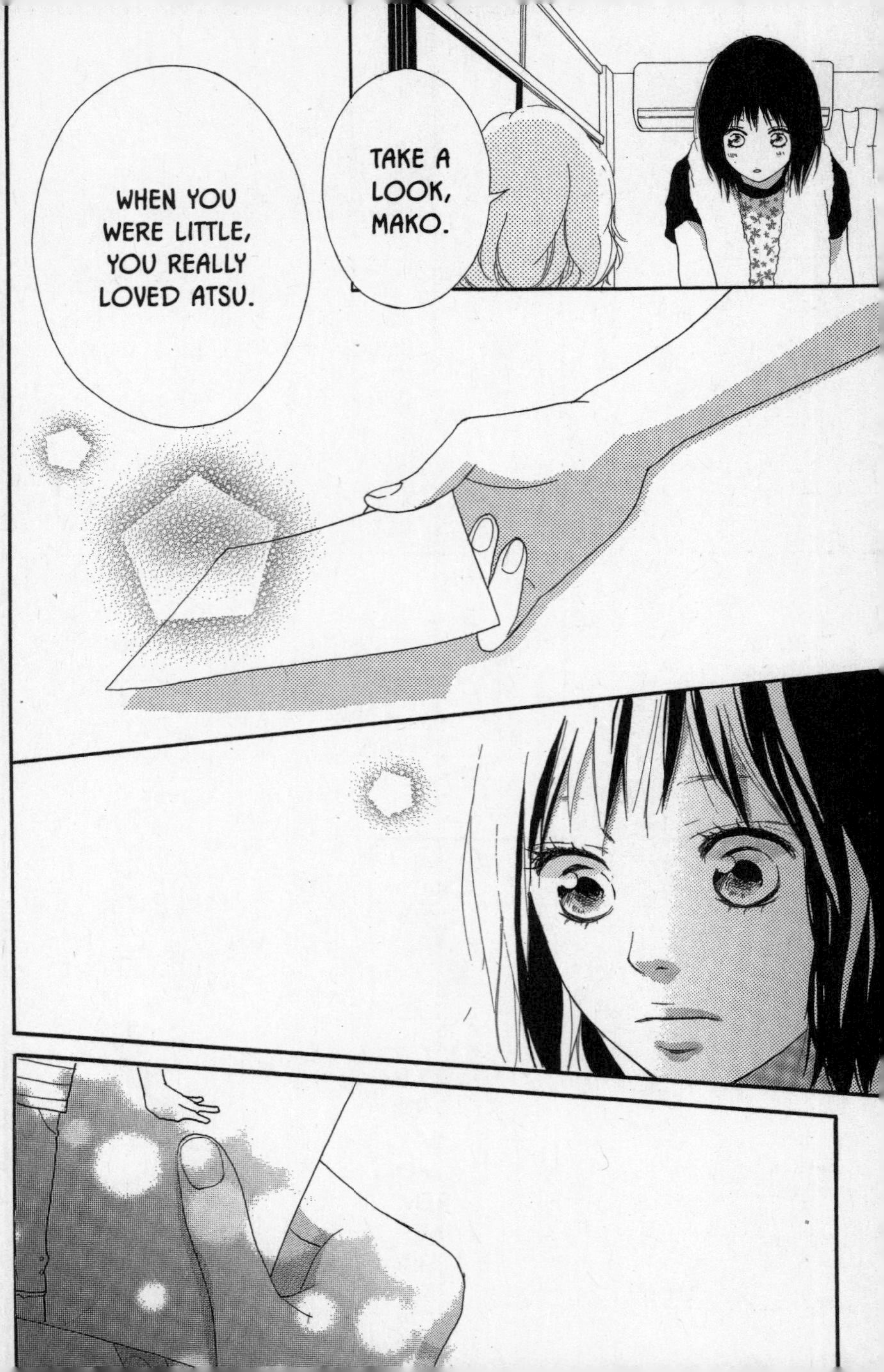
TAKE A LOOK, MAKO.
WHEN YOU WERE LITTLE, YOU REALLY LOVED ATSU.

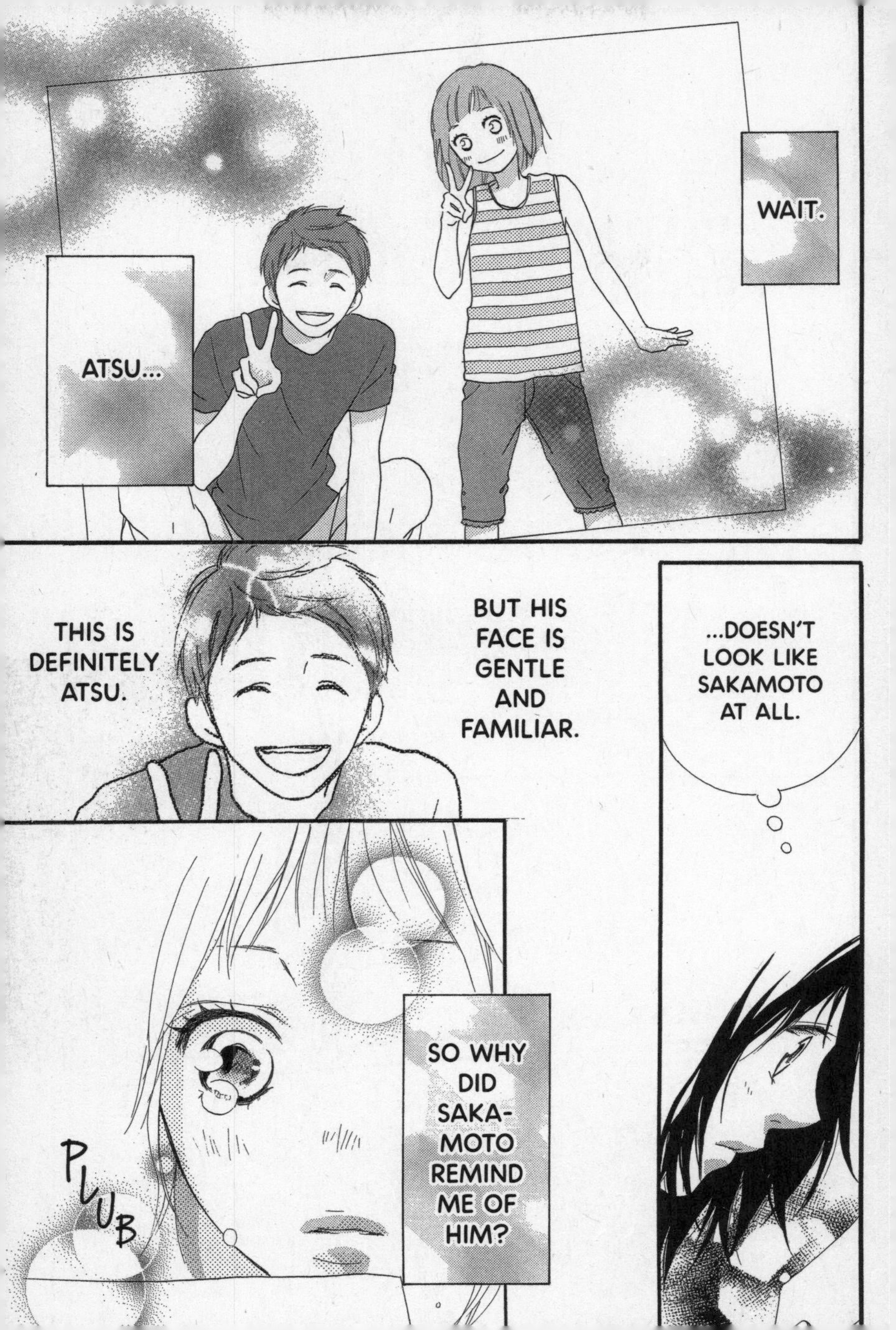
WAIT.
ATSU...
...DOESN'T LOOK LIKE SAKAMOTO AT ALL.
BUT HIS FACE IS GENTLE AND FAMILIAR.
THIS IS DEFINITELY ATSU.
SO WHY DID SAKA-MOTO REMIND ME OF HIM?
PLUB

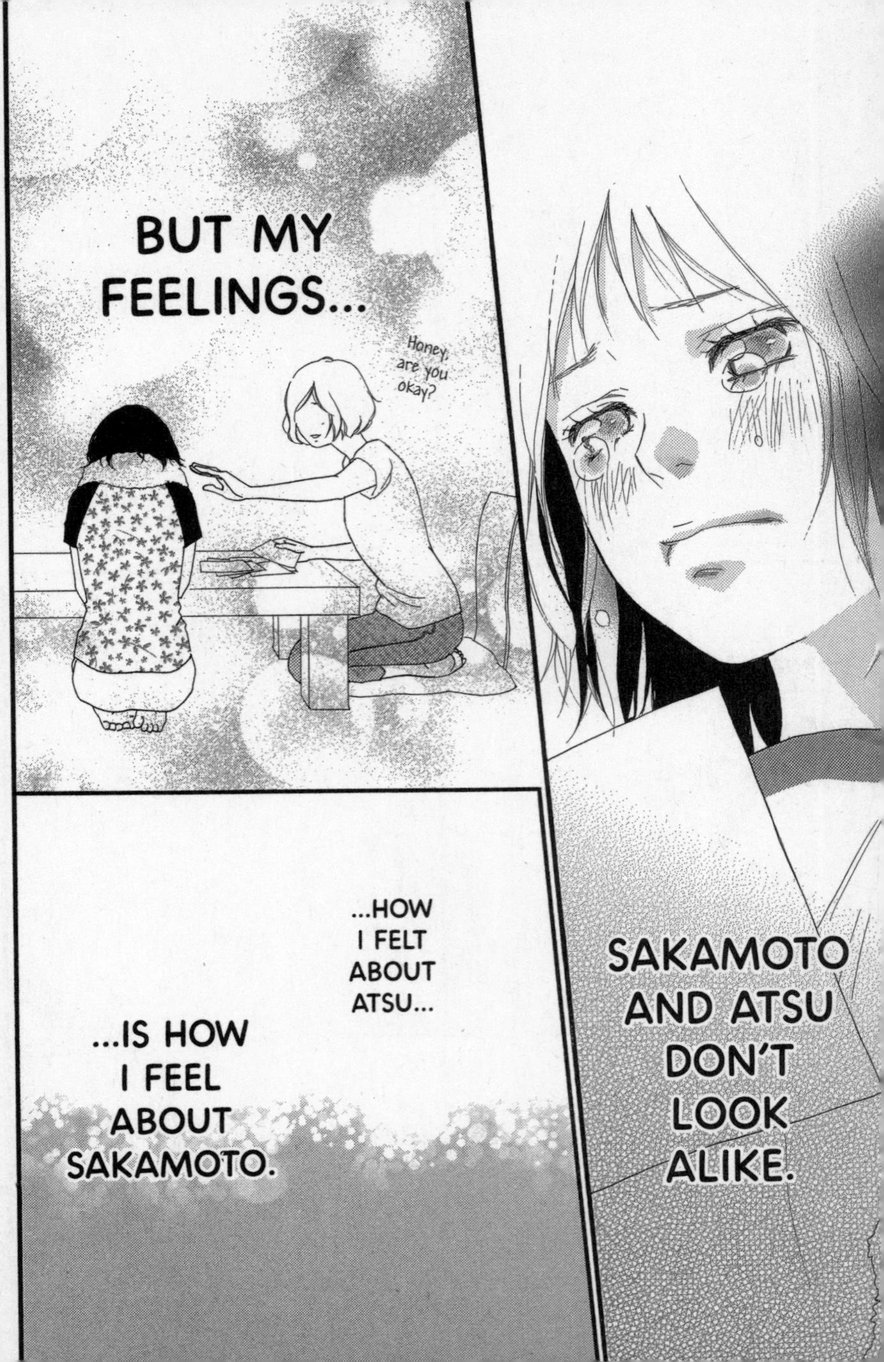
SAKAMOTO AND ATSU DON'T LOOK ALIKE.
BUT MY FEELINGS...
Honey, are you okay?
...HOW I FELT ABOUT ATSU...
...IS HOW I FEEL ABOUT SAKAMOTO.

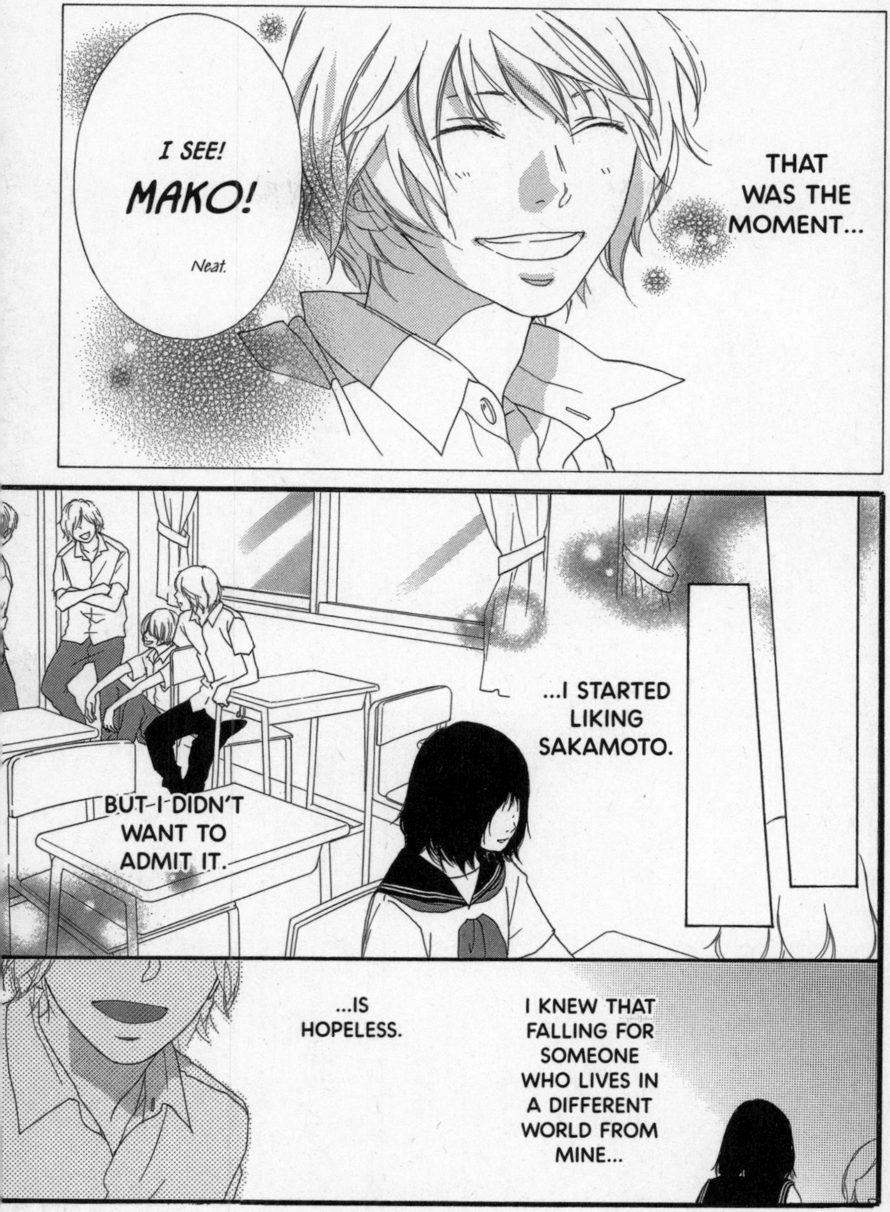
THAT WAS THE MOMENT...
I SEE! MAKO!
Neat.
...I STARTED LIKING SAKAMOTO.
BUT I DIDN'T WANT TO ADMIT IT.
I KNEW THAT FALLING FOR SOMEONE WHO LIVES IN A DIFFERENT WORLD FROM MINE...
...IS HOPELESS.

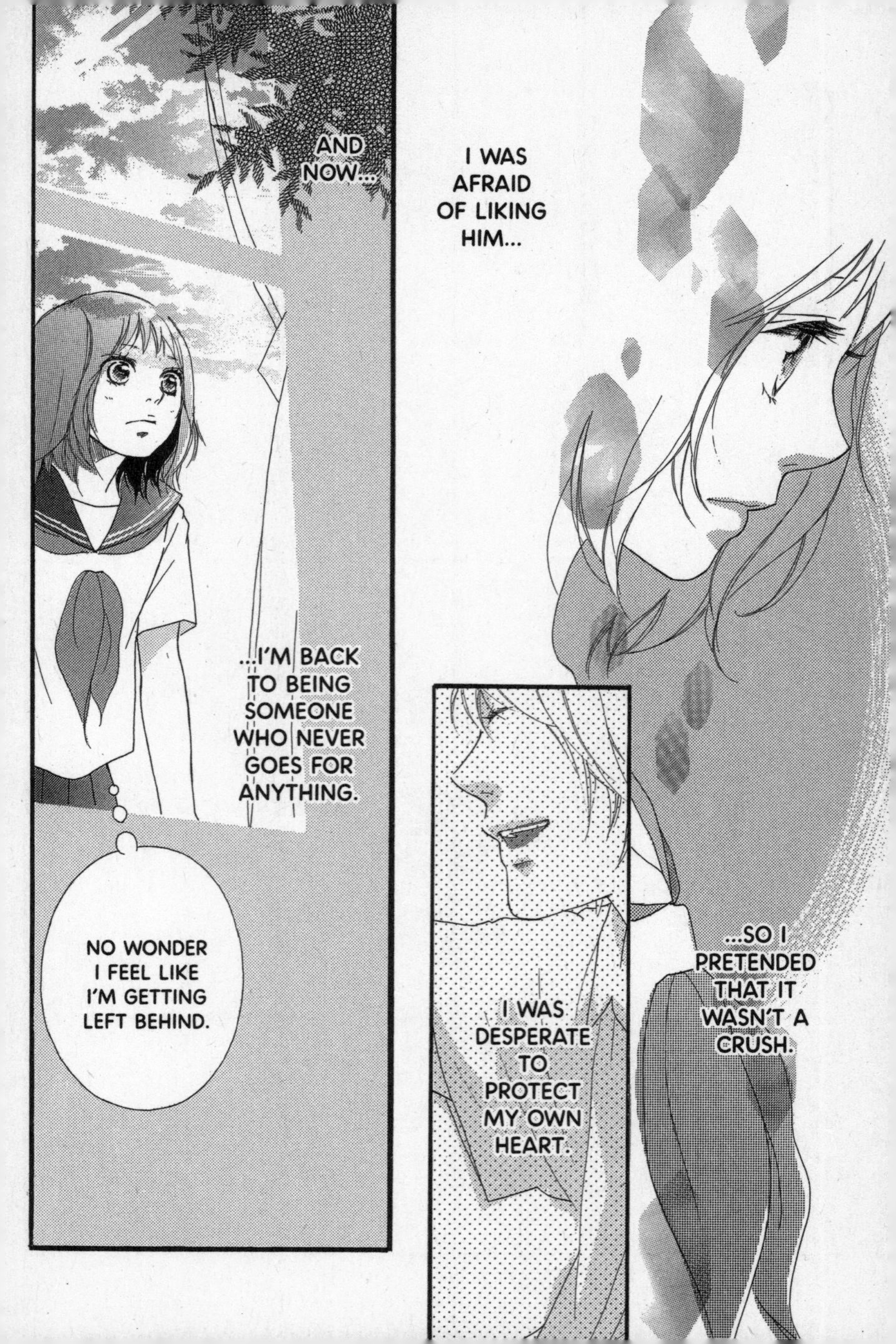
I WAS AFRAID OF LIKING HIM...
...SO I PRETENDED THAT IT WASN'T A CRUSH.
I WAS DESPERATE TO PROTECT MY OWN HEART.
AND NOW...
...I'M BACK TO BEING SOMEONE WHO NEVER GOES FOR ANYTHING.
NO WONDER I FEEL LIKE I'M GETTING LEFT BEHIND.

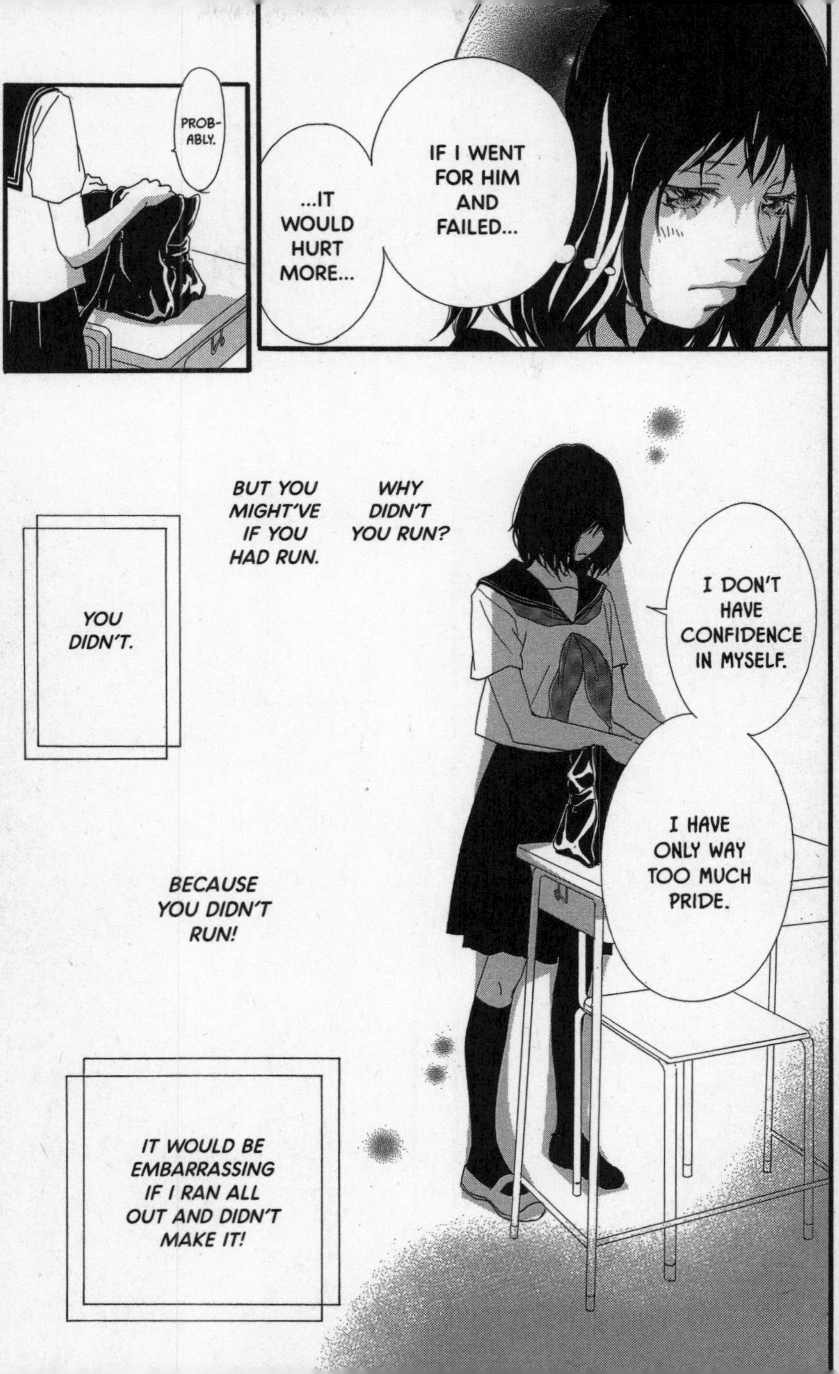
IF I WENT FOR HIM AND FAILED...
...IT WOULD HURT MORE...
PROB-ABLY.
I DON'T HAVE CONFIDENCE IN MYSELF.
I HAVE ONLY WAY TOO MUCH PRIDE.
WHY DIDN'T YOU RUN?
BUT YOU MIGHT'VE IF YOU HAD RUN.
YOU DIDN'T.
BECAUSE YOU DIDN'T RUN!
IT WOULD BE EMBARRASSING IF I RAN ALL OUT AND DIDN'T MAKE IT!

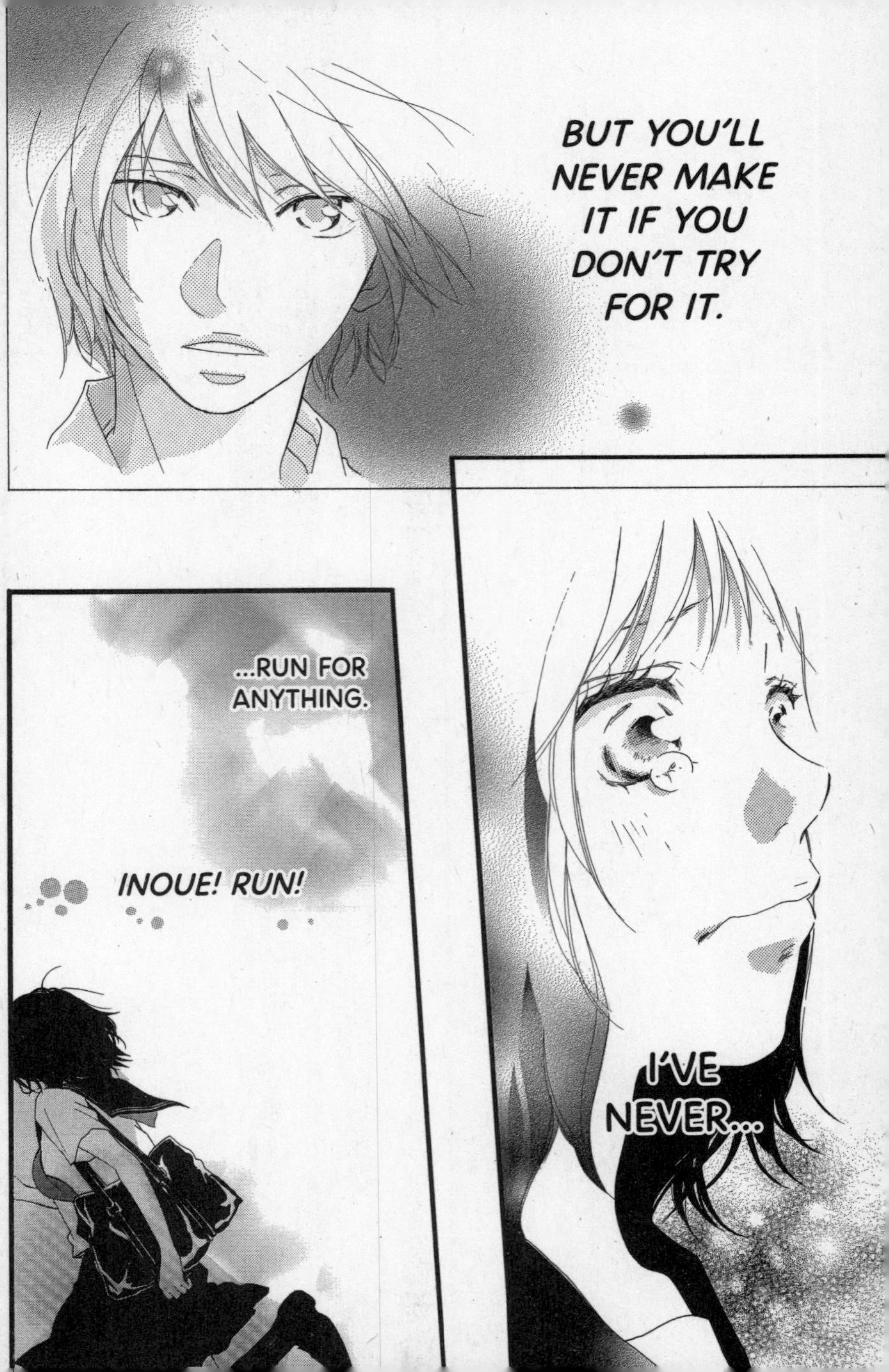
BUT YOU'LL NEVER MAKE IT IF YOU DON'T TRY FOR IT.
I'VE NEVER...
...RUN FOR ANYTHING.
INOUE! RUN!

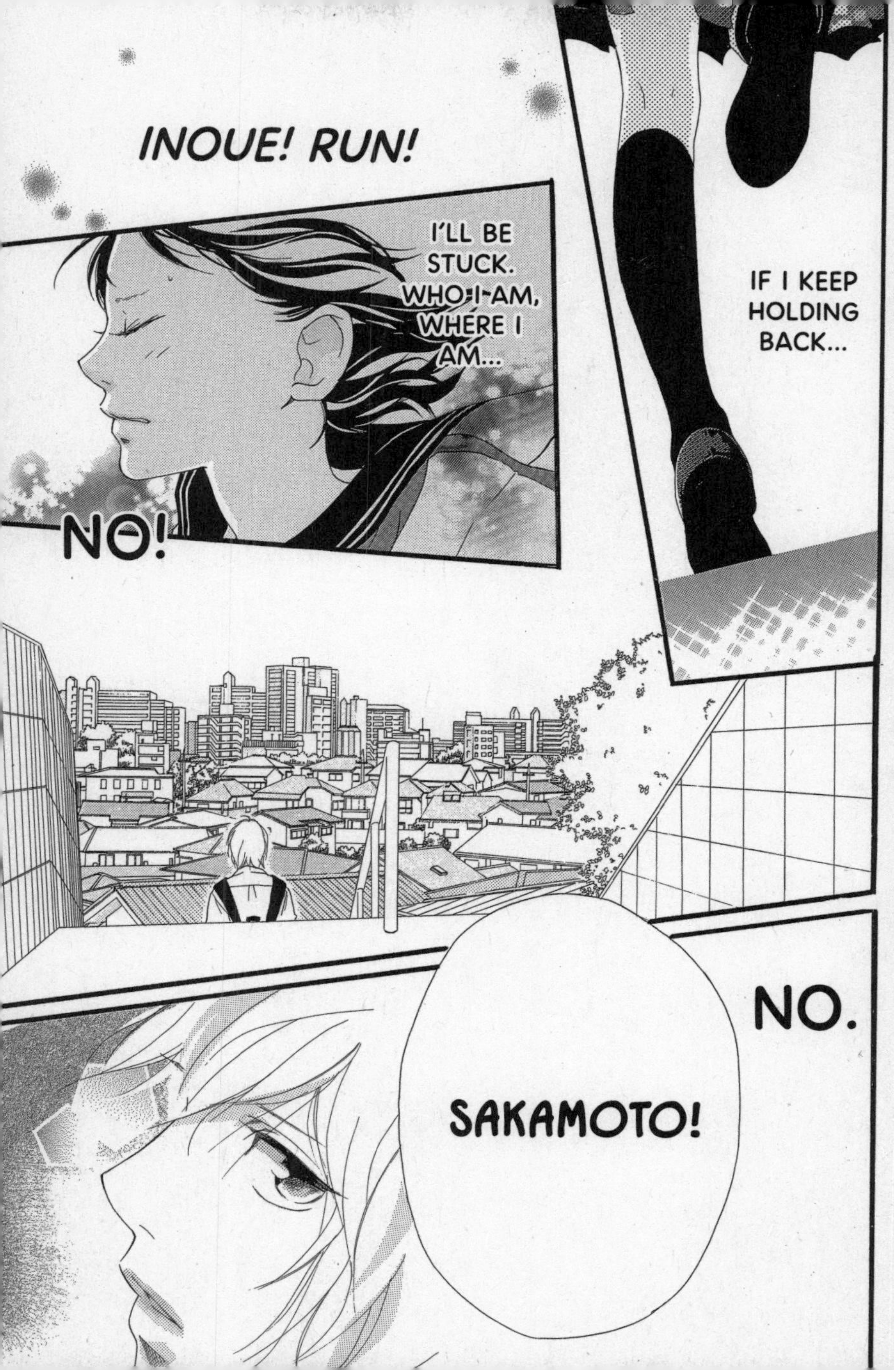
IF I KEEP HOLDING BACK...
INOUE! RUN!
I'LL BE STUCK. WHO I AM, WHERE I AM...
NO!
NO.
SAKAMOTO!

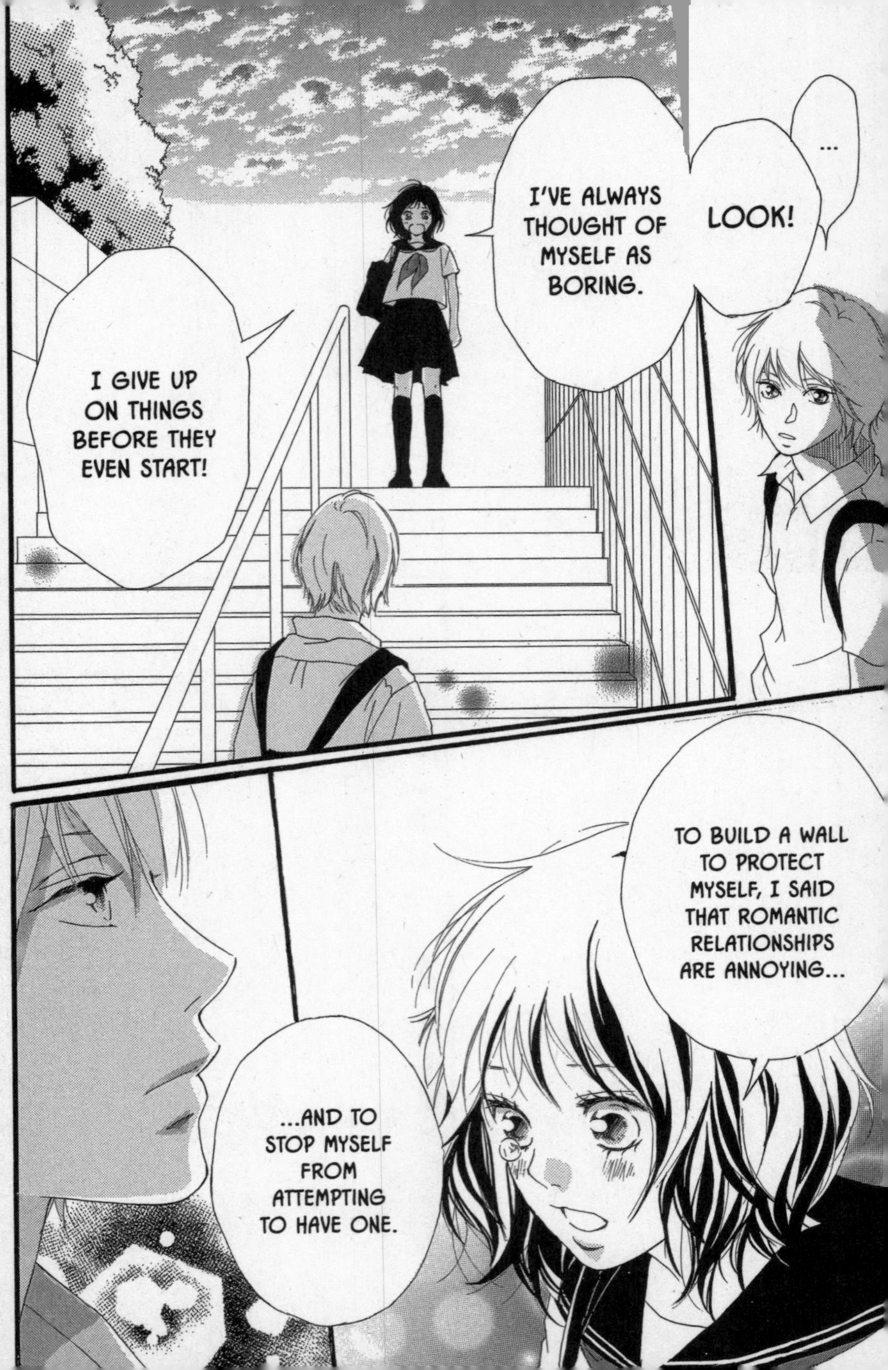
...
LOOK!
I'VE ALWAYS THOUGHT OF MYSELF AS BORING.
I GIVE UP ON THINGS BEFORE THEY EVEN START!
TO BUILD A WALL TO PROTECT MYSELF, I SAID THAT ROMANTIC RELATIONSHIPS ARE ANNOYING...
...AND TO STOP MYSELF FROM ATTEMPTING TO HAVE ONE.

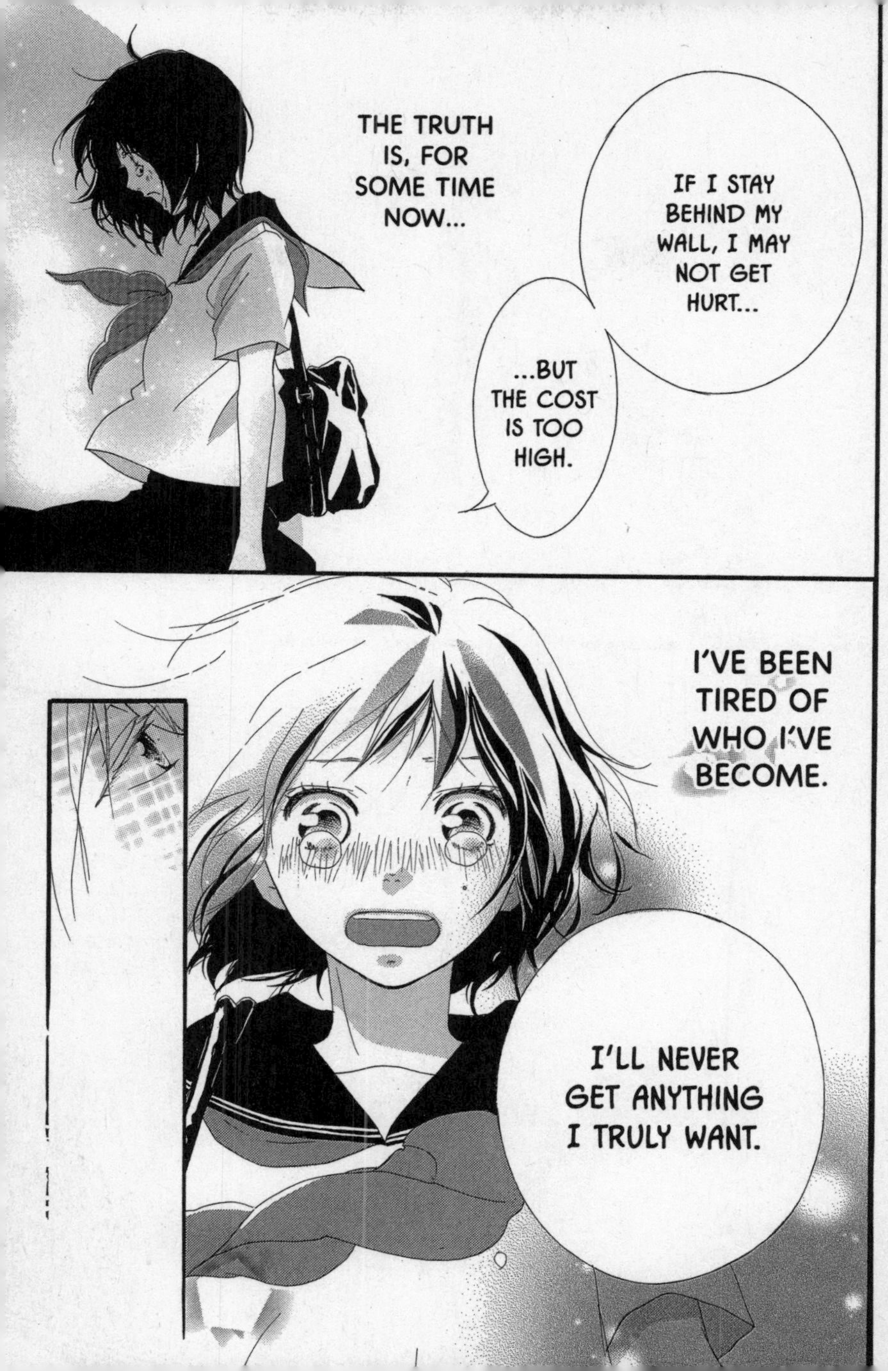
IF I STAY BEHIND MY WALL, I MAY NOT GET HURT...
...BUT THE COST IS TOO HIGH.
THE TRUTH IS, FOR SOME TIME NOW...
I'VE BEEN TIRED OF WHO I'VE BECOME.
I'LL NEVER GET ANYTHING I TRULY WANT.

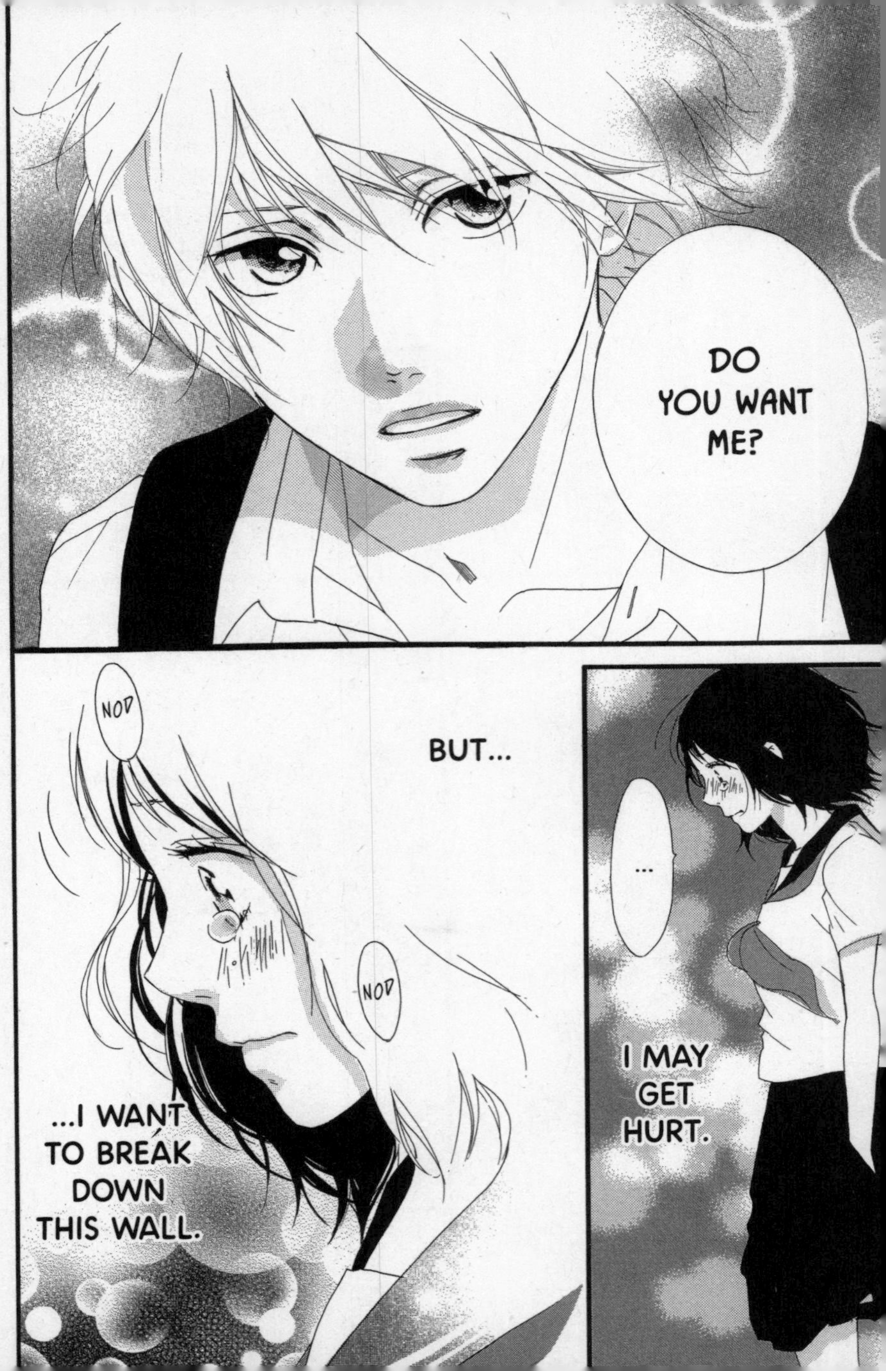
DO YOU WANT ME?
...
I MAY GET HURT.
BUT...
NOD
NOD
...I WANT TO BREAK DOWN THIS WALL.

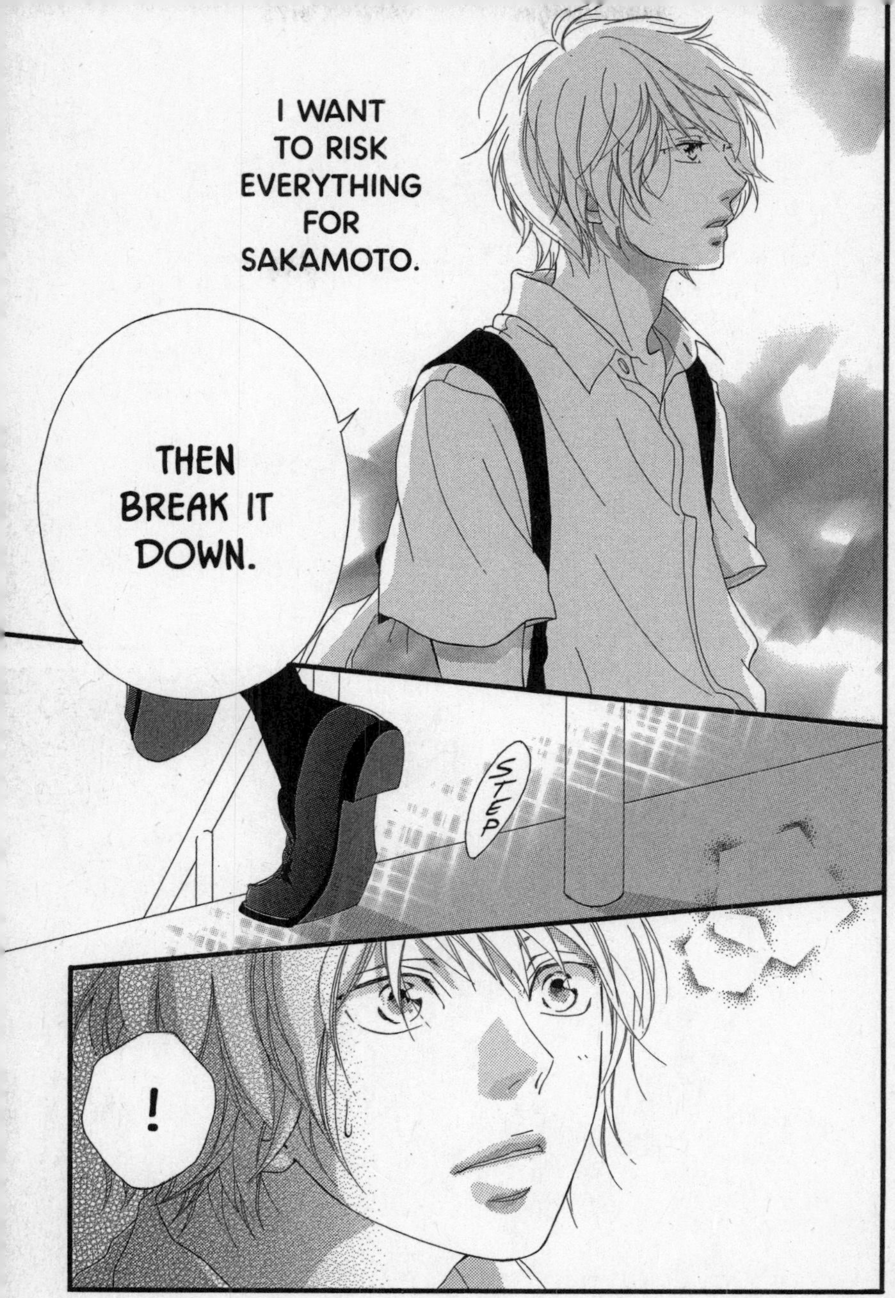
I WANT TO RISK EVERYTHING FOR SAKAMOTO.
THEN BREAK IT DOWN.
STEP
!

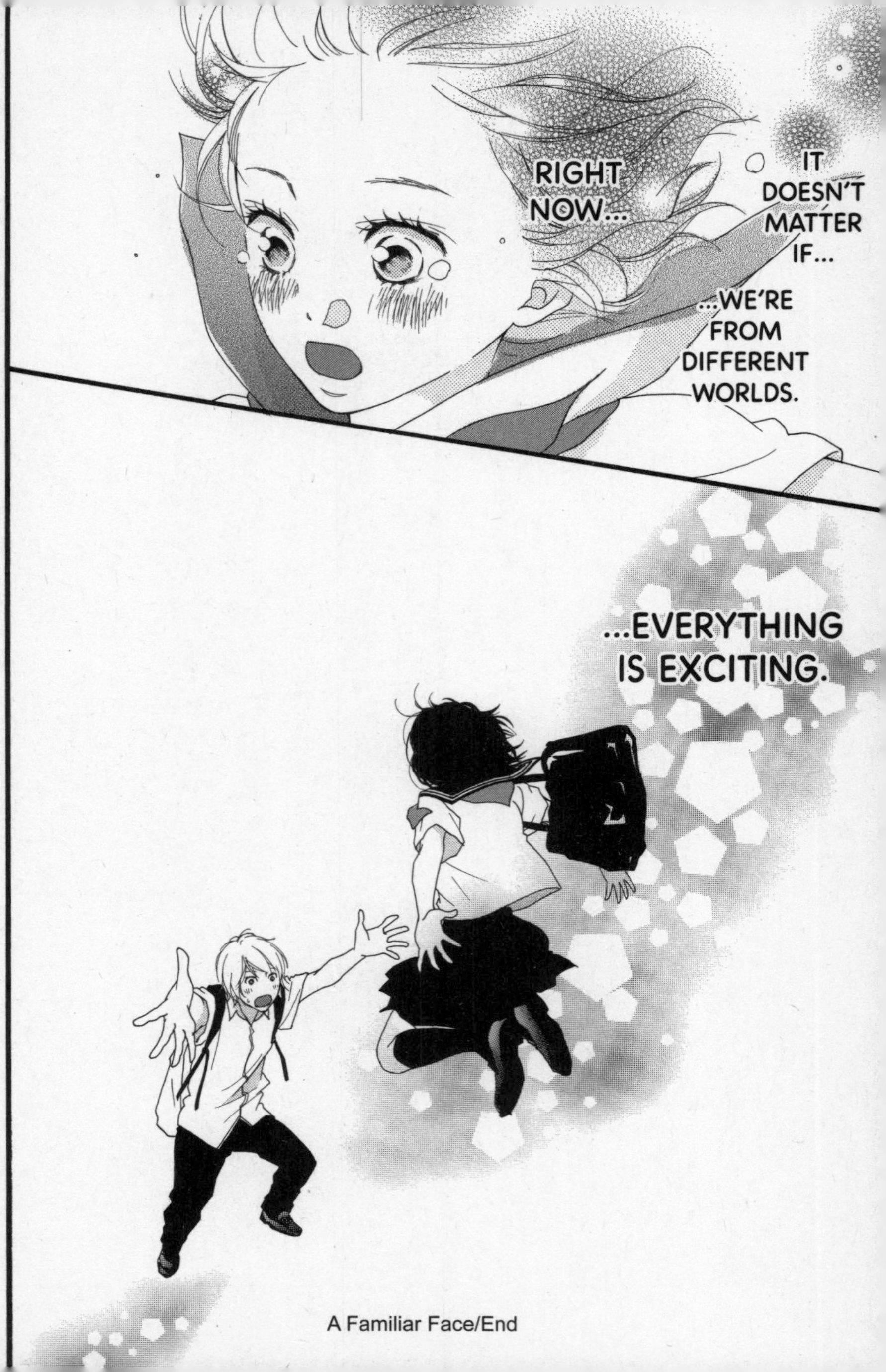
IT DOESN'T MATTER IF...
...WE'RE FROM DIFFERENT WORLDS.
RIGHT NOW...
...EVERYTHING IS EXCITING.

A Familiar Face/End

I keep buying washi tape.

It takes me months to get through one roll, but when I go to the store and see the cute patterns, I can't help but buy a ton.

I've accumulated so many now that when I open up my desk drawers they're all crammed in there. It's getting to be a bit crazy.

But I'm sure I'll keep buying more...

IO SAKISAKA

Born on June 8, Io Sakisaka made her debut as a manga creator with *Sakura, Chiru*. Her works include *Call My Name*, *Gate of Planet* and *Blue*. *Strobe Edge*, her previous work, is also published by VIZ Media's Shojo Beat imprint. *Ao Haru Ride* was adapted into an anime series in 2014. In her spare time, Sakisaka likes to paint things and sleep.

Ao Haru Ride

VOLUME 8
SHOJO BEAT EDITION

STORY AND ART BY **IO SAKISAKA**

TRANSLATION **Emi Louie-Nishikawa**
TOUCH-UP ART + LETTERING **Inori Fukuda Trant**
DESIGN **Shawn Carrico**
EDITOR **Nancy Thistlethwaite**

AOHA RIDE © 2011 by Io Sakisaka
All rights reserved.
First published in Japan in 2011 by SHUEISHA Inc., Tokyo.
English translation rights arranged by SHUEISHA Inc.

The stories, characters and incidents mentioned
in this publication are entirely fictional.

Printed in the U.S.A.

Published by VIZ Media, LLC
P.O. Box 77010
San Francisco, CA 94107

10 9 8 7 6 5 4 3 2 1
First printing, December 2019

PARENTAL ADVISORY
AO HARU RIDE is rated T for Teen and
is recommended for ages 13 and up.
This volume contains the courage of youth.

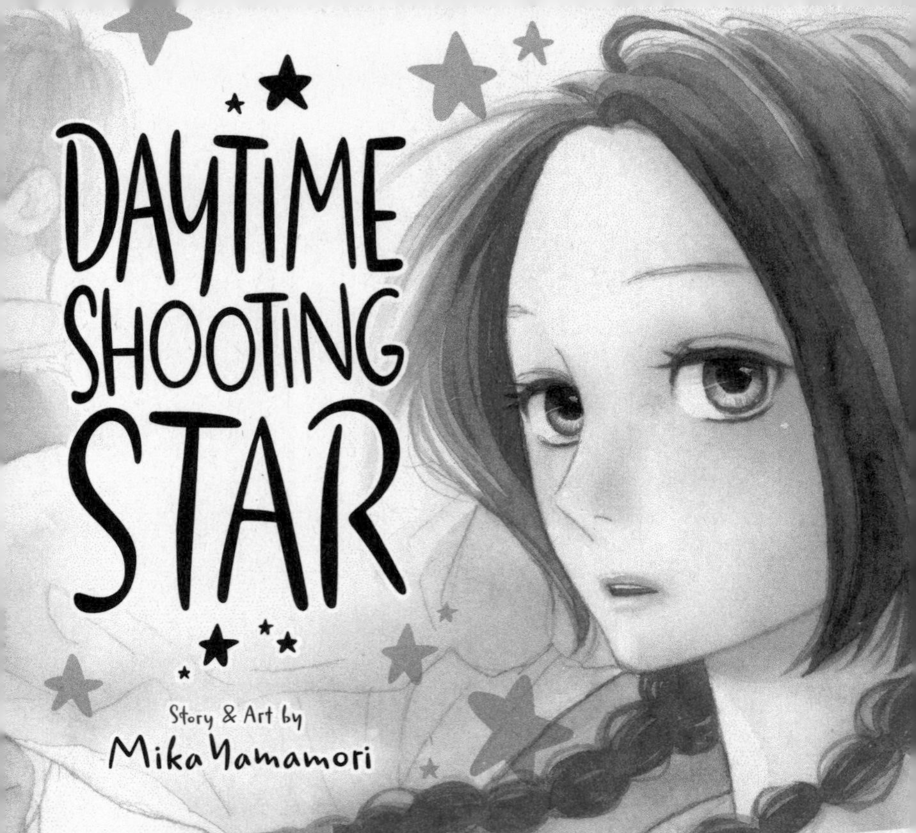

DAYTIME SHOOTING STAR

Story & Art by
Mika Yamamori

Small town girl Suzume moves to Tokyo and finds her heart caught between two men!

After arriving in Tokyo to live with her uncle, Suzume collapses in a nearby park when she remembers once seeing a shooting star during the day. A handsome stranger brings her to her new home and tells her they'll meet again. Suzume starts her first day at her new high school sitting next to a boy who blushes furiously at her touch. And her homeroom teacher is none other than the handsome stranger!

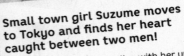

High School DEBUT

By Kazune Kawahara

When Haruna Nagashima was in junior high, softball and comics were her life. Now that she's in high school, she's ready to find a boyfriend. But will hard work (and the right coach) be enough?

Find out in the *High School Debut* manga series—available now!

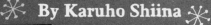

SHORTCAKE CAKE

CAKE

STORY AND ART BY
suu Morishita

**An unflappable girl and a cast of
lovable roommates at a boardinghouse
create bonds of friendship and romance!**

When Ten moves out of her parents' home
in the mountains to live in a boardinghouse,
she finds herself becoming fast friends with
her male roommates. But can love and
romance be far behind?

VIZ

Honey
So Sweet

Story and Art by Amu Meguro

Little did Nao Kogure realize back in middle school that when she left an umbrella and a box of bandages in the rain for injured delinquent Taiga Onise that she would meet him again in high school. Nao wants nothing to do with the gruff and frightening Taiga, but he suddenly presents her with a huge bouquet of flowers and asks her to date him—with marriage in mind! Is Taiga really so scary, or is he a sweetheart in disguise?

ratings.viz.com

viz.com

STOP!

YOU MAY BE READING THE WRONG WAY.

In keeping with the original Japanese comic format, this book reads from right to left—so action, sound effects and word balloons are completely reversed to preserve the orientation of the original artwork.